Stuck In The Onsies Series – Book Three

Ginger

A prequal

Star

To my good friend Elaine. Enjoy!

Diana

Diana McDonough

Dedication

I WOULD LIKE to dedicate this book to my late husband, Jeff, who passed away in 2015. We first visited Jamaica together in 1995 to prepare for our church's first mission trip there. I immediately fell in love with the island and its people. We would return on mission trips at least annually, sometimes more, for over twenty years.

We often vacationed there, and while Jeff liked Jamaica, he would fuss every time I planned our next trip to the island. He was always wanting to go somewhere else, but I held fast. However, when we landed in Jamaica, one would have thought it was all his idea. He embraced the people just like he did everyone in his life, with open arms.

My precious Jeff had health issues off and on for about ten years. The last few years of his life, he was in and out of the hospital countless times. We were planning a vacation and for once, I wanted to stay in the USA thinking if he needed help, we'd be better off in the States. However, he insisted we go to Jamaica, so we did. Little did I know, it would be his last trip. Something tells me he knew.

Jeff always supported my writing time (unless I talked about quitting the day job!). I would get up on Saturday mornings before dawn to work on *Stuck in the Onesies* (anyone that knows me, realizes I rarely get up that early) and would work on it all weekend. He never complained—probably happy to have the remote completely to himself.

Jeff also never complained about his illnesses. He was sad to retire on medical disability, but jumped right in to do the marketing for Woman to Woman Global (WWG), a non-profit I'd started years before. We would have a Bam-Bam (Jamaican term) fundraiser and he would hit the bricks begging for donations for the auctions. He did such an amazing job and was a natural born salesman, that and the fact that he'd never met a stranger made for a perfect combination. He admitted carrying around a wound vac and wearing a surgical boot were great props to initiate conversation. He lovingly earned the nickname "Mr. Bam Bam" from the WWG team.

Now that I'm retired from the 'day job' and writing full time, I know if he were here he'd be the best marketing manager any author ever had. Our dream of Jeff driving our RV while I wrote never came to fruition, but so many others did. Thanks for the memories and so much more.

"If you would not be forgotten as soon as you are dead and rotten, either write things worth reading, or do things worth writing about."

—Benjamin Franklin
Poor Richard's Almanack, 1738

Contents

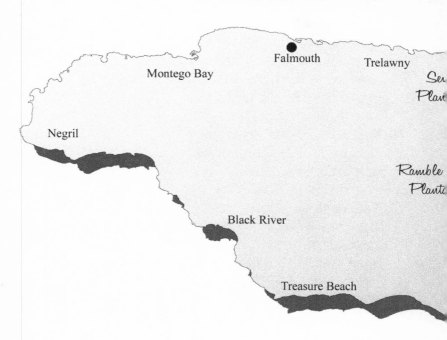

Jamaica

Montego Bay

Falmouth

Trelawny

Se
Plan

Negril

Ramble
Plant

Black River

Treasure Beach

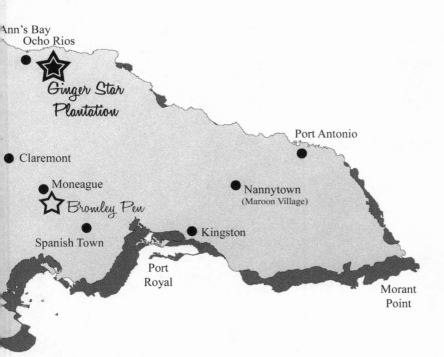

North Coast

Ann's Bay
Ocho Rios

Ginger Star
Plantation

Port Antonio

Claremont

Moneague

Bromley Pen

Nannytown
(Maroon Village)

Spanish Town

Kingston

Port
Royal

Morant
Point

—Chapter One—

"When there is no Law, there's no Bread." —Benjamin Franklin

1719, Ghana

Amari chased the rabbit across the meadow and into the wooded trail. The sun gleamed through the green leaves giving him just enough light to see. He stopped, let his eyes adjust, and stood still listening for the rustling leaves that would reveal his prey's location. His tall stature allowed him to peek over the brush and into the small pathway that had been worn down by animals. The sweat on his dark skin glistened in the sun's rays. He wore his normal hunting gear and already had a few prizes hanging from his belt.

He wondered if his friend, Kwasi, had any luck in the forest today. The two had a friendly hunting competition that would end tomorrow. They had agreed the loser would have to clean the winner's catch for the coming week. Counting what he had on his belt, Amari thought he might be in the lead, but he didn't want to give up just yet. "There is always tomorrow's hunt," he thought and grinned to himself, planning to get up earlier than normal to ensure a win. He would have a good time teasing Kwasi about having to do Amari's dirty work.

Amari could hear nothing but the beating of his own heart until a muffled sound came from his left and he turned toward the noise. Nothing. He looked to the right but saw only bushes. The rabbit must have found its den. He closed his eyes and let out a deep breath as he often did when trying to decide his next move. He held onto his bow with one hand and an arrow in his other. Amari was always ready for his next move. Until now.

Before his eyes opened, something grabbed his arm. His eyes flashed wide and he looked down to see the dark hand of another gripping him. As Amari looked up into the eyes of a Fante warrior, his heart sank, realizing his father's warnings had come true. The markings on the man's face told him what he didn't want to know. Half of his face was painted in white, the other half in red, a sure sign he was a Fante warrior.

"The Fantes are working with the slave ships and every one of us has a bounty on our head," his father had explained after attending the chief's tribal council meeting just the week before. His father wasn't sure where the ships went, but they both knew the captives never came back.

"I thought the treaty we signed with them last year was still good," Amari said, confused. The Fantes have always been a rival of their tribe, the Ewes (U-ways).

"Rain beats on a leopard's skin, but it does not wash out the spots," his father reminded him. The Fante tribe had never been one to keep its word to the Ewes.

Amari pulled away from the Fante, who appeared to be alone. He thought he could break away, but another, stronger arm came around his neck and held him tight. Amari could feel the cold blade of what he assumed was a knife pricking his throat. He gasped for air as his bow and arrow fell from his hands. He could see the second Fante out of the corner of his eye, realizing he was outnumbered as the two Fantes pushed and held him to the ground, knocking the breath out of his lungs.

His face in the dirt, he gasped for air and could see his bow lying in the dirt next to him.

"Tie him up! The ship is due to leave soon," one Fante said to the other in their native tongue. Amari didn't speak their dialect but understood the Fante's language well enough. They pulled his hands behind his back and used a strap to bind them together. Air finally filled his lungs and he tried to yell, but not before someone put a cloth over his mouth, gagging him silent. His abductor pulled on the back of Amari's hair, told him to stand, and he struggled to his feet. The shorter Fante tied the remainder of the strap around his own waist to prevent Amari from escaping.

Amari never thought he would have been a captive of anyone. He was half-dazed as they trudged down the path. He'd always taken pride in his ability to run faster, work harder, and out-think his opponents. Until today. He'd discovered there was no pride in being a hostage.

The Fantes argued with each other as they pushed Amari down the path toward the shore. The taller one accused the shorter of slowing down the day's progress. Evidently their bounty hunting had not gone as well as they had hoped, but they redeemed themselves when they captured Amari at the last minute. Amari looked for a way to escape, but his heart sank as he knew there was no hope, at least for now. He prayed to Lisa and Mawu, the gods of the Ewe tribe. He knew they were his only hope.

His captors walked him for many miles to a clearing on the beach and joined a group of Africans being held by other Fante warriors. "Those are the ones from the fort," the taller Fante said to the shorter. Amari could see at least 100 of his people, many that he recognized, nearly naked and huddled by the shore. He'd grown up hearing the horrific stories about the white castles that housed the "door of no return," a place where the Fante or white man would take their captives, never to be seen or heard from again.

A few white men, apparently the ones that would pay the bounties, stood off to the side looking Amari's way with little interest other than to size up the Fantes' catch. Amari had heard about these white men but had never seen one before. He could not help but stare at their white skin — so unlike his own, seeming translucent. Their hair was long and flowing, nothing like his.

A huge ship rocked on the sea in the distance. Only half its sails were up. He had seen ships riding down the coast before, but never this close. The slavers' sloop was pulled up onto the beach and a few captives were already on board, waiting for their journey into darkness.

Amari scanned the crowd wondering if he would recognize anyone. He feared that he would see a face he knew. His heart leapt as he recognized Kwasi on the other side of the group. "Kwasi, how this happen to you?" He looked up and locked eyes with him and before he could answer, his Fante captor struck him upside his head and Amari found himself falling to the ground as if in slow motion. In the distance, he could hear Kwasi scream his name. He opened his eyes to see the sky with people standing over him. Feeling his own his warm blood spill over his face, his eyes closed despite his resistance. He felt the coolness of something hard being clamped around his ankle and then his wrists forced him back to reality. The pain in his head made him want to drift away.

"Hey! Take it easy, boy," the white man with the beard and black hat yelled at the Fante. He ran over to see how badly Amari was hurt. "He was a strong one and could've been worth at least 20 pounds, Charlie!"

"Well, the bounty on him just went down." Charlie walked over and saw the blood pouring from Amari's head. He tossed

Amari a rag to wipe up the mess. "Here, clean yourself up." He kicked Amari on the arm. "You'll not get 40, maybe only 24 pounds for this one. Hardly worth what it costs to keep him alive," Charlie said. The red-haired sailor chuckled and looked at Amari. "Keep it up and you will find yourself at the bottom of the ocean!"

"Go ahead, get him up!" the Fante said as he nudged Kwasi, almost knocking him over. Amari could only see the outline of a man as he faded in and out. The voice was that of Kwasi, his friend. He held onto Kwasi's hand and struggled to stand on his feet. Kwasi held him up as they walked toward the others.

The small group of white men herded their captives toward the sloops. Their chains clunked on the sides of the boats as they struggled to hoist their bodies on board. Once the sloops were full and the bounties paid, the white men jumped on board and the Fantes pushed the sloops into the water. They walked inland, not turning to witness the human horror they had helped set in motion.

THE SLOOPS PITCHED up and down as they headed the ship. Several of the captives were forced to row in tandem until they floated up alongside the large vessel. Amari fought dizziness and closed his eyes but found the effort made him sick, so he kept them open, looking down in his lap only to see his empty hands bound in chains. He looked up to see the name of the other ship painted on its side. "Neptune."

The sloop pulled up alongside the ship and the captives were herded off the sloops and up the rope ladder onto the deck. The chains impeded their progress and served to irritate the white men, yet again. "Watch what you're doing!" the red-haired sailor hollered and pulled a leather whip from his belt. He cracked it on the side of the ship with a loud snap, as he found just the sound was enough of a threat to keep the Africans on task. Once on deck, they were pushed in close to one another.

"Women and children over here!" the captain shouted, as the crew members herded them away from the men. Captain Lewis was excited about their haul and knew it would be best to separate the men away from the rest.

Charlie called to the men, "Ase ko! (hurry up)" the first mate hollered. He had managed to glean a few Ewe phrases from the Fantes as the sailor pointed down into the dark hole that was to become their home.

Amari was seeing better now, but his head still throbbed. Kwasi managed to position himself next to Amari when they boarded the ship and helped him along. They followed the others single file down the ladder into a dark, musty hold. They could not stand erect but had to double over to walk until they could go no further. The red-headed sailor and another crew member came through and removed the shackles from the hands of their captives, but left their ankles tied together. Amari rubbed his wrists, grateful that his hands were free. His hand went to his wounded forehead, but even a light touch brought forth a stinging pain. They were instructed to sit with their backs against the wall. Once done, the crew marched another row of captives to sit between the legs of the ones already there. Amari's head jerked as the ship pulled away from the shore with the wind filling the unfurled sails.

His head throbbed and he drifted in and out of consciousness. Kwasi sat next to him, grateful he was able to help his friend. He woke Amari when bread and water were passed down the line a few hours after they had set sail. Amari slept more than he was awake and Kwasi thought his friend might be the luckier of the two. At least he didn't have to sit and ponder his fate as the rest of them did. Kwasi found himself wishing Amari would wake up so they could talk. They had always been able to figure things out together.

The ship pitched back and forth, bringing on sea sickness for many. The stench and humidity combined to create an acrid odor that made one want to wretch. Their captors soon donned kerchiefs over their nose to try and hold the smell at bay.

Kwasi covered his ears in vain as his fellow captives reacted to their fates. Some cried aloud, not caring who heard. The sound of wailing men was something he'd never before witnessed. Sadness and fear filled his heart.

"How will Afi feed the children?" one man cried about his wife and family's fate. "Our third child will soon come," he said as tears flowed down his cheeks.

"We must lean on Mawu and Lisa to show us what to do!" Kwasi tried to encourage everyone, including himself, to seek the Ewe tribe gods' counsel.

"Where were your gods when these devils took us from our homeland?" the husband of Afi asked, staring at him in disbelief.

"They were with us then as now. They will help us through." Kwasi leaned back on the wall and closed his eyes, hoping his words were true. He prayed to Mawu and Lisa as he never had before. He knew his village would seek the chief's advice when they did not return from their hunt and the Voodoo prayers and ceremonies would be relentless until they found favor. That he knew for sure.

Amari floated in and out of consciousness; he could sometimes hear the conversations going on between his fellow captives as they talked about ways they would try to escape. "Are we not bound in chains?" he asked himself as he drifted back into darkness.

"Me know the Fante prey 'pon us," the man next to Amari said. "Must be a Ewe dat tell dem about where we hunt," he said as he shook his head.

"That's enough!" Kwasi yelled at two Ewe captives as they wailed their sad stories. "Do you not think we all feel as you?" The two stopped and looked at him, their faces wet with tears. "No shame shall come upon you unless you give up," he tried to assure them, yet hoped that his own uncertainty remained hidden. "We must keep our eyes and ears open so we can find an opportunity for Mawu and Lisa to show us what to do!" He knew that positive thoughts and dependence on their gods was essential were they to survive.

The ship moved slowly, and darkness covered what little light they had below deck as the sun sank into the sea. Kwasi struggled for a comfortable position, but sleep eluded him. He could smell the stench that was starting to build as they were forced to sit in their own waste. Every time he would drift off to sleep, the sounds of the crew laughing and singing up on the deck woke him. Once the effects of the excess rum took hold of the crew members, they passed out and slept, helping Kwasi to drift into sleep with only the sound of creaking wood and snoring as the waves pushed them through the ocean.

THE DAWN OF morning woke Kwasi along with the sounds of footsteps above. For just a second, he had hoped someone was on board aiding in their escape, but the reality of being a hostage set in again. He could hear the captain they called "Lewis" shouting instructions to his crew.

Amari stirred as the sun and its heat worked its way into the room through cracks in the deck above. His hand touched his forehead and he winced. Kwasi looked at him and smiled. "So, you are awake, my friend." He touched Amari's head and turned it toward him. "How are you feeling?"

Amari took a deep breath and grunted, shaking his head. He put his head in his hands. "What is happening? Where are we now?"

"The Fantes turned us over to the slave traders and we are on their ship, but I do not know where we are headed," Kwasi said as he put his hand on his friend's shoulder.

"How do you feel?" Kwasi asked.

"I can see better, but am still unsure," he said, feeling grateful for Kwasi.

Charlie, the red-headed sailor, had indicated through hand signs that they would be going up on deck. "It appears they will be taking us onto the upper deck to bathe and exercise this morning," Kwasi said. "Do you think you can do that?"

Amari nodded. "I suppose so. No one willingly walks to his own death, but today I feel as though I would gladly," he confessed.

"I understand, my friend." Kwasi patted him on the back.

Before noon, the red-haired sailor and his sidekick, whom he referred to as, "Martin" came down to the hull to herd their captives up onto the deck. They were small men, obviously performing this task since they could stand up straight under the low ceiling. "Hurry up, you sluggards!" Martin shouted. He pushed each one as they walked by, hunched over to avoid hitting their heads on the low-hanging beams. They climbed the stairs, trying not to step on the chains that clung to their ankles. A few stumbled but managed to get on deck. "They're all here, Charlie," Martin said to the red-haired sailor.

The sun glared as Kwasi and Amari shielded their eyes, hoping to see all they could. "Our home is there," Kwasi nodded toward the coastline. Kwasi could see his homeland in the distance. He noticed they were headed north and, from what he could ascertain by listening to Charlie, they would be stopping to load up on supplies before heading out to sea. A white fort shone on the distant shore. "They say the 'Door of No Return' is in the white castles," Kwasi said as nodded toward the shoreline. They both stared. "Many on this ship say they were held in one for many moons before boarding this ship."

The crew handed out buckets of water and pieces of soap for the Africans to clean themselves. "Hurry up!" Charlie barked.

When they were soaped and rinsed, Martin went around retrieving the buckets and soap. "Get in line!" he said as he pulled and shoved each one until they understood what a line was. "Do as I do," Charlie hollered, raising his arms, showing them how to exercise in place.

Martin grabbed Kwasi's arms and raised them until everyone understood they were to do as Charlie did. Charlie made simple movements and simulated walking in place as they followed suit. "A strong African is a good African," Martin said impressed with his own joke.

Another night of whooping and hollering from the drunken crew followed in the same fashion as the night before, making sleep scarce and fitful. The next morning the ship slowed and pulled close to shore to purchase food and other supplies. A few crew members boarded a sloop to head ashore and the rest stayed put while the captives were put through their daily ritual of bathing and exercise and put back into the belly of the ship. The Neptune rocked slowly. The humidity and intense heat increased as the day wore on. No air moved and Kwasi found that simply taking a breath was laborious. Sweat beaded on Amari's brow and flowed down his face. Kwasi was concerned as his friend was sleeping more than he had the day before.

"I don't think this one can make it up the ladder," Martin said to Charlie as he nudged Amari with his boot.

"Well, leave him behind and if he's not better soon, we'll toss him over."

THE SLOOP RETURNED and the supplies were loaded on the Neptune. Captain Wells barked orders to the crew as the ship took sail. "Dark clouds ahead, Captain," the tall and lanky sailmaster reported.

Wells looked toward the horizon. His long black hair was pulled behind and tied with a piece of leather twine. He had commanded the Neptune for two years now. Two years of low paying bounties from robbing other ships with less than expected cargoes. His crew was growing restless with less than expected paydays. But recently, his fortune had turned when he met Robert Anderson, a wealthy businessman, in Nassau. Thanks to Mr. Anderson's bankroll, Wells was now in the slave-trading business. He hoped to hang onto his crew by cashing in on this payload.

"Do what you have to do, but get around it," Wells bellowed. "We must set sail before nightfall in order to catch the winds from the other side of the storm!"

The Neptune sailed north of the storm but was unable to avoid the high seas created by the winds. It pitched up, down, and sideways, making many seasick. Several of the mates hung over the railing heaving their dinners into the sea. The captives were not as fortunate, as they heaved where they sat.

CAPTAIN LEWIS WALKED back and forth on the deck of the Vulture, spyglass in hand. He looked through the telescope once again and decided they were close enough. They'd been following the Neptune for several days at a safe distance, waiting for the opportunity to swoop in and capture the ship.

He had been tipped off that the Neptune had planned to travel up the Ivory Coast to fill its belly with captured Africans and then further up as they purchased supplies for the month-long trip across the ocean.

Lewis turned and looked at his quartermaster, Harris, an older man with strong navigational skills. Lewis had hired him on the spot, knowing his reputation was solid. "We are not interested in the human cargo, only the vessel itself," Lewis said as they raised their glasses in agreement. "It's fast and has a huge hull to carry much more valuable assets." The thought of selling slaves was abhorrent to him and Harris agreed. He was confident they'd make a great team.

The deep and spacious belly of the Neptune could carry greater amounts of sugarcane and coffee from Jamaica to Britain at a fast pace despite its size and weight. Lewis had sought a ship of this design for a long while. He'd seen the storm advancing and knew the Neptune would have to navigate around it to avoid the gales. Now that she was frantic, he saw his window of opportunity.

"AHOY! LOOK STARBOARD!" Charlie shouted. He quickly descended the mast of the Neptune. "It looks to be the Vulture! All hands on deck!" The Vulture was known to prey on ships as they were preparing for a voyage and the Neptune was her target today. The officers of the Neptune had been distracted because of the storm and didn't realize they'd been in the Vulture's sights for some time.

"Get the powder monkeys down there for supplies!" Charlie yelled.

"What's happening?" roused by the noise, Amari asked as the commotion above intensified. He leaned up on his elbow and rubbed his eyes, trying to focus. The sound of boots running and cannons rolling on the deck above drowned out voices. The young boys on the crew were the powder monkeys and they ran up and down the ladder taking gun powder and other weapons up to Neptune's deck. "They're gonna ram us!" Captain Wells bellowed.

Seconds glided by as if in slow motion when suddenly, the ship jolted as the Vulture struck its port bow. The Neptune groaned with the sound of splintering wood and equipment sliding from one side to the other. Gunfire drowned out the panicked cries. Before the Neptune could retaliate, a cannon fired and hit its deck. "Fire!" someone yelled from above. Amari drifted in and out of consciousness. The smell of smoke filtered into the belly of the ship. Powder monkeys ran back and forth with buckets of water while the rest of the crew manned cannons that refused to fire. The crew of the Vulture clambered onto the Neptune's deck. Charlie grabbed his sword, half-afraid this fight might be his last.

The crews from the two ships fought man-to-man with swords. An occasional gunshot echoed in the air. Men fell, blood flowing from their bodies, writhing on the deck, gasping for air, as they struggled to hold onto life. Charlie caught his breath after stabbing a Vulture crew member and looked over to see Captain Wells in shackles, along with several other members of the crew. He heard a thud at his feet and looked down to see Martin lying there in a pool of blood. He knelt down to help his friend, laying his sword down beside him. Picking up Martin's head, he laid it on his lap. His friend's eyes closed. "No, Martin, wake up!" Charlie hollered. Martin's body bled all over Charlie when he tried to rouse him. Martin fell limp in his arms. The next thing Charlie knew, someone grabbed him from behind, yanking his arms behind him and tied his hands together.

What was left of the crew of the Neptune was subdued and shackled. The Vulture's Captain Lewis instructed his men to herd them onto the sloops along with the Africans. The fallen Neptune crew was forced to step over the dead and climb into the boat.

"Throw these bodies overboard!" Lewis bellowed. Corpses were heaved over the rail into the sea. The ropes to the sloops were dropped and they drifted out to sea. Charlie sat in the sloop alongside his fellow crew members as well as some of the Africans. He could see them tossing bodies overboard from the ship. He looked down to see that he was covered in the blood of what belonged to his friend, Martin.

The storm caught up with them, and rain began to wash over the craft. As the raindrops streamed over his body, they rinsed away the blood in tiny rivers over his skin. Tears he hoped didn't show, streamed down his face as he looked at the unforgiving sea that was certain to swallow them whole.

Lewis instructed the crew to unload the leftover Africans into the remaining sloops. They unlocked the shackles as they came on deck, one after the other.

"What is going on?" Kwasi asked. He looked around at the unlikely sight of Africans and white men being held captive together. The chatter of the captives continued as they talked amongst themselves trying to figure out their fate. When it became clear they were being freed, cheers broke out among the Africans along with hidden smiles not one of them had ever thought would cross their face again. The expressions of their white counterparts were that of shock and disbelief.

Kwasi looked around but couldn't see Amari on the deck. His friend had been drifting in and out of consciousness all day and Kwasi had been unable to pull Amari to his feet before they'd herded everyone upstairs. He looked around again, but still didn't see him.

Kwasi asked a Vulture crew member where Amari was, but the language barrier kept him from being understood. He was shoved back in line to board the sloops along with everyone else. As he boarded the sloop, he looked back over his shoulder several times, but never saw Amari. While he wanted to rejoice in his newfound freedom, his emotions were tempered with worry. He sat in the sloop as it pitched to and fro in the waves. Where were they headed? How would they get anywhere without oars? As he watched the Neptune and Vulture sail in the opposite direction, he looked toward the shore. He hoped to see land or even just a bird and prayed to Mawu and Lisa. It was obvious to him they were looking over all of them.

Captain Lewis watched as the boats filled with Africans and Neptune crew members floated between the two ships. "They aren't sure where to go," Harris, the quartermaster, said as they pulled up the anchor.

The Africans responded and began to row with the sloop threatening to capsize as every wave tossed them one way and then the other. In just a few minutes, they were out of sight and sound.

"You gave them oars?" The surprise was evident in Lewis' voice. He looked at Harris in disbelief.

"Yes, if they are to stand a chance, they have to at least be able to row in the direction of the shore," Harris answered. "Over there!" he pointed to the shore. Nightfall had hidden the coast from their sight. "Go that way!" Somehow giving them a direction made him feel better about setting them loose in a sea that seemed determined to swallow them.

—Chapter Two—

"He that drinks fast, pays slow." —Benjamin Franklin

1719, Atlantic Ocean

Captain Lewis decided that he and Harris would stay on the Neptune and follow the other ship to Jamaica, leaving their trusted Boyle in charge of the navigation from the Vulture. He had been the quartermaster on the Vulture's crew from its inception. Both men trusted in Boyle's loyalty and skill. They all three agreed that once they made a drop of supplies in Ocho Rios, both ships would head over to Port Royal where he would sell their cargo and fill the hulls of both the Neptune and Vulture with sugar and rum to take back to England and cash in again. Port Royal was the unofficial gathering site for pirate and merchant ships. Some called it the Sodom of the seas — and not without reason. The crew would spend a few heady days filled with rum and women before heading back across the ocean.

Captain Lewis climbed down into the belly of the Neptune, covering his face with a handkerchief. The stench threatened to make the stomach of a strong man weak. He heard a groaning noise and saw Amari lying on the floor. "What is he doing here?" he asked Harris.

"He was injured and couldn't board the boat. It appears they forgot to come back for him." Harris nudged the African with his foot. Amari raised his head and looked at the two men. He took a deep breath and laid his head back down, trying with little success to keep his eyes open. He drifted back into a dreamlike state.

"I suppose we should just drop him into the water," Lewis said as he shook his head and sighed. A voice came out of the darkness.

"Why don't we keep him, sir?" A young crew member walked up behind them. "He looks strong enough." The mate wore a brown cap and white shirt tucked into his trousers. His lack of a beard revealed his youth. "I have some medical background. I think I can get him well enough to be of some service here on the Neptune."

Captain Lewis looked at the young mate, "Who are you?" he asked. "You're not one of my crew!"

A white bird squawked from across the room, walking back and forth on the deck.

Lewis glared at the parrot. "I do, however, remember that blasted bird. Is it yours?"

"I'm Ronnie Shepherd," the cabin boy answered. "The Neptune crew chief, Masterson, hired me on in Nassau." He looked over at the parrot he called Scottie. "The bird doesn't belong to me but seems to think he does." At first, Ronnie was annoyed the bird wouldn't leave him alone, but soon came to enjoy his company more than anyone else on board. He was the only friend he had at the moment.

"How did you manage to stay on this ship?" Harris asked Ronnie. He looked at Captain Lewis, afraid his legendary temper would flare.

"I stayed below to look after this one," Ronnie said, nudging Amari with his foot in an attempt to show disdain for the

African. The truth was, he had hidden under the stairs as the fighting took place, knowing if he were to board a sloop, there was a good chance he would be doomed with the rest.

Lewis shook his head. "We don't have time to nurse Africans back to health!"

"What is wrong with him?" Harris stooped down and looked closer at Amari.

"I believe he just had a severe knock to the head and should be better in a day or two. Other than that, he appears to be quite strong," Ronnie replied.

"Perhaps we should reconsider, Captain." Harris said. "We lost more of our men in the fight than we should have and could use an extra pair of hands."

Captain Lewis stroked his beard as he considered the possibility. He knew former slaves sometimes turned into strong crew members. "How do I know I can trust you?" Lewis asked Ronnie.

"I have no allegiance to Wells and the Neptune. I can help you bring this one back to usefulness."

Harris stood back up and looked at Lewis. "If he thinks he's able to get him into shape, the African could be of use. Now and later." Ronnie knew what "later" meant. A good price in Kingston.

Turning to look at Harris, Lewis said, "Alright, but any issues with either of them, they go overboard." Harris nodded in agreement and made a mental note to permanently silence that bird.

"Awwk! Harris!" Scottie repeated as he hopped up and down on the rungs of the ladder.

"Whatever you say, sir," Harris agreed looking down at the African and cut his eyes over at the bird that continued to annoy him. Harris looked at Ronnie. "You are responsible for him! You have three days to get him in shape or we will have to throw him overboard and your stupid bird will follow."

"Aye, aye, sir," Ronnie nodded. The thought of Harris trying to throw Scottie overboard amused him, but he thought better of saying so, knowing that one round from his gun could send him over the rail.

"And what is that?" Harris asked as he pointed to a large wooden bin. He walked over to see.

"It's turtles for soup. I've been keeping them fed," Ronnie answered

"Well, do continue. Turtle soup sounds like a delicacy compared to what I'm used to these days," Harris said.

Lewis and Harris headed back up the ladder to the deck. Ronnie turned, looked at the African, and crouched down to look closer at the gash on his forehead. "It looks like you're going to be fine. I'll find some wet cloths and come back to clean you up."

Amari lifted his head to say thank you. He didn't understand their language but was able to discern what had just happened. He wanted to acknowledge his gratitude to the one who apparently had just saved his life, instead he merely groaned in pain. As he laid there in the silence of the hold, his vision began to spin. He involuntarily closed his eyes. Darkness welcomed him like a blanket.

Ronnie found a moderately clean rag, wet it from a barrel of drinking water, and scooped up a cupful to take to the African, knowing that he had to stay hydrated. The line Ronnie had given Lewis and Harris about being familiar with medical practices was somewhat of a stretch, but he had been privy to the care given by Doctor Graves to Ronnie's brother after he had been injured in a fight on the docks.

Ronnie quietly knelt down next to the sleeping African and checked his pulse. There was a strong heartbeat. He pressed the man's fingernails and saw the blood leave and return, indicating his heart was good. Amari awoke again, this time feeling steadier and more focused. Scottie walked around the two men and stretched his wings a few times before settling down.

"Well, I see you're awake," Ronnie said as he looked at the African. "Hopefully, we can get you better soon so we can keep you on the ship."

Amari looked at Ronnie. "Me daa si," Amari said as his hand reached out in thanks. He touched his forehead with his other hand in response to the pain.

Ronnie waved him off. "Take it easy. Here, let's clean you up." Ronnie reached for the supplies he'd brought from upstairs. Catching air in its sails, the ship lurched, Ronnie reached over to touch the African's arm to steady himself. "It appears we have set sail."

Touching Amari's forehead and he gently wiped the wound. Next, he poured some of the water over it. He caught the excess with the cloth, dabbing the gash to further clean it. The African winced but stayed still.

"Amari, alright?" Ronnie repeated and the African nodded in the universal language "yes." "Alright then, Amari, I suppose we'll need to work on your English." Amari looked at Ronnie and wondered how much he should trust this person, but decided he had no choice. While he'd slept, he'd suspected the captain and his first mate were discussing his fate and deduced that the third voice had been Ronnie's.

Ronnie picked up the candle that he'd carried down and lit it from another that was nearly out. Amari pulled back, unsure of what Ronnie had planned. Ronnie smiled and touched Amari's arm. "It's fine. I just want you to look at the flame and follow it with your eyes." He pointed to his own eyes, held the candle in front, and moved it back and forth to demonstrate. Amari understood and followed the flame back and forth. Ronnie could see that Amari appeared to be able to focus. "Well, it appears that all is good," he said and blew out the flame. "That, my friend, is the extent of my medical expertise. We need to get you better quickly before Harris decides you're fish bait."

Ronnie felt better when he could say these things out loud. There was little he felt good about saying out loud on this or any other ship, for that matter. He'd found himself confiding in Scottie when there was no one else to hear and other than that, had kept to himself on the ship as best he could. The less people knew about him, the better.

As Ronnie stood, he offered his hand to Amari. The black hand hesitated and then reached for the white one. Amari sat up slowly as Ronnie pulled on him. "Take it slow." Ronnie put his hand up to indicate Amari should be cautious. "Slow," he said and pointed to his mouth for Amari to repeat and he did.

"Slow," Amari sounded out the word. He nodded at Ronnie after he sat up, indicating that he felt alright. His hand touched his forehead, involuntarily checking on the bandage that Ronnie had wrapped around his head.

"Your head will be fine," Ronnie said and touched his own forehead, "Just a small cut." He indicated the size of the gash with his fingers.

"Cut," Amari repeated.

"Yes," Ronnie nodded. "Small." He held up his fingers again, "small," he repeated.

"Small," Amari repeated and held his fingers up. The two smiled at one another.

They both jumped when a bucket came crashing down from the upper deck onto the floor in front of them. Harris ducked his head in the hole, looked down, and hollered to Ronnie. "Start swabbing up this hell hole. Get the African to help you!" Harris ordered as he threw down two chunks of lye, rags, and a dirty mop.

Ronnie and Amari looked at each other. Ronnie shrugged. "I suppose our respite is over." He reached for the bucket and walked over to the drum of water that sat in the corner, pulled off the lid and dipped the bucket inside until it was full. "Here," Ronnie handed Amari a clean wet rag and a bar of the soap. "Wash up," he said holding up the soap. Amari remembered and followed his lead.

Once Amari had washed up, Ronnie began the process of filling the bucket with water from the rain barrel to swab the deck and added lye. He threw the water down and swabbed as best he could, following with a bucket of clean water. He used the mop to push the water down the trough that drained to the outside of the ship. Amari stood and walked slowly over to the barrel to fill up the bucket, dragging the shackles that bound his ankles with him.

The stench was intense. Ronnie grabbed a kerchief and covered his nose to try and ward off some of the foul smell. He motioned for Amari to turn around and he covered his face as well with a piece of a dry rag.

"Try not to bend over," Ronnie told him, bending over and shaking his head to convey his meaning. "It will make your head hurt again."

Amari nodded.

It occurred to Ronnie that Amari could attack him since his hands were not bound, but for whatever reason, he felt no threat from the African. He reached into his pocket and took out the key Harris had given him earlier. He held his hand out to tell Amari to stand still and crouched down to unlock the shackles that held him captive. The metal chains fell to the floor with a clunk. Ronnie stood up to see Amari smile, something he hadn't done in a long while. The two looked at each other. No words were needed to convey the feeling of freedom and trust between them. We've both experienced being in bondage, and not just by chains. Ronnie was pretty sure he would have to fight for his own freedom from Harris and Lewis when the time came.

"Just kneel like this," Ronnie demonstrated for Amari, and he knelt on the deck. The two worked side by side for several hours. They used the time to work on Amari's vocabulary. "You will need to learn the language if you want to stay on board," Ronnie said to Amari and began teaching him the meaning of words. "Bucket," he pointed to the pail that Harris had thrown down the ladder.

"Buck it," Amari repeated and grinned. He did the same with the brush, water, lye, and mop.

"I have to go to the head," Ronnie stood and stretched.

"Head?" Amari pointed to his own head.

"No, not that one," Ronnie laughed. He made a gesture as if he was peeing and Amari tilted his head not understanding.

"Two," Ronnie held up two fingers, "Two meanings for head," he said trying to explain. He pointed to his head and the door of the head. Shrugging his shoulders, he chuckled, opened the door, and walked inside.

Amari continued to clean the floor and when Ronnie returned, he got back down on his knees and they worked in tandem. The air didn't move in the belly of the ship and the sweat poured off them both. Ronnie took another handkerchief from his pocket and wiped the sweat from his brow and neck. He handed the cloth to Amari who did the same.

"Well, my belly tells me it's time for some food." Ronnie placed his hand on his belly and then to his mouth. "Belly, food," Amari repeated each word. Ronnie then pointed to the bucket. Amari thought for a few seconds, trying to remember. "Bucket," he said, and Ronnie smiled.

"You're a quick study!" Amari nodded. They gathered up their cleaning supplies and headed up the ladder to the deck. Ronnie shielded his eyes, but Amari embraced the bright sunshine. He had made a deal with himself that he would never again complain when daylight dawned.

The scorching sun beat down on him and beads of sweat began to cover his skin. He could hear Ronnie talking to Harris but didn't understand what they were saying. Who is this person that has agreed to help me? Where am I? Will I ever be home again? Amari scanned the horizon but saw no land. Nothing that resembled home. He turned and watched the two men converse, tracking their body language to try and gain an idea of what they said.

"If you want to keep him here, make sure he stays out of my way. If he causes any trouble at all, he's going overboard!" Harris's hand swept toward the rail. Amari didn't like the gesture Harris had made and stepped back. "Crocker can get you some grub." He pointed in the starboard direction.

"Aye, aye, sir." He looked at Amari and gestured, "Come." They headed down to the galley where the sweaty Crocker stood preparing the evening meal. He wiped his brow with his sleeve and handed over bread, beans, and rice on metal plates. Ronnie handed one to Amari and walked over to sit on the top of a trunk. The two sat and ate silently, using the bread as a utensil as best they could.

"Slow," Ronnie said to Amari, using his hand to remind him of the meaning of the word with regards to the food. "You have not eaten in some time and if you go too fast, you could get sick and give them a reason to cast you overboard." Ronnie pointed to his stomach and made a sad face, getting the idea across.

Ronnie reflected on his task at hand with Amari. He had never owned a slave and was grateful it was not a part of his life. While he himself was an indentured servant now, where he came from, in the name of economic growth, enslaving another human was becoming commonplace. A practice he was never at ease with, it was now a concept that sat next to him. While technically, Amari was no longer a "slave," his future was uncertain at best. It was Ronnie's responsibility to educate him in his language. He knew that without the ability to communicate, Amari's value to the crew was limited.

Ronnie tossed Scottie a piece of crust and downed his own food quickly. He looked over at the African and wondered. Amari's food was about half gone. He had followed the instructions to move slowly. *Either he's pretty smart and catches on fast, or I'm a great instructor. Hopefully, both. He'll need all the brains he can get to survive what lays ahead.* Ronnie sighed and declined to imagine what that might be. Memories of the slave auctions in Nassau tried to crowd his thoughts, but he did his best to shake them off and found himself laying in his hammock, praying that would not be Amari's fate. *Why do I even care?*

THE TWO WORKED side-by-side every day taking the jobs at hand seriously. Scottie followed them from task to task when he wasn't perched on the sails. Amari proved himself to be strong and reliable and as Ronnie had suspected that first day, a fast learner. He easily picked up the necessary phrases of the language and they both became quick studies of their own sign language in an effort to understand one another better when time didn't permit an actual lesson.

Ronnie crept down to his hammock for a little privacy while Amari was, for the first time, enjoying the company of some of the crew. Most of the men were busy playing cards and drinking rum. Amari watched and studied what was happening. He was able to communicate with them via hand gestures and a mutual laugh when he would botch a word or meaning of one. Ronnie smiled to himself to think that Amari could ever fit in. Who would have believed it?

The days turned into weeks and Ronnie yearned to see land again. He sometimes wondered if they ever would walk on solid ground again. Amari proved to be a quick study and loyal. He would share whatever rations he was given. Ronnie shared some of the clothing he had packed in his satchel. *It fits him better than me anyway.*

Ronnie was careful to avoid Lewis and Harris, keeping both himself and Amari busy and productive. Amari was tall and strong and had learned to help with the sails on the ship. His height was an asset as he was able to reach higher than most.

"Hoist the sail!" Harris shouted to the crew. Ronnie and Amari stood up from their task of cleaning the floor in the galley and ran up the steps to the deck. There was a dark cloud only half a mile or so in the distance and it didn't look like a storm they wanted to sail through. Harris would normally steer them in the opposite direction, but it appeared to be too late. Rain began to fall before the sails were changed. The wind whipped and snapped making it difficult to position them correctly.

Amari stood tall fighting the gusts until he was able to grab hold of the ropes. The muscles across his shoulders tightened as he secured the lines, grimacing until they were tied down. All of the other crew members had given up, but Amari's perseverance paid off. The ship began to pick up the wind from the storm and pushed it further away from the dark clouds.

As the rain let up, the ship left the lightning in the distance. "Amari, Amari, Amari!" the crew shouted in respect. He descended the steps to head to the galley and his broad smile lit up the darkness of the room as the crew gathered, slapping him on the back. He hung his head in embarrassment from the attention.

Harris walked up to him and extended his hand. Amari took it as he had seen others do. "Well done! A smooth sea never made for a skilled sailor. You're definitely learning fast." Amari stared at Harris, pretending to understand, but knew enough to know he had earned some respect. He smiled and looked down, embarrassed at all the attention.

Ronnie could hear the celebration below and was the last one to climb down the steps to head to the galley. He was soaked from the rain, arms crossed in front of him trying to keep warm, but as he hit the last step, he slipped and lost his balance, falling to the floor. Amari's eyes flashed wide and he quickly went to the aid of his friend, pulling him to his feet.

His eyes rested on Ronnie's wet shirt that had caught on a nail and ripped open to reveal what appeared to be a woman's chest and not a man's. Ronnie quickly pulled it closed, but not before seeing the recognition in Amari's eyes. She put her fingers to her lips using their universal sign language to be quiet.

Could this man really be a woman? Amari looked away and wondered what had just happened. How could that be and why? He didn't have to wonder long. Common sense told him that being a female on board this ship could be a worse fate than that of an African. He looked back at Ronnie and nodded letting her know he would keep her secret.

Ronnie made her exit from the galley as soon as she could. Her identity was revealed to Amari, but she wasn't sure if anyone else had seen. She hoped not and tried to convince herself that her secret was safe. She had hidden her true identity knowing that, as a woman, she would never have been allowed on the ship. Her desire to leave Nassau and begin a new life was stronger than her fear of the unknown. She hoped her friendship with Amari was enough to solicit his silence. Crawling into her hammock she sought sleep, but it remained elusive. *Now, I have to depend on Amari's loyalty to keep us both safe.* Ronnie sighed and hoped she could trust him.

When the storm was far enough in the distance, the crew was released to hit their hammocks for the night. They had fashioned a hammock bunkroom over the former slave quarters.

Amari sat on the edge of his hammock and when Ronnie saw him, she sat up in hers and swung her legs over the side, rocking back and forth. She once again put her fingers to her lips indicating that he tell no one about her identity. He nodded and turned his hands upward and shrugged his shoulders as if to say, "What is going on?"

"The captain would throw me overboard if he knew," she whispered, using their personal sign language to help get her point across, "Please, don't say anything!" She vehemently shook her head.

He understood what she was saying and replied, "I will no," he said, meaning "I will not" and he shook his head in universal sign language. Ronnie smiled in reply.

"I knew I could count on you, Amari," she whispered and laid back down. *At least I hope I can.* She turned her back to him, afraid of saying anything more should someone overhear. Her hammock swayed as the ship pitched back and forth, struggling to stay in front of the storm. Several crew members were sick before the night was over, but in the morning, the skies parted way for the steamy sunshine.

Amari laid in his hammock feeling good about his beginning to fit in, but still yearned for his homeland. Ronnie's revelation confused him even more. *Please, Lisa and Mawu, I pray that Kwasi and the others reached the shore safely.* He prayed this every night and imagined their homecoming. A tear slipped out of his eye wishing he had been on the sloop with them. Part of him was grateful for the second chance he had been given here on the Neptune, but visions of Kwasi and other tribal members being launched to an uncertain fate in the sea haunted his dreams. His thoughts of escape were quickly thwarted with the factual realization that he had nowhere to go. Perhaps, when the Neptune found land, he would stand a chance. But each day as he scanned the horizon, he saw none. *Will I ever walk on land again?*

He comforted himself by drumming with his fingers on his belly at night as he prepared for sleep, remembering the sounds that wafted through his village at the end of each day, calling the hunters in before dark. He longed to be in the jungle hearing that sound just one more time, calling him home. *Never again will I complain that the hunt is over. Never.*

The weeks churned by and chatter about landing began to grow among the crew members. The ship was due to arrive in Jamaica any day now. They had passed Cuba just the day before. "The land of wood and water, that's what they call it," Harris told the junior members of the crew, including Ronnie and Amari. "The place has the clearest sea you've ever seen and waterfalls around every turn." His arm swept the horizon. "There's no way any man should go hungry with the fruit on the hills and the fish in the sea."

"Hotter than blue blazes, I'm told!" another crew member bellowed.

"Hot it is, Mac," Harris said, lighting his pipe and shielding the flame from the breeze with his hand. He took a long drag and let the smoke go. "But when we get to Port Royal and Kingston, let the fun begin!"

The crew laughed and mused at what their definitions of "fun" entailed. "Yeah, a handful of coins in my pocket, one hand around a willing wench, and a pint of ale in the other!" Masterson said.

"Forget the ale, all I want is the wench!" another sailor added.

"You'd better take two fistfuls of coins to get any woman to bed down with you!" Masterson chuckled and everyone laughed.

Ronnie didn't laugh but wondered what lay ahead for Amari and her in Port Royal. She had begun to formulate a plan to barter for Amari's release when they arrived in Jamaica. She knew she had to build a strong case as he would bring a good price on the open market in Port Royal, the slave trader's capital of the Caribbean and the Americas.

She motioned for Amari to meet her on the lower deck. It was time to formulate a plan. They each sat on the edge of their hammocks facing each other. "When the time comes and I find a moment for us to slip away," she used her arms to indicate fleeing from the others, "I will give you a signal like this." Ronnie put both hands behind her head with her elbows pointing away from each other. "Then, we run like the wind!" She pumped her arms indicating she was running. She had given a lot of thought to their escape but knew that to try and translate too much to him now would be futile.

The bell rang calling all hands on deck. They climbed up the ladder faster than normal, hoping for landfall. "Land ho!" the first mate called out as he squinted into the eyeglass. Ronnie shielded her eyes from the sun and looked at the horizon.

"Look, Amari!" They both smiled, knowing that soon it would be time to put their plan in motion. It had been a long time since they had seen land and Amari was thrilled at the thought of finding a way to be free again. He hoped that Ronnie's plan would work and once they were on the island, he knew his survival skills would help them both.

Jamaica stood tall with mountains reaching from the shoreline to the sky. Huge clumps of clouds floated on the clear blue sky, providing shade off and on from the relentless sunshine. The heat and humidity clung to them like skin, but the sea breeze provided welcome relief. They drew closer to the dock in Ocho Rios on the north shore of the island. The tropical setting was a beautiful contrast to the blue sky and multicolored sea.

The Neptune was planning to stop in Ocho Rios to see if they could sell any of the supplies that were left from the slave traders, but the Vulture would continue on to Port Royal and Kingston.

Harris gathered the crew in to give them their instructions. "Just like we discussed yesterday, gather everything that is to be sold and once we land, carry it all to the shore." He pointed to the supplies. "Separate the food from the other supplies to make for an easy sale. Once everything has been unloaded and sold, return to the deck and you will be given your pay for half the journey." He knew if they gave them all of their salary, half of them would not come back for the rest of their trip to Kingston. After weeks at sea, a man and his money could get lost in the arms of a prostitute, but the promise of more gold would hopefully sober him up enough to get him back to the ship.

As the ship glided into the sleepy little fishing village of Ocho Rios, the town came alive. The residents knew these were most likely pirates, but there were surely supplies to be sold and they didn't waste the opportunity to buy them here in their own town as opposed to traveling to the other side of the island to Kingston. The ladies were especially excited when a pirate ship had been to India. They usually brought chintz fabric with them, a cotton textile that had gained popularity. The British government had banned the importation of chintz as they wanted to protect their silk, linen, and woolen industries. However, their efforts did little to dispel chintz's popularity, especially in the tropics where perpetual heat was a constant. By the time the ship dropped anchor close to the rickety pier, there were horse-drawn wagons lined up with people hoping to purchase what they needed. The crew began to unload supplies they thought the village residents would purchase. Lewis set the prices and took in the coins or bartered with them for live turtles, soap, and other ship necessities.

Ronnie suspected Amari would not be allowed to go ashore. Harris and Lewis had been ambiguous whenever she would inquire as to his fate. She was afraid they would sell him into slavery in Port Royal or force him to stay on the ship as an indentured servant. Just the thought of either fate was deplorable. She had an agreement in writing with Captain Wells that she would be permitted to stay in Jamaica after they docked in Port Royal but held little hope they would hold fast to Wells' promise. Ronnie had no idea how she would survive, but decided she would worry about that when the time came.

The crew carried the supplies out in wheelbarrows. Once everything was off the ship and the bartering and selling was over, they lined up for their pay. Ronnie waited her turn and Harris handed her a few coins. Amari stepped up next. "Sorry, chap," he shook his head, "but your pay will have to wait until we get to Kingston." Amari frowned.

"What do you mean?" Ronnie asked. "He's worked harder than most on this ship!"

"The funds will not be available until we reach Kingston and sell the rest of the supplies from the Vulture," Harris replied and turned his back on the two indicating the conversation was over. Ronnie looked at Amari and shook her head. She knew what this meant. A knot filled her stomach. Chills crawled up her back to her neck at the thought. They were not going to pay him in Kingston. Instead, their plan was to sell him into slavery in nearby Port Royal. It was time to put their plan into action.

Rather than go ashore with the other crew members for recreation, she stayed on the ship with Amari. Two crew members had been left on the ship to watch the cargo, but she was certain the real reason was to make sure that Amari went nowhere.

They spent their time packing up the few belongings they had, making them ready to depart at a moment's notice. They played a few hands of cards with other crew members before heading to bed for the night, but Ronnie couldn't fake interest any longer. She excused herself knowing she wouldn't be missed and headed to her hammock. She laid on her back playing their escape plan over and over in her mind. Between her anxiety and the drunken mates that returned to the ship a few at a time, stumbling down the ladder to their bunks, sleep kept its distance. She twisted and turned in her hammock finding her heart raced if she thought too much about the horrific "what ifs."

She realized she must have slept for a while when she woke to the sound of a rooster crowing and could feel the ship begin to move out of the port. She got out of the hammock and pulled on her trousers. She always slept with her shirt on, no matter how hot it might be, for fear of being discovered.

Climbing up the ladder to the deck, she could see the sun peeking out from behind huge clouds that headed up the coast from the eastern side of the island. She pulled the bill of her hat down to shield her eyes. Jamaica's beauty masked her fear for a moment as she stared at the mountains that climbed up from the sea. She could sometimes see a bird flying near the shoreline. "Well, look there, Scottie," she pointed as she saw him perched on the railing next to her. "I think you have a few cousins here." Scottie responded to her voice by inching closer. "Stick close to us today. When we make a break for it, I hope you'll follow." She looked the bird in the eye.

"Break for it!" he repeated.

"Shhh!" She hushed him. Sometimes she wished Scottie weren't so bright.

She leaned on the rail staring at the shoreline, trying to keep her nerves at bay. The best plan she could muster was for the two of them to quietly lower themselves overboard under the cover of darkness, the first chance they got. It didn't appear they would be able to wait for the ship to dock again as that would be in Kingston and then it would be too late. There would be too many people there who could chase after them. The first mate rang the morning bell indicating all hands on deck. Amari was the first one to join her.

"Morning, Amari," she said as she moved over to make room for him at the rail. "Did you sleep?" she asked as she used their personal sign language to remind him of what the word, sleep meant.

"A small," he replied.

She grinned and said, "I think you mean a little!"

He nodded and repeated the words, "Yes, little."

One by one, the crew members climbed the ladder to the deck. The Jamaican shoreline slowly slipped by as they waited in line for their morning meal. Ronnie had eaten before any of them had come up, so she took the opportunity to head to her hammock for a few minutes alone.

She straightened up her sleeping area and pulled out the pouch with her mother's stone and put it into her trouser pocket. The cool green jade stone always brought her comfort when she ran a finger over it several times a day. Her mother had died when she was twelve, leaving her with a despondent father and no siblings.

She heard a noise over by the ladder and turned around to find Captain Lewis standing just two feet away. She jumped as if she'd seen a ghost.

"Oh, Captain!" She quickly put her cap back on. "I didn't know you were there!"

"No need to worry, my lady." He stepped closer. "I wanted to come down here before anyone else showed up." She realized he knew what she was and felt the hair on the back of her neck stand as fear gripped her. Before she could move away, he reached over and pulled her to him by the waist. Ronnie gasped when his hand reached inside her shirt. He pulled on the batting that she used as a girdle to hold in her breasts down and revealed what she had tried in vain to hide. She jerked away and ran toward the ladder, but he caught her wrist.

"No one pulls a stunt on me and gets away with it, Miss Shepherd," he grabbed her second wrist from the ladder and pulled her hands behind her back and said in her ear, "Now, it's time for you to pay for your passage!" She struggled, but her strength was no match for his.

AMARI WIPED HIS mouth with the back of his hand as he took the last bite. He looked around the galley and noticed Ronnie was gone. It wasn't like her to leave him alone in the company of others. He headed out of the galley and climbed up the starboard ladder to the upper deck. He walked toward the bow of the ship, but she was nowhere. He deduced she must have gone back to her hammock and decided to check. He started down the ladder and could hear voices, one being Ronnie's. When he heard her cry out, he skipped the last half of the ladder jumping the rest of the way down, landing on both feet facing Lewis who had Ronnie pushed up against a wall.

Ronnie jumped when Amari seemed to come out of nowhere. Lewis' back was to him and before he could turn around, Amari reached over from behind, and throttled him by the throat with his forearm. He turned the man around and shoved him up against the wall, his hand pinning his throat. Amari said something in Ewe that neither Ronnie or Lewis understood, but the tone of his voice and actions were enough of a translation for both. Lewis' face went red as he gasped for air. Amari grabbed him, pulling his arm back to plant a punch, when Ronnie stopped him.

"No, Amari! Let's go before we have to fight off the whole crew!" Ronnie grabbed the Captain's weapon from his belt and

tucked it into hers. "Let go of me!" Lewis bellowed, threatening
to bring unwanted attention from the rest of the crew. Amari's
hand quickly covered Lewis' mouth. Ronnie grabbed a kerchief
from the Captain's pocket and together, they gagged him as best
they could. Amari removed the Captain's belt and swiftly tied
Lewis' hands behind him. The irony of taking someone else
captive did not escape him. Ronnie opened the door to a storage
closet and the African shoved Lewis inside as he fell to the floor.
Amari slammed the door shut. Ronnie helped him to shove a
water barrel in front of the door to delay Lewis' escape.

"Come on, we have to get out of here fast!" Ronnie said,
forgetting that Amari didn't know exactly what she was saying.
She remembered their signal and put her hands behind her
head. He immediately understood. She motioned for them to
be as quiet as possible.

She grabbed the satchel from her bunk and they climbed
the ladder onto the deck. Trying not to draw attention to themselves, they walked to the railing of the ship. The ship was close
enough to the cliff lined shore and a waterfall roared in the
distance. Ronnie looked behind them to see if they were being
watched. It appeared everyone was busy with their daily tasks
and paid them no mind.

They looked over their shoulders and Ronnie nodded at
Amari indicating the coast was clear. Amari helped her to
the top of the railing. She looked down, but only briefly, and
jumped into the water, forgetting that she couldn't swim very
well. Amari's initial reaction was to look down and check on her
but thought better of it when the sound of her hitting the water
drew unwanted attention. He hoisted his body to the top of the
rail and plummeted through the air with his arms flailing to join
her. He was an adequate swimmer from his days of fishing with
his father but was still grateful it was shallow enough for him to
touch the bottom and start running after just a few strokes. He

could see Ronnie heading toward the shore in front of him and he ran through the water feeling as if he were in slow motion. He could hear the crew shouting through the muffled sound of the falls.

Ronnie's boots, clothing, and satchel weighed her down. She felt like she was never going to reach the shore, certain they would catch up with them, but Harris just stood on deck barking orders. She glanced back to see him leaning over the railing waving his arms. Amari splashed close behind her.

Finally, one of the crew members jumped in to chase them down, but they were already on shore, looking for a place to hide. Running down the beach, they ducked into the bushes.

"Get back on board! She's not worth it. Someone's coming!" Harris hollered to the mate. He could see a person descending a set of steps leading down to the beach. He was not eager for anyone to identify his ship in the middle of what might look like a mutiny.

Ronnie and Amari heard the worried shouts that someone was coming and peeked through the leaves to see them hoist the sails on the ship and leave the cove. Whoever was on the steps had saved them, at least for now

—Chapter Three—

"The end of Passion is the beginning of Repentance." —Benjamin Franklin

1719, Ocho Rios, Jamaica

Adria had never been very good at keeping secrets but this one had her by the throat. The irony was not lost on her as she'd never been one to keep things to herself. When she was a youngster, she tried to hold her tongue when it came to Christmas presents, but no one ever received a gift from her that was a surprise. This time was different. Some days she could almost forget, but on others, and more often in the past few weeks, it was getting harder and harder to push the secret to the cobwebs of her mind.

She repeated the stanza on the harpsichord over and over, her slender fingers reaching over the black and white keys. One, two, three, one, two three. Her mind struggled to focus as she stared out the window. A doctor bird darted from one blossom to another. She wished she could disappear as quickly as the hummingbird; here one second and gone the next. Her life in Jamaica had been one of advantage, compared to most, but not without its sacrifices. She allowed her mind to use the music to transport her past the secret. Her mind traveled back to their first days at Ginger Star while her fingers slid over the keys. This time she remembered the beginning, but she couldn't bear to imagine the future.

THE COURTNEY, THE ship that had carried them across the ocean, nosed its bow into the cove at Ginger Star after two months at sea. Once in the harbor, the first mate dropped anchor, the crew lowered the schooner, and Papa helped her and Mummy into the smaller craft. "My goodness, John, the water is crystal clear."

"Look, there's a fish!" Adria pointed down to the water as she stepped into the smaller boat.

"We won't go hungry living here, that is for sure," John put his oar down as the mate jumped in the water and pulled the boat up onto the sand. John joined him and carried Sarah to the shore, keeping her feet out of the water. "Just like on our honeymoon," Sarah whispered in his ear with one arm wrapped around his neck and the other on top of her head holding onto her hat.

"No better way to start our new life together, my dear." He kissed her on the cheek before he let her down on the sandy shore. He walked over and took Adria's hand as Robert, the first mate, handed her over.

"Thank you, my friend. Safe travels to you and the crew as you round the island to Port Royal," John said and shook Robert's hand padding it with a few shillings in gratitude.

"Should be there by nightfall, John. We certainly are ready for a hot meal and jug of ale!" He raised his hand that held the coins. Privateers and pirate ships congregated in Port Royal for food, trading, and debauchery. "We will see you on your next trip," John said. Ginger Star had a standing order of supplies to be delivered the next time the Courtney traveled the north coast of Jamaica.

They turned and walked along the shoreline that led to a steep hill. Adria looked over her shoulder to watch the ship disappear out of the cove. The women followed John to a set of steps that he and Sam, the family's trusted slave, had built to give access to their property from the shore. "Stay here until I get Adria up the steps, dear," John said as he took Adria's hand. She lifted her skirts to climb to the top. When she reached the last step, she turned towards the sea and the view took her breath away. "Oh my, Papa. What a beautiful view of the sea!" Papa laughed and headed back down the steps to help her mother. Small white caps broke over the reef that was outside the cove. The sea went from royal blue to crystal-clear aqua as it closed in on the shoreline. Her gaze landed across the cove on a waterfall that spilled into the sea with fresh water from one of the eight rivers in and near Ocho Rios. "Oh my, it's even more beautiful than you said, Papa!" She looked at her parents as they joined her at the top of the steps.

"Look at the waterfall, Mummy." Adria pointed across the cove.

"Oh my," Sarah agreed. "What type of flower is that?" she nodded toward a red waxy pointed flower. "That's a heliconia, but we call it a Ginger Star," John answered. "I knew you'd love it, so I had the crew plant them all around the perimeter. The doctor birds love them too."

"What's a doctor bird?" Adria asked.

"It's the nickname for the Jamaican hummingbird," Papa answered as he turned to lead the way up the path. "The male has the most beautiful long tail as you will no doubt soon see."

They continued walking through the foliage along the path that had been created with stones from the river. Adria pulled her fan from her pocket and her mother followed suit. John had warned them to keep a fan handy. "I know it's hot. The cottage is just ahead," John said as they came up the path. It was a modest house with a thatched roof that stood in the small clearing. A large black man ducked as he walked out of the front door and waved a greeting. "Sam! It's good to see you! Come meet my family," John said, and the two men shook hands. Sam wore a white shirt that was unbuttoned in an effort to cool off. It revealed his muscular build and Adria diverted her eyes as he buttoned up. He greeted the ladies with a bow from the waist as he continued to work on the buttons.

"It is my pleasure," Sarah said and extended her hand in greeting. Sam's hand swallowed hers in comparison. "This is our daughter, Adria," she looked at Adria who was fanning herself furiously, sweat dripping from her forehead.

"Sorry about the sweat, this heat is incredible and it's not even noon yet!" Adria wiped her forehead with her sleeve. She swept her dark auburn hair up and secured it with her hat, with the exception of a few loose curls. Her green eyes complimented her hair and olive skin tone.

Sam and Papa laughed. "The heat can be fierce. Everyone handles it differently, my dear. It appears you are one of the unlucky ones," Papa said, handing her his kerchief.

"We'll find ways to cool you off, Miss Adria," Sam smiled and took her small hand in his. "Come in, we have lemonade Mum Lettie send sent down from kitchen." The great house was under construction, but the kitchen and slave quarters had been completed first. They walked inside the cottage to find three cots, a table with chairs, and a fireplace.

"I warned you that it's not very large, but we won't be staying in here for much longer," John said.

"John, it's lovely. Our own little cottage and private beach as well. What more could two ladies want?"

John and Sam held out chairs for the women and they sat down, each one still waving their fans. Sam pulled the towels off the platters of fish, plantains, callaloo, and yams. "Oh my, all of a sudden, I'm famished!" Adria admitted. The three of them sat and ate, but not before giving thanks. They reached around the table to take each other's hands. Adria reached for one of Sam's hands and Sarah took his other. They bowed their heads and John gave thanks for the safe journey and the bounty before them.

Adria opened her eyes. "What is this?" Adria asked holding up a forkful of yams.

"Those are yams, Jamaica's version of a potato," Papa explained as he took another helping from the bowl. "Want more?"

"No, still getting used to them. They don't look or taste like British yams!"

Sarah looked around the cottage. "I'm impressed, John," she picked up a tea cup that she recognized from home. "How did you get these here without my knowledge?"

"I have my ways, my love." He kissed her on the head as he stood up from the table. "Shall we take a ride and see how the house is coming along?"

They cleared off the table and headed outside. Sam was ready with the horse drawn wagon that doubled as a lumber and construction wagon at the rear of the cottage. The men helped the ladies into the back of the wagon and jumped on the front bench. The horse pawed at the ground, anxious to get started.

"Adria, meet Chance," Papa said to his daughter. Her eyes flew open. The black stallion whinnied.

"Is that the stallion you talked about, Papa?"

"Yes, this is him and he loves to comb the shoreline and wander in the salt water when he's not pulling us around in the wagon.

"I will surely take him for a ride soon," she promised. This was one piece of home she could hold onto. She was an accomplished equestrian. Her thoughts turned to her time riding with abandon with her best friend, Jeffrey, and she reminded herself to post her letter to him soon.

Sam grabbed the reigns. The road turned into a trail and then back into a road riddled with ruts and sparse gravel. The wagon tossed back and forth as Adria and Sarah both clung to the wagon's sides, trying keep from tumbling off the makeshift seats. They were used to cobblestone streets that were well maintained, where there were shops and inns for entertaining. They traveled the worn trail that doubled as a road until Sam turned the horses onto a lane with two field stone pillars that held a sign between it that read, "Ginger Star."

"Oh, John, it's lovely!" Sarah exclaimed. She marveled at the yellow and red hibiscus blooms that were overcome with color and the bounce of the pink bougainvillea in the breeze. The lane was bordered with bamboo on both sides that tried to meet in the middle of the road to create an archway.

"Papa, this is amazing. You have quite the eye for landscaping, it seems," Adria said.

"I would love to take the credit, but I must admit Sam has come up with most of the ideas for Ginger Star's beauty. I will, however, take some credit for the house," and as he said that they headed up the hill towards their soon-to-be home.

They approached the driveway that wound around the front of the house in a circle. The wagon pulled up in front of the half-moon steps that led to the massive door and the men helped the ladies down from the wagon. Arm-in-arm they ascended the steps together. At the top of the steps, there was mahogany paneling with inlaid carvings. The ceiling arched over the steps provided a welcoming atmosphere. John led them up through the doorway and into a large room with sixteen-foot ceilings.

The windows opened to allow the Caribbean breeze easy access. The slaves that had been working to stain more of the mahogany trim, scattered and disappeared down the back steps to allow the family its privacy. Adria felt strange at the thought of owning slaves, but understood they were needed to make plantation crops profitable. Nevertheless, she felt a pang of guilt at the thought of owning someone. That was now a reality.

"John, this is just breathtaking," Sarah said as she looked out the rear windows that gave way to the mountains of Jamaica. She walked to the front window to see the Caribbean looking back at her.

Adria walked to look out the rear veranda. "Oh my! The views just get better and better!" She reveled in the warm breeze that worked to cool her off. Having pulled her petticoat off while they were at the cottage, she found that she was much cooler.

"Nothing but the best for the two ladies in my life," his chest puffed out with pride.

"John! You didn't tell me." Sarah's hand flew to cover her mouth in surprise. She walked towards the fireplace and touched the Italian marble with her hand. The carving was flawless with a green vein running through the ivory stone. The mantle appeared to be one piece connected to the sides that ran down the front of the firebox. The hearth matched the mantle and the glow of the afternoon sunlight reflected itself giving the illusion of a cozy evening fire. It was an exact replica of their fireplace back in London.

He slid his arm around the back of her waist, and they stood silently together, mesmerized by the fireplace. "I know how hard it was for you to move so far away from everything and everyone you love," he pulled her closer. "I wanted to give you as much as I could to make you feel at home, my love." He kissed the top of her head.

They walked through the great house and talked about its progress. They were at the mercy of the shipments of supplies, but John assured them both they should be able to move into their living quarters within the next few months. Now that the kitchen was finished, their sleeping quarters would be the main focus.

Every day, Adria and her mother would visit Ginger Star and pitch in with the work in any way they could. Painting turned out to be Adria's skill and Sarah worked with the garden crew to create English gardens and walkways throughout the grounds.

Although the cottage was small, they enjoyed their close quarters and passed the time playing chess and backgammon. Papa had brought a deck of cards from England and taught them how to play whist, but since there were only three of them, he modified the rules to accommodate. They laughed and kept an ongoing scorecard, adding to the total each night.

Adria missed her friends and relatives, but her closest friend had always been her mother anyway. Sarah had schooled her, taught her to play the piano, how to embroider, and all the needed social graces.

They walked into the kitchen where the slaves were working on their dinner. An older woman looked up. Her head was wrapped in a blue kerchief and sweat glistened on her forehead.

"Mum Lettie, this is my wife, Sarah and daughter, Adria," John said.

The older woman wiped her hands on her apron and dipped a small curtsy. "Good to meet you," Mum Lettie said. "Massa John very happy you here."

Sarah took Mum Lettie's hand in hers and said, "Thank you for the lemonade and delicious meal that was waiting for us in the cottage."

"Yes, everything was wonderful," Adria said. "Papa says you're the best cook on the island!"

Mum Lettie's head bowed, and she giggled a little, not used to such praise. "I have much help from others," she said nodding toward the rest of her staff that had made a hasty exit when the family walked in. "Welcome to Jamaica," she said wondering how such a young woman as Adria might acclimate to life on the island.

TWO YEARS HAD passed and Adria's family had acclimated very well, enjoying the climate and surroundings on the island of Jamaica, but the isolation could be daunting. There were few families that had moved here and stayed permanently. Too many missed the social whirl of London and its advantages.

Adria missed all of her friends, but mostly Jeffrey. They had grown up together. Their mothers were best of friends and the two had been like brother and sister. At first, they traded letters often, however the communication had gotten slower and slower. Adria suspected Jeffrey had found a young lady to pursue. After all, he was seventeen, the same as her. It was time to get on with his life. He never said so in his letters, but she was good at picking up the nuances of his words. She'd hoped he would find happiness.

Adria loved the harpsichord, however lately, it was difficult to keep her concentration on her practice. The sewing circle was nearly impossible, trying to make small talk with her mother and whatever friend might have been visiting. It was much easier for her to hide behind the lid of the harpsichord and feign interest in her music in an effort to keep others at bay. Nevertheless, the secret made her feel like an imposter. She was a true friend to no one.

The insidious click-click of the grandfather clock quieted as it chimed two o'clock and put an end to her daydream. Adria slid to the end of the bench and stood. She picked up her skirts, smoothing the fabric in the front. The house was quiet as Father and Sam had gone to town for more building supplies and Mother was taking her afternoon rest. The only sound was the whispering from the kitchen with an occasional clink of a dish or pan where Mum Lettie and the kitchen help worked quietly prepping for dinner. Adria was expected to nap after her harpsichord practice, but more often than not, she stole away to the gardens or the seaside.

Tiptoeing out of the house, she held her skirt up to quiet the rustling of the crinoline and walked down the path toward the beach. She reminded herself to be extra careful not to harm her dress as it was made of the special aqua-colored brocade fabric Mama had ordered just for her from back home.

Plucking a yellow hibiscus bloom from a bush, she stared at its perfection. Hibiscus blooms always reminded her of happiness, something that had eluded her of late. She tucked the flower behind her ear and ducked under the lower limb of a bread fruit tree. As she brushed the offending tree limb from her hair she gently touched the flower to ensure it hadn't fallen away.

Adria walked to the top of the cliff and headed down the stone steps to the shoreline. The little cove that ducked in from the sea shone like a jewel in the sunshine. As she reached the bottom step, her eyes, shielded by her bonnet, scanned the sea's edge as always, looking for shells. Bending over, she picked up a one-inch conch, her favorite size. It was white with brown stripes. Her collection grew almost daily. She'd taken the larger shells and dotted the steps leading up the cliff to the lawn.

She'd found most of them after what many had called a hurricane. She hoped not to experience that frightful event ever again. The fierce winds and sideways rain had been frightful and kept them huddled inside for two long, dreary days. When they finally ventured outside, the damage to Ginger Star was startling.

Trees had fallen and the roof was severely damaged, but as Papa had pointed out, everyone at Ginger Star was still alive and unharmed. Not everyone had been so fortunate. Several slaves at the Seville Plantation had been washed away in rushing water that came quickly down from the mountains after a storm. It took months for the repairs to be completed and everything cleaned up at Ginger Star with Adria and her mother pitching in to help where they could.

Determined to head back to the main house, she tucked the shell inside her dress pocket. She was about halfway up the steps when shouts came from the sea.

"Hey, over there maybe!" a man's voice bellowed.

Why would anyone be shouting? Without thinking, she stopped to listen closer. She froze when she saw the bow of a ship. It was tucked in her favorite swimming hole at the bottom of the falls. She frowned as she'd never seen a vessel there before and by the looks of it, Papa wouldn't think it a friendly one. Adria ducked up against the cool roots of the banyan tree. Distant shouts made it clear that the vessel's inhabitants weren't happy ones. She leaned on the tree and peeked around the side to see what was happening, clutching the seashell to her chest.

A burly man trudged through the water trying to run toward the shore waving what appeared to be a gun. Suddenly, he slowed to a stop before reaching the beach. He looked back at the ship with his hands lifted up as if to ask a question.

"Get back on board. She's not worth it. Someone's coming!" a man's voice shouted from the bow of the ship. The man looked back at the shore's edge and tugged the black bandana down that threatened to fall off his head into the water. He sloshed back to the ship's side and climbed the rope ladder.

Why would they be looking for me? Didn't he say 'she'? Her heart threatened to leap up through her throat. Adria leaned against the tree, afraid to breathe. Her eyes darted back and forth frightened of what she might see.

She? Does he know I am here? An unfamiliar feeling of terror crept up the back of her neck and her imagination took flight. Adria knew about pirates and merchant ships and had seen a few of them pass through in the early morning hours. A few had anchored at Ginger Star delivering construction materials and supplies that Papa had ordered for the plantation. On occasion, she'd heard Papa and his friends talk about unsavory ships while smoking their pipes in the parlor after dinner. She realized this ship was what they had talked about. Seeing it while she was alone was enough to make her knees want to buckle.

Adria watched as the man slosh through the water back to the ship. Words were exchanged, but the sound of the falls muffled them. The next time she peeked, she saw him nimbly climb the rope ladder onto the ship. While she stood silently observing the men, she strained to discern their angry words. No matter how attentively she listened, Adria was only able to discern a word now and then. The ship slowly turned and made its exit, hoisting its big sails to catch the breeze. When she was certain they wouldn't see her, she came out from behind the enormous banyan tree and walked toward the cove to investigate.

"Awwwwk!" squawked a white parrot as it flew from one branch to the other, catching Adria's hair in his wake. She screamed without thinking and swatted at the bird that had already landed on a nearby branch. "Gbrrrr!" the parrot shook his head and shrugged his shoulders.

"Geez! You scratch me and I'm the one that's in trouble?" Adria talked to the bird as if he could answer.

"Yes, trouble," the bird cocked his head and stared at her. "Trouble!"

"Wait, you can talk?" She was shocked at the parrot's vocabulary. Wild parrots didn't talk; only those that spent a lot of time with people.

"He can when he wants to."

Adria whirled around toward the voice and dropped the conch shell. A female voice. There was no one in sight.

"Who? Where are you?" Adria bent down and picked up a piece of driftwood to try and fend off the intruder. The sound of the falls mingled with the tiny ripples of water lapping the shore failed to convince her she was alone. "Come out, I tell you!" She looked from side-to-side.

"Come out!" The white bird mimicked her.

The leaves of a hibiscus wiggled, and a head poked through the foliage. What appeared to be a pirate stepped forward, wearing obviously way too large men's clothing, a long-sleeved dirty blue shirt, and soggy black baggy pants stuffed into oversized boots. Nevertheless, the clothes couldn't hide the fact that the sailor was a woman.

"Are they gone yet?" Ronnie asked, looking from side to side. Adria glanced back at the ship.

"Yes, but who are you?" Adria stepped back still holding the driftwood. Her eyes settled on the pistol handle that stuck out of the sailor's beltline.

"My name is Ronnie Shepherd."

"What are you doing here?" Adria stepped back again, and the sailor reached for the pistol. Adria turned to run.

"Don't go! Here!" Ronnie threw the long-handled pistol to the ground, landing in the sand near Adria's feet. "It's not loaded anyway."

"Awwwk! Not loaded," mimicked the parrot.

Adria stopped and bent over to retrieve the gun, realizing that it was a fruitless act since she'd never handled one before, but hoped that Ronnie didn't notice.

"Again, what are you doing here?" Adria asked.

The sailor took the hat off revealing cropped brown hair that fell to her shoulders.

"You're a. . ." Adria gasped, "woman!"

"Yeah, and that's why I'm here. They just figured it out," she pointed toward the ship. "After two months at sea, the realization really irritated them, I must say." Ronnie's voice cracked and she sat on the low-hanging sea grape tree limb that almost reached the ground to gain her composure. She stared down at the sand. Adria noticed Ronnie's shirt was torn and the buttons were missing. There were bruises where her skin was exposed. It wasn't hard to figure out that Ronnie had been running for more than her life.

Ronnie pulled the sides of her shirt back together and shivered despite the Jamaican summer heat. She cringed when she remembered Captain Lewis' dirty hands reaching under her shirt as she struggled to get away from his grasp.

"Lucky for me, the water wasn't too deep when we jumped in and ran to shore." Ronnie looked back up at Adria, quickly wiping away the tears that revealed her recent terror, as they trickled down her cheeks.

"We? There are more of you?"

Ronnie realized her mistake. She looked back along the shoreline in the direction of Amari. "Yes, a man named Amari. They would have killed us both had we not jumped off the ship."

"Where is he?" Adria looked over Ronnie's shoulder.

"I'm not sure," Ronnie looked behind her. "Amari! Are you here?" she called.

Scottie flew back down the shoreline to another tree as Amari stepped out from behind the bushes. He was crouched down, ready to run if necessary. Where to, he wasn't sure. His eyes shifted back and forth looking for danger.

"Oh, my goodness, a slave?" Adria's hand jumped to her throat. She looked from Amari, to Ronnie, and back at him again.

"No, he's not," Ronnie stammered, not wanting to lie, "he almost was." Ronnie explained the capture of the slave ship and why Amari was with her.

"That's just awful," Adria processed the story. "No one deserves to be treated that way. Neither of you." She looked from Amari back to Ronnie and asked, "But why were you on the ship?"

"It's a long story." Ronnie fiddled with the black scarf and cap, pulling out the knot. "I wanted to leave Nassau behind and the only way I could do it, was on the sea."

"Awwwk, long story!" the parrot squawked.

"And who is he?" Adria asked looking up at the parrot, holding onto the pistol with both hands.

"That's Scottie. I guess he didn't like those rotten scoundrels any more than we did." Ronnie reached up and stroked his back. "Evidently, he flew the coop too. He's been a good companion to us over the past few months."

"Adria!" Papa's voice called from a distance. They turned their heads in unison and looked up the steps.

"Oh my, Papa's back from town!" Adria started toward the steps and turned back to face them. They stood up ready to bolt at the sound of his voice. "Stay here." She thought for a quick second. "No, get back in the bushes so no one sees you," she pointed to the spot that Amari had been hiding. "I'll be back!"

Adria stared at the pistol in her hand, unsure of what to do. She looked at Ronnie but didn't trust her enough to hand it back. She tossed it into the water, figuring if it were wet, it wouldn't do anyone any good for a least a little while. She gathered up her skirts and headed up the steps of the cliff. "Coming, Papa!" she called as she hurried toward her father.

—Chapter Four—

"How can we expect another to keep our secret if we cannot keep it ourselves."
—Francois de La Rochefoucauld

1720, Jamaica

Ronnie tried to hide her nervousness from Amari. She talked aloud, although she realized he didn't understand and she was really just talking to herself, so she tried to stop. Frantic thoughts gave way to shaking hands and trembling knees. Before she knew what was happening, tears slid down her cheeks and fear crept in.

Her shoulders heaved as she cried into her hands. Tears were something she'd not allowed herself on board the Neptune. The African walked over and sat down next to her. "I'm sorry, Amari," she sobbed. "I don't know what is wrong with me!" Amari cautiously put his arm around her shoulder, not sure how she would react. Their silent communication was once again a comfort. She laid her head on his shoulder and closed her eyes as he placed his hand on the top of her head. Ronnie felt safe in Amari's arms but realized that was probably foolish. He was in more danger than she. Even so, she allowed herself the momentary lapse in judgment. Both of them knew that Amari ran the risk of being sold as a slave were he to be captured again.

It occurred to her that his fate would be even worse were anyone to see him showing her any affection at all. She raised her head off his shoulder when the thought crossed her mind.

"Amari take care you," he said to her, pointing his finger from himself to her. Ronnie's heart sank, as she knew there was little chance of that ever happening for any length of time. The thought of what Amari's future might bring him brought more silent tears, but she didn't share their origin with him. She took several deep breaths and looked around. Scottie reappeared on the ground in front of them. He was tearing into an over-ripened mango he'd found.

"Well, I suppose we need to think about what our plan is going to be," Ronnie said to them. *Alright, now you're talking to a bird and someone that can't speak your language . . . What in the world?* She didn't know where they would sleep for the night or where their next meal would come from, but she did know the emotions bubbling up in her were strange, strong, and dangerous on so many levels.

Amari stood staring intently at the sea. He motioned to Ronnie to stay put. Walking slowly into the water, he pointed at his prey and she shielded her eyes to see. He'd spotted a school of fish. Standing incredibly still for a few minutes, he barely breathed. The only thing that moved were his eyes darting back and forth as he studied the fish. Without warning, he dove with his arms slicing through the water, his arms and legs flailing in the waist high water. He stood up with both hands holding on to a silver fish of good size. "Incredible work!" Ronnie called out. The fish struggled for its freedom, but Amari's hunger and determination won the fight. He carried the fish back to the shore and allowed it to flop out of his hands onto the sandy beach. Amari turned and went back to wait for another opportunity, but the school had left the shoreline.

Ronnie took the fish from him with both hands and laid it in the shade. Laughing, she said, "I suppose there is no reason to go hungry in this place of plenty, we just need to figure out how to cook him."

"Hungry," Amari said and put his hand on his belly.

"Yes, hungry." Ronnie smiled. She looked around at the trees that lined the beach. "Scottie is eating, so there's got to be something close by." She spotted the tree and pointed, "There is food," she pointed. "I'm not sure what it is, but it looks like we could eat one." They walked a few yards down the beach. The fruit was orange, yellow, and green. He reached to find one that appeared soft enough to be ripe. He took a bite and chewed the yellow fruit. The juice ran down his chin. Wiping it with the back of his hand, he smiled and offered the fruit to Ronnie. She leaned over and took a bite. The taste was sweet, smooth, and delicious. "I'm not sure what it is, but it's wonderful!" They smiled at each other. It was the first time Ronnie could remember smiling in what seemed like a lifetime. Amari was tall enough to reach more of the low-hanging fruit. Each time he picked a promising fruit, he handed it to Ronnie who carefully piled it in the shade next to the fish.

Voices could be heard from a distance. "We'd best duck back into the bush until we see who it is," Ronnie said. Leaving their stash of food, they ran back and hid in the bushes.

Sitting as still as they could they listened attentively as the voices faded. "No duck," Amari said and shook his head.

"What do you mean?" she asked leaning over so he could whisper and not be heard. She shrugged showing him she didn't understand.

"Where?" he asked. "Where duck?" Amari used his arms trying to imitate a quacking duck.

It occurred to her that he misunderstood "duck in here" and she laughed aloud, but quickly threw her hand over her mouth.

She giggled. "Not that kind of duck," she whispered. "Duck means," and she dipped her head down as if trying to hide, "hide away." Amari frowned, not sure he understood.

"Are you there?" They heard Adria call in a quiet voice. She looked around, not sure if the runaways had stayed put. Ronnie peeked out from behind a branch.

Once she was sure it was Adria, Ronnie pulled back the leaves and said, "Yes, we're here."

"Oh my! I didn't see you!" Adria's hand flew to her throat as she jumped back.

"So sorry," Ronnie said and came out from behind the tree branches and put her hand on Adria's shoulder. "The last thing I want to do is scare off our only ally."

"Not to worry," Adria said straightening her bodice and lifted up a sack, handing it to Ronnie. "It's just a few things that I thought you might need." Ronnie peeked inside and saw clothes and food.

"Thank you so much. We found some fruit on a tree," she pointed to the pile in the shade. "I'm not sure what kind it is, and Amari caught that fish." Ronnie pointed to the silver fish laying under the tree in the shade.

"You caught that?" Adria asked Amari pointing at the fish.

Amari grinned and nodded.

"And those are mangos," Adria said. "They provide good food almost year-round. Did you like them?"

"Like them!" Amari nodded and smiled.

"Well, you are a quick study with English, Amari!" Adria was impressed.

Ronnie reached in the pouch, pulled out the clothing, and said, "He's very smart."

"How did he catch the fish?" Adria asked.

"With his bare hands, wading in the water," Ronnie said. "It was really something to watch." She looked at Amari who knew they were talking about him. "So much for the opinions of folks saying Africans can't think for themselves!"

"Quite true," Adria answered. "I've seen that by getting to know the servants here at Ginger Star."

"You have servants and not slaves?" Ronnie's head leaned to one side.

"Well, we have both. Sam and Mum Lettie are emancipated, but the rest are not," Adria said sitting down on the branch next to Ronnie. She kicked off her shoes, pulled off her stockings, and put her toes in the sand. "My father began to see the error of slavery and how unfair it was to expect God or anyone to understand any logic with regards to one person owning another." She leaned back and stared off into the vibrant blue sky.

Their conversation was penetrated by the sounds of drums in the distance. Amari frowned and turned his head to try and hear it better. Seeing the frown on Amari's face, Ronnie asked, "Amari, what's wrong?" He recognized the cadence of the drums. It was an Ewe cadence. His heart leapt and he jumped to his feet, with his hand to his ear signaling for the women to listen up. The drums and a horn continued off and on for a minute.

"The Maroons often start their___" Adria's voice trailed off when Amari put his hand up asking her to hush. Ronnie and Adria just looked at each other and shrugged, not understanding what he said and then looked back at him.

"It's like he understands what they're saying," Adria whispered and Ronnie nodded.

Looking back at Ronnie and then Adria, he asked "Where?" When neither knew what to say, he asked, "Go?" His hands pointed up into the hills.

Shaking her head, Adria said, "Oh, no, I wouldn't do that!" She looked from Amari to Ronnie. "It can be very dangerous. They're somewhere up in the hills hiding in the steepest of mountains where they cannot be found or caught." She looked at Ronnie and nodded toward Amari, her head tilted sideways. "How much does he understand?"

"More than you think," Ronnie stood and walked over to Amari and put her hand on his arm. "What did the drums say?" She used their sign language to convey her question. He understood.

"Drums," he replied using his hands to imitate them pounding on the drum itself.

"Yes, it is," Ronnie said.

"Say bad come, be warned." He looked up into the mountains again. The drums were silent now, but the sound of a horn moaned through the air. A few long sounds followed by two short blows. Amari nodded as if he understood the code.

"Perhaps we should head up that way since he understands the sounds," Ronnie said with hope in her voice. She didn't know what their plan would be but knew they couldn't stay on the beach indefinitely.

"You wouldn't get far in those hills these days," Adria sighed.

"Why is that?" she took the last bite of the mango and tossed the seed aside, wiping her mouth with her sleeve.

Adria said, "The Maroons have been restless of late. I've heard they are scaring people back down from the hills."

"What are 'Maroons'?" Ronnie asked as she closed the sack up.

"They're a tribe of escaped slaves and Taino Indians that have fought against the British since the Spanish left in 1655, some 65 years ago."

"How did they manage to band together like that?" Ronnie asked.

"Many managed to slip away from plantations over the years, but originally, the Spanish retaliated against the British when they surrendered Jamaica by releasing all their slaves into the mountains. They joined up with the Taino Indians who were indigenous to Jamaica and formed their own militia. They stand ready to fight and are very good at it." Adria stood up. "Papa has not been able to go to Claremont to check on our sugar crops for some time now. They have the roads blocked."

"Surely the Brits can stop them with the Royal Army!" Ronnie surmised.

"One would think so, but the Maroons are cunning. They're positioned from a high vantage point so we cannot approach them without being seen and they are very good at camouflaging themselves in the jungle, coming at us with no warning. Our only choice is to stay away." She lent her hand to Ronnie and pulled her up from the branch.

"Come with me," Adria said turning toward the sound of the falls. "I'll show you where you can stay until we figure out what you should do." Ronnie motioned to Amari to follow them. Putting the mangoes inside the satchel and picking up the fish with his other hand, he followed them down the shoreline to another set of steps that were overgrown and less traveled than the others. Adria picked up her skirt with one hand and held on to the tree branch-turned-into-railing with the other.

"It must be hard getting around here wearing a skirt," Ronnie said as they trudged up the steps. "And hot, too."

"Yes, it is, but I have become accustomed to them and try to stay out of the sun as much as I can. I have found that skirts are cooler than trousers. I put one in the sack for you." They came to the top of the stairs and Adria motioned for them to stand back. She looked both ways to be sure no one was there and waved them on. Ronnie and Amari followed her to a small cottage hidden by a few mango and breadfruit trees laden with fruit. The thatched roof sagged in the middle, but other than that, the little house appeared to be in good shape. Sunlight filtered through the shade of the dense foliage bringing with it the Jamaican heat.

Adria opened the door and grabbed an old broom from the corner to knock down a few cobwebs she'd missed earlier. They followed her inside. Sunlight filtered through the slatted window shades to reveal three small cots on one side of the room and a table with three chairs on the other. "This used to be Papa's cottage before he brought Mummy and me to Jamaica." She pulled out one of the chairs, sat down, and fanned herself. Realizing Ronnie might appreciate one as well, she reached in the sack and pulled out a second fan and handed it to her. "He and Sam stayed here for a while, and we all stayed here for a few months until Ginger Star was finished. No one uses it anymore and you should be fine to stay for a while until you decide what it is you want to do."

"Who is Sam?" Ronnie asked.

"He was a slave, but now emancipated and a servant. A very trusted friend," Adria explained. "I'm sure that you'll meet him before long. By the way, keep the fan with you. It's a good way to make this heat bearable."

Ronnie opened the blue fan and waved it at her face. "Well, it seems like I'm constantly thanking you, but I have a feeling I owe you tremendously for this favor!" Glancing out the window, she saw Scottie sitting on a branch of the breadfruit tree keeping an eye on them. "Aren't you worried someone will find us here?" Ronnie asked. The bird was not about to let them out of his sight.

Adria walked over to the counter and opened the basket she'd dropped off earlier, pulling out a flask of tea. "My parents are so busy planning Mummy's next trip to London you could probably sit down for dinner and they wouldn't notice," She giggled as she pulled two cups out of the satchel and poured some tea in each.

Ronnie laughed at the thought. "I could just introduce myself as an almost sailor with a big African shadow and a crazy bird that follows me everywhere!" Scottie squawked in protest.

The two laughed and Amari smiled quizzically wondering what was so funny. "It has been so long since I've laughed, Ronnie," Adria said. "It feels so good!"

They talked until it was time for Adria to head back to the house for afternoon tea. "I can miss a lot, but tea is not a good idea. Mummy would send out a search party."

"Please go and enjoy. We'll be just fine." Ronnie sat down on the edge of the small bed. "The excitement of the day has tuckered me out." She stretched her arms toward the thatched roof.

"I will and you do the same. There are sandwiches in the basket," she pointed toward the small fireplace. "You can make tea there and even cook up the fish. There is a flint and striker in there to start your fire." She nodded toward the basket.

"Aren't you worried about the smoke?"

"No, this is far enough away, no one will notice." Adria said. "I put some clean linens on the beds and a few dishes on the shelf." She pulled the door closed behind her and headed up the trail.

Ronnie looked around the cottage. It was obvious Adria had cleaned it up earlier. Weariness set in as she thought about the events of their first day on the island. Pulling out the cheese sandwiches, she shared them with Amari. "Well, folks," she said to Amari and Scottie, who had come in when Adria went out, "It looks like this is our new home for now." She tossed a crust of bread his way and he swooped down to the floor. Amari looked around the cottage. He smiled at the bird and then at Ronnie.

"Here, let's make the bed," Ronnie said pointing to the cot. "Why make bed when have one?" he asked.

Ronnie laughed when she realized he was confused as to what "making" the bed meant. "Our words have two meanings sometimes." She raised two fingers. He just shook his head, not sure what she meant. They pulled off the old linens and replaced them with clean ones.

Closing the door and shutters on the windows, Ronnie remembered Adria had mentioned there were blankets inside the trunk against the wall. Pulling them out, she wrapped one around her shoulders and offered the other to Amari. "I think I'll rest for a while." She put her prayer-like posed hands up to her head so he would understand.

"Sleep?" he asked.

"Yes, just a little nap," she held her thumb and finger up showing him "just a little."

"Little," he said and held his hand up in the same way. He walked over to the second cot and sat down.

Ronnie laid her head on the pillow and smiled at the parrot as he chopped up the bread with his beak. She rolled over onto her side and folded her arm under her head. Closing her eyes, she remembered Captain Lewis' fury as she managed to tear away from his grip. She closed her eyes tighter recalling the fear she felt as she jumped from the ship into the water. Then, she quickly reminded herself of her relief as she recalled the sight of Adria walking toward her while the ship glided away. She could hear the Jamaican crickets begin their lullaby outside the cottage window and sleep embraced her.

Amari lay down on the other cot. His mind raced as he remembered the sound of the drums and horn. Memories of home flooded him more than ever since he was captured. He prayed again for Kwasi and the others. He wondered how he would find the drums. He could follow their sound and get to where they were. Adria had told him that it would be difficult, that much he knew. He also knew that somewhere in Jamaica, there were free Africans and his heart filled with hope for the first time since he'd left home. Closing his eyes as hope filled his heart, sleep greeted him with dreams of freedom.

OPENING HER EYES, Ronnie looked around the cottage, and realized she'd taken more than just a nap. The afternoon had turned to night as she was reminded where she was. Exhausted from their ordeal, she hadn't even rolled over in the night. Sunlight peeked through the slats of the closed shutters. The cricket lullaby was gone and, in its place, the sound of Scottie pacing back and forth clucking reached her ears. She chuckled, "Sorry, boy, I didn't mean to pen you up last night." Throwing back the lightweight blanket, she put her feet on the floor and walked over to open the door allowing the bird to make a hasty exit. His white wings fluttered as he hopped up to a neighboring branch. Amari's dark brown back lay facing her as he slept. She followed the bird outside and ducked into the outhouse to the rear of the cottage. She came out and walked over to a wooden bench by the door and sat down.

Ronnie reached in her pocket to see if it was still there and it was. Sighing with relief, she pulled the smooth, round stone wrapped in a handkerchief, out of her pocket. She unwrapped it to see the shiny green jade that had once been her mother's brooch that had fallen out of its setting. She reached into her other pocket and pulled out her journal. It was soaked, so she opened it and laid it on the ground, hoping it would dry.

Since she'd lost her mother, she'd developed the habit of talking to her as if she was there with her. It was a relief that finally, she was pretty much alone. There was no one within earshot that would deem her crazy for talking to herself. Amari had been a great sounding board, but she missed her comfortable one-sided talks. "Mummy, what will I do now? Look at this place." Ronnie looked around. "It's beautiful, but I don't know what to do." She put her head in her hands and allowed her fears to come out as tearless sobs from inside. She could feel her mother's words assuring her "all is good," and immediately felt a calm confident assurance overtake her. Looking up she heard Scottie tap, tap, tap as he scurried across the path toward her. He always kept close when he sensed she was upset.

"Sorry, boy," she lifted her head and grinned. "You're always there to make me feel better." She reached out to touch him, but he scurried out of her arm's reach.

Leaning her chin on her hand, she let out a heavy sigh. She stood, tucking the stone back in her pocket and walked inside the door as Amari began to stir. Rolling over, he opened his eyes to see her. "Well, good morning, Sleepyhead," she said to him and smiled. "I see you slept as good as I did."

Amari smiled, sat up on the edge of the cot, and rubbed his eyes. He yawned and stretched his long dark arms into the already warm tropical air. "I'll let you wake up and wait for you outside," Ronnie said.

She stood and walked outside stretching her arms toward the sky. Birds flitted from branch to branch, and the leaves waved slowly in the warm breeze. Flowers dotted the foliage with such vivid colors. Hues that she'd never before seen on a bush.

Amari walked outside and looked at her. "Go to head," he said. She nodded and giggled to herself as he ducked behind the cottage and walked to the outhouse.

When he came back to where she stood, she looked at him and said, "My goodness, Amari." She picked up a fallen hibiscus bloom and tucked it behind her ear as he walked out to join her. It felt good to be female again. "Just look at the beauty of this place," she pointed to the flower in her hair: "Flower."

"Flower," he repeated and reached over and touched the blossom.

Holding her hand up, she said, "Wait a second. Let's go back
to the waterfall. Adria said we could bathe there." She made
hand signals as if taking a bath. Walking back inside, she gathered up the satchel that held clothing and linens. They followed
the path back down to the shoreline steps. Holding onto the
makeshift railing, they walked carefully down the cliff to the
beach and followed the edge of the water. The sea was choppy
from a strong, welcome breeze. Ronnie began picking up shells
that had washed ashore and tucked them in her pockets. The
waterfall beckoned them with the sound of rushing water. "I can
hear it," she said to him, holding her hand to her ear.

He nodded and said, "Hear," putting his hand to his ear
showing he understood. They continued walking as the shoreline took a bend. As they walked, the sound grew louder. When
they rounded the curve, they stopped, shoulder to shoulder,
looking at the amazing falls. The water fell from 50 feet above to
a stone plateau, splashing onto a huge flat rock and falling over
into the pool below that emptied into the sea.

"Oh my, Amari," Ronnie gasped. "Have you ever seen anything more beautiful?"

"Beau-tee-full," he repeated and nodded. The sound of the
rushing water was so loud, they had to yell to hear one another.
The power of the water was tremendous, and they stood in
awe as the mist floated out in every direction.

Walking closer, the mist wrapped around them, and Ronnie
said, "Adria suggested we climb up the side to where there are
some steps we can take to get into the pool below the falls."
Ronnie explained, knowing that he didn't understand, but
Amari's lack of understanding didn't keep her from talking.
Sometimes she wondered if she was going mad chatting without
expecting an answer. But she consoled herself with the idea that
the more she talked, the more he would learn and eventually

understand. She also knew that talking helped her to feel less alone. She was tired of being alone.

She reached over and grabbed hold of the ginger flower that Adria had explained how to use for washing her hair. She snapped off a blossom from the bush. The flower was cone shaped with thick waxy petals. Ronnie pulled off a petal from the bloom and squeezed. Just as Adria had described, a scented gel came out into her hand. She took it and rubbed it into her hair so that it would be there when she got in the water. She did it a few more times to make sure she had enough and passed it over to Amari. He looked at her in question. "It's alright, wash," she pretended to wash her hair, "your hair with it." He nodded and followed her lead.

They stood looking at the pool of water. She kicked off her shoes and sticking her toe in to check the temperature, she said, "Brrr! That's cold!" Amari smiled and pretended to shiver with his arms crossed. They both laughed at his ability to understand and make fun of her. She turned away and quickly took off her dress, leaving on her drawers and chemise and grabbed the chunk of soap Adria had put in the satchel.

Ronnie jumped into the chilly pool as far away from the pounding falls as she could. She went under the water and popped back up with an involuntary "Wow!" at the coldness of the water. Looking up she shook her head and hollered for Amari to join her. He removed his shoes and shirt and jumped in. He let out a whooping holler when he surfaced, and they both laughed. "Well, lucky for us the falls is so loud, I don't think anyone heard!" she said.

Ronnie swam over to the edge until she found shallows that allowed her to get her footing. She scrubbed the gel into her hair and ducked under the water to rinse it off. Taking the soap, she reached under her garments to wash off, keeping her back to Amari. He responded in respect and swam to the other side of the pool, watching Scottie as he flitted from branch to branch in the distance.

"It's alright, you can turn around now!" Ronnie hollered and swam to the middle to meet Amari. She handed him the bar of soap and stayed to float in the middle while he went to the shallow side. She laid back and stared at the sky and huge white clouds that floated slowly by. This must be what heaven is like. No worries, nothing to fear. For just a minute, her worries disappeared and she felt nothing but gratitude. She willed herself to stop wondering about where life would lead her now knowing her past was many miles behind her. Focus on the future, not the past, she reminded herself as she floated at the bottom of the falls. Ronnie could hear the pounding of the water dim as she glided to the edge of the pool. She looked for Amari and found him in the middle of the pool, headed her way. She turned over and swam out to meet him.

They treaded water and did their best to communicate. They giggled as she tried to give hand communications while struggling to stay afloat. He reached over and grabbed her arm as her body tried to sink while she used her hands to talk instead of swim. They laughed and she let him know with her hand signals and words that she would get out of the water and get dressed first. He nodded, let go, and headed to the other side yet again to look the other way.

Swimming to the shallow end, she got out of the water and dried off with a towel from the satchel. It felt so good to be clean. She hadn't felt this good since long before she boarded the Neptune. She stopped for a second and remembered Amari's touch. She shook her head as if to shake the memory away. It had been so long since anyone had touched her with kindness. With a heavy sigh, she reached in the bag, pulled out the clothing and put on a blue and white dress that reached down to her ankles. Then, she pulled out the shirt and trousers for Amari and laid them on a dry rock.

Turning toward him, she yelled, "The coast is clear!" He looked over and waved. She walked back down to the shoreline. Once he was out of the water, she signaled that she would wait around the bend for him to change clothes.

She found the stump of a fallen tree and sat. She could see Scottie flying across the inlet from the beach to meet her. "Staying away from that mist, I see," she called to him as he landed on the sand in front of her. The bird walked back and forth as they waited for Amari. When he appeared, she was amazed at how well the clothing fit him. "You look great!"

"Great!" he said, nodding and his smile radiated. "Feel good." She chuckled to herself as she realized that both of her companions would repeat just about anything she said.

They washed their soiled clothes in the shallows of the falls and packed them up to take back to the cottage.

Ronnie smiled at Amari and nodded in agreement. "Well, I suppose we'd better get back." She stood, and together they walked back up the beach and cliff steps to the cottage in silence. Once they arrived, she pulled the wet clothing out of the satchel and strung them over a few bushes to dry. She gazed at the cottage with gratitude in her heart. It was good to be on solid ground again.

A FEW DAYS went by and Ronnie and Adria fell into a routine of spending afternoons together getting to know each other. Ronnie sat on the edge of her cot folding her now dry clothes. She could hear Adria's whistle announcing her approach to the cottage and looked out to see her striding purposefully down the path.

Ronnie motioned for her to come inside and sit down at the table. "I've just sliced up some mangos." Smiling at her new friend, she handed Adria a slice.

"Perfect, I brought some scones." Adria popped the mango into her mouth and pulled out the second chair, sitting the satchel on the table. They served themselves and were quiet for a few seconds. "Amari, come and eat," Ronnie said pointing to her mouth. Amari nodded but waved them on as he wanted to finish trimming back the bushes that surrounded the pathway to the cottage. Ronnie's appetite got the better of her and she started without him.

Pulling out the scones and a jar of jam, Adria said, "I want to bring Mummy down to meet you this afternoon."

Ronnie looked at Adria and frowned. "Are you sure that's a good idea?"

"Yes, I think so. Mummy is very benevolent and will find ways to help," Adria said. She could see the worry in Ronnie's eyes and reached over to pat her hand to reassure her.

They spent most of the afternoon talking. "I'd better take it easy on the scones. Having to eat again when I get back to Ginger Star, my belly is getting bigger by the day," she patted her stomach. They had felt an immediate connection with each other and never seemed to run out of things to share, each one always wondering just how much she should tell the other.

"It's getting warm in here," Adria said as she fanned herself. "Let's head down to the shoreline." Adria cleared the table and Ronnie took some scones and mango outside to Amari.

"T'ank you," he said and flashed his winning smile at her.

"Want to go to the sea with us?" Ronnie asked and pointed the shoreline. He shook his head and pointed to the roof. She looked up and saw the recently cut foliage from the pathway that he had used to cover the sinking thatched roof.

"Oh my!" Ronnie said. "And I thought you were just trimming the pathway." She looked back at Amari and smiled. His heart leapt at her approval. "Adria, look at what he's done!" She pointed to the roof as Adria came out of the cottage.

"Good heavens, that's a great job, Amari!" She looked back at him and smiled. "I don't suppose the rain will get inside now!"

The two women walked the pathway and down the cliff steps to the shoreline.

"It's strange," Ronnie said as she plopped down on the sand. As usual, Adria sat on the sea grape tree branch.

"What's strange?" Adria asked.

"Here I am technically homeless, yet I don't recall ever having been happier. Maybe it's just because I escaped the grip of those awful men. I now wake up when the sun peeks through the slats of the window and go to sleep when the shadows cover the hills at night. I'm living with a bird and a runaway African that can't speak much English," Ronnie laughed. "It really doesn't make any sense when I say it out loud!"

Adria's eyes betrayed her, filling with tears that overflowed down her cheeks.

"I'm so sorry! Did I upset you?"

Adria let Ronnie think her feelings were hurt. It was easier than confessing the secret that claimed her every thought. She'd rehearsed her confession over and over again in her head, but nothing was right. Nothing.

THE NEXT AFTERNOON, Adria rode her horse, Chance, over to the cottage. "Amari, come see Adria's horse!" Ronnie said as she walked outside the cottage.

Amari was on the roof adding a few more reinforcements when he looked down and saw the horse. His eyes flashed open at the sight of the horse's stature as he stomped and chuffed, hoping for a snack. "No come der!" Amari said and sat down on the roof shaking his head, refusing to budge.

The women laughed and Ronnie stroked Chance's neck. He was chestnut brown with a white face. "What a gorgeous animal, Adria."

"Yes, he is. Papa had him waiting for me when we arrived from London." She reached behind her and pulled a carrot from the saddlebag and gave it to Chance. "You know all my secrets, don't you, fella?"

"And what secrets would those be?" Ronnie said jokingly.

Adria's countenance changed and her grin left, but she quickly recovered. "Oh, just silly things about my dreams of the future." She put her grin back on and said, "Come on, let's go for a ride!" She reached down and pulled Ronnie up onto Chance's back behind her. Ronnie hung onto Adria's waist smelling the waft of a gardenias' scent as they rode through the sandy cove, into the aqua blue water. Together they sauntered further down the coast where there would be less chance of being noticed.

Adria slowed the horse down and let Chance stop for a much-needed drink from the waterfall's pool. Ronnie slid off Chance's back to the ground. Adria swung her legs around and tried to jump to the ground when she realized she couldn't without falling. Her arm swung around as Ronnie reached over to help her keep her balance. Adria's blouse pulled loose from her skirt revealing her protruding tummy for just an instant. Adria quickly tucked it back in when she landed on her feet.

"Wow! Are you alright?" Ronnie asked as she grabbed hold of her friend's arm. Adria's head turned and she answered with a quick nod. She took a deep breath with the realization that Ronnie had probably recognized her secret. They walked over and sat on a flat part of the rocks down from the waterfall. The flutter of Scottie's wings mingled with the sound of the falls, but just for a few seconds. He landed stealthily on a flat rock halfway up the falls, away from the mist. The leaves of the banyan dipped in the water from the splash created by the soft breeze caused by the force of the water. The heat of the Jamaican afternoon was dashed by the rush of the waterfall that infused the air with a cool breeze.

Adria opened the sack she brought and pulled out the nappies that she had used for her monthly issue. "I thought you might need these soon, if not already." Ronnie grinned sheepishly and agreed. "Yes, as a matter of fact, just this morning." She took the sack from Adria. "I will put them to good use. Thank you so much for being so very thoughtful. Again."

"Well, I don't need them right now, that's for sure," Adria confessed and looked Ronnie in the eye.

"I wondered," Ronnie said as she tossed her last bite of a scone to Scottie. The bird swooped down and caught it in midair.

They shared a silence that spoke volumes, both knowing that having a child out of wedlock could be devastating to a woman and her family.

Staring at the crystal sea, Adria said, "Well, this secret is the biggest one Chance is aware of and now you're the only one besides him who knows." She put her head in her hands and said, "No matter what I do, I can't keep life from changing when it wants to." Lazy afternoon sunlight created glittering diamonds of happiness on the water's surface as if to mock her. Adria continued, "All of the hopes and dreams I shared with you are ones that will never come true for me."

"What do you mean?" Ronnie asked. "You're the only heir and one day you will run Ginger Star as your own." Ronnie swept her arm through the air pointing at the great house. "The world is yours."

"But I'm having a baby and I am not married with no hope of being so."

"Why not? Where is the father?"

Adria sighed and said, "When I told you I had never loved a man, that was a lie." She stood and walked to the waterfall's edge. Ronnie followed and took hold of her friend's arm; almost afraid she would fall on purpose.

"You don't have to share this, Adria."

"I have to tell someone or my heart will explode. Our friendship is a farce unless I do. I feel guilty every time you share something with me while I hold back on what rules my world." Ronnie stood behind Adria and rubbed her shoulders trying to relieve the tenseness she could feel in her muscles.

"Go ahead, nothing you can say will make a difference to me."

Adria stood with her arms crossed staring at the rushing water of the falls. "There was a merchant ship much like the one you jumped from called the Matilda." She closed her eyes and leaned her head back. "Papa allowed them to anchor here since the docks were full in Ocho Rios. They stayed for three weeks. His name was Eric. We were friends and before he set sail, we were intimate." Adria talked about the sweet way he spoke to her, stroked her hair, and told her she was beautiful. "When I woke one morning, I saw the Matilda sailing into the distance, and he was gone." Ronnie continued massaging her shoulders. "I feel like such a fool to have believed anything he said to me." Tears slid down her cheeks as she shook her head.

"You're not the first woman to be led astray by a sweet-talking man, my friend." Ronnie's own thoughts tapped her on the shoulder bringing back unwelcome memories. "I'm guilty of the same."

"Perhaps, but your sin has been left behind you. Mine will never leave."

Ronnie paused for a moment, knowing that her own pain failed to give up its grip on her. She saw no point in sharing her not-so-perfect past just now. "That's not true. You mustn't allow love to create guilty feelings that bring you such pain," Ronnie said, knowing her statement had a double meaning. Her own guilt would follow her forever, no matter what words she came up with that said otherwise.

Adria twirled around to face her friend and slipped. Ronnie's other arm caught her on the slick surface. "It's not my feelings that causes such sadness, it's the reality of my situation." She placed her hands on her belly. "Without the help of corsets, my secret would no longer be one." Ronnie watched as Adria unlaced her dress from behind. Her stomach protruded, revealing the roundness of her belly.

Ronnie stared at her stomach realizing the pregnancy was well advanced and then looked into the eyes of her friend, swollen with shame and sadness. Adria fell into Ronnie's arms and sobbed until she was spent.

Ronnie led her back to solid ground and down the shoreline to their favorite spot on the sea grape branch. They sat in silence except for the sound of Scottie's wings fluttering from spot to spot as he searched for rotted mangoes on the ground. He always seemed to know when to keep quiet.

Adria's voice broke the hushing sound of the falls, "I don't know how to tell Mummy and Papa. This will break their hearts." Ronnie slid her arm around her friend's shoulders and hugged her close. Adria laid her head on her shoulder. "They will probably send me back to England."

"When will the baby come?"

"I'm not sure, I think in a month or so." Ronnie didn't bother to let her know that it was probably too late for a trip back to England. The trip was at least a month-long journey which no expectant mother should endure.

"I feel the movement of hands and feet that must be well on their way to being whole." Her fingertips touched her stomach and rested there. Her stomach jumped causing her hand to pop up. "See! Did you see?" Her eyes flew open flashing their green smile.

Ronnie's whole face lit up, "Oh my, that was really something!" Their smiles connected. "Here, you feel." Adria placed Ronnie's hand on her stomach. The baby's hand rolled across her tummy.

"That is incredible! What's it like?"

Adria paused to find the words. "Like my body has taken on a life of its own, and I suppose it has." She looked at her stomach and her hand laid on top as if to protect its precious cargo.

"I just know they will make me give it away." Saying the words aloud for the first time broke her. She could hardly catch her breath as she wept leaning hard onto Ronnie's shoulder. Ronnie dried her tears with a napkin from the sack and found a few tears of her own to wipe away.

"Give it away?" Ronnie asked. "Who would you give it to?"

Adria took a deep breath and lifted her head staring across the cove. She let out a heavy sigh, her shoulders slumped, and her hands rested on her belly. Sorrow clung to her like a baby holding onto its momma's breast.

"Do you want to be a mother?" Ronnie looked at her slowly.

"More than anything in the world! It's all I've ever dreamt of since I was a little girl."

Adria gazed at the ground and shook her head. She put her head in her hands. Ronnie rubbed her back trying to provide encouragement but felt the depth Adria's helpless. "I don't know, I just know they won't let me keep it," Adria said. She could hear the coldness of her statement by calling her baby, "it," but she made a conscious decision not to correct herself. It was somehow easier that way.

They sat on the tree branch for a long while with their separate thoughts swirling in their heads. The water of the cove lapped harder than normal and small breakers created white caps as they broke over the reef in the distance.

"So, you've not told me much about the father," Ronnie said as she took Adria's hand back, immediately regretted the question as Adria's smile faded. "I'm so sorry! I should not have asked." Adria nodded and took a deep breath, trying not to break down again.

"He's been gone for months now, just a distant memory of shared moments that I foolishly thought would continue. To think I finally thought I had found my forever love. Not even so much as a letter. I'm such a fool!" She stood and walked a few steps away staring at the sea. "This is the first time I've spoken of him aloud to another living soul except the one living inside me."

Ronnie stood and wished she could put the words back in her mouth. *Why can you not keep your mouth shut?*

Adria continued, "He was a British sailor docked here in Ocho Rios for a few days. He was the son of a friend of Papa's."

"So, why did you not tell your father about your feelings? You didn't think he would understand falling in love?"

"It was more complicated than that." Adria kicked off her shoes, pulled off her stockings, and walked to the water's edge, allowing her feet to get wet. "Papa would not have approved of him."

"But you said he was his friend's son, right?" Ronnie kicked off her shoes too and followed her. They both held their skirts up as the water washed over their feet.

"Yes, but he is not," Adria turned and looked Ronnie in the eyes, "like us."

Ronnie shook her head. "What do you mean?"

"He's African, he and his father were our former slaves," Adria said. "Both Eric and his father chose to sign on as crew members instead of staying with us when Papa emancipated them."

Ronnie drew in her breath and looked at Adria. "Oh, my dear." Her hand covered her mouth involuntarily. Ronnie knew the prejudices that came with caring for someone with a different skin color. "I do know that love knows no boundaries and one can have a hard time taming the heart." They stood in a comfortable silence as only friends can do.

"But he was only here for a short while? How did your romance move so quickly?"

"We had known each other for a long time prior to his ship docking here. Our friendship, or so I thought it was a 'friendship' was already there and we crossed the line of intimacy." Adria stood up and reached around to tie up her corset. Ronnie reached over to help and followed her down the shoreline toward Chance, stopping to pick up an occasional shell, or a piece of fruit for Scottie. Suddenly, Adria bent down beside a piece of driftwood. "This looks the way I feel sometimes. Broken and weathered, wanting to grow again, but knowing that my life is over."

The sun began its descent below the mountains signaling it was time for her to head back to the great house. They mounted the horse and rode back to the cottage in silence. They could see Amari in the distance climbing down from the roof. Adria slowed Chance to a stop at the fork in the path that led back to Ginger Star. Ronnie slid off the horse and looked up at her friend and said, "Can you stay for a bit? It's not quite time for tea."

"I wish I could, but I must sit for a portrait with an artist Mummy has commissioned."

Ronnie nodded and reached up to touch her hands that held the reins. "Please know you're not alone in this. I owe you my life and will do anything I can to help." Now that Ronnie knew Adria was expecting, she could see the roundness of her tummy even with the corset intact. *I hope the artist doesn't notice. I'm not sure how he couldn't.* She couldn't bring herself to say it aloud. "I don't know what that could be, but anything at all."

Adria nodded and said, "I think I will bring Mummy to meet you tomorrow morning. Just an introduction to you and Amari. One revelation at a time is all she can take, I'm sure."

"I look forward to meeting her. We'll figure this out together."

Adria nodded, afraid to talk again for fear of breaking down. She grinned in acknowledgement, turning Chance toward Ginger Star and rode away. It was time.

RONNIE SIGHED AND watched the horse carry her new friend away. Walking toward the cottage, she saw Amari heading to the outhouse. She walked inside the cottage and picked up the bowl from the counter that she had left there earlier. She decided to wait and wash it in the morning down at the falls. The afternoon began to cast its shadows through the room. She had always been scared of shadows and afraid of the dark, but living in the cottage for the past week, she'd been forced to confront her fears only to find that the darkness brought with it the promise of good rest and morning light. The melodies of the Jamaican crickets lulled her to calmness in the evenings and were there in the middle of the night when she'd wake. Since she'd jumped ship and come ashore, Ronnie found a peace had come over her and she felt a strange sense of belonging on this island that was quickly becoming her home.

Ronnie pondered Adria's plight. How can I bring any kind of hope to her? How will her parents react to us? The baby? Lying in bed that night, sleep was longer in coming. She dreamt of a baby. The one she'd never had.

ADRIA STOOD AS still as she could while the artist, Terrance, worked on the draft of her portrait. Telling Ronnie about Eric brought everything back and made her love for him come alive again. She couldn't help but remember the quick passion she'd felt when he kissed her. Their initial friendship from when they were younger at Ginger Star had quickly transformed as she fell in love with him in the few short weeks they shared before he'd left on the ship that they both knew would tear them apart. Knowing their time together was not long enough to bridge the reality of their differences, they chose to ignore the harshness of what culture dictated.

And now, for the first time in her life, she felt out of control. Never had she known she was running out of time, never had she felt love for another being like this before and she stopped to feel the baby's feet kicking once again. She looked at Terrance hoping he didn't notice. Thankfully, he was looking for something in his case.

She felt a twinge of what felt like a cramp that stopped her in midbreath. She stopped breathing for a few seconds and then, taking a deep breath, didn't feel anything more, and continued with the session. Time was running short, but she couldn't tell her parents about the baby tonight. Marshall Fergusson from Ramble House was coming to dinner. She would first introduce Ronnie and Amari to them. Then, the baby. One thing at a time. She resolved that tomorrow would be the day she would change all their lives forever.

"MUMMY, THIS IS Veronica, or Ronnie as she likes to be called." Adria turned toward Ronnie. They stood just inside the doorway of the cottage. A small black woman stood in the background and Ronnie assumed she was a house slave. Amari had ducked behind their makeshift dressing room curtain when he saw Adria and Sarah approaching. "She is the woman I was telling you about." Sarah turned and cocked her head to one side. She looked at the young woman, leery about her intentions, but at the same time, admired the beauty that she tried unsuccessfully to hide beneath her oversized clothing.

"So, Adria tells me you are new to Jamaica." Sarah extended her hand, took Ronnie's, and stared into her eyes. The shade offered by the cottage gave some relief, but the air was still. Dust slowly floated in the sunlight, filtering through the cracks in the shutters.

"Yes, ma'am. I've only been here a short time." Ronnie wasn't sure exactly what Adria had told her mother. "Thank you so much for allowing me to stay in your cottage. I hope I've not inconvenienced you."

"I trust my daughter's judgement, Ronnie. It seems your arrival was unexpected, but I am glad you landed here. It sounds as if things could have been disastrous for you both." Sarah looked over Ronnie's shoulder hoping to meet Amari. *What in the world would they do with a runaway slave?* "Where is the African?" Ronnie turned and walked over to the curtain that doubled as a wall to a dressing room. She pulled the curtain aside and nodded at Amari as he stood in front of them. "Oh my," Sarah said as she stepped back just a little. He was tall and lean, obviously strong and able, should he decide to push them aside and run.

"He scared but friendly," the older black woman spoke out of turn and stepped in front of Sarah toward Amari. They all turned to look at her. Her hair was tucked under her signature blue bandana scarf and her white apron hinted at time spent in the kitchen. Her gift of seeing into a person's soul and discerning their true intent was well known at Ginger Star and beyond. Knowing this, Adria had insisted she attend the meeting. The woman had already sized up Ronnie from a distance and was confident she was of good character.

"Ronnie, Amari, this is Mum Lettie," Adria said introducing the woman that helped all of them acclimate to Jamaica. "She is a valued member of our family and the one who made you the food I brought from her kitchen."

Reaching out, Ronnie shook Mum Lettie's hand and said, "Well, I must say, I've never tasted a better scone and your guava jam is truly incredible. Thank you, Mum Lettie. Adria's told me so much about you." Looking at Mum Lettie's brown eyes, she felt as if the older woman's gaze peered into her soul. In just a few seconds, she was left feeling the woman knew more about her than she did herself.

Adria patted her mother and Mum Lettie on their shoulders as she stood between the two. She looked toward the African. "This is Amari. He doesn't speak much English but is very gentle and friendly." Amari looked from Sarah to Mum Lettie and then broke into a wide smile when he looked at the small lady with skin the same color as his. Realizing his error, afraid he was being inappropriate, he looked down at the wooden floor, unsure of what to do.

A shadow filled the doorway. They all turned around to see a large black man standing there. He looked at them, holding his hat in his hand and said, "Sorry I late. Solomon needed my help in stable." Again, Amari smiled when he saw another person that resembled himself.

"Not a problem," Sarah said. "Ronnie and Amari, this is Sam, our trusted servant and friend. Another member of the Ginger Star family." Sam stepped up and shook Ronnie and Amari's hands. Sarah nodded and continued, "Sam, we have to figure something out for Amari's safety. We don't want him to get caught up with the law." Looking at Mum Lettie, she continued, "We should not want to see him end up a slave and if word gets out, we could have an issue since I'm assuming he has no papers."

"Could we let him work for us here at Ginger Star?" Adria asked.

Sarah looked from Adria to Amari and back again. "I doubt that would be a good idea. We have more than enough help already, but I shall talk to your father when he returns from Claremont tonight and see if he has any ideas."

"Maybe Maroons take him," Mum Lettie suggested. They all turned to look at her. "We send message to dem through Danquah and see?" She looked at Sam for an answer to her question. They stood in silence as Mum Lettie's idea sank in. Danquah was Sam's brother, so they had a connection. Sam shrugged, unsure of the answer.

"You know, Mum Lettie, that just might be a good idea." Sarah untied the bow under her hat and took it off revealing blonde hair pulled up into a bun on top of her head. She looked at Sam and said, "What do you think?"

"Me t'inks I talk wid Danquah and ask," Sam said.

"Alright, we'll try to figure out how to do that, but it will take some time. Meanwhile," Sarah looked at Ronnie, "I suggest Amari stay very close to the cottage. Maybe slip down to the waterfall for bathing, but other than that, it could be dangerous should he draw any attention." Sarah turned to leave and then turned back to Ronnie. "Remember to be careful."

"Absolutely, my lady. I cannot thank you enough for your kindness. I hope one day I can return the favor you extend so graciously." Ronnie nodded her head and dipped a small curtsy in Sarah's direction, realizing it had been a long time since she could acknowledge someone in that manner.

Adria turned and they all followed Sam out of the cottage with Amari close behind, leaving Ronnie and Sarah alone.

Sarah looked into Ronnie's eyes. "I haven't seen Adria this happy in months. The past few days she has almost returned to her old self." It was true. Her daughter's smile had been missing for a long time until she met Ronnie. "Welcome to Ginger Star." Sarah smiled. "I'm thinking it was a good day when you came ashore." She turned and they walked outside the cottage. Sarah tied her hat back on. "Adria, we should head back to the house. Mum Lettie, can you and Sam discuss the Maroon idea and come up with a plan?" Mum Lettie nodded, and she and Sam headed back to the great house.

Adria breathed a sigh of relief at her mother's reaction and realized for the first time in a while, the secret was not her primary concern. She had a twinge of guilt at not sharing her pregnancy with her mother, especially since she had been so accommodating to her new friends, but she quickly pushed that thought aside, for now. Soon, she promised herself. There was always tomorrow.

—Chapter Five—

"When the well's dry, we know the worth of water." —Benjamin Franklin

1719, Ocho Rios, Jamaica

*A*dria slid out of the great house, down the half-moon steps to the side garden before another contraction took control of her body. She ducked into the shadows, leaned up against the cool stone wall of the house, slid down and tucked her head between her knees. She held her breath and tried not to make a sound. After the pain subsided again, she figured she had another ten minutes before the next flooded her. Taking a deep breath, she pulled herself to her feet and continued around the side of the house to the pathway that led to the cottage.

She was grateful for the full moon that guided her way. She'd been afraid to bring a candle along lest someone see her. Another sharper cramp doubled her over. "Not already!" she said louder than she intended. She let out an involuntary groan and slumped to the ground. *This must be labor, but I'm not ready. Not yet. I must tell Mummy first.* Her body refused to listen. The contractions came at their own will.

"Miss Adria!" Mum Lettie ran down the path to her. She put her lantern on the ground and crouched down next to her. "Yuh

having di pickney tonight?" Adria looked at the older woman
and slowly nodded. The contraction continued. "Look at me!"
Mum Lettie grabbed hold of Adria's hands and looked her in the
eye. "Breathe deep and let out slow."

Adria focused on Mum Lettie's face as she squeezed Mum
Lettie's hands hard and then let go as the contraction subsided.
Her heart swelled with love for her surrogate mother who had
been with her through so much since she'd come to Jamaica. It
only made sense she was here now. Taking a deep breath, she
laid her head back, and sighed.

Turning her head to look at Mum Lettie, she said, "You
knew?" As soon as she voiced the words, she thought better of
it and answered her own question while shaking her head. "Of
course you did." She sighed in resignation and placed her hands
on her stomach. She spoke to the baby inside her, "Mum Lettie's
here, little one. With her here, we'll be just fine." Suddenly, Adria
was flooded with anticipation of becoming a mother. "We can
do this together." She laid her head back to rest on the grass and
catch her breath. She stared at the stars and the full moon. "How
long have you known, Mum Lettie?"

"A while now." She sat next to her stroking Adria's hair and
pulled it back from her face.

"How did you know?" Adria asked. She stared into the
galaxy above, something she didn't do often. She found staring
at the stars made her feel insignificant and small. Tonight, it
did the opposite. She felt a part of something bigger. Something
important.

"How yuh walked. Yuh breasts dem get bigga. Yuh sigh when
yuh bend ova an' you no can catch yuh breath." She reached over
and wiped the sweat from Adria's forehead.

Why didn't it dawn on her that Mum Lettie would realize
what was happening to her all these months? Her intuitiveness
was legendary.

Adria asked, "Why did you not tell me what you suspected?"

"Me know yuh scared. Yuh wi tell me in yuh own time."

"Well, I waited longer than I should have, for sure."

"It alright, chile, we get yuh trough dis." Mum Lettie looked up as she saw a candle coming up the path from the cottage. Ronnie and Amari hurried to meet them. She looked at Ronnie and said, "She in labor. Come, let us get her to the cottage."

"Amari?" They all looked up at the African. The night wrapped around his dark skin and kept him almost hidden. He bent down, scooped up Adria, and carried her to the cottage. He laid her on his bed. Ronnie hurried inside and lit all the candles in the cottage. "Help her out of these clothes and cover her with dis." Mum Lettie reached up and grabbed a blanket from a shelf. "I bring linen back." Ronnie helped Adria change and pointed Amari to the water and then the fireplace. He followed her instructions and put a pot of water over the fire to boil, grateful for leftover embers from last night's supper. He cleared away their belongings to make space, for what he did not know.

Ronnie walked over and crouched down on her knees and stroked Adria's hair. "How are you?" Adria opened her eyes and sighed.

"As good as I can be, I suppose," she said looking at Ronnie who sat in a chair next to her bed. She pulled the blanket close around her body. Amari stood over them both. "I never got the chance to tell Mummy and Papa."

"It's alright. Everything will be fine. You'll see." Ronnie looked into Adria's eyes, hoping she was right, and was determined not to let her friend see her doubt. "You will be an exemplary mother." Adria nodded and closed her eyes. Mum Lettie walked into the cottage carrying towels and sheets. They rolled Adria over and covered the cot with the fresh linens.

"It's coming again!" Adria struggled to focus.

"Memba to focus and breathe," Mum Lettie reminded her.

Ronnie held her hand. "They say it keeps you from tensing up so much." Ronnie had attended a few births back in Nassau, but always as an onlooker. Never a midwife.

Adria's labor continued as the rooster crowed and the sun tried to peek out from behind the rain forest clouds threatening to make their way down the coast.

Sam called from the pathway, "Where?" It surprised him to see so many candles illuminating the little house so early in the morning. He walked to the doorway. The bulk of his frame cast a shadow into the candlelight. He blinked twice as he tried to register the scene before him. "Wat in di worl'?" Sam asked, confused.

"Mi find har on pass inna labor and we bring har inna here," Mum Lettie answered.

Sam stepped into the room. Not knowing what else to say, he asked, "What can I do?"

"A time fuh wake di Missus and Massa," Mum Lettie said.

"I go find dem," Sam said and nodded, glad to have a reason to leave the cottage.

"No!" Adria screamed. She heard Mum Lettie's instructions to Sam. "You can't! Not yet!" Another contraction forced her to gasp lean back on the pillow in resignation.

Mum Lettie didn't argue with her, but looked at Sam, nodded and said, "When you at de house, go my room and get basket wid red lid. Inside are supplies to use when dis happen," Mum Lettie said to Sam. She kept the basket packed as she was frequently called upon to be a midwife on the plantation and surrounding homes. He turned and took off for the great house.

Sam ran to the house and went straight through to Mum Lettie's room behind the kitchen and grabbed the basket she'd described. Walking back into the kitchen where a few house slaves were peeling yams he asked, "Weh di Massa and di Missus?" Although he was on a first name basis with

Adria's parents, he always referred to them in that way around the others.

Olivia, Ginger Star's head cook, looked up from stirring a pot over the kitchen fireplace. "Mi did see di Missus inna di dining room." She turned back to her kettle of stew. Sam headed to the dining room where Sarah sat in her dark-red robe, drinking a glass of orange juice. Her blonde hair was wrapped up into a bun on top of her head. She looked up when she heard him coming. He was breathing hard and seemed confused.

"Why, Sam." Her eyebrows raised. "Is something wrong?" She'd known this man for years and rarely saw him upset.

"Well, mi lady, I," he stuttered. "I s'pose so." He shifted from foot to foot and held his hat in his hands. "Miss Adria in bad way." He knew that wasn't how he wanted to start the conversation, and he tried to recover. "She 'ave pickney dis mornin.'"

"What? Pickney?" She didn't know much Patois, but that word, she knew. Sarah stood up and stepped toward Sam. "A baby? I don't understand. Where did she get a baby?" She sat the glass of orange juice on the table with an unsteady hand.

"She givin' birth. She hide it from all a wi." He looked over her shoulder to see Massa John standing in the doorway but continued. "Mum Lettie find har on di pass to di cottage in di darkness. She der in labor." Knowing Mum Lettie was waiting for the basket, he said, "I have get dis to Mum Lettie!" He turned and ran out of the house toward the cottage.

Sarah turned and looked at John, her heart pounding in confusion.

"How could she be having a child and we not know it?" John asked. His voice echoed into the foyer. "What in the world is going on, Sarah?"

Swirling around, she darted out of the dining room, through the foyer, and down the stone steps. Picking up her skirts, she ran down the pathway with abandon to her daughter. John followed close behind. She could hear the murmur of voices as she approached the cottage. Standing breathless in the doorway she tried to process the scene before her.

Sam stood next to the bed holding the basket. Adria laid on a cot with Mum Lettie coaching her and Ronnie stood at her side. Looking up to see Sarah, Ronnie stepped back in deference to Adria's mother. Sarah rushed over and took Adria's hand. "Oh, Mummy, please forgive me!"

"Not now, Darling, just listen to Mum Lettie!" Sarah said while John looked on from the doorway.

Sam opened the basket and took its contents out, and arranged them on the table next to the cot. First there was a Bible, a Jamaica-must, to be on display for favor during birth, a bottle of castor oil to anoint Adria's belly, a knife to cut the cord, and nutmeg for the baby's navel. Mum Lettie's old clay pipe was there filled with tobacco, a flint and striker, and a small flask of Jamaican rum, all standard Jamaican midwifery tools. "Open the Bible to Psalm 30," Mum Lettie said to Ronnie.

As Adria rested on her side in between contractions, Mum Lettie grabbed the flask of rum, pouring some into her hands, and splashing her face with the spirit. She took a swig to give her eyesight since the witnessing of each birth was said to affect the midwife's sight. She went back down to the end of the bed and said, "Now a time fi push, Miss Adria." She anointed Adria's belly with the castor oil. Mum Lettie knelt back down at the bottom of the bed. "Get back on de knees," the old woman said. Adria groaned as she struggled to get back onto her hands and knees. She was too tired for the squatting position any longer. She cried out when another contraction seized her body and she grunted and pushed. Adria looked to her side where her mother sat as she felt the baby's head emerge. "Dat good, dat good. Now rest a little and wen di next pain here, da pickney soon come."

Mum Lettie glanced around and caught Adria's gaze. She laid her forehead on the bed waiting for the next pain to come.

Sarah felt that familiar feeling of inadequacy as she watched Mum Lettie so easily take charge of this and any other situation she'd ever encountered. Once again, she was grateful to have this woman in their lives. Sarah pulled Adria's hair back and wiped her brow with a towel Ronnie handed her. "It's almost over, my sweet," she said to Adria in that familiar tone that only a mother can muster in the midst of turmoil. She kissed her little girl's cheek. Adria closed her eyes and moaned as her body took over once again.

"I'm so sorry," Adria gasped and continued. "About the baby." The contraction took control of her.

Sarah reached over, grabbed Adria's hand, and stroked her head. "Just listen to Mum Lettie, my dear. She will get us through this." Sarah's blue eyes locked with Mum Lettie's brown ones in mutual understanding. The love they both shared for Adria transcended any familiar pangs of jealousy the younger woman had for the older.

Light began to fill the cottage as it filtered in from behind the clouds. Birds sang, dogs barked, and a baby cried. A few seconds later, Mum Lettie smiled and said, "Yuh hav' a bwoy." She laid the baby on Adria's belly as he let out another cry. Handing Ronnie the knife Sam had pulled from her basket, she showed her where to sever the umbilical cord. Mum Lettie tied off two parts of the cord with the twine Amari had used for fishing and said to Ronnie, "Cut it der." Reaching over, Sarah grabbed a towel, and wiped the sweat from Mum Lettie's face. "T'anks," Mum Lettie said as she turned and tended to the afterbirth. Adria lifted her head to see her son. Reaching down, she touched his little head as he opened his eyes for the first time. He squirmed and whimpered. "When di next pain come, push again an' wi should be finish," Mum Lettie instructed. Adria nodded.

"Here, let me clean him up for you while you push." Ronnie reached over and picked up the baby. She laid him down on the table she had covered with a sheet, and gently wiped the blood from him with a wet cloth. He wriggled and cried whenever his little arms would reach too far. "Not used to being outside of your mum's tummy, little one?" Ronnie swaddled him in a clean sheet, picked him up as he calmed down, and cradled him in her arms while his mother let out an involuntary yelp and pushed again. Adria sighed when the contraction ended, laid her head back on the pillow, and turned her eyes back to her son.

Ronnie placed him in his mother's arms as Sarah looked down at her daughter holding her grandson. She tried to make sense of what had just played out in front of her. *Who is his father? How did Adria manage to keep this a secret from us for so long?* She looked up to see John standing in the doorway looking as confounded as she felt. Sarah bent over and kissed Adria on her forehead, then stood and walked over to her husband.

"How did this happen?" John asked his wife as she followed him outside the cottage. The crease in his frown was deeper than she'd ever seen it before. "How could you not know?" Sarah felt his disapproval and saw the anger in his eyes. She had already asked herself the same question, but still had no answer. She stepped back from him. Sarah had always prided herself on her close relationship with her daughter. Now it was apparent she'd been fooling herself. Tears betrayed her as she felt the shame of her failure as a mother and friend of her daughter.

"What will we do? She cannot raise a child on her own! Who is the father?" John pounded her with questions as he paced back and forth on the pathway. Neither of them had any answers.

Before Sarah could respond, Ronnie cried out. "Adria! What's wrong?" She took the baby from his mother's arms. Sarah and John ran back to the doorway. Adria's eyes were closed, and

beads of sweat broke out on her brow. She didn't answer. Mum
Lettie handed the pail of blood and placenta to Sam and rushed
to Adria's side. She wiped the sweat away and felt her forehead.

"She too warm." The old woman looked at Sarah. Their blue
and brown eyes locked again. "Sumtime childbed fever come."

"What can we do?" Sarah asked the woman she felt always
had a resolution for everything. "Should we call Doc Walton?"

"We can't call anyone!" John's voice boomed. "No one must
know what's happened here." Sarah recognized the look of
resolve in John's eyes. She knew there was no sense in arguing.
Everything had happened way too fast.

"Di pickney need fi eat," Mum Lettie said. She looked at
Sam and said, "Go get Martha. She can be di wet nurse 'til
Miss Adria wake up." Martha was a young mother who served
at Ginger Star as a house slave. Sam turned to head toward the
kitchen. "Fetch some wormwood. It der in a jar on di kitchen
shelf. Olivia know which one it tis." Sarah knew Mum Lettie was
well versed in the care of a new mother. Wormwood was used
to help in cases of extreme fever. She cultivated it for situations
such as this. They all knew Mum Lettie was as skilled as any
doctor would be in this situation. Sam turned and ran toward
the house.

"Will she be alright?" Sarah asked Mum Lettie as she walked
up next to the woman who once again had helped them through
a catastrophe. Mum Lettie's years were showing on her this day.
Her gray hair escaped more than usual from under her blue
bandana, and she seemed shorter than the day before.

"Mi nuh for certain, but dem things jes run dem course."

John looked at Ronnie and shook his head as if trying to
clear away the confusion and asked, "Who the hell are you?"
He stared unable to comprehend all that was happening
around him.

"I, uh," she stumbled for words, "I'm Ronnie Shepherd," she said looking over to Sarah for help.

Sarah stepped toward John and said, "She's the one that escaped the pirate ship with him." She pointed to Amari who stood in the corner, his head down, wishing he were invisible. "Adria has been giving them food and shelter the past few days."

"This is all getting stranger by the minute!" John shouted. "Come outside, I want to talk to you both." He looked over her shoulder at Amari who stood stoically in the background trying to look away from what was happening. He didn't know what information the African might have, but he had to ask. They followed him outside to the pathway. Ronnie had never met John before now and had no idea what to expect. Sarah squeezed Mum Lettie's hand in gratitude, bent over and kissed Adria on the forehead, and followed them outside. Sarah had told John about Ronnie and Amari the night before when he'd come home from Claremont. He'd agreed that the Maroons were Amari's best option.

John turned and looked at Ronnie. "You knew about this?"

She saw the anger in his eyes, gulped and replied, "Yes, sir." She looked down at her feet and then back up at him. "But only for a few days now. I know she was trying to find a way to tell you both." She looked at Sarah, hoping for empathy and understanding.

Looking at Ronnie he asked, "Who is the father?" Ronnie hesitated and stepped back a little. "Tell me now!"

Ronnie took a deep breath and said, "She said his name was Eric. A merchant marine and a former resident of Ginger Star."

Sarah's hand flew to her mouth. "Oh my god!" She remembered the ship that had docked in their cove for several weeks last year. Eric and his father, Nigel, had been trusted emancipated slaves at Ginger Star. She and John knew this meant the baby was half negro. Not something they or their culture would ever accept. She looked at her husband. He ran his fingers through his black hair as he shook his head in an effort to shake off the truth. "What can we do?" Sarah asked.

"We must find a home for the baby. A home that will accept who he is." John answered. Ronnie shivered in the heat of the steamy Jamaican morning. Adria had been right. Her parents would never allow her to keep the baby.

Sam hurried down the path with the jar of wormwood.

"Martha soon come," Sam said, stopping in the pathway. It was clear things were not going well. Hearing the conversation, Mum Lettie came out of the cottage and grabbed the jar of wormwood and went back to Adria.

"Sam," John stepped toward his friend. "We talked about Amari going to live with the Maroons. Can we take the baby to them as well? Will they take him?"

Sam stood with his mouth open not knowing what to say. He would do anything to help John. He owed him his freedom, but helping to give away Adria's baby? He wasn't sure he could.

Before Sam could respond, Sarah cried out, "Oh my god, John!" She whirled around to look at her husband. "You court a disastrous plan. How can we possibly send our grandchild into the hills to be raised by savages?" She rarely disagreed with her husband, but a grandmotherly love had unwittingly taken up space in her heart.

"For heaven's sake, Sarah," John walked toward his wife, and for once, she stepped back, both repulsed at his suggestion and just a little fearful. She'd never seen him so angry. He stopped. He'd never seen her so upset, but then again, he couldn't remember being so scared himself. Pirates, hurricanes, and slave rebellions had never brought him such pain and worry. How would he protect his daughter from such scrutiny, having a child not only out of wedlock, but half negro as well? It was a scenario with no happy ending, no plausible solution that would make everyone whole again, let alone happy. In that moment, he doubted they would ever find happiness again. "We have to think about Adria's future."

A chill crept up her spine and Sarah knew he was right.

ADRIA FELL INTO a coma the rest of the day and next night. The young house slave, Martha, nursed the baby every few hours. He latched on to her breast and wrapped his little hand around her finger, as she said, "Come now, little one," offering the infant her breast. He rooted around and instinctively latched on and settled down. She rocked back and forth and hummed a lullaby. Sam brought two more cots into the cottage. One for Martha so she could be close to the baby, and the other for Sarah who refused to leave her daughter's side.

Sarah realized what she was doing and said to Mum Lettie, "Martha cannot stay here. She has to care for her daughter as well." She stood and looked at Martha and the baby. "I believe she should take the baby to her quarters and care for him there." Ronnie looked at Mum Lettie in disbelief. She worried about Adria's reaction when she woke and her son wasn't in the cottage. "That way, she can nurse both babies when needed. We certainly don't have room here for another child in this small space." Ronnie searched her mind for options, but came up with none, so she said nothing. The look in Mum Lettie's eyes showed Ronnie they shared the same thoughts, but both knew neither one of them were free to speak their minds.

With Sam's help, Martha took the baby boy to her quarters in the rear of Ginger Star. Adria continued to sleep, sometimes thrashing about, soaking the bed linens in sweat. She called out,

"Come back!" over and over again, but to whom, they weren't certain. Ronnie suspected she called for Eric, but also wondered if she had heard the plan being formed outside her door.

The plan to give away her son.

—Chapter Six—

"Twant me, 'twas the Lord. I always told Him, 'I trust you. I don't know where to go or what to do, but I expect You to lead me,' and He always did." —Harriet Tubman

1719, Interior Jamaica

Ronnie, Amari, and Sam took the two-day-old baby and left Ginger Star before dawn. Ronnie and the baby trudged behind Sam and Amari, following from the rear through the jungles of Jamaica. Mum Lettie had helped her to fashion a sling to carry the baby across her stomach. They had to hurry to keep him from crying. The makeshift bottle with a pewter bottom and a nipple fashioned from a piece of leather stretched over the bottle's neck was almost empty. They only had one more.

"How much farther, Sam?" Ronnie asked as she struggled to catch her breath. They had just climbed up a steep dirt road that threatened to drain all her energy. She wasn't sure she could go much further. They'd abandoned the horse-drawn wagon a few miles back, pulling it into the woods near a waterfall so as not to be seen by passersby. The last thing they needed was anyone questioning what Sam was doing traveling with Ronnie, Amari, and a baby. On foot, they would be less conspicuous as they made the rest of their way up into the mountains.

"We be der in jus' few miles, Miss Ronnie." Sam stopped to let her catch up. "Casa Daley jus up round the bend." He pointed up the path that doubled as a road. The sound of horses' hooves rattled the ground from the distance. "Come!" He motioned with his hand as he dove into the bushes. They followed him, and a pineapple stalk scratched Ronnie's face as she ducked for cover. They huddled together with only the moon for a lamp. Sam looked at Ronnie and Amari and nodded, letting them know to remain as still as possible. They prayed a collective silent prayer that the baby would stay asleep despite the increasing sound of the horse's hooves and creaking carriage heading their way. The three of them crouched under the bushes as the lanterns on the carriage swayed wildly back and forth as the wagon worked to avoid the ruts in the dirt road created by the latest downpour.

"Whoa!" the driver shouted, as he slowed the team of horses to dodge the ruts in the road. "Keep 'em to di right!" the second man hollered. The baby startled and began to cry. Ronnie pulled him out of the sling and cuddled him close, but he kept wailing. Thankfully, the drivers' fussing at the horses, the creaking wagon, and the clanging of the lanterns drowned out the infant's cries.

Soon, the sound of the carriage faded and the baby calmed down. Sam handed Ronnie the last bottle and she put it to the baby's lips. He eagerly began to eat.

"Here, let's sit down ova der." Sam reached over and held onto her elbow as she cradled the baby in her left arm and held the bottle with her right. They walked a few feet over to a fallen tree and sat with Amari following close behind.

Ronnie continued to feed the baby as sweat poured down her face in the cool nighttime breeze. Amari reached over with his ragged handkerchief and wiped the droplets from her face. She grinned a weak thanks.

"I don't know how much farther I can go, Sam," she said, nodding toward a clearing in the forest. "Can't we stop and bed down here for the night?" She pointed to an open area.

"Only a mile or so to go, Miss Ronnie. Jus up di road." He pointed in the direction the carriage had traveled. "'Sides, wi only got a little more lef' in dat bottle. Wi need to get to da wet nurse at Casa Daley before sunlight." Ronnie could see a bank of lights at the top of the hill.

"But that's where the carriage went, Sam." She pulled the makeshift bottle away from the baby's mouth, wiping his chin with her torn shirt. The infant had fallen back to sleep. She knew enough to lean him over her shoulder and pat him on the back.

"No, a no problem, Miss Ronnie." Sam patted her on the shoulder. "Henry be waitin' for us at di bottom of di drive," he pointed up the road. "Me sen' Matthew, the stable bwoy, up here on Chance and he deliver di message before wi lef Ginger Star."

"But that carriage just arrived, they'll see us coming," Ronnie said as she worried out loud. "How will we get inside without being noticed?"

Whispering out loud, he said, "Jes trust Big Sam." He patted her shoulder. "It be alright."

Once the baby was changed and sleeping again, Ronnie placed him back in her sling. The four of them slipped up the road, guided by the Jamaican moonlight, as bright as any lantern they could have carried. Ronnie struggled to continue and managed to put one foot in front of the other despite her fatigue. They approached what appeared to be the rear of a large house at the top of a hill where lights flickered outside the buildings. The carriage that had passed them was parked toward the front of the house. As they drew near, the horse snorted his acknowledgement of their approach, but no one noticed. Overgrown trees and bushes lined both sides of the pathway, providing some cover from the sight of the house.

Sam motioned for Ronnie and Amari to follow him into the brush. She climbed over the lava rock wall and followed him to a clearing. He walked over to a pile of stones lying next to a tall palm tree. Sam pulled them down, one at a time, reached in the middle of the pile, and pulled out several candles. He reached under another stone to find a flint and striker wrapped in a char cloth to keep dry.

Sam struck the flint against the steel using the char cloth to catch fire and lit the candles carrying them to the edge of the forest holding several in one hand. He held the light up for a few seconds and then lowered them, repeating the exercise several times. Finally, a blinking lantern answered his beacon in return. He turned and the moonlight lit up his smile. "Dey see us. Soon come." Grabbing her hand, the three of them hurried back to the clearing.

"How did you know what to do?" Ronnie whispered. The baby began to stir, and Sam put his finger up to his lips to shush her.

"Old Maroon secret." He nodded his head toward the road-side. "Pile of rock next to clearing give clue to others that one has a need."

"What do we do now?"

"We wait."

"How long?"

"Me not know," Sam said as he lay the thin blanket down. "Could be long time." He motioned for her to sit down on the blanket. She pulled the sling from around her neck and cradled the baby. The infant opened his eyes and tried to focus on the three adults that stared at him. He was tiny, smaller than he should have been at full term, yet he appeared to be healthy. His skin was a milky tan and the springy curls on his head shone in the moonlight.

"He doesn't even have a name," Ronnie whispered out loud. It was the first time it had occurred to her. "What should we call him?"

"This chile will overcome many tings. He have hard beginning and should be rewarded with strong name," Sam said. He lightly touched the baby's head as he stared at Ronnie. This woman was different from any he had ever met. Slave, English, or Spanish, she was unusual. Perhaps it was because she'd been forced to be tougher than she really was. She'd endured a lot and now was risking so much for an African man and a baby that wasn't even hers to give away.

She looked at the little one and then up at Sam. "What do you have in mind, Sam?"

"Elijah. It mean 'God is strong.'"

Amari nodded in agreement. "E-li-jah," he repeated and nodded again.

Ronnie smiled at them both and looked back to the baby who had fallen back asleep with the coaxing of the Jamaican crickets' lullaby. "I think that suits him well." Ronnie laid Elijah down in the bed of banana leaves Amari had made for him and covered him with the blanket. "He will need God's strength, that is for certain." Sam smiled back at her. "I hope they come soon. We're getting low on the baby's . . ." she looked Sam and smirked, "I mean Elijah's milk."

"Wi rest now. They soon come," Sam said as Ronnie laid down next to Elijah with her arm over top of him. Sam and Amari laid on each side of Ronnie and Elijah as if guarding them. Ronnie enjoyed the sense of security, however misguided.

Amari stared at Ronnie and baby Elijah as they drifted off to sleep in tandem. He closed his eyes, but only for a bit before opening them again. He knew that soon enough he and Ronnie would part ways and he wanted never to forget this woman who had saved his life many times in just a few short months.

They woke to the rustling of leaves. "What was that?" Ronnie asked before she realized Sam was already standing. She gathered Elijah onto her lap. He stirred. His nappy was damp, but there was no time to worry about that now. Amari stood ready to provide backup for Sam, if needed.

A thin black man, so dark that had it not been for the light of the full moon he would have been hard to find, stood at the edge of the clearing. Sam towered over him. They spoke back and forth in Patois, a language indigenous to slaves across the island, created to keep the British wondering what was being said. Ronnie couldn't follow the conversation, but the tone of the man's voice told her all she needed to know. He had slipped down here to guide them into the slave quarters of Casa Daley. Sam turned to see Ronnie standing with Elijah cradled in her arms. Amari bent down and gathered up their few belongings and fell in line behind Ronnie and the man from the plantation.

"What did he say?" Ronnie asked.

"Dis Henry. We to follow him to Casa Daley up di road. We stay in di bushes, so keep behind me," Sam said. Henry looked back over his shoulder and motioned for them to follow.

"Elijah is getting restless. We should stop and put a dry nappy on him first," Ronnie protested. "We don't want him getting fussy at the wrong time."

Sam tapped Henry on the shoulder and started whispering. Henry scratched his head, wanting to hurry, but realized the need to keep Elijah quiet and nodded.

Sam turned back to Ronnie and pointed to a felled tree. "Sit down an' change him quick, for wi fightin' di dawn," he said wiping the sweat off his brow. It occurred to Ronnie that was what Sam did when he was worried. Sweat rolled down his forehead. They sat while Sam and Henry chatted back and forth in flowing Patois.

"What's he saying, Sam?" she asked as she swaddled Elijah and rocked him back and forth in an attempt to lull him back to sleep.

"He say that we need to get to Casa Daley 'foe the massa wakes." Sam nodded toward the great house. He looked at Elijah. "Miss Melinda help us send dem to Maroons."

"Give him a minute, then I think we can go." She kissed Elijah on the forehead, shaking off the maternal feelings, and rocked and cooed him back to sleep after she'd tucked him back in the sling. Once she was sure he was snoozing again, she looked at Henry and Sam and nodded. Silently, they picked up their few belongings and walked single file through the thick Jamaican forest.

Ronnie held Elijah close and prayed he wouldn't wake. *When did you learn how to pray?* She ignored her thoughts and continued toward the blinking lights that came from the smaller outbuildings of the great house. Sam turned to check on them every so often and she'd nod to assure him they were alright.

Henry signaled to slow down as they got closer to the lower level of the house. Tucking themselves behind the brush on the side of the road, Henry whistled a shrill "Whip-o-will!"

Before too long, a light came closer, swinging back and forth. Henry motioned for them to follow. The only sounds were that of their feet crunching on the rocky road. The lantern got brighter until it revealed the face of a young brown woman. She wasn't black and she wasn't white, but somewhere in between. She spoke Spanish to Henry who answered her in kind.

The woman turned and looked at Ronnie. "My name is Melinda," she said.

Ronnie nodded. "And I'm Ronnie."

Melinda looked at Ronnie and was surprised to see they were close to the same age. She realized her expectation of a woman that would bring the crossbred pickney to them was not what she expected at all. She'd figured Mum Lettie or another Ginger Star slave would be given the task. They hurried as fast as their feet would take them back to the rear buildings of the great house while she wondered where the infant came from.

What Ronnie saw as they followed Melinda inside the house wasn't a great house at all, but a rather elaborate cottage when compared to Ginger Star. Dark stone buildings stood to the side and beneath a larger structure that was hard to discern in the blackness of night. Melinda extinguished the flame as they approached the building. Turning, she put her finger to her lips telling them all to be quiet. Ronnie looked down at Elijah who was, to her surprise, still sleeping soundly. He must be used to being tossed around, first in his momma's tummy and now in my arms.

They ducked down a short set of steps, through a narrow opening, and into an underground part of the building. Ronnie grabbed the side of the door jamb, trying to gain her bearings as she carried Elijah down the narrow stairwell. Her eyes adjusted slowly to the darkness. There was someone already in the room which felt more like the opening to a tunnel. Candlelight flickered on the walls.

"Haniah, these are our visitors." Melinda bent down and lit a small candle giving a little light to the dark room. Haniah was tall and slender with her hair pulled into a bun on top of her head. The woman's skin glowed against the candlelight and her eyes bore a history only Haniah could tell. She looked from Ronnie to Elijah. Haniah glanced back at Melinda as if waiting for permission to do something.

"You can give the baby to Haniah now," Melinda said to her.

Ronnie stood still for a moment and felt as if all the air inside her lungs had been sucked away. She wasn't ready to surrender Elijah. Not yet. Looking down at him as he stirred, his little fingers were still wound around her pinky. She couldn't bring herself to pull her hand away. "I'm not sure if he's ready." She tried to stall her separation from this little one that mistook her for his mother. She blinked hard and took a deep breath as she slowly pulled her pinky finger away from him. Immediately Elijah began to stir. She looked up to see Amari's eyes looking into hers. The sight of his tears unleashed hers. A different kind of heartache hit her as she realized Amari would be leaving with Elijah. They would both be gone.

"Here, give him to Haniah," Melinda whispered. "Quickly, before he wakes."

Ronnie knew Elijah's cries would draw fast attention from the cottage. She pulled his little hand away from her finger and handed the swaddled Elijah over to Haniah. The older woman grasped Elijah with the familiarity of a mother and cradled him in her arms. Elijah began to stir. The woman opened her blouse and put her breast to his lips. His little head turned back and forth as he tried to decide between crying and sucking. Elijah's fingers touched her brown skin and instantly raised his other hand in grateful comfort. He eagerly latched on to her breast instead of Ronnie's makeshift bottle. His little fingers found Haniah's finger instead of hers. Ronnie blinked hard once again. Turning toward Amari she felt a sadness she'd not had since Nassau. She remembered to reach into her pocket to pull out her mother's jade stone. "I want you to have this." She looked at Amari and placed the cool green stone in his hand. He looked down and shook his head. He knew how much the stone meant to her. She'd shown him while they were still on the ship. He had noticed she held it whenever she was worried. Amari handed it back to her.

Ronnie reached up, touched Amari's cheek, and shook her head. She placed the stone back in his palm, curling his hand with hers around the cool gem. Her almond fingers laid on top of his ebony hand, a contrast she no longer noticed. Looking into his eyes overflowing with tears, she leaned over and hugged him, laying her head on his chest and said, "I know God has great things in mind for you, my friend." She took a deep breath so she could continue without breaking down. "I thank Him for bringing you into my life, if only for such a brief time." They held each other in silent protest of separation. No translation or hand gestures were needed this time.

Amari had trusted Ronnie with his life and once again he owed his future to her. The thought of creating a new life for himself without her at his side was an idea he didn't want to entertain, even though knew that was going to be the outcome. After being ripped from his homeland, and the hurt he endured every day from its memory, the thought of losing her friendship and protection was tortuous. The two of them bonded out of necessity. Now, they were being torn apart for the same reason. Necessity.

Amari sobbed and Ronnie let her silent tears flow onto his chest. Her life had changed so much in such a short span of time. The grief she had tried to escape by joining the Neptune months ago in Nassau came raging back with a vengeance. Her body shook with that old familiar fear. She felt Sam's light touch on her shoulder. "Wi got to go now," Sam whispered to Ronnie.

She pulled away from Amari. "I'm so tired, but I guess you're right," she said looking around the room. Elijah was nursing quietly. Amari kissed Ronnie on the top of her head, let her go, and walked over to stand next to Haniah and Elijah.

"It seems he much prefers you to the bottle," Ronnie said to Haniah. She reached over and stroked Elijah's black curls. "Goodbye, little one. Remember, God is strong and always with you," she whispered. It occurred to her she needed to remember it as well. Unexpected tears sprang into her eyes again and she tried to blink them back, but they cascaded down her cheeks anyway. She didn't mind it this time though. She knew she was doing the right thing, the only thing. At least for Amari.

The African looked at her with wet cheeks. He took a deep breath and instead of gaining his composure, it left him completely. Through his sobs, he looked at her and said, "I love," as he placed his hands over his heart, "you," and pointed to her. Ronnie fell into his arms.

"Oh, Amari, I will miss you!" She hugged him and he buried his face in her blonde hair that had fallen free. He breathed in her scent, steeled himself, and lifted his head. She looked up at him. "I will think of you every day and pray you'll find a better life up in the hills with the Maroons."

Amari nodded as if he understood.

Sam's hand lay on her shoulder in an effort to encourage her to leave, but she didn't budge from where she stood. She reached up and touched Amari's face, tracing his bearded jawline amidst the tears. "We will miss one another, but I know your life will be better this way." She stood on her tiptoes, held his face, and kissed both of his cheeks. "Go with God, my friend." She didn't wait for his response, knowing neither of them wanted to let go. She turned and followed Sam outside into the darkness that was slowly giving way to dawn. She could hear Amari breaking down again, but kept one foot in front of the other as she willed herself to leave. Glancing over her shoulder, she could see the lights of Casa Daley as they faded into the distance.

Ronnie followed Sam with only the moon for guidance and tried not to allow herself to think about whom or what she had left behind. She attempted to push her memories of pulling Elijah's little hand away from hers. A profound sadness overtook her as she realized she would have to live a lie. In her heart she knew she had no choice but to deceive Adria, her friend that given her refuge on the island. If Adria were to survive the fever,

Ronnie knew she would experience the greatest sadness of all, the loss of a child.

Ronnie had confidence that Amari would settle in and be alright. He would create a new life for himself; just how, she didn't know. It would be a comfort to think she'd see him again, but she couldn't imagine how that would ever happen. Their worlds were not meant to intertwine.

It perplexed her that John and Sarah chose never to embrace their grandson and watch him grow up as a he was a part of their daughter. Yes, the initial embarrassment would have been difficult, but with time, Ronnie thought much could be forgiven and forgotten. But Sarah and John had chosen to live a lie. *How will I ever keep from telling Adria the truth? How can I let her think her baby died?* She hadn't wanted to be a part of such a deceitful scheme, to give away Adria's baby, but knew she had to take part in the plan in order to ensure Amari's safety. Unless he went to live with the Maroons, he faced life as a slave. John had made that painfully clear.

Ronnie tried to focus on getting down the rough terrain without falling. She brushed a stray tree limb aside as they headed across the steep mountain ridge and wondered what she would find when they arrived back at Ginger Star. Would Adria still be with them, or did she succumb to the childbed fever? Her mind swirled with the possibilities. There didn't seem to be any "good" scenarios.

She'd learned to live with secrets before, and she made up her mind; she would do it again.

—Chapter Seven—

"A good example is the best sermon." —Benjamin Franklin

Claremont, Jamaica

Sam and Ronnie headed west of Casa Daley to stay at Ramble House Plantation, the home of Marshall Fergusson. John had told Sam that he would send a message to Marshall asking for accommodations for the two of them for a night, figuring they would be too tired to travel all the way back to Ocho Rios after dropping off the baby.

The unlikely couple trudged up one path and down another along the mountain ridges. "Mr. Marshall, he da son of Dr. and Mrs. Fergusson. The doctor, he pass some years back. Mr. Marshall stay and take good care of his momma till she gone too. He run di plantation and help folk back in di holler." Sam pointed to the mountains in the background. "We gonna stay der for the night. Massa John work it out."

"Is Marshall married?" she couldn't help but ask, wondering why she cared.

"No," Sam replied. Ronnie blinked back her surprise. *Why would anyone live in such an isolated place alone?* Sam looked at her and shared, "Massa John send note an' tell him 'bout Amari, but not baby."

"I understand," said Ronnie. She was not surprised.

They could hear the bleating of goats and saw a herd of them trotting down the hillside. A young black boy ran to catch up carrying a tall bamboo stick as a staff. The lad hollered at a stray goat and used his staff to guide him back to the pack. The goats ranged in size and colors with the kids staying close to their mothers.

"That must be Massa Marshall's goats," Sam said. Ronnie walked next to him taking in her surroundings. There was Ramble House, a fairly large house, built mostly with stone, with a cistern to the side on the top of the hill. A separate building that appeared to be a greenhouse stood off to the side along with a building in the back. A dog barked and ran out toward them announcing their arrival. Sam reached down and stroked his ears. "Willie, it good see you," he said crouching down to look the dog in the eye. The animal sat and licked Sam's face.

"My, he really knows you, Sam." Ronnie took a cautious step toward Willie.

"Massa Marshall often bring him to Ochi when he come." Sam patted the brown short-haired dog, then looked up to see a tall man wearing knickers and a white blouse at the top of the stairs.

"Sam! You made it safely," the young man said. His blue eyes immediately settled on Ronnie. She blushed and silently admonished herself. She looked at this hearty handsome man in the middle of absolutely nowhere and was amazed at the presence he gave off. His black hair dipped in front of his forehead, giving him a debonair presence, intended or not. The men shook hands, but it was obvious to Ronnie that had they not been of different colored skin, it would have been a hearty slap on the back and hug.

"Yes, Massa Marshall. We thanks ya for de offa." Sam looked back at Ronnie.

Ronnie found herself swooping up her loose hair and tucking it back under her hat, trying to look presentable. She wiped the sweat from her forehead with the back of her hand. Marshall quickly reached in his pocket and pulled out a fresh handkerchief. "Here, may I offer some assistance?" He held out the kerchief to her and she took it.

"Thank you very much. This Jamaican heat wreaks havoc with me, I'm afraid," she said. Grinning, she felt herself blush and her eyes fell to the ground. "I will make sure to return it."

"Oh, please keep it. I have more than I need." Marshall bowed a little.

Lifting her eyes, they met his blue ones. He bent and kissed the top of her hand. A shiver in contrast to the hot afternoon ran up her spine.

As Marshall and Sam talked, she took in the view and was impressed by God's tapestry of the mountains, flowering trees, and waterfalls flowing from untold rivers that gave it life. Birds flew, large and small, seeming to live together in harmony. She could see the neighboring hillside had been cleared and recently planted.

Giving them some privacy as the men caught up on the local gossip, she walked around the lawn and admired the view. She could hear voices from afar and assumed it came from the slave quarters. She was still not accustomed to the slavery part of the island's culture and hoped she never would be.

Marshall turned and waved her back to join them. She walked over and said, "Well, Marshall, your property is certainly beautiful. What is that planted on the next hillside?"

Marshall looked across the way. "Oh, that's tea. We planted them just last year when, not long ago, it was discovered we had the perfect climate for it here in Jamaica."

"Well, you are certainly an astute businessman to be in the forefront of such an opportunity." Ronnie was impressed with his intuitiveness. "But, please let me be so bold as to ask a question." She looked at him with eyebrows raised. "How many more people did it take to man the operation?" In other words, how many more slaves did you need?

Marshall looked at this outspoken young woman with renewed interest. He was impressed with her boldness, knowing what it was she referenced. "Well, I suppose you refer to those that do the laborious work in the fields. I was fortunate enough to purchase twelve more field hands and have been able to plant and tend to the tea as well as more sugarcane over on the north ridge." He pointed to the cane flowing in the breeze to their right.

She noticed he referred to them as "field hands" and not slaves. Interesting. "I'm sure it takes a lot of people and hard work to keep all of this going."

"Yes, it do," Sam replied. He feared he knew where this conversation was headed and tried to help Ronnie exit it graciously.

Marshall chuckled, knowing what Sam was up to. "It is definitely a full-time job for many of us," Marshall said. He offered his arm to Ronnie which she coyly accepted. They walked toward the house. "Rosalie is here to show you to your room." He nodded toward the top of the steps that led inside the house where a young black woman stood. "You have a little while to freshen up and rest before dinner."

"Why thank you, sir." She turned his way and dipped in respect.

"Please, call me Marshall."

"Yes, of course, Marshall." She smiled and walked up the steps to meet Rosalie.

"This way, mi lady." Rosalie swept her arm in the direction of the stairs. The dark woman had a regal look to her with her hair swept up on top of her head and wore what appeared to be a uniform of sorts: a black dress with a white apron. Ronnie followed her inside, all the while admiring the carved paneling and Italian tiles that lined the walls and floors. Rosalie opened a door and Ronnie walked inside. High ceilings gave the room an airiness that was most welcome in the Jamaican heat, and windows were thrown open allowing a breeze to make its way through.

"Mista Marshall said supper is to be served on the veranda, Miss," Rosalie said as she handed Ronnie a white cotton robe. "There is more clothing for you there." She pointed to a skirt and blouse lying on the bed.

"Oh my! How very thoughtful. Thank you, Rosalie," Ronnie touched her on the shoulder. "How long have you worked here?" Having never had the opportunity to speak intimately with a female slave, she felt the need to connect with her, even if it was just to make small talk.

Rosalie looked at her, surprised at the question. "Oh, I been with Mr. Marshall's family since they come to Jamaica. Since I was pickney." Rosalie nodded toward a tub. "I draw you bat." She pointed to the tub hidden behind a screen. "Der more hot wata in de kettle." Rosalie held it up and headed toward the tub to pour it in, but Ronnie stopped her.

"There's no need for you to do that. I can certainly handle things from here." Ronnie was not used to anyone taking care of her like this. She smiled at Rosalie and gently took the kettle from her hand. Rosalie nodded and slipped out of the room.

Ronnie pulled off her soiled clothing and draped them over a chair. She dipped her finger into the lukewarm bath water and emptied the hot kettle into the tub. After she stepped over the edge and lowered herself into the water, she leaned her head back onto the cool porcelain. Closing her eyes, she found the solace of solitude for the first time since she could remember.

Her thoughts drifted back to Amari and Elijah, wondering where they were right now. Then she remembered Adria, wondering how this would all play out. *What will I say to her? How will we get through this?* She mourned their friendship, knowing it could never survive now that it was wrapped in deceit.

Ronnie was keenly aware that she had left Adria's baby behind in a slave quarters at Casa Daley. *Dear God, please watch over them all. Please forgive me.* It was all she could come up with and then prayed that it was enough. Sighing deeply, she lowered her body further into the water, wetting her hair and submerging her face. Staring at the ceiling from under the water, she closed her eyes until she had to come up for a breath.

Ronnie languished in the tub until the water chilled. She stood and grabbed the towel Rosalie had left draped over a chair. She stepped out of the tub, dried her body off, and looked at the clothes on the bed. She picked up a cerulean blue dress with delicate white flowers, a loose fit on the bodice, and gathered at the waist. As she pulled on the clothes, she was delighted at the feeling of wearing a skirt again. She'd become so accustomed to wearing pants on the ship. It felt surprisingly good to dress like a woman and feel feminine.

Ronnie pulled her damp hair into a makeshift bun at the nape of her neck, giving up on the loose strands that insisted on springing loose around her face. She sat down at the vanity with a mirror and stared at her reflection. It had been a long time since she had seen her own face. "Well, there you are," she said aloud to herself and sighed. Ronnie reached into her satchel she had dropped on the floor and retrieved her tattered journal. The pages were crinkled from getting wet. She stood and easily found a pen that sat next to an ink well on a desk. Sitting down in the desk chair, she dipped the tip of the pen in the ebony liquid.

"This must be a heaven of sorts for some," she wrote in her journal. "Were it not for my predicament, I believe I could learn to love the isolation." She continued to write about her thoughts that had swirled in her head while lying in the tub. She hoped for some type of future here in Jamaica, but she couldn't even imagine what that might be. Ronnie prayed, in writing, for Amari, Elijah, and Adria. Yawning, she closed the book and looked over at the bed. I'll lay down, just for a minute. The white linen was soft and cool against her skin. As she pulled the coverlet over her body, the murmur of voices from the slave quarters lulled her to sleep.

She woke to the light touch of Rosalie's hand. "Dinner is ready, Miss Ronnie," she said.

Ronnie sat up and rubbed her eyes. "Oh, my goodness! I must have drifted off."

Rosalie smiled. "Must be real tired, Miss! You been on long journey."

Ronnie stretched her arms out and stood up. Rosalie reached over to straighten up the coverlet. "You go on now. I take care of dis."

"Thank you, Rosalie. I so appreciate all you are doing for me." The slave looked at her, a bit confused, but continued with her duties. She wasn't accustomed to such small talk from a white lady. Yet, she welcomed it just the same. "I'll see you later, I'm sure."

"Yes'm." Rosalie said as she straightened up the bed and slipped out of the room.

RONNIE WALKED OUT of the bedroom and down the hall to the landing. Walking up the steps to the veranda off the dining room, she marveled at the hand-painted ceramic tiles that appeared to be laid with care on the walls of the dining room and veranda. The green-marble fireplace was the centerpiece of the dining room. She ran her hand over the cool marble and stared at the images, wondering how difficult it must have been to get any type of supplies, let alone building materials of this quality, so far up into the mountains of the island. Hearing footsteps, she looked up to see Marshall stroll into the dining room. He whispered something to Rosalie and walked to the veranda to join Ronnie.

"My goodness, my lady, you do transform as no other. So, how was your afternoon?" He said as he handed her a single purple orchid. Her finger traced the circular petal and she tried to tuck it behind her ear. "Here, allow me." He took the flower, gently pulled aside her silky hair that had sprung loose, and tucked the flower behind her ear using her hair to keep it there. The feeling of someone touching her chilled her spine. She turned and looked at her reflection in the glass door.

"It's lovely, thank you." She dipped a little curtsy of gratitude and again thought about how long it had been since she'd made the automatic show of respect. She was reminded of how many times she stopped herself from curtsying in respect to someone when she was back on the Neptune.

"I certainly did not expect such gracious accommodations." Her arm swept toward the back of the property. "I had no idea the grounds of Ramble House were so lovely, Mr. Fer . . ." She corrected herself, "I mean, Marshall."

Marshall chuckled. "It is Jamaica that makes Ramble House what it is. Without her beauty, it's just another house."

She nodded. "Hmm, yes, you are so right." Orchids were planted in such a way that the Bird of Paradise looked like a crown in the middle. "What a beautiful view, Marshall. You have done a wonderful job with the gardens." She took a deep breath. "If I didn't know better, I would swear I could smell the flowers all the way up here."

"Well, I must give credit to my mum who designed the gardens and had the greenhouse built." He pointed to the building that stood to the side of the doctor's quarters. "She was quite the horticulturist."

"She sure must have been. Sam told me she passed not that long ago. I'm so sorry for your loss."

"Thank you. Those are her clothes you are wearing."

Ronnie's hand went to her neck feeling the ruffled fabric. "Oh my, I didn't know." She realized it must be hard seeing her in his mother's garments.

"Don't fret my dear lady, it makes me feel good to see you in them. Take more with you, if you like. It will do my heart good to know they are being put to good use. They are doing no one any good hidden in boxes."

"I would be most grateful," Ronnie said. She had very little choice of things to wear and knew she could use them.

"I will send you with what you can carry and bring the rest to you on my next trip to Ocho Rios. Assuming you will be there." He didn't know Ronnie's background, but understood she was new to the island.

"Why, Marshall, that would be very nice of you. Right now, I do hope to stay here in Jamaica, but just don't know. Not yet."

They looked over the rail of the veranda to the grounds of Ramble House and could see Sam as he walked across the courtyard. She was grateful for the diversion as she could sense Marshall's curiosity regarding her past and future.

Sam walked up from the slave quarters where he had gone to freshen up and change for dinner.

"Sam, we're up here!" she called.

Sam smiled and waved, continuing to amble toward the house. "Oh, Sam won't be joining us for dinner. I'm sure he's already eaten with the rest."

Rest? Rest of what? Ronnie checked her thoughts. "Oh, I didn't realize," she said. Marshall offered his arm and she took it as they turned and walked into the dining room. Rosalie and two other slaves were there, ready to dish up their dinner from the sideboard. Marshall pulled out a chair and she sat, trying to remember how to dine properly, which fork to use first and so on. She thought it best to just follow his lead.

Ronnie found it foreign to have anyone serve her, but Marshall seemed to take it for granted. "So, tell me about Ronnie," Marshall said.

She took a deep breath and was prepared for the question. She knew her past would be a topic of discussion sooner than later. Might as well get it over with. "Well, there's not much to tell really. I found myself alone in Nassau as the war between the British and the pirates of New Providence Island began to break out. With the offer of pardons from Woodes Rogers, things were in quite a state of confusion. I knew I had nowhere else to go, so I was hired on as a crew member of the Neptune."

"A woman on a merchant ship?"

"Oh no! I hid my identity." She looked down and touched the sleeve on the blouse she wore. "Wearing this outfit tonight, reminds me that's it's been too long."

He looked at Ronnie in his mother's clothes Rosalie had laid out for her. "Well, I must say, it suits you quite well." Trying not to be too obvious about his attraction to her he said, "So, how did you end up in Jamaica?"

Ronnie explained to him how her identity was uncovered and her swift exit from the ship to the shore of Ocho Rios. She explained a little about Amari, but didn't elaborate, unsure how much she could trust this man, despite his helpfulness.

"Well, I must say, you are an amazing young lady. How do you know Sam?" Marshall asked.

"I met him when I landed on the shore of Ginger Star."

Marshall could sense there was more to the story but didn't press her for more.

They finished their meal of curried goat, callaloo, and yams—all of which, Marshall had boasted, having been homegrown at the Ramble House plantation. Ronnie declined Rosalie's offer of dessert. "Thank you, but if I want to fit into any more of these clothes," she said as she smoothed her skirt and stood, "I had best decline, but the meal was beyond delicious, Rosalie."

"T'ank you, Miss Ronnie," Rosalie said and, not being used to compliments, could feel herself blush as she began to clear the table. "I will save should you want it later." Marshall escorted Ronnie out to the veranda overlooking the front lawn of Ramble House.

Ronnie could hear the rhythm of drums making music she'd not heard before. People in the distance sang songs to each other. One would start and others joined in. The soulful sound soothed Ronnie's fears of the future for the first time since she could remember. "What's that sound?" she asked. He looked into the distance to hear what she went on to describe. "It sounds almost like drums, but more intricate and detailed," she said stopping to stare into the Jamaican night. The beat of the drums harnessed a melody of their own.

Marshall smiled and said, "That's Kimar playing the drums." He stood close to her at the railing. He chuckled at the puzzled look on her face.

"It almost tickles my ears. He's quite good." She leaned on the railing, trying to see him better. Staring at the young man as he flitted his hands back and forth on the surface of the multiple sized drums, she involuntarily tapped her toe. Kimar looked up at her, grinned, and stepped up the pace.

"Many massas nuh allow slaves to 'av drums, Miss Ronnie," Sam said as he walked onto the veranda to join them. He stood on the other side of Ronnie.

"Why on earth not?" Her fingers involuntarily tapped on the railing to the beat of the drum.

"Plantation owners fear that their slaves will try to communicate with one another to plan an escape. They're very adept at using the Gumbah drum to communicate." Marshall said.

"I notice you oftentimes refer to them as *servants*. Why is that?"

"Probably lessens the guilt of knowing that I legally own another man's life." Pulling a pipe from his breast pocket, he lit the end of a small stick by using a nearby candle. Marshall puffed on the carved wooden pipe until it lit. The curl of smoke seemed to dance to the drums as it twirled its way to the Jamaican sky lit with stars.

"Perhaps I should retire," she said backing away from the veranda, waving a nod of appreciation to Kimar.

"I'll have Kimar stop playing." Marshall sat his drink down on the sill.

"Oh no, please don't," Ronnie said, "at least not on my account."

Marshall smiled. "I've found it certainly can be a lullaby," he took Ronnie's hand in his. "Sleep well, my lady." He brushed his lips across the top of her hand.

Ronnie smiled and let his hand go slowly. Following Rosalie back to her room, she turned back to glance at Marshall. Finding him looking after her, their eyes locked for a brief moment. Her heart skipped a beat as she turned and continued toward her room, the sound of the drums growing softer and softer.

As she slid under the covers in her bed, the breeze lifted the curtains and their shadow danced on the wall in the candlelight. She remembered the softness of Elijah's skin as she stroked his

cheek and the smell of his baby-soft hair. She prayed again that
he and Amari would be safe and healthy in their new home,
and then she realized she didn't know where that would be.
She remembered Adria's loyalty, protecting her and Amari, and
she hoped that Adria would somehow forgive her for giving
her baby away to live a life with the Maroons in the mountains
of Jamaica. She drifted into a restless sleep with the sound of
Kimar's lullaby carrying her away.

Waking to the morning song of a rooster, Ronnie rolled
over and stretched. She looked around at the shuttered windows
that kept the leaves of the banana tree from reaching out to her.
Jamaican sunshine peeked through the green leaves and filtered
into the room. She recalled her last conscious moment, the
tinkling sound of the drums, and the memory of Marshall's eyes
that had visited her dreams.

She climbed out of the four-poster bed and sat at the vanity.
Pulling her hair up into a ribbon that Rosalie had left her, she
noticed the woman's comb with a silver hand mirror were more
than a guest set. She intuitively knew it was his mother's comb.
Somehow, it made her feel not so alone in this ménage of mountaintops. Rosalie had laundered her travel clothes and she put
them back on for the trip back down the mountains.

AFTER BREAKFAST ALONE in the dining room, Ronnie joined
Sam in the courtyard and said their goodbyes as Marshall rode
up. "Sorry I missed breakfast," he said to Ronnie.

"Oh, not to worry. Rosalie took good care of me," Ronnie
replied.

Marshall reached for Sam's hand and shook it. "Safe travels,
Sam. Look after this lovely lady."

Sam nodded and said, "She in good hands."

"Yes, indeed I am," Ronnie said, flattered at Marshall's concern. She looked at Marshall and continued, "Your hospitality was a most welcome respite." She smiled at him and turned toward Sam. "Well, I suppose we need to get on with our trip."

Handing Sam an envelope, Marshall said, "Please deliver this to John for me."

"Yessir, I surely will," Sam said tucking the envelope into the saddlebag. "And I take good care of Silver for you till you come back to Ginger Star." Marshall had insisted they borrow his dapple-gray horse for their trip down the mountain.

"I know you will. She's happy to get out of the pasture and take a trip," Marshall said.

Turning to Ronnie, Marshall said, "And these are the clothes I promised you." He handed a satchel to her. As she took it with her right hand, he lifted her left and lightly kissed it.

There's that shiver again. She shook her head and offered, "You didn't have to do that, but I do greatly appreciate the kindness. I'm sorry I have no way to repay you."

"Perhaps our paths will cross again someday, and you can figure out a way." He smiled at her and nodded, then, turned and shook Sam's hand. "You two travel safely now."

Sam hopped up on Silver. Ronnie tucked the satchel away in the saddlebag and Sam offered her his hand to mount the horse. She declined, easily putting her foot in the stirrup, pulling herself up into the saddle behind him. Sam guided the horse down the rugged mountain paths substituting for roads toward Ocho Rios and she turned to wave goodbye. "Marshall seems to be right, it's as if Silver really does know the way to the coast," Ronnie said over Sam's shoulder.

"Yep, it do," said Sam. The afternoon sun began its descent back over the mountains and allowed the evening cool to set in. "We be back at Ginger Star in jes a little while now," he said to Ronnie. They made the stop at the falls and picked up the wagon and horse they had left behind on their trek to Casa Daley. Ronnie rode Silver the rest of the way and Sam drove the wagon.

Finding herself alone with her thoughts too much, she called to Sam, "I wonder what we will find back at Ginger Star. My mind keeps going to Adria, I cannot imagine what there is to say." They both had played scenarios over and over in their minds, unable to articulate their biggest fears to one another. Sam nodded and kept his attention on the road, trying to avoid ruts and gullies created by the latest shower coming from the rain forest just east from where they came. "I must think about where I'll go from here, Sam. I can't stay at Ginger Star much longer, if at all."

"Maybe you go with Miss Mavis in Ocho Rios. She good friend of Mum Lettie's."

She followed the wagon and had to practically shout for Sam to hear her over the creaking wheels. "Adria mentioned her to me more than once. Mavis owns a mercantile?"

Sam nodded again. "Her husband die suddenly 'bout a year ago. She work it alone now."

They rode in silence for a long stretch, lost in their own thoughts. The sun set behind the mountains as they turned down the lane that led to Ginger Star. The grounds were unusually quiet. Normally, as the sun was setting, slaves were bustling around preparing dinner, but things were calmer than normal. They could see candles slowly lighting up the great house as the evening's shadows approached. Sam pulled up to the front steps. He jumped down and tied the horse and wagon to the hitching post. Ronnie dismounted Silver, sliding off to the ground. The front door opened and John stepped outside carrying a candle. He looked much older than he had the last time she saw him. His hair was pulled back and the frown on his forehead was deeper than Ronnie remembered. "I'm grateful you returned safely. I trust your mission was accomplished." He looked from Sam to Ronnie and back again.

That is correct, the mission of giving away your grandson. Ronnie knew she had to stop herself from these thoughts before they betrayed her and she slipped and said them out loud. After all, didn't she share just as much guilt as anyone else standing on these steps? She stared at John and nodded. Thankfully, Sam took charge of the conversation.

"Yessir, Elijah now wit di Maroon tribe."

John tilted his head and said, "Who?"

"Sorry, sir. Dat di name wi give him."

John took a deep breath and sighed. "Well no need to mention that to anyone here." He walked the rest of the way down the steps.

Ronnie looked toward the cottage, but there were no candles burning. She'd wrongly assumed Adria was still down there. Turning back to John, she asked, "How is Adria?"

"Gratefully, she has recovered from the fever." John looked back over his shoulder, making sure the door was closed.

"Does she. . .?" Sam's voice trailed off. His eyes fell away from John's and down to his own hands shifting his hat from hand to hand.

"Know about the baby?" John finished the question. He looked at Sam, his friend, employee, and confidante for many years. They'd built Ginger Star side by side, sweating in the sun during the heat of the days and cooling off in the falls in the evenings. John considered Sam a brother, but this was asking way too much of anyone and John knew it. He also knew he had to protect his wife and daughter from scandal and repercussions of poor choices. Sam nodded. "Yes," John said. He looked at Ronnie. "And now knows her child did not survive." John looked away from Ronnie and Sam and stared up at the mountains not seeing anything. He couldn't bring himself to use the word "died." He took a deep breath, but his shoulders now sagged where they had not before. "She and her mother are leaving for London in the morning."

"So soon? May I see her?" Ronnie asked. She saw the fear in his eyes. "To say goodbye."

John didn't hesitate to answer. "That is not a good idea. The less contact she has with anyone who knows what happened, the better off all involved will be."

Ronnie had no argument for his logic. While it broke her heart to think she may never see Adria again, her friend that saved both her and Amari, a part of her was relieved. She didn't know how well she would have mastered being Adria's friend and not be honest about her son. Part of her was grateful she would not have to live the lie in front of Adria. Ronnie felt awful taking part in this deception. She consoled herself knowing that she had to help Amari find a future and that Elijah would be much better off with people who accepted him. She knew in her heart Amari would watch over Elijah.

"I understand." Ronnie knew she was in no position to argue the merits of her feelings. Feelings, she knew, could get one in all kinds of trouble.

"You are welcome to remain in the cottage until you can find suitable lodging," John said to Ronnie.

"Thank you, sir. I shall head back down to the cottage and begin my search for a home tomorrow." Her stomach twisted into a knot. Finding a new place would not be easy.

"Here, you'll need this." John handed her his candlelit lantern.

Grateful for his act of kindness, Ronnie said, "Thank you again." She nodded and took the lantern in both hands.

"Massa John, I was thinking that Miss Mavis might be able to help Ronnie."

John cocked his head to one side. "That might just be a good idea, Sam."

"Wi a go see har tomorrow," Sam said.

John looked back at Ronnie. He reached in his pants pocket and pulled out a bag of coins and handed it to her. "There should be enough in here to help you get on your feet."

Ronnie didn't move. She was stunned. Was John paying for her silence? The mere thought made her stomach wretch and with greater force this time. She swallowed hard trying to keep her composure. "Thank you, sir. Your generosity is far above any expectation I could have. I will certainly remain here at the cottage, but only until I can find a suitable place of my own. However, I cannot accept your offer of money."

"Well, while I admire your upstanding virtue, Miss Shepherd, I am also fairly certain you have no means by which to support yourself or secure a home for that matter." John looked her square in the eyes and stepped closer making her feel just a little intimidated. He extended the envelope once more. "I can understand if you think this gesture has a false motive, but you can rest assured, that is not the case. If you would feel better were it a loan, then so be it."

She looked at the bag in his hand and realized she had no choice but to accept his offer. Slowly she reached for it, sighed, and hung her head. "Please consider it a loan," she whispered.

"Sam can give you an introduction to Mavis, she knows everyone along the north coast. If there are opportunities for honest work, she will know of them." John looked at Sam who nodded and handed her a satchel. "There is food in here and fresh water in the basin in the cottage."

Ronnie acquiesced. "Thank you, sir." She hung her head, turned, and walked down the path. The lantern provided aid to the now-emerging moonlight guiding her way. She slung the satchel over her shoulder, held the candle and bag of coins in one hand, and turned the knob of the cottage door with the other. Walking inside, the lantern struggled to illuminate the room. Everything had been put back in its original place. There was no sign of a birth. No sign of Amari. The lantern's meager efforts to light the room only made it more desolate. Her heart sank. Here she was again, alone. Loneliness swept over her like the waterfalls, crashing down, leaving her empty and alone. Again.

She found a few more candles and lit them from the lantern's flame. Somehow, the added light brought a small comfort. The sun had set and the long night stretched out before her. Alone. She didn't realize until now how much Amari's presence made her feel protected. Walking outside the cottage door, she sat on the bench Amari had fashioned with a few fallen logs from the forest. She surprised herself when she chuckled at the memory of him working on it, trying to carve a bird into the back of the seat. "What is that?" she had asked Amari as he fussed something in Ewe tossing the carving knife to the ground.

"No make good!" Amari said.

She turned her head to one side and looked at it closely. "Is it a bird?"

He nodded in response and then shook his head. "No do good."

She offered to help, but Amari insisted he could do it, and did finish. The carving was primitive, but the reflection of Amari was definitely there.

The flutter of Scottie's white wings brought her back to the present that very moment as if to say, "Welcome back!" The bird landed on a nearby branch of an almond tree. "Awwk!" Scottie squawked. His white feathers shined in the moonlight.

Ronnie's heart lifted at the sight of him. "Well, hello there, my friend. My only friend. I'm so happy you waited for me!" Scottie clucked a greeting, happy she was back. "How is it a bird can bring me such comfort?" He squawked at her comment and she managed a grin. Somehow Scottie's being there gave her hope, making her feel safe, and at least a little more confident than five minutes before. Sitting down on the bench, she tossed him a few bites of the scone she pulled from the satchel.

Wondering how Amari was doing and praying his new community would accept him, she thought of Elijah. Sadness found overwhelmed her again as guilt and worry broke into her thoughts. *How will I live with myself knowing I gave away my friend's son? How can I ever forgive myself for taking part in such an evil act? The deed of giving away someone's child without their consent.* "How did I get caught up in such a web of deceit?" she said to the bird who gobbled up the last bit of the scone.

Is it because of my past? My life in Nassau? Is this my punishment?

Ronnie felt a soft touch on her shoulder and looked up to see Mum Lettie whose kind face and wise presence seemed to unleash even more of her emotions. The older woman sat down next to her, putting her arm over her shoulder. Ronnie collapsed into her arms. Mum Lettie stroked her head and whispered into her ear. "There, there, chile. I know your heart tis breaking. Let it out. Mum Lettie here." It occurred to the older woman she had said the same words to Adria time and again.

"I don't know how I can ever get past any of this," Ronnie cried. "To think I didn't even know Amari or Elijah just a short time ago. How can this hurt so much?"

Mum Lettie figured Elijah to be Adria's baby. "So, pickney now has name?"

"Yes." Ronnie took the kerchief Mum Lettie offered and wiped her tears and blew her nose. "It means 'God is near.'"

"Well, that good choice."

She took a deep breath. "Mum Lettie, I miss Amari terribly, but am grateful he has a chance for freedom. I just can't stop thinking about Elijah and Adria. How can we allow her to believe her son is dead? How do we permit her to leave and go to London when her son is crying for her up in the hills on this island? How do I go on hiding the truth?"

"Well, that many questions, my dear. Come wid me inside. Wi sort through dem." Ronnie stood and Mum Lettie put her arm around her waist as they walked into the cottage. Mum Lettie smoothed the younger woman's hair and Ronnie's crushed spirit soaked up her kindness.

"I carry you food. Figured you hungry." She pulled out an apple, started slicing it, and offered a piece to Ronnie. "First," Mum Lettie said, "God nuh let tings happen. Sumtimes wi mek decisions dat cause these tings happen. He der to pull us through it an' we learn much while we do it."

"But how can we just ignore what's happened? I'll never forget the past few days. Adria should know the truth."

"You never forget, but dat not decision for you or Mum Lettie to do. We mus' allow Miss Adria's parents to know what best for der daughter and 'ave faith dat God protect Elijah. His new name will make sure dat happen."

Ronnie began to eat the apple and biscuit Mum Lettie sat before her, her appetite showing up unannounced.

"Sometimes we have to let God sort out de mess made by odda people's choices." Mum Lettie poured tea into a cup from the jar she had brought down from the great house and pushed it toward Ronnie.

Feeling the need to share some of her past with Ronnie, Mum Lettie said, "I come here when I was young girl, maybe six-year-old. First time I sold to a cruel man and stay there till I grown. He beat us for no reason." She looked off as if seeing right back into those days. Her eyes widened and she looked at Ronnie. "Den his wife die and he too sad to grow cane, so I get sold to Mr. John and tings get much betta. I been on dis island close to thirty year now."

Ronnie took a deep breath, "I can't imagine what it was like to be ripped away from your home and then forced to be a slave." She shook her head. "How did you live through that?" She spoke softly as she knew it was taboo to discuss a slave's unfortunate circumstance, but her defenses were down and her vulnerability high.

"Well, I was sad and upset as you is. But what da Bible say tis true, 'joy come in de morning.'" Mum Lettie looked up from peeling another apple. "But it take many mornings." She would always be grateful to Sarah for sharing her faith with her and teaching her to read by using the Bible. "My heart, it always long to be home." She cut the apple core away. "But me like dis apple, I whole and den the white folk, dey cut me up to little pieces. But de core still der." Mum Lettie held up what was left of the apple. "Nobody tink dey want it, and me glad of dat." Putting down the apple, she took Ronnie's face into her hands and stared into her eyes. "Da core be me soul dat no white or black man can touch."

"I feel as if my core has been torn to shreds," Ronnie said.

"Yes, me know, but dis I know too. Da seeds in your core remain and will grow." Mum Lettie shook her finger, not at Ronnie, but at life's injustices. "God will turn this horrible ting to a blessin'. Only He know how." She pulled out a biscuit sandwich from her apron pocket. "But first, you must eat to keep strong." Ronnie nodded and gratefully took another piece of the apple.

Mum Lettie squeezed Ronnie's thigh and said, "Let's git you down to see Miss Mavis 'morrow. She good friend and done tole me she help you."

"Thank you, Mum Lettie. I only hope I can carry your optimism with me."

"Hope is born in da heart, my dear." The older woman touched Ronnie's chest. "You find yours hiding beneath your ache."

Ronnie nodded and half-heartedly grinned. It wasn't much, but Mum Lettie felt a little better about the young woman's state of mind. They both sat and ate in silence until the food was gone.

"Well, wi get you to bed for good night's rest." She stood and pulled Ronnie up by her hand. The two women looked at each other. Mum Lettie pulled Ronnie into a hug. "Joy come in di mornin', my dear." The older woman patted the younger's back.

After she left, Ronnie laid on the cot and stared at the ceiling, one forearm laid on top her forehead. Hope was all Mum Lettie had to offer, and all Ronnie had to hold onto. She prayed it was enough.

Ronnie sat up, reached into her satchel, and pulled out her journal. Trying to smooth out the crinkled pages of the little book, she stared at the journal that held so many memories and secrets. She remembered when she got it for Christmas the year she turned eight. One lone present sat on the kitchen table. Her mother had wrapped the journal in a reused green ribbon. Ronnie was thrilled. She saved the ribbon and used it as a bookmark.

She recalled her mother's words: "Write down your thoughts, it helps when the days stretch too long and the nights stare you in the face." Ronnie had found her to be right. Once written down, her problems seemed to take on a better perspective. She hoped this was one of those times. Ronnie walked over to the table and sat down. Memories of the past few days swirled in her mind as she picked up a pen and dipped it in the jar of ink. As the words committed themselves to paper, she felt the tension ease. She had learned to keep the book with her always. Leaving her journal around for someone else to read could tempt fate in a dangerous way. Ronnie had found that out the hard way.

After waiting for the ink to dry, she closed her journal whose pages were almost used up and tucked it back in her pants pocket. Climbing into bed, she laid down and pulled the blanket up to her chin. The sound of crickets soothed her core. In the inky darkness, Ronnie sighed, rolled over onto her side, closed her eyes, and saw Amari holding Elijah. "Sweet dreams," she whispered and hoped that sometimes dreams really did come true.

—Chapter Eight—

"The way to see by faith is to shut the eye of reason." —Benjamin Franklin

Ocho Rios, Jamaica

H ere, take dis and no lose it," Mum Lettie said and threw Ronnie a small purple quilt. "I make it. If you have to get inside di chest to hide, Sam can cover it up. You keep it when you get der," she said. "Me gift to you." The chatter of the tree frogs helped to drown the sound of their whispers. Heavy clouds hid the moon, shrouding the landscape. Ronnie had gotten used to taking orders from Mum Lettie.

"I have learned enough not to argue with you, Mum Lettie. I'll treasure it always. I'm going to miss you!" Ronnie again felt she was walking away from the only people she trusted, Mum Lettie and Sam, but she reminded herself yet again that joy does come in the morning.

The older woman looked at Ronnie. "We meet again, my sweet." She sensed Ronnie's reticence. "I hear back from Miss Mavis." She patted the younger woman on the back as they walked toward the wagon. "She waitin' and take good care you."

The lights from the Ginger Star great house were dim. A lantern shone through the leaves of the palm tree that flowed in the breeze next to the kitchen window where the house slaves clanged pots and prepared for the morning meal. Ronnie could hear murmurs of conversation coming from behind the open window. The sound of soft footsteps grew closer. Mum Lettie looked over her shoulder and saw Sam walking toward them.

"Are you ready, Ms. Ronnie?" Sam whispered as he glanced over Mum Lettie's shoulder to get a look at her. Sam had received specific instructions from John via Mum Lettie to keep Ronnie's presence at Ginger Star under cover.

"Sure am, Sam." He motioned for her to follow, and she did. Chance was tethered to a wagon and tucked back behind the low-hanging branches of a banyan tree. Taking his hand, she pulled up her skirt to climb onto the wagon. Handing him the satchel that carried what few belongings she could call hers, and a second sack including the extra set of clothes Marshall had given her, she checked her pocket to ensure her journal was safely tucked away. The horse chuffed in anticipation.

"You know what do, right?" Mum Lettie asked Sam.

"Yes'm. We head straight to Ochi to see Miss Mavis," he climbed onto the front of the wagon next to Ronnie.

"Dat right, make sure you give her dis," she said, tucking an envelope into his large, calloused hand.

"Yes'm." Sam took the envelope, nodded, and grabbed the reigns with his other hand.

"I head inside and tell dem you have to go git some nuts and screws 'fore Massa John come down to start work," Mum Lettie looked at Ronnie and reached up to pat her hand. "You trust Miss Mavis, chile. I see you soon." Sensing Ronnie's reluctance, she added, "Me promise."

"Alright." Ronnie leaned over the side of the wagon and hugged the old woman she had grown to care for so much in such a short time. Ronnie waved to her as Sam got the wagon on its way. She looked around for Scottie but didn't see him.

She had reminded him when she first got out of bed that they would be going soon. Her heart sank at the thought of leaving him behind. The wheels creaked enough to make her wish they wouldn't. Looking back at Ginger Star, Ronnie noticed the carriage was pulled up to the front steps of the great house. She could only assume it was waiting for Adria and Sarah to head to the dock to board their ship. Her heart ached as she realized she would never see Adria again.

The clip-clop of Chance and Brownie's hooves soothed her. Part of her feared this next step in her journey, but another part was relieved to leave Ginger Star behind. At least she had put some space between her and the secrets of the past few days. Secrets that threatened to swallow her peace of mind and sink her back into her past. Ronnie turned to look back at Ginger Star and saw Mum Lettie walk back inside the kitchen. The whirring sound of wings came closer, and she could see Scottie's white glow in the dark. The bird landed in the back of the wagon, dancing around trying to get his footing, but slipped in spite of himself.

"You made it!" Ronnie said to her sidekick. Her heart smiled, if only for a second. Scottie was all she had left. His presence gave her just enough familiarity to offer her a little comfort. Ronnie had bared her soul to the bird. He was the only living soul that really knew her.

"Dat your bird?" Sam looked back over his shoulder. His surprise was highlighted by the whites of his eyes shining in the early morning darkness.

"Yes, Sam. This is my close friend, Scottie." Ronnie held her arm out back toward Scottie who was perched on Sam's wagon, trying hard to hang on. "He's been with me since I boarded the ship."

Sam shook his head, "I suppose him can come, but not sure how Miss Mavis and her cat, Shadow, gonna take to him." Scottie gave up trying to hold on and instead followed them flying from tree to tree as they traveled down the bumpy road. The wagon groaned with every rut it encountered.

"I think he's learned to keep at a distance of late," Ronnie answered. "So, have you lived in Jamaica all your life, Sam?" She purposely tried to shift the focus away from her.

"No, I come to Ginger Star same time as Mum Lettie. Long time ago from across the sea."

"I know about your brother, Danquah, but do you have other brothers and sisters?" Ronnie was relieved that Sam seemed willing to talk.

"Sure do. Tree sistas and tree bruddas." He slapped the reigns on the back of the horses and brought their walk to a trot now that the road was smoother. The sun started to peek out from behind the huge clouds that hugged the eastern end of the island making it easier to see the road. For that, Ronnie was grateful.

"Do they all live on Ginger Star too?"

"Oh, no," Sam took both reigns in one hand and leaned back a little. "Only me still at Ginga Star." He pulled the horses to the right and slowed down to avoid a ditch that the recent flash floods from the mountains had created the week before.

"Few of us sold off and da rest done run off to da mountains." Sam picked up speed when the road flattened out. Ronnie could see the Caribbean in the early morning dawn as the road hugged the coastline.

"In the mountains? Where in the mountains, Sam?"

"You sure is curious, ma'am." Sam looked at Ronnie. "If'n you don't mind me sayin' so." He looked away, afraid he had said too much.

"No, not at all, Sam. And please try not to call me 'ma'am'. Makes me feel like an old dowager!" Ronnie said and Sam grinned. "So where in the mountains did they go? Far away?"

"Pretty far. They run off and joined wid da Maroons."

"Is that how the connection was made for Elijah and Amari? Through you?"

"Yes, my brudda, Danquah, help us."

"Why did your brothers run off, Sam?"

"Some folks just don't wanna be owned by nobody. They hung up on bein' they own massa."

"I know what you mean," Ronnie agreed staring off at the coastline. "But sometimes, that too can get you in trouble." She tried not to think of her life back in Nassau.

"Shhh!" Sam put his finger to his lips and looked ahead, slowing Chance and Brownie down to a walk.

What sounded like a horse coming in their direction had drawn his attention. Ronnie looked at Sam and he nodded his head toward the back of the wagon. Ronnie hiked up her skirt, jumped in the back of the wagon, and climbed inside the wooden chest. Sam reached back, lowered the lid and latch, and threw Mum Lettie's purple quilt over the top while he kept his eyes on the road. Scottie seemed to sense the need to keep his distance, landing in a nearby tree as if standing guard.

The horse slowed to a trot as the rider drew near to them. "Mornin' Massa Fergusson," Sam said tipping his hat as he pulled the wagon to a stop. As he did, the right front wagon wheel dipped down into a rut, leaning the wagon sideways. The chest slid with a thump as it hit the sideboard of the wagon.

"Morning, Sam. It's good to see you again so soon!" The young Marshall Fergusson tipped his hat in response. "What's John got you out so early for today?"

"Just going to Ochi to fetch screws for the new conservatory the missus will use to grow her orchids." Sam wondered what Marshall would be doing heading from Ochi so early in the morning.

"You don't say?" Marshall glanced at the chest covered in Mum Lettie's purple quilt. "So, Miss Sarah is to become a nursery entrepreneur?"

"It appear so, sir," Sam shifted his weight in the seat. He hoped when he pulled up out of the rut, the wheel would stay on, and the chest remain closed.

"Are you going to be able to pull up out of there?" Marshall cocked his head and looked at the wagon leaning in the ditch. His horse snorted and stomped as if eager to get back on the road.

"Yes, I tink so, Sir," Sam glanced at the chest that was now hugging the side of the wagon.

"Well, you go first as I won't leave until I know you're on your way." Marshall moved his horse over for Sam to pull the wagon to the center of the road.

"Yessir," Sam nodded and picked up the reigns. The horses instinctively knew their role and moved slowly to the left. The wagon creaked and moaned.

Marshall leaned on his saddle pummel and said, "I had to come to town unexpectedly and left before dawn. Turns out we don't have enough supplies to finish the roof on the new quarters. I need to be sure to be here when the next shipment arrives." He looked at Chance and Brownie.

"Silver back at Ginga Star resting in stable," Sam said before Marshall could ask, hoping he didn't mention Ronnie. "Solomon take good care of him."

"Well, I had best get a move on. Take care, Sam, and be sure to tell Miss Ronnie I said hello," Marshall tipped his hat. Truth was, he was hoping to run into Ronnie at Ginger Star when he retrieved Silver. Sam nodded and slapped the reins to get the horses moving again as fast as he could.

Ronnie stared at mostly blackness from inside the chest. Just what you need is for Marshall to find you hiding in a trunk.

She could see the faint light of dawn through the keyhole, but nothing else. She braced herself inside the wooden box so as not to roll back and forth. She unconsciously bit her lip to keep from groaning as the wagon tipped back and forth until the horses landed the wagon on solid ground once again.

Listening intently, she heard Sam and Marshall exchange goodbyes and it was only a few minutes before all she could hear was the wagon and horses pulling her to her destination, wherever that was. All she knew was that Mavis owned a mercantile in the middle of Ocho Rios.

Once they were back on the road again, Sam leaned back toward the rear of the wagon. "You good, Miss Ronnie?"

"Yes, I think so." She continued to keep her arms and feet braced. "Was that Marshall you ran into?"

"Yes'm it was. I fear you'd best stay der in di chest till we gets to Ochi, 'less someone else come."

"Yes indeed!" She hoped it wouldn't take much longer though. It was getting warm inside the trunk.

She'd been alone before, but never this far away from everyone she knew. Growing up as she did, sometimes she found that being alone was often preferable to being with someone she didn't trust. And finding others to trust, well, it didn't turn out to be as easy as she had once believed. As the wagon tossed her back and forth on the bumpy road to Ochi, she realized that she had once again put her life in the hands of strangers. At that moment, she did something she found herself doing a lot lately, she prayed. Closing her eyes despite the darkness the box provided, she prayed that this time, her life would be different. Where was the "joy" Mum Lettie had talked about last night? Ronnie hoped to find it with Mavis, yet another stranger.

The wagon made a few turns, but Ronnie had figured out how to lock her feet up against the wall of the chest to keep from rolling around quite so much. They slowed to a stop and she felt the wagon lift, just a bit, when Sam jumped off the wagon.

Sam leaned close to the wooden chest and whispered, "Stay put, Miss Ronnie." He looked back over his shoulder. "I gonna check for Miss Mavis and will come back to get ya."

Sam stepped up onto the wooden sidewalk. A few lights glowed from windows up the street, but for the most part, it appeared that the residents of Ocho Rios were still fast asleep. The street was empty with the exception of a stray chicken and a cat that darted between the buildings. The sign hanging over Mavis's mercantile swung in the Caribbean breeze, creaking as it swayed. He didn't see any lamps lit in the storefront, so he walked around to the back of the building. A brown dog woke, looked up, and put his head back down, not interested in protecting anyone.

Sam noticed the soft glow of a lamp inside the window and knocked softly on the door. After a few seconds, the door slowly opened and Mavis stood there with her head cocked to one side. Her dark hair was tied back into a long braid, and she was dressed in a green dress that matched the color of her eyes. "Morning, Sam." Mavis stood on her toes trying to see over his shoulder. "Where is our stowaway?"

"Miss Ronnie is hiding in the chest in the back of the wagon," Sam nodded his head in the direction of the street. He handed her the envelope that Mum Lettie had sent.

"What's this?" Mavis looked down at the envelope.

"Not sure, Ma'am. Mum Lettie ask dat I give to you." Sam looked toward the street.

"Well, stay here and I'll go fetch my new friend." Mavis put the envelope on the kitchen table, grabbed a white shawl, and wrapped it around her shoulders. "Help yourself to a biscuit, Sam," she said and pointed to a tray on the kitchen counter.

Mavis left the door open and headed around the building. Chance chuffed and pawed the ground as Mavis walked closer. She patted him on his back as she walked by. Reaching over the side of the wagon, she lifted the purple quilt, unlatched and lifted the lid.

Ronnie's head turned up to look at Mavis, but her hair fell over her face. Pushing it away from her eyes, she sat up stiffly and wiggled her neck.

"Well, good morning, my dear," Mavis said. Her British accent had a French lilt to it as she extended her hand. Ronnie crouched and then stood up. She pulled up her skirt, grabbed the side of the wagon, and jumped down to the ground. In a sweeping motion, she brushed the hair from her face again and extended her hand to Mavis, shivering in the morning breeze. Mavis grabbed the quilt from the wagon and placed it over Ronnie's shoulders.

"Thank you," Ronnie said and pulled the purple quilt tightly around her shivering form. "How do you do, ma'am?" Ronnie shook her hand and looked into her blue eyes.

"Ma'am was my momma. Call me Mavis." She put her hand on Ronnie's arm. "Come on, now. Let's get you inside and figure out what needs to get done." Mavis put her arm around Ronnie's shoulder and led her to the rear of the mercantile.

Ronnie glanced sideways at the older woman whose dark hair had wisps of gray betraying her age, giving her a mature look that framed her beauty. Ronnie wondered if this woman was the answer to the prayers she'd whispered not that long ago. Perhaps this was part of the answered prayer Mum Lettie spoke of.

When they walked into the kitchen, Sam was sitting by the fireplace wiping the biscuit crumbs from his face. He stood up and extinguished the lantern as the morning sun peeked through the windows.

"Have a seat near the stove and we'll throw on some more wood to heat water for a bath," Mavis said pointing to the white wicker chair. Ronnie sat down. Sam handed her a biscuit and proceeded to pump water into two large kettles for the stove. She looked at the back room of the mercantile. While it was small, it was cozy and welcoming with a wooden table with chairs colorfully painted that helped to brighten the otherwise drab room. The cool morning breeze lifted the lacy curtains.

As Sam stoked the stove, Mavis took off her shawl and sat down in the rocker across from Ronnie and began to quietly rock.

"So, Mum Lettie tells me that you were a stowaway on a ship and landed on the beach at Ginger Star."

"Well, kind of," Ronnie stuttered and added, "yes, ma'am." Mavis raised her eyebrows. Ronnie grinned at her mistake. "I mean, Mavis."

"Well, I suppose the obvious question is why would you hide on a ship?" Mavis asked.

Ronnie bit her lip, not sure how much to say. She wanted to be honest, but. She took a deep breath.

"I found myself in Nassau on the island of New Providence." Ronnie decided too many details would raise her eyebrows, so she kept things in generalities, for now. "When they named Woodes Rogers as the new governor, and Hornigold linked arms with the Royal Navy to pull in his former pirate buddies, I knew things would soon get out of hand." Hornigold had always refused to raid British ships, remaining loyal to the Royal Navy. He became a privateer and hunted pirate ships that refused the pardon. Britain was serious about going to war with the pirates to gain control of the island. Ronnie had seen firsthand how ruthless they could be.

"When I watched men in the pirate community unite with one another for a common purpose as opposed to fighting against each other, I realized an all-out war was more of a reality than a possibility. I knew I had to get off the island before the fighting broke out."

Sam handed Ronnie and Mavis each a cup of tea. Ronnie took a sip and held the cup to keep her hands from shaking, but not before Mavis noticed. Just talking about Nassau, her former home, made her shake with a familiar fear.

"Well, we can talk more about that later." She could see she was upsetting Ronnie and decided to keep her inquisition short, for now. "Right now, we need to figure out a way to introduce you to the community without raising a lot of curiosity. Let me take care of that." She reached over and covered Ronnie's shaking hand with hers. "How would you like to be my niece?" The women smiled at each other.

"I would like nothing better," Ronnie said, feeling better already. *Maybe joy really does come in the morning.*

The sun peeked through the side window of the store front. A black cat with a white chest and nose rubbed up against Ronnie's leg and she reached down to rub its back. The sound of rustling wings caught the cat's attention. Jumping up onto the table and then to Mavis' lap, the cat's ears pointed backwards. Shadow meowed her concern.

"I tink Scottie done caught up wid us," Sam said as he walked to the window and parted the curtains. The parrot bobbed his head in acknowledgement and walked back and forth on the window sill. His feathers shone brightly in the morning sunshine that had peeked through a heavy cluster of clouds.

Ronnie saw the surprise in Mavis' eyes. "This is Scottie, my fellow stowaway and closest confidant." She stood and walked over to the window, reached out and stroked his back. Scottie responded with a soft caw. "I hope it is alright that he followed me here." Ronnie cupped her hand under the parrot's neck. He'd become much easier for her to pet since they had arrived on the island. "I didn't think of it before, but I suppose we are very much a package deal."

"I suppose you'd best ask Shadow's opinion." Mavis laughed. "Looks like she's not too sure, but I must say, I've never met a friendlier parrot."

"Awwk!" Scottie agreed. Mavis and Sam jumped at the sound and Ronnie giggled.

"He doesn't think of himself as a parrot, really. Once he gets comfortable, he'll reveal his conversational abilities. He's really quite a chatty fellow." Ronnie walked back to her chair.

Mavis watched Ronnie as she moved about the small kitchen. There was something wounded about her spirit. Horses' hooves and voices rolled down the street in front of the store. Ocho Rios was waking. "Well, I had best get the shop opened for the day. Sam, would you mind adding the hot water kettles to the bath for Ronnie? I am sure she would like to freshen up."

"Yes'm." Sam rose and nodded.

"Pardon me, Mavis, but perhaps Sam should head back to Ginger Star. I can certainly draw my own bath. Thanks just the same, Sam." Ronnie said.

"Yes, I suppose you're right, my dear." Mavis stood and Shadow jumped to the floor, keeping an eye on Scottie.

"Sam, thank you for the safe transfer. I will always be in debt to you," Ronnie said as she shook Sam's hand and pulled close for a hug. They both knew they shared a bond that would always be there.

"Thank you, Miss Ronnie." He leaned back and looked at her. "I take my leave now and go get those nuts and bolts for Mister John." Sam nodded at Mavis and headed toward the back door. Turning, he looked at the two women and said, "You take care of each other now," and closed the door behind him.

"Awwk! Take care!" Scottie chimed in. Mavis and Ronnie looked at one another and laughed.

"Well, go ahead and make yourself at home. I'll go out front and open the store."

Ronnie poured both kettles carefully into the tub. She heard the wheels of Sam's wagon creak as he pulled away and turned toward the sound. While she was grateful to be here with Mavis, it occurred to her that the one person who made her feel safe was headed in the opposite direction. Yet again.

—Chapter Nine—

"Tis easy to see, hard to foresee." —Benjamin Franklin

Ocho Rios, Jamaica

Once the water was warm enough, Ronnie undressed and stepped into the tub. She leaned back and relaxed in the water, closing her eyes. Mavis seemed nice enough, but Ronnie wondered what would happen next. She clung to Mum Lettie's promise of hope.

Ronnie pushed back the memories of Nassau and vowed to not live in the past any longer. Her new-found life in Jamaica held promise just with its beauty alone. She made a conscious decision to settle here, but the memories of Amari and Elijah held on tight haunting her thoughts.

"Here are some clothes that I thought might fit you," Mavis whispered from behind the curtain that acted as a privacy screen. She tossed a sack onto the floor. Ronnie, startled back to consciousness, and realized she had succumbed to her body's need for rest.

"Thank you so much!" Splashing a little in the tub as she sat upright, she reached for the towel on the chair. Ronnie stood up to cover herself and then realized there was no need, she could see Mavis' feet under the curtain turn and walk away. She dried off and stepped out of the tub, taking care not to get the floor too wet. When Ronnie opened the sack, she found a yellow cotton dress, perfect for the Jamaican humidity. She also discovered clean undergarments and was surprised at the good fit. *I'm acquiring a nice wardrobe thanks to the generosity of strangers.*

Ronnie turned to look at the clouded mirror above the wash basin. Her hand reached up, touched her wet blonde hair, pulling it up and tied it just above her neck. It was still shorter than she liked but had started to grow out from the cropping she'd given her hair right before she boarded the Neptune. A few strands strayed down the side and she tucked them behind her ears. The neckline of the dress reached up to the middle of her throat and gave her a soft look that reminded her of her life before Nassau in South Carolina. She still wasn't used to looking in a mirror to see a woman looking back. The woman she once was. Shaking off the thought, Ronnie turned, and walked out into the kitchen.

Shadow jumped down from a chair and Scottie cawed in approval. "My, you do clean up nicely!" Mavis said as she walked out to the kitchen from the store.

"Thank you so much for the clothes, Mavis. Everything fits perfectly. It feels wonderful to finally be cleaned up properly."

"I'm so happy to hear that. I suppose we should decide how to introduce you to the community, so we don't have to answer a lot of questions. Come, let's go out front and we can talk as I open up." Ronnie dutifully followed her into the store. Mavis walked back behind the counter. Sacks of salt, flour, and sugar lay in barrels on the floor. The shelves were full of staples to supply just about any need a household might have.

Mavis sat down on a stool behind the cash box as she pulled out a sack to fill it with needed change for the day. Mavis pushed a stool toward Ronnie who immediately sat down next to her.

Sorting the coins into the slots in the drawer, Mavis asked, "So, do you want to use your given name . . . or would that be an issue?"

Ronnie thought for a second, "My name does not pose a problem. No one cares where I am," she said and settled down on the stool. *Most people in Nassau only knew my first name anyway.*

"Well then. If you would like, you can work here at the store. That will certainly help you meet the local folk as most of them need something on my shelves at one time or another."

The bell hanging on the storefront door tinkled as it opened. A tall dark-haired man walked in and looked from Ronnie to Mavis and back to Ronnie.

"So, we meet again so soon!" Marshall said to Ronnie.

"Uh, yes, so we have, Marshall. Good to see you as well." Her eyes locked with his. That familiar feeling of interest came back to her as her mind swirled. How would she explain all this to Mavis?

"I thought I might run into you at Ginger Star. Do you work here?" Marshall asked. He looked over to Mavis who stepped up.

"Yes, Ronnie is my niece and employee. She also lives here with me."

"Well, you should have mentioned you were related to Mavis!" He smiled at Ronnie and wondered again why she had neglected to tell him. "This is welcome news. I stop here a good bit when in town, so we should cross paths often."

He took off his hat as he nodded at Ronnie. His black hair set off the blue of his eyes. The wooden floor creaked under the scuffing of his boots.

"Well, Marshall, it's good to see you," Mavis rose and walked to the counter. "What brings you here today?"

"I had hoped to find some jerky and hard tack this morning. I'm heading back to Claremont after the next ship arrives. I'm not sure that I'll make it all the way back to Ramble House, so I need to have it handy," he grinned at Mavis. "I have several stops to make in the fields to check on things."

"I'm sorry, but I still have to stop and think when folks call it Claremont," Mavis said looking at Ronnie to explain. "It was called Finger Post for years. Ramble was the first great house in that area and then the Claremont House was built. That's when the name of the town changed." She looked back at Marshall. "And you are in luck, my dear." Mavis turned and reaching up on the shelf, grabbed a large glass jar. "I just finished a new batch of both yesterday." She sat the jars on the counter. Mavis pulled out a piece of cheesecloth and laid it next to the jar. "Just get what you want and I'll weigh it when you're done."

Marshall walked toward the counter and looked at Ronnie. "I believe I just might take all you have. It could be a long few days getting back." His blue eyes settled on Ronnie. It had been a long time since she'd felt a man look at her in that way. She could feel her cheeks blush. He couldn't help but notice how the hair she'd pulled back struggled to get free, one strand at a time. Wishing he had another orchid for her hair, he turned and began to make his selection. "I don't know if you're aware, Miss Shepherd, but Mavis makes the best jerky on the island."

"Here, try some for yourself," Mavis said as she reached in and handed Ronnie a piece.

Ronnie examined the brown leathery piece of beef and looked at Mavis with her eyebrows raised. Marshall chuckled. "Quite a strange name, I must say," Ronnie said.

Pulling a tin down from the shelf, Mavis replied, "Well, it was called 'ch'arki' by the Indians, but the name has evolved to 'jerky' over the years."

"Just bite off a piece and give it a chew." Marshall demonstrated and Ronnie followed suit.

"Hmm, it's sweet and spicy," Ronnie said, delighted with the taste of the otherwise not so appetizing looking snack.

Marshall filled up the cheesecloth bag with the contents of the jar. "Do you have any hard tack left?" he asked.

Mavis opened the tin she still held to reveal the biscuit-like hard tack crackers and filled up a small paper bag. "Is that all you need, Marshall?" she asked.

"I think that will take care of me for this trip, much obliged and sorry to deplete your stock." He followed Mavis to the register. Mavis showed Ronnie how to weigh the jerky on the scales with the different bars to counter balance the purchase. Once the jerky was weighed, Mavis handed Ronnie the cheesecloth sack, and showed her how to calculate the cost.

Marshall reached in the bag and pulled out another piece of jerky. "I saw Sam from Ginger Star earlier this morning," Marshall said. "He said he was headed to town to get supplies for John's conservatory. It will be interesting to see how that plan goes."

The two women looked at each other. Ronnie's heart seemed to skip a beat, but Mavis responded in short order, "That's one-fifty," Mavis said as Ronnie handed over the hard tack. "Yes, I saw him. He stopped in to drop off a message from Mum Lettie." She hoped her answer would quell any question in the event Marshall had seen Sam's wagon at the mercantile. Her answer seemed to satisfy him.

"Just add that amount to my account, if that's alright, and we will settle up when I get back in town next week." Mavis nodded and pulled out her ledger to make note of his purchase, showing Ronnie where to log the purchase. She slid the ledger across the counter toward Marshall. He leaned on the counter, took the pen Mavis handed to him, and signed the page. "Thank you, Mavis." Heading for the door, he turned and looked at Ronnie. "Welcome to Ocho Rios, Miss Shepherd." He tipped his hat in her direction. Ronnie looked up and smiled as he walked out the door.

"What do you suppose Marshall will do in Claremont?" Ronnie asked and then added, "Not that it is any of my concern really."

"It's no secret," Mavis smiled. "He has tea and sugarcane growing up in the mountains. He'll spend time checking on its progress." Sitting back down on her stool, Mavis asked, "So, how is it you know Marshall already?"

Ronnie took a deep breath and shook her head, not knowing what to say. The last thing she wanted to do was lie to her new ally. She bit her lip for a second.

Mavis could sense Ronnie's hesitation to share more. "Before you answer that question, I should tell you that I know about Amari. The note Sam delivered was from John, the owner of Ginger Star. He explained about Amari and the need to unite him with the Maroon tribe."

Ronnie tried to process the information. *So, John had mentioned Amari and not Elijah. Makes sense.* "Yes, Sam and I took him to meet the Maroons. We stopped at Ramble House for the night on the way back. That's where I met Marshall." Her entire being sighed with relief as there was no need to lie.

"Well, it's obvious you made quite an impression on him."

"I must say, the impression was mutual."

Mavis smiled, "I could see that as well."

AS THE WEEKS passed, Ronnie grew to like Mavis more and more. They spent time working in the store together during the day and walked on the shore in the evenings. Their long talks revealed more about their lives as the days went by. Ronnie came very close to confiding her past in Nassau, but so far had only given sparse details.

On their way back from their walk, they sat on the low-lying branch of an almond tree near the water. "When my Jared died two years ago," Mavis said as she looked out at the sea and sighed, "I was stunned and horribly alone. We were never able to have children. All we had was each other. I was inconsolable and useless for the better part of a year." Her shoulders slumped in an unusual sign of resignation. "Everyone seemed convinced I was a strong woman and would be fine. While that was true, I found an emptiness I never knew was there." Ronnie reached her arm around Mavis' shoulders and pulled her close. Mavis gratefully laid her head on Ronnie's shoulder. "I must say, having you with me has been such a comfort. The evenings don't hold the dreaded loneliness as much as before."

They had shared laughs and tears over Mavis' tales of her life with her husband. Jared was quite the jokester. "I love hearing the stories of you and Jared. I wish I'd known him, but your stories make me feel as if I did."

After attending the Methodist church one Sunday, they visited Jared's grave in the small cemetery to the side. Mavis laid a bouquet of lilies at the bottom of his headstone. "These were his favorite because of their fragrance," Mavis said, taking a sniff. "Although I doubt he can smell them now!"

"You never know. From what you've told me about him, just about anything is possible!" Ronnie slipped her arm around Mavis' shoulders and they both chuckled as they walked away.

AFTER REPLENISHING THE dry goods on the shelf of the mercantile, Ronnie climbed down off the ladder. Wiping the sweat from her brow, she picked up the woven fan Adria had given her and waved it back and forth to cool herself off. "I hope the ship shows up soon. We're almost out of so many things," Ronnie said to Mavis.

"True enough, Looks like the afternoon heat has taken its toll on you." The mercantile had enjoyed a constant flow of customers that day. Mavis reached over and brushed Ronnie's hair out of her eyes. "Take a break and go down to the sea for a bit. I'll keep watch over the store."

"Only if you allow me to return the favor for you when you need a break." Mavis agreed and guided her to the door.

"Go and enjoy yourself." Ronnie walked out the door, turned, and waved back to her friend, realizing what a good feeling it was to have someone on this island who cared about her.

Ronnie nodded in greeting to several of the residents as she walked down the dirt road to the sea. She knew most of Mavis' neighbors. Strings of fish hung from the rafters of the fish market and Lucky, the tabby cat who lived there, lazed in the afternoon sunshine. Lucky raised his head when he heard Scottie's squawk but lazily decided against a chase today. Normally, Scottie and Lucky would taunt one another when Ronnie visited with Belinda and Arnold, the owners of the fish market. Belinda had laughed when Ronnie asked why she named her cat Lucky.

"He lives in a fish market. For a cat, how 'lucky' can one get?" Belinda's brown eyes twinkled as she teased Ronnie.

Today, Belinda and Arnold were busy bartering with a local fisherman over the cost of his catch. Hands flew in all directions and their voices carried as they chided the fisherman for the price he was asking. She chuckled and shook her head as she could not understand what they were saying in Patois, but the tone and animation told her all she needed to know. She waved and kept walking toward the beach. Scottie followed her and flew from tree to tree until they reached the shoreline.

The late afternoon sun began to duck behind the mountains of Ocho Rios. The shadows stayed behind to cool the air. Ronnie glanced over to see a flock of white egrets flying back up the mountainside to roost for the night. She never tired of the sight. Each time she imagined the same egrets chose to roost close to Amari and Elijah. The thought brought her comfort.

Several months had passed since she landed on Jamaica and some days she couldn't will herself to stop thinking about Elijah. This was one of those days. Sometimes she would daydream about his first step or word and wonder what he now looked like. She had to constantly remind herself he was in God's hands, not hers. *All I can do is pray.* She sighed. *Why does so much of my life fit into that category?*

However, it was thoughts of Adria that troubled her the most. Ronnie wondered if Adria still cried every day and if her sadness would ever abate. She'd also come to the realization Adria would never forgive her for what she'd done. But, then again, how could she when she didn't even know of her crime?

She approached her same almond tree branch and sat down to stare at the sea. It had been six months since Ronnie had landed in Jamaica, but it seemed like just weeks before. "So, Scottie, what do you think of our new home?" She looked over at the fluffy white bird. He was gaining weight since they arrived and looked much healthier than on the ship. "I think I'm going to stay here. It's starting to feel like home to me." Scottie clucked as if in agreement and shook his tail feathers.

Sometimes she worried about her ability to talk with a bird but had decided he was too much of a comfort to be concerned about it. While she'd made many acquaintances in Ochi since working at the mercantile, other than Mum Lettie and Mavis, she didn't know any of them all that well. Besides her journal, Scottie was still her closest confidant. She pulled her book, pen, and covered inkwell, out of her pocket. Carefully she opened the inkwell and gently placed it on the sand. Her thoughts flowed on the paper. Before she realized it, darkness had fallen. Sighing, she closed the book, put the lid back on the inkwell, and shoved all back into her pocket. Ronnie stood, brushing herself off, and headed back to the mercantile.

When Ronnie opened the door of the store, she noticed that Mavis had lit candles, in anticipation of her return. Scottie scooted through the door in front of her. Shadow jumped from the floor to the counter, let out an irritated meow, turned, and sat looking down at the bird.

Scottie piped up, "Gotta stay here!" Scottie walked back and forth on the wooden floor betraying Ronnie's confidence. "Going to stay."

"What did you say?" Mavis put her hands on her hips as she looked at Scottie.

"My, I know now that I can't say a word in front of that bird!" Ronnie looked at Mavis and then back to Scottie. "But he's right, Jamaica is definitely our home now." Ronnie reached over and scratched Shadow under the neck. "Thanks to you, Sam, and Mum Lettie." Shadow jumped up onto her lap. "And Shadow, of course!"

THE FRONT DOORBELL jingled as the door opened. Ronnie and Mavis looked up. A short, light-skinned, black woman walked in. In her hand she carried a cane, sliding it back and forth in front of her on the floor. Wearing dark wire-rimmed glasses, her hair was tucked under a turban giving her a regal air. It was obvious to Ronnie that she knew her way around this room.

"Queenie! How are you, my dear?" Mavis asked as she strode toward the woman. Queenie turned in Mavis' direction.

"I am grateful for yet another day on our beautiful island." Queenie smiled and faced Mavis. "How are you, my friend?"

Mavis smiled and reached out to pull Queenie in for a hug. "I am wonderful, my dear."

"And I as well." Queenie's head turned in Ronnie's direction. "Who may I have the pleasure of meeting today?" Mavis was familiar with Queenie's ability to see beyond her sightless eyes, but Ronnie was taken aback.

Mavis looked at Ronnie and nodded. "Queenie, this is Ronnie Shepherd, my niece, roommate, and coworker."

Ronnie walked over to Queenie. Uncertain, she looked at Mavis and tentatively offered the blind woman her hand. Queenie reached out and took Ronnie's hand in both of hers. "Your niece? Well, tis always my pleasure to meet a new friend." Her hands felt Ronnie's palms. "But your hands feel like you've been doing a man's work. Why is your name Ronnie when you are a woman?"

Ronnie and Mavis looked at each other and then Ronnie realized it was her name that was confusing. "Why yes, that's true, Miss Queenie. My given name is Veronica, but Ronnie has always been my everyday name."

"Well, I certainly understand that. I'm not really a queen, you know!" They all laughed.

"That depends on who one would ask, Queenie,".

"Quite true, Mavis. Let your perception be my reality!" The women laughed.

"Well, Queenie, what brings you here so early in the morning?" Mavis said as she walked over to the woman and put her arm across her shoulder. The brown of her skin was complimented by the yellow turban-like kerchief that held Queenie's hair. Mavis looked into Queenie's sightless eyes. "The sun is barely up."

Queenie grinned. "Well, you know my bones can tell when bad weather is coming. It woke me up long before the rooster crow this morning. 'Tis my responsibility to promulgate the warning to everyone."

"I was hoping for the Eagle to arrive before now, but if there is a storm out there, that explains their delay." Mavis looked at Ronnie. They'd been wondering when the ship with her order would arrive. "They will certainly hang back or take another route to keep out of its way until it passes."

"No ships will come for some time. Of that I'm sure." She turned toward Ronnie. "Now, my dear, what brought you to Jamaica?"

Ronnie shifted to the other foot and looked at Mavis wondering what to say. "Well, I really just wanted a fresh start and I've never seen a more beautiful place than this island of yours." Ronnie instantly wanted to take her words back since Queenie had never seen Jamaica with her eyes. "Um, I'm sorry. I did not mean . . ."

"Not to worry, my dear. The beauty of this place only escapes those that fail to see it. Sight is not only through the eyes, but the spirit. Many with seeing eyes are often very much blind."

"I would imagine that is true," Ronnie said, feeling better at her acquittal.

"Queenie, is there anything I can get you from the shelves this morning?"

"No, Mavis. I can tell you don't have any jerky left." Queenie knew from the scents in the mercantile there was none of her favorite on the shelf.

"You are quite right. Marshall wiped me out this morning, but I will have some ready tomorrow. We're happy to drop it off to you then."

"Make sure you save plenty for yourselves given the storm that 'tis coming," Queenie turned toward Mavis. "I must be on my way. Have to share the forecast." Mavis stepped closer and wrapped her arms around Queenie, and hugged her tight. Queenie turned toward Ronnie who stepped up to shake her hand, but Queenie pushed Ronnie's hand aside. She stepped closer and pulled Ronnie in for a hug. Queenie said into her ear, "My dear, you are a kind soul, but I sense a desire not to draw close to people." Ronnie felt the woman's fingers hold tighter on her arms. "In order to heal, you must allow your heart to feel again."

Ronnie was stunned. She opened her mouth to respond but could come up with nothing. *How did this woman, who could not physically see, peer into my soul the way she did?*

Mavis came to her rescue. "You're correct, Queenie. Ronnie can be closed off, but she has been through so much of late."

Ronnie's heart pounded at hearing the truth voiced aloud. "You are most discerning, Queenie. I promise I'll take your words to heart."

"Permit your heart to soak in the love that seeks to abide in your life, my sweet." With that, Queenie turned, held onto her cane, and found her way out of the shop.

Ronnie stared after her for a few seconds and then looked at Mavis. Cocking her head, she asked, "What just happened?"

"You are the beneficiary of Queenie's keen senses." Mavis replied as she walked back behind the counter. "Many of us have been, from time to time. Wise folks take her counsel, fools discount her foresight. I would advise you to be one of the former."

"Where does Queenie live? Does she own Queenie's?" Queenie's was a hotel and restaurant of sorts, but more popular than that, it included a brothel.

"Yes," Mavis said. "She opened it many years ago. Queenie is the innkeeper and madam." Ronnie had seen the establishment many times during her walks up the shoreline. She'd noticed women dressed in provocative clothing with bright red lips coming and going. Once in a while, one of them named Joanie came to the mercantile and bought supplies for Queenie's restaurant.

Not only does she feel the weather coming, but without sight, manages to read my mind and feelings. Might be someone for me to avoid for a while.

—Chapter Ten—

"Work as if you were to live a hundred years..." —Benjamin Franklin

Ocho Rios, Jamaica

A strong breeze came through the windows and slammed the door shut with a loud bang. The blue curtains seemed to stand sideways from the constant wind. Mavis walked over and started throwing the shutters closed. Ronnie followed and closed up the windows in the back. Mavis looked at Ronnie and said, "I thought something was brewing even before Queenie came by but I didn't want to worry you. Something is definitely coming toward us off the coast," Mavis hollered over the sound of the wind, and pushed the door hard, throwing the latch.

Ronnie sighed and wished Mavis would not try to protect her so much, even though somehow it felt good. "What's it like during a hurricane, Mavis?" Ronnie had heard horror stories when she was on board the ship.

"Well, it can be pretty bad and if we have time, we should head up into the hills to weather the worst of it." Mavis didn't normally evacuate, but she could feel the intensity was different this time and wasn't sure she should subject Ronnie to the wrath of a possible hurricane quite so soon. She walked around and threw the bolts on the bottom of the shutters.

It was the first time Ronnie had seen her take that precaution although they had already had several stormy bouts of weather. Maybe Jamaica wasn't the idyllic place she thought it was.

"Where would we go?" Ronnie asked.

"Well, there's always Ginger Star."

"Ginger Star?" Ronnie was terrified at the thought. She knew the flood of memories the estate carried with it. Memories she fought every day with worry and imagination, wondering how Adria, Elijah, and Amari were.

"Your reluctance shows," Mavis said Ronnie hung her head in resignation. She already knew better than to argue with Mavis. The older woman grinned and said to the younger, "My dear, the best way to get beyond the past is to face it." Seeing the fear in Ronnie's eyes, Mavis took pity on her and decided to let her in on her real plan. "Or if it's really bad, we could head up to Ramble House."

"Mr. Fergusson's place?" She tried not to smile with anticipation.

"Yes, but either way, we still need to pay a quick visit to Ginger Star," Mavis said. Ronnie was disappointed they would have to visit Ginger Star but breathed a sigh of relief knowing they wouldn't stay there.

Mavis pounded the bolt closed on the window in the store and tested its resolve. "I saw Marshall in town yesterday and he extended the invitation to us." She cut her eyes over to Ronnie to check her reaction. It was as she thought it would be. Noticing the smile Ronnie was trying to hide, she said, "I take it that agrees with you." Ronnie had told her she met Marshall with Sam on their way back to Ochie.

Grinning, Ronnie asked, "It shows?"

"It is like looking through an open window with you, my dear." They both chuckled and prepared to leave.

Mavis picked up Shadow, tucking her inside the rear of the store and closed the door. She had fashioned a sandbox for the cat to use instead of allowing her to go outside as usual. Shadow protested. "Aww girl, you know you need to stay and look after things. Besides, you know you don't travel well." She reached over and stroked her feline friend. Shadow relented noisily. "All will be good, my love," said Mavis as the cat continued to bellow.

"It's fine, Shadow. Your mama just wants you to be safe." Ronnie called back over her shoulder in the cat's direction. She looked over at Scottie who sat on the rail of Stars' stall. The bird paced back and forth knowing he wasn't included in the trip. "Oh, my friend, I'll be back soon. I promise. You stay home this time and hold down the fort with Shadow." The bird squawked and Ronnie laughed. "I'm not sure if you're agreeing or arguing with me this time!"

"I'm thinking the latter," Mavis smiled. "He'll be fine. Scottie can fly to higher ground, if needed, and we already know he can find his way home."

Throwing the latch on the final shutter, Mavis said, "Bring a few days' clothing with you. You'll want something warm because of all the rain and wind that is sure to come."

After packing their saddlebags, Mavis mounted her horse, Moxie, a black and white stallion. Ronnie got up on, Jared's horse, Stars. "I want you to have Stars for your very own," Mavis said.

Ronnie looked over at her. "Mavis, I . . ." her voice trailed. "I can't accept such a lofty gift."

"You'd be doing her and me a favor as I can't ride her the way she wants to be ridden since I'm always riding Moxie. I know you'll set her free in the meadows." Ronnie smiled and did just that every time they hit an open space, racing Mavis and Moxie.

It had been a long time since she was able to recall the freedom and oneness of her and a horse. It was a feeling she welcomed each time it happened.

Ronnie loved the way Stars' light-tan coat with white speckles gave the illusion of white stars splashed on her side and forehead.

MAVIS AND RONNIE pulled Moxie and Stars to a stop in front of the steps of Ginger Star. Holding onto the door with both hands, fighting the wind, John came outside and pushed the door shut behind him. It was the first time Ronnie had seen him since she left Ginger Star several months before. She saw him stiffen when his eyes met hers. It was clear he was no happier to see her than she him.

"Morning, John," Mavis said as she jumped off of Moxie and walked up one step toward him. He walked down to meet her.

"Mavis," he said looking slightly toward Ronnie. "Miss Shepherd." He nodded in her direction.

"Good day, sir," Ronnie said.

He looked back at Mavis.

"I just wanted to drop off the hardware that Sam ordered last week. I thought you might need them given the storm that seems to be on its way," Mavis said as she reached inside her saddlebag and pulled out a small satchel.

"Why, Mavis, I certainly appreciate your concern and help!" He smiled at her.

"I'm happy to oblige. We've closed up the mercantile and will be on our way up to Ramble Estate in Claremont to ride out the storm later today. Is Ginger Star all battened down?"

"We're just about ready. You're most welcome to stay here if you like." He looked at Ronnie, knowing what her answer would be. "Both of you."

Ronnie held her breath hoping Mavis would turn him down. "Well, that's most generous of you, but Marshall's expecting us at Ramble House this evening. We'll be heading up the mountain straight away."

"My lord," Ronnie said as she reached into her pocket and pulled out an envelope. "I would like to thank you once again for helping me. Here is repayment of the loan you graciously extended to me when I first arrived."

John looked at the envelope in his hand, surprised to ever see this money again. Nodding his head, he looked at Ronnie and said, "Thank you, Miss Shepherd. Your assiduous repayment is unexpected and appreciated." He reached over and shook Ronnie's hand. She could see he was surprised. She so wanted to ask about Adria but resisted, knowing it wouldn't be a welcome question.

As if reading her thoughts, he added, "Adria and her mother are doing well back in London. I shall head home next month for a visit." John turned, reached up, and patted Mavis on the arm. "Well, Godspeed to you, my friend. Wishing you traveling mercies."

"Thank you so much, John. May God keep you safe as well. Please give our regards to Adria and Sarah when you see them," Mavis stated as she mounted Moxie. Ronnie breathed a sigh of relief as she and Stars followed them, waving back at John as they trotted out of the driveway to the mercantile.

The two rode side-by-side back through the village of Ocho Rios and down the road that wound around the northern coastline of the island. "The water's churning," Ronnie said. Waves were crashing over the reef as she had never seen before.

"It'll become much worse before it gets better. I'm grateful we're headed to higher ground at Ramble House." Once they reached Saint Ann's Bay, they turned their horses off the road heading single file up the mountain toward Claremont, as the road narrowed. The hairpin turns going up the mountain prevented one from seeing an oncoming traveler. The green foliage shaded much of their climb, helping to keep the sweltering Jamaican sun at bay. Steadily, they wove their way up the mountain past waterfalls, both large and small, with the temperature cooling as they climbed.

"Mavis!" Ronnie called ahead. Mavis slowed to a stop and turned to look at her. "Look!" Ronnie pointed to a waterfall spilling down the mountain to their left. The sound drowned out their conversation, so the two just sat and stared. Green parrots flitted around, some dipping in to bathe at the foot of the falls. Mavis motioned for Ronnie to continue following her. As they came to the crest of the mountain, Mavis stopped and pointed to the mountaintops off in the distance and said, "Ramble House is just beyond that first ridge." They continued to ride through the small town of Claremont. The streets of the town were nearly empty as most of its villagers had already headed home to prepare for the storm. The road was somewhat wider here, which enabled them to ride side-by-side.

"Did you and your husband ever evacuate for a hurricane?" Ronnie asked.

"Only once. Jared was not one to abandon his property in times of trouble, but when the hurricane of 1718 was coming, we knew it was worse than others we'd experienced and headed up here to Ramble House."

Mavis pulled off the road and Ronnie followed suit to allow a large wagon to pass from behind. Two horses pulled the wagon and the drivers nodded, waving hello and thanks. As the wagon pulled past, Ronnie could see it was overflowing with African

men and women bound in chains. Many pairs of hopeless brown
eyes stared at them. One woman raised her shackled wrists
toward Mavis and their eyes locked. The driver happened to
look back and struck her in the back, sending her to the floor of
the wagon.

"Oh my God!" Ronnie shouted. They looked at each other in
horror. Once the wagon passed, Ronnie pulled Star up next to
Moxie. "Where do you suppose they are headed?"

Mavis steered Moxie around a rut in the road and said, "Not
sure, but plantations are expanding their sugarcane and tea
endeavors, so it is hard to tell. Now they're talking about planting coffee. But where will the labor come from?"

Ronnie sighed, "I think we both know the answer to that."

Mavis nodded, "It appears they were coming from the
direction of Port Royal where most slave trade takes place." The
importation of slaves in Jamaica had greatly increased with the
growing sugarcane, tea, and now coffee over the past few years.
The process required a lot of manual labor to sustain profitability
and increase production.

"Let's pull off for a bit and give the horses a rest," Mavis
announced. There was a small waterfall in the hairpin bend of
the road. Quickly, they dismounted and walked the horses over
to the creek that flowed from the cascading water. Ronnie bent
down, cupped her hands, and took a drink next to Stars who
gratefully lapped the water.

"How much further is Ramble House?" She stood and wiped
her mouth with the back of her hand.

"Not too far. Just through town and a few miles beyond."
Mavis turned Moxie around and remounted with Ronnie following suit. As they rode along, Ronnie's thoughts kept going
back to the woman on the wagon lifting her hands for help. The
memory wouldn't leave her alone.

Ronnie followed Mavis as she turned off the main road onto a path, traveling around pastures of cattle grazing and headed up a hill. "There's Ramble House." Mavis pointed toward the estate.

Ronnie nodded, saying, "As I remember it."

To one side, the road gave way to a sharp drop. Ronnie kept Stars as far to the right as she could, not enjoying the view of the cliffside. They wound around the hillside and turned left onto the little road leading up to Ramble House. Even though, the great house was not as grand as Ginger Star it possessed a genteel quality of its own. The flowers produced in the greenhouse had been transplanted in a circular garden in the middle of the driveway. The bird of paradise popped out from the center as if in greeting.

"Marshall took over Ramble House when his father passed," Mavis said, pointing down the path that led to the valley between two steep mountains. They heard goats fussing and could see the herd of twelve or so trotting down the hillside. Ronnie wondered if it was the same young boy she had seen the last time she was here.

After dismounting and tethering Stars and Moxie, they reached in their saddlebags to grab their clothes. The same brown and white dog Ronnie had met before barked and ran up to them. Mavis reached down and stroked his ears. "Willie, it's good to see you." She crouched down to look the dog in the eye. The animal sat down and smiled as only a dog could.

Ronnie took a slow step toward Willie and lowered her hand for him to sniff. He recognized her scent right away and she stooped down to greet him. He gave her a big wet welcome kiss. "Well, that sure feels good after a ride on a hot day, Willie!"

After she hugged the dog, she stood and looked up toward the house and caught sight of Marshall at the top of the stairs. Walking across the grassy knoll, she admired the shoots of Bird of Paradise growing along the path. She still wasn't accustomed to the tropical flowers of Jamaica growing on a whim.

"Ladies, I see you made it safely!" Marshall's blue eyes immediately settled on Ronnie. He jogged down off the steps and walked over to them. Ronnie's face felt flushed and she silently admonished herself. Looking at this hearty, handsome man in the middle of absolute nowhere, she was mesmerized by his regal presence. He and Mavis shook hands and, without hesitation, he pulled her close for a hug.

"Yes, my dear, Marshall. We are most grateful for your offer of shelter during the storm." Mavis looked back at Ronnie who found herself swooping up her loose hair and tucking it back under her hat, trying to look presentable. She wiped the sweat from her forehead with the back of her sleeve.

Marshall quickly reached in his pocket and pulled out a fresh handkerchief. "Here, may I offer some assistance?" He held out the kerchief to her and she took it. His hand brushed hers lightly.

"It seems you are always coming to my rescue, Marshall." Ronnie smiled. "Thank you so much. This Jamaican heat wreaks havoc with me, I'm afraid." Ronnie grinned shyly and lowered her gaze to the ground.

"Please keep it. You can start a collection," Marshall smiled and bowed a little. "It is wonderful to see you again and I am at your service mi'lady." He reached out for her hand, and she placed hers in his.

"Thank you for your offer of refuge." She looked into his blue eyes. He bent and kissed the top of her hand in the customary way. *Will I ever get used to being treated like a real lady?*

The sound of a wagon drew their attention at the rear of the house. They turned to see what looked to be the same wagon they had met on the road. "Is that?" Ronnie's eyes grew wide as she looked from the wagon to Mavis.

"I believe it is," Mavis said and looked at Marshall. "They passed us on the road a few miles back."

He understood their reaction. "The spoils of this situation I find myself in." He shook his head. "Trying to run a tea plantation on the heels of sugarcane creates a need for unprecedented manpower." Marshall sighed. "And when I was told they were from Kenya, I knew I needed them."

"Why?" Ronnie asked.

Marshall looked at her. "Kenya is a leader in tea production. Their climate is similar, and I require their expertise."

Ronnie stared after the wagon. "Where are they going?" she asked.

"The new camp on the estate is about a mile down that path." He pointed to the side of the house. "We are building new accommodations as well as a tea harvesting plant."

Mavis could sense the need to change the subject. She knew Ronnie was uncomfortable with the slavery part of the culture on the island. "When will your first tea crop come in?"

"It will take a while yet. The first seedlings were planted just a little over two years ago. It can take three years for them to mature, but once that happens, we can harvest every week or so, just picking from the top of the bush."

"How many different types of tea have you planted?" Mavis asked.

"We only need to plant one type. Each bush will give us different types of tea, depending on the part of the bush we harvest."

"Well, let me be first in line to place an order for the mercantile when it is ready!" Mavis exclaimed. Marshall smiled at her enthusiasm.

"Rosalie has readied your rooms." He turned to address the young slave as she walked toward them. "Rosalie, please take the ladies to their rooms so they can get some rest and freshen up before dinner." Rosalie wore a black and white servant's uniform of sorts, just like the last time Ronnie was at Ramble House. Ronnie noticed those that worked in the great house all dressed alike.

"Thank you so much for your gracious hospitality, Marshall." Mavis extended her hand and dipped just a little. Marshall took her hand and responded with a nod.

He looked up and reached for Ronnie's hand. She placed her hand in his. She enjoyed the feel of his hand on her skin, but she shook off the attraction and nodded. "Rosalie will show you what we call the hurricane room so you will know where to go if I sound the alarm bell," Marshall said.

Letting go of his hand, Ronnie said, "Thank you for taking such good care of us. It's my first hurricane and you've made me feel safer already."

"My pleasure, my dear." He looked in her eyes just a second longer than was socially acceptable.

She nodded and followed Rosalie and Mavis across the yard. Rosalie stopped in front of a door in the middle of the bottom floor of the house. She grabbed the handle and pulled it open.

"That's strange that it pulls open instead of pushes," Ronnie said. She and Mavis walked inside a dark room.

"That so wind no push it open, Miss Ronnie," Rosalie offered.

"Well, that makes good sense!" Ronnie replied.

They walked inside the windowless room. Light from the doorway revealed a table with a few lanterns and a couple of baskets with food and linens, a chamber pot, and buckets of water. Single cots lined the walls. "This where you come if you hear alarm bell."

"Thank you, Rosalie," Mavis said. "This will be easy to find." They followed her out of the room and Ronnie pushed the door shut behind them. Following her into the great house, they walked down the dark hallway. Rosalie opened the door to Mavis' room. "Thank you, Rosalie. You can take Ronnie to her room. I know my way around." Mavis smiled at Rosalie.

"You bat' is drawn and ready for you, Miss Mavis," Rosalie said.

"Thank you, my dear. Your hospitality is always wonderful." She turned and looked at Ronnie. "Rest well, and I'll see you in at dinner."

"See you then." Mavis smiled and closed the door behind her.

Ronnie continued following Rosalie down the hallway while she once again, admired the woodwork throughout the house. Carved wooden paneling covered many of the walls, flickering in the candlelight while the breeze threatened to extinguish its flame. Beautiful hand painted tiles and the green Italian marble fireplace mantle in the dining room added contrast and color. She ran her hand over the tiles feeling the coolness of their surface as she walked down the hallway.

Rosalie opened the door to Ronnie's room. It was the same room she had occupied the first time when she and Sam were returning to Ochi. The tall ceilings accommodated a large four-poster bed with matching furniture. Lacy curtains flowed in the mountain breeze, welcoming her back.

"Oh my, this will soon be labeled as my room if I keep this up!" Ronnie said as they walked in. Rosalie showed her where her bag had been placed and pointed out the essentials like candles, a flint and striker, as well as a chamber pot.

"I draw mi lady a bath behind da screen." Rosalie pointed to the tub and pulled the privacy screen in front of it. The fireplace flickered its light on the walls.

"An' der is more hot wata here in de kettle when you ready." She nodded toward the fireplace.

"Well, I pretty much feel like a princess, Rosalie. You are quite the hostess and spoil me yet again." Ronnie enjoyed seeing a smile cross Rosalie's face at the compliment. "This will be wonderful after the long day of travel up the mountains. Thank you so much!"

"You welcome, mi'lady. I will knock when dinna ready." Rosalie nodded and pulled the door closed after her.

Once Rosalie departed, Ronnie sat on the edge of the bed and stared out the window. *This place is just so relaxing and serene.* But when she recalled the woman on the wagon, the idea of harmony left her with a heaviness in her chest. Would she never become accustomed to that dark side of their culture? She hoped she would not. She could see a hillside in the distance that had been cleared and planted with what she assumed was tea.

Ronnie pulled off her soiled clothes, put them on a chair, poured the remaining hot water in the tub, and carefully stepped over the edge of the white porcelain tub. She sank down into the water. Reaching for a towel, she put it under her head as a pillow and closed her eyes as images of the day ran through her mind.

First, it was John accepting the repayment of her loan. It felt good to have retired that obligation. She remembered the waterfalls that cascaded down the mountains as they traveled. In contrast, there was the sight of a wagon-full of people that were now owned by another, Marshall. The irony of the feel of Marshall's kiss on her hand was not lost on her. Quite a day indeed. She found a bar of soap Rosalie had left next to the towel and began to bathe. Once finished, she stood and found the towel once again. Stepping out of the tub, she was careful to stay on the extra towel she had placed on the floor. What once felt like hot sticky air, was now cool and refreshing on her cleansed skin.

Ronnie slid her slip over her head, pulled out her journal from the pocket of her pants, and laid down across the large bed. "This must be a heaven (of sorts) for some," she wrote. "And a definite hell for others." She went on to describe the woman in the wagon and how they were needed to run the new tea plantation. When the pen ran low on ink again, she put it on the nightstand and laid her head down. The woman's brown eyes from the wagon stared into hers as she drifted off.

"Supper be ready on the veranda soon, Miss Ronnie." Rosalie lightly touched Ronnie's shoulder. She had fallen asleep on the bed with her journal lying beside her, wearing only her slip. Ronnie sat up slowly, rubbed her eyes, and closed her journal. She could only hope that Rosalie had not been able to read what she'd written. She could see the sun had begun to set. Rosalie laid a white robe across the bed.

"Thank you, Rosalie. I suppose I dozed off. This room seems to have that effect on me!" She sat up, stretched like a cat, and rubbed her eyes. "How long have you worked here?"

"Oh, I been wit Massa Marshall's family since dey come to Jamaica," Rosalie was surprised that Ronnie was showing an interest in her. She lit a few candles to ward off the shadows of the evening. "Many years now. Since I was pickney."

"Well, you do a wonderful job making your guests feel welcome." Rosalie held up the skirt she had hung in the closet for Ronnie and helped her dress for dinner. Ronnie found it strange to have someone help her get ready. *Will I ever grow accustomed to the advantages of being born into this favored race I find myself a part of?* Her station in life was never one of luxury, but it was certainly one of advantage here in Jamaica compared to Rosalie's.

RONNIE WALKED UP the front steps of Ramble House to the landing and then the veranda off the dining room. Her hand traced the carving on the marble fireplace mantle. Soon she discerned footsteps. When she looked up she watched as Marshall entered the dining room. He whispered something to Rosalie and quickly walked to the veranda to join Ronnie.

"So, my lady, how was your afternoon?" He handed her a single purple orchid.

"Quite restful and your hospitality is beyond measure." She looked at the orchid in her hand. "Why thank you, Marshall." Her finger traced the circular petal and she tried to tuck it behind her ear.

"Allow me." Once again, he took the flower from her, pulled her silky hair behind her ear, and tucked the flower behind it using her hair to keep it in place. *Why do I have such a physical reaction every time he touches me*? Taking a deep breath, she tried to ignore the growing warmth of her attraction, and looked at her reflection in the glass door.

"Thank you." Her hand reached up to touch the flower and she dipped a slight curtsy of gratitude.

He offered his arm and she took it as they headed into the dining room. The perfect gentleman, he pulled out a chair for her and she sat. He seated himself next to her at the head of the table. The candlelight on the walls danced betraying the winds which were beginning to show signs of an impending storm.

Her view was directly over the garden. Today, the wind tossed the orchids and Bird of Paradise back and forth, as if trying to knock them down. "It appears the storm is beginning to reveal itself."

"I'm afraid so. We should go over some hurricane protocol before we turn in. We want all to be safe," Marshall stated.

"Absolutely. Thank you again for all of your consideration." Ronnie nodded and smiled at him.

Her smile reminded him of a woman he'd known in London, but Ronnie had a quality that he'd never encountered before. She had a grit and seeming determination not found in many women these days, but definitely qualities required of those living on the island.

From where they sat, they could see over the rail of the veranda to the grounds of Ramble House. Ronnie waived at Mavis as she walked across the courtyard. She was grateful for the diversion as she could sense Marshall's curiosity.

"Mavis, we're up here!" She waved to attract her attention.

"Coming. Don't start without me!" Mavis wore a green dress that blended in nicely with the plush Jamaican countryside. Her raven hair was pulled into a bun. Marshall rose and met her at the dining room door, escorting her to the chair across from Ronnie.

They were served a dinner of roasted chicken and vegetables, all grown on the estate. "Let's enjoy this tonight. As for tomorrow, we could be closed up waiting out the storm," Marshall said.

They could hear the hammering as the slaves closed up the windows of the great house, leaving the dining room open until dinner was over. Over the breeze, they could hear McClintock, the overseer, hollering orders in the distance. The sun was setting and Rosalie walked around lighting candles throughout the room.

Soon, the food was brought in by several house slaves, all wearing the same black and white clothing. They sat the food on the sideboard that sat against the wall, behind the dining room table. Rosalie plated the food and put a dish in front of each of them.

"It is a rare treat that I have guests to dine with me here at Ramble House." Marshall raised his glass of port. "To friends," he looked from Mavis to Ronnie. "Both old and new." They clinked their glasses of port and took a sip. The liquid warmed Ronnie and she could feel her cheeks blush. Why, she wasn't sure. They enjoyed easy conversation and the roasted chicken.

"So, it appears the storm is still off the coast from what passing wagons have reported this afternoon. For that reason, I suggest when we retire, we do so to our respective rooms. In the event the storm gets too strong, I will sound the plantation bell to wake you. I believe Rosalie pointed out the hurricane room earlier."

"Yes, she did. That sounds like a fine plan, Marshall," Mavis said.

Eating their dinner, they could hear the rhythm of drums and voices of men and women as they rang out in the distance. The soulful sound soothed Ronnie's fear of the storm. Once they finished dinner, Rosalie served tea when the women declined dessert.

Marshall walked the ladies out onto the veranda. Rosalie handed him a pipe, already lit. It was obvious this was an evening ritual. Marshall puffed on the pipe until the curl of smoke seemed to dance to the drums as it twirled its way into the inky Jamaican sky.

"Is that Kimar playing the drums again?" she asked Marshall. She stopped and stared into the Jamaican night as the tinkling soulful sounds drifted in the night air.

Marshall smiled. "Yes. It's pretty much a daily ritual around here in the evenings." He pointed at Kimar sitting in the yard. Before long, they could hear the singing of those in the slave quarters.

"I would never tire of the sound," Ronnie said. She stared down at the young man who sat at the edge of the yard. He flitted the stick back and forth, around the surface of the drums, taking turns allowing his left hand to tap the drums directly. Kimar grinned when he realized he had an audience and greeted them by waving his drumstick.

Ronnie's toe involuntarily tapped to the beat of the drum. The house slaves sang as they continued to close up the house and wash up the dinner dishes.

"So, Mavis, what is the latest news about the pirates fighting against Rogers in Nassau?" Marshall asked. He knew she was privy to many rumors that floated around the islands from her customers at the mercantile.

Leaning against the veranda railing, Mavis said, "Well from what I've heard, Hornigold met his demise a while back and the Flying Gang is no more. His ship wrecked on a coral reef during a storm. He was doing a pretty good job rounding up those that fought against the Crown after the King's pardon was issued."

Ronnie listened intently as she'd not heard Hornigold's name in a while.

"Yes, I heard he turned against his pirate community and accepted the pardon along with a commission to take down as many pirates as he could," Marshall said. "Sounds like an astute businessman to me!"

"Yes, he was always very careful not to attack British ships. Seems he did have a true allegiance to the Crown," Mavis offered.

Ronnie remembered Hornigold well. He was very charismatic and could talk anyone into anything. Having no desire to bring attention to her past, she listened attentively, hoping for more details.

"It seems as if Vane has truly lost his mind thinking he can take on the Crown," Mavis said. Ronnie had to really subdue her urge to speak as she knew Vane was indeed crazy, and that was putting it mildly. Examples of his violence were legendary, not to mention she'd seen plenty of his madness first hand.

"Well, let's just be grateful we're not in Nassau. It's bound to get much worse if Rogers has anything to do with it. Seems he's handling the restructuring very well for the Crown," Marshall said. Woodes Rogers had been named governor of the Bahamas and New Providence Island where the town of Nassau was located. He arrived in 1718 and his job was to bring law and order to this unruly and decadent colony of Britain.

MAVIS YAWNED AND covered her mouth with her hand. "Oh, please forgive me. I'm more tired than I realized." She turned to Marshall. "Seems as if we could talk about the madness of this world we live in all night." She looked at Marshall and said, "I hope it's alright if I were to retire for the evening."

"Absolutely, my dear. I pray you rest well and the storm doesn't keep you awake." He smiled at the thought of having Ronnie all to himself. "Please let me know if there is anything at all you need." He looked over toward the slave quarters. "Perhaps I should request Kimar stop playing." Marshall sat his drink down on the railing.

"Oh no, please don't," Mavis said, "at least not on my account. It will be most pleasant to drift to sleep with such a melody." Mavis leaned in for a kiss on her cheek from Marshall and hugged Ronnie. Turning, she walked back into the dining room and down the steps toward her bedroom, smiling to herself. She knew the two of them relished the idea of some time alone.

"I believe I should do the same," Ronnie said, not wanting to leave, but thinking protocol dictated that she do so.

"Oh, why be in such haste? Are you tired as well?"

"Well, I believe the nap I took this afternoon has rejuvenated me enough to last a while longer." Ronnie grinned. She was delighted and tried not to let it show.

Marshall smiled. Ronnie was glad to see his somber mood had lifted. She wondered if she were the reason. He was certainly the reason for hers. She found him to be quite interesting and this part of the interior of Jamaica kept her intrigued.

He held a chair on the veranda for her and she sat down overlooking the yard with the orchid garden on the far side. They talked about the upcoming storm and politics abroad.

"It appears that Woodes Rogers is serious about the outlawing of piracy." Marshall shook his head.

Ronnie nodded and said, "Many have taken advantage of the King's pardon for piracy, but just as many have not. It was all just beginning when I first left Nassau. It will be a difficult thing to accomplish, for sure." She didn't reveal that she knew much more about the subject than she let on. She found him very easy to be with and enjoyed the comfortable silence when talking slowed.

"What was it like living in a place like Nassau?" Marshall asked.

Ronnie shifted in her seat suddenly wishing she'd retired when Mavis had. Clearing her throat, she said, "It was always a rough place. I was only there for a short while," Ronnie answered demurely. "I met lots of those nefarious characters when I was there. Many of the rumors are true, unfortunately.

Marshall could sense she wasn't eager to share more, so he shifted the conversation saying, "Well, our world is certainly changing. Let's hope the Crown's efforts are successful." They continued talking about the events happening in London with the Quadruple Alliance that was signed between France, Britain, Austria, and the Dutch Republic against Spain back in August of 1718. "When Spain invaded Sicily in July, 1718," Marshall said, "the alliance was formed and war broke out."

"Hadn't Spain already captured Sardinia from Austria a year earlier?" she asked.

"Yes, they did indeed," Marshall said, surprised and impressed at her knowledge of current events.

"It appears countries tend to trade properties like we do with sugarcane for fabric and oils," Ronnie said. They continued talking politics until the sun dipped behind the last mountain range, adding the Jamaican crickets to Kimar's drum lullaby.

He looked at her. "I'm relieved you and Mavis are here at Ramble House instead of down in Ocho Rios."

"I'm grateful. It seems Ramble House continues to be a refuge for me." Ronnie's eyes met his for a second and she looked away as she felt her cheeks blush. *Why does he have this effect on me?* "Having Mavis in my life has introduced me to many good friends."

"It seems we have much in common. I'm grateful to have met you, Ronnie." He took her hand in his and leaned over, brushing the back of it lightly with his lips. Looking into her eyes again he said, "I suppose we should both retire. There's no telling what the storm might bring, and we'll want to be as rested as possible."

She laughed , "You're right. Sleep might be difficult to find once the storm kicks in." The wind was beginning to pick up and drops of rain splattered on the railing.

Ronnie smiled and slowly let go of his hand. She turned and he followed her down the steps to the foyer of the great house. As she walked toward her room, she glanced back at Marshall to find him staring after her. Pushing her hair out of her face, she pulled the purple orchid from behind her ear as the breeze found its way into the hallway. Their eyes locked. Her heart skipped a beat and she grinned, dipping her head as she turned and walked to her room. Kimar's lullaby grew softer and softer.

Ronnie planned to latch the windows tight if the storm kicked up during the night, but it appeared Rosalie had already taken care of it. After changing, she slid under the covers. The

breeze that made it through the closed shutters lifted the curtains and their shadow traveled up and down the wall in the
flickering candlelight. She could still feel the effects of Marshall
staring at her as she walked to her room. Tracing the edges of
the purple orchid and sliding her finger over its soft petals, she
laid it on her night stand. Dismissing the thoughts of Marshall,
she gave in to images of Elijah and Amari. She compared the
silkiness of the orchid to the softness of Elijah's skin as she
stroked his cheek.

Clasping her hands together, she offered her daily prayer for
his health and safety in his new home. She remembered Adria
with her loyalty, how she protected Ronnie and Amari. Praying
again that one day Adria would somehow forgive her, she drifted
into a dream-filled sleep with the tinkling sound of Kimar's
lullaby rising on the wind.

Chapter Eleven

"Pray as if you were to die tomorrow." —Benjamin Franklin

1720, Claremont, Jamaica

Ronnie woke with a start to the sound of a clanging bell. It took a second for her to realize it was the warning Marshall had talked about. She raised up on her elbow to find the shutter had blown open and the rain blew in sideways. Rushing to the window, she slammed the shutter closed, and threw the bolt, quickly closing up the slats. Grabbing her robe, she took the almost burnt-out candle and lit the wick of another larger one. Holding the light in front of her, she opened her door and found Marshall standing there.

"Come on, let's go!" Marshall grabbed her arm and pulled the door shut behind them. "Mavis, where are you?" Marshall hollered.

Mavis answered, "I'm here. On my way!" Ronnie could see a flickering light coming toward them.

"Let's get to the hurricane room fast!" Marshall said. The sound of the wind crashed around the house whirling down the open hallways. Rain continued to pound sideways, making it impossible not to get soaked. Branches darted around as they broke away from their trunks while lightning flashed almost constantly, providing light to see. Palm fronds flew as if they were wings. The three ran across the yard, shielding their eyes from whatever might be flying through the air. Marshall grabbed the handle of the hurricane room door, pulling with both hands and yanked it open. He stood in the rain waving them inside. Mavis hurried past him when he noticed Ronnie was not there. He turned to see her lying in the yard. "Stay here!" he said to Mavis, pushing the door closed behind him. Marshall ran back into the storm, rain pelting him while the wind threatened to knock him flat. He knelt beside Ronnie. "Are you alright?" He could see she was trembling.

"I think so," Ronnie said raising her head, blood streaming down her face.

"Let's get you inside!" Ronnie took his hand and struggled to stand against the wind and rain. Her clothes were a muddy mess.

Marshall moved behind her, scooping Ronnie up into his arms. Mavis peeked through the hole in the door and saw them coming. Pushing the door open with all her might, it finally opened. The door swung out of her hands and banged against the wall as Marshall carried Ronnie inside. "Hold on tight, Mavis! Don't let the wind knock you down!" he said.

She grabbed onto the door with both hands, dug in her heels, and using her weight against the wind, pulled it closed. Marshall sat Ronnie down in a chair and he and Mavis both pushed the deadbolt closed. Leaning back on the door, darkness surrounded them with the exception of the flickering light of a few lanterns.

Pushing his wet black hair back out of his eyes, he looked at Ronnie. "Are you alright?"

Ronnie touched her forehead. "Something hit me in the head when we were running across the yard." She looked at her hand, feeling faint. Marshall knelt down next to her.

"Here, let's take a look." Marshall held her shoulders protectively and pushed her hair back to find a gash about a half-inch long along her hair line. "I think we have just the thing to get you fixed up." He reached over and pulled a box from across the table toward him. "It's amazing just how much a scratch on the head can bleed." He opened the latch to find bandages and alcohol. Mavis handed him a pitcher of water and wet a towel to clean up the wound. Ronnie winced but stayed still. Mavis stood next to him trying to anticipate what he needed next. She handed him a bandage and he wrapped it around Ronnie's head like a bandana.

Wetting a towel with the pitcher of water on the table, Mavis helped Ronnie to wipe off the mud and blood from her face and arms.

"Well, there you are, my lady." Marshall stood back to review his work. He tilted Ronnie's chin up a little to see if the bandage would hold. It did.

"How do you feel?" Mavis asked.

Ronnie sighed. "I'm fine, really." Her hand touched the bandage. "From what I can tell, the two of you make a really good team."

"I'm so grateful you're alright," Mavis said.

Ronnie felt Marshall lay a blanket over her shoulders.

"You two need to dry off as best you can," he said. He picked up a basket from the floor and put it on the table. "I know these won't fit just right, but they should be good enough to allow you to dry off and escape your wet clothes." He turned away and went to the fireplace with his back to them. He crouched down to stoke the fire he had started an hour earlier when the storm had picked up strength. "Let me know when you are finished changing." He thought about taking a peek but knew better.

Mavis giggled. "Well, Marshall, it appears that once again, you've remembered everything." The two women each found a suitable shirt and pants and changed. They hung their wet clothes around the room to dry.

Marshall pulled out his pocket watch and held it close to a lantern to see the time. "It is almost 4 am. Just a few hours until dawn." The wind continued to blow a gale. "It sounds as if the rain has slowed which could mean it is coming to an end. However, it could also be just the eye of the storm which can give us a false sense of security. It's hard to tell just yet."

Mavis nodded. "It is more often than not just a waiting game."

"I suggest we all lay down and try to get some rest. There's no telling what we may face in the morning," Marshall said.

They each laid down on a cot that lined the wall of the windowless room. The darkness helped to bring sleep for a while as the storm calmed.

Ronnie laid there feeling somewhat afraid, yet somehow safe at the same time. She had not felt so cared for since she left Nassau. A familiar, yet new, feeling of security came over her. She closed her eyes and wondered how long it would last.

A ROOSTER CROWED and Marshall sat up on the edge of his cot. Walking to the door, he threw the deadbolt and opened it. Light flooded the room. The wind and rain had ended as the heavy clouds floated slowly across the top of the mountains.

Ronnie walked over to join him. "Well, for once the sound of a rooster crowing is a welcome sound." Their hands touched. Marshall turned and looked her in the eyes as he pulled her toward him. His arms slipped around her waist. She wondered briefly where Mavis was. Their eyes met as he tilted her chin up to place his lips on hers. Her heart raced and reality betrayed her as she opened her eyes to the sound of the plantation bell ringing in the distance.

"Oh my!" Ronnie said. She sat up on the edge of her cot. It appeared Marshall had slipped out before she woke and was already outside assessing the damages. She was grateful the dream was hers alone, but found she was sorry it was over so soon.

Mavis walked over to her. "What's wrong?"

Ronnie shook her head. "Oh, just a dumb dream. Funny the tricks one's mind can play when asleep!"

Mavis grinned. She had heard Ronnie mumble in her sleep and the dream had indeed been a happy one. "How's your head this morning?"

Ronnie's hand went to the bandaged. "It feels fine. Should we take this off?" she asked.

Mavis walked over and peeked under the bandage. "Yes, I think it's fine." She unwrapped the bandage and put it on the table. "As good as new, I'm thinking."

Pushing her hair back from her face, Ronnie said, "Thanks so much, Mavis."

"Well, I believe we need to go outside and see how things are. Marshall left right before you woke up." They slipped into their shoes and Mavis opened the door.

"There he is," Ronnie said. Marshall was walking in the yard assessing the damage. Tree limbs were scattered along with shutters and a few buckets were laying here and there.

He looked up to see the two women walking out to join him. "There's no telling how far some of this stuff has blown. I certainly don't recognize much of it," Marshall said as he picked up a bucket. "The good news is that the roof seems to be intact and for that, I'm grateful." He turned and looked at them.

"How are you feeling this morning, my dear?" he said to Ronnie as he walked closer to check out the wound. "I see you've taken your bandage off."

"I feel fine, thank you." Ronnie said as she lifted her hair for him to see. "I'm healing up fast."

Smiling he said, "You sure are. I'm grateful for that." He looked at Mavis. "I hope you managed to get at least a little rest."

"We both did. Ronnie woke talking and dreaming."

Ronnie tried not to blush, without success. "I suppose I did!" She hoped her attraction didn't show but wasn't so sure that was the case.

"Well, if you ladies will excuse me, I'll be off to assess any damages and put together a plan to restore the grounds as needed. Rosalie will see to your breakfast."

"Of course," Ronnie said. "Where was Rosalie last night?"

"She stayed in the slave quarters with the others. Mr. McClintock, my overseer, said all appeared to be good there. I'm headed down now to check it out."

"You go ahead. We will do what we can and help clean up around here," Mavis said.

Ronnie walked over and picked up a stray limb. "We'll begin here in the yard, but if you find something more urgent that needs to be done, please let us know." She continued to pick up loose debris and stuff it in a stray bucket.

He stared after her for a second. This woman's determination combined with her political awareness, social abilities, and grace intrigued him. Shaking off his infatuation, he jumped on his horse, Rebel. "Thank you, ladies!"

Marshall headed toward the camp to assess the damage, riding Rebel slowly down the hill toward the camp. The rain had dug deep ruts all over the road and Rebel slipped just a little, making Marshall grateful he'd just had new shoes put on him.

Marshall spent most of the day riding throughout the Ramble House plantation, making lists and assigning tasks. First, the slaves' quarters. Gratefully, only one minor injury to speak of and some random repairs that needed to be made. He rode Rebel down to the valley below checking on the sugarcane fields, and once finished there, went on to the tea fields. His list grew with each stop, but it was apparent the hurricane had stayed closer to the shore. Traveling back toward the great house, he could see his overseer's horse standing next to a wagon about a mile away and he tracked him down. "Mr. McClintock," Marshall said as he pulled on Rebel's reins stopping the horse alongside the wagon. The bulky man looked up from changing a wheel. "Looks like you have your hands full!"

McClintock stood and wiped his brow with a kerchief and said, "Just one of those aggravating delays is all!"

Marshall handed McClintock a piece of paper. "Here's a list of repairs that need to be made in the southern fields. Just some fencing and a few simple tasks. I was grateful to see that Trudy will be alright." Trudy was a cook in the slave quarters. "I sent her to the house for first aid. She took a knock in the head but seems to be fine."

McClintock checked his tongue. He was annoyed that Trudy had gone against his directions by tending to the open gate of the pig pen instead of staying inside even though she'd prevented the pigs from escaping. "That's good. I'm glad to know it wasn't any worse than that," McClintock said.

"Yes indeed. Once you look over the list, please let me know if there are any supplies you'll need."

McClintock stood up and wiped his brow with a kerchief. He took the list and read it over. "Yes sir. I'll get right on it."

"Looks like you could use some sustenance." Marshall pulled out what was left of his lunch and tossed it to McClintock.

The overseer stood and looked in the satchel. "Why thank you, sir. I have worked up an appetite!" He pulled out a piece of Mavis' jerky and yanked off a bite.

"Well, take a break. You deserve it. I'll check in with you later." He pulled on Rebel's reins and took off toward the great house, wondering what Ronnie was up to. She crowded his thoughts more and more. He returned to find Ronnie and Mavis sitting in front on the retaining wall next to of a pile of debris they'd collected from all over the property. They waved as he got closer.

"Is this yours?" Cocking her head to one side, Ronnie held up a chamber pot for Marshall to see.

He sat on Rebel trying to decide how to answer. Taking the leap, he said, "Well, I was wondering where that had gotten to." He smiled sheepishly and added, "Sorry if it was a little smelly when you found it!"

"I think the rain took care of that." Ronnie said and smiled, sitting the pot down on the ground. She dusted her hands off. "I suppose I should, however, still wash my hands." She pretended to sniff them and made a face. Marshall and Mavis laughed.

After cleaning up, they all sat down to dinner on the veranda to enjoy the cool mountain breeze left behind by the hurricane. "Thank you, Rosalie. You can take a break now. I'll call when we're finished. I think we're capable of serving ourselves tonight, right ladies?"

They both nodded and Mavis said, "We're more than able. Enjoy your evening, Rosalie, and thanks." The slave ducked out the door, grateful for a little time to go check on things in the slave quarters. She'd promised Trudy she would check in on her since she'd been feeling poorly that morning.

The three enjoyed their meal and retired to the veranda for some fresh air. "It's been a long day, I can see we are all tuckered out," Marshall said.

"Yes, I'm afraid I'm withering fast tonight," Ronnie replied. "I believe I'll say good night and head up to my room." She realized how that sounded and added, "Well, maybe it's not 'my room,' but it's beginning to feel like it!"

"I'm happy to hear you feel that way," Marshall said. "I trust you'll have pleasant dreams." He picked up her hand and kissed it. Turning to Mavis, he added, "The rooster crows early around here, so I'll say my good night to you both." He kissed Mavis' hand and turned to leave, adding, "I need to check on some things down at the slave quarters and will retire soon myself."

Wondering what might need to be checked on in the slave quarters, Ronnie decided not to ask and proceeded to her room. *Don't ask the question if you don't want to hear the answer.*

THE FOLLOWING MORNING, Ronnie woke to the cockerel's crowing again. "'Tis one song I'll never learn to enjoy," she said aloud to herself. Rolling over, she stretched her arms and rubbed her eyes, giving way to a wide yawn. Ronnie rose from her bed and pushed the shutter open to allow the sunshine to warm her.

Pulling her hair up in the ribbon Rosalie had left her on the vanity, she lifted her hair to inspect the scratch on her forehead. Talking to herself again she said, "Well, it's always been said you've a 'hard head,' I suppose this is proof enough." She sighed and finished getting dressed.

The sun was beginning to peek over the mountain range. Ronnie guessed it to be around 6 am. The estate was sleepy this morning with no one moving around that she could see.

Everyone was probably worn out from the hard day's work recovering from the storm. *I doubt the slaves get the day off.*

Grabbing her shawl, she stole down the stairs and headed to the back yard. Willie trotted over to her. Reaching down to pat his head, she said, "Want to take a walk with me, Willie?" The dog answered by following her through the yard, past the outbuildings and cistern, and headed down a road that was little more than a path.

Ronnie held her skirt up so it wouldn't get muddy. She found a bamboo branch lying on the ground and picked it up to use as a walking stick. Smelling wood burning in the distance, she guessed the slaves were preparing breakfast. Down the hill, Ronnie could see the smoke curling up between the rooftops of the slave quarters in the distance. As she got closer, she could see a few people milling about. She recognized Rosalie who was bent over stoking a campfire that served as a stove. *Does she ever quit working?* A black horse snorted as if to protest that he was tied to a post. Willie wove in and out of the horse's legs. "You had best be careful, my friend, lest you get kicked!" Ronnie warned him.

"Oh, he knows his way around Rebel. You needn't worry." Ronnie whirled around to find Marshall standing behind her. "They're old friends."

"Well, hello there. I didn't know you were here!" Her hand covered her mouth.

"Nor I you, I must admit."

"I'm sorry if I have wandered too far. Willie and I were just taking a stroll."

"Not at all. Would you like for me to show you around?"

"Very much." She put her hand on his arm that was already extended, his warmth and smile being all the encouragement she needed. "I'm so happy the storm didn't cause more damage than it did," Ronnie said.

"As am I. The mountains often provide enough of a buffer to keep the biggest threat at bay." He looked toward the distant Blue Mountain range and squinted. "However, it is difficult to tell how we fared down on the coast." He steered her around a rut the hard rain had dug into the road. She slipped a little and he caught her arm.

"Careful there! This red clay dirt is really slick after a rain," he said.

"It certainly is!" Ronnie said and felt herself blush at being so clumsy. "So, what brings you down here so early in the day?" Ronnie asked.

Marshall glanced sideways at her as they walked. "I wanted to check on our new residents and make sure they were well tended." He felt her hand tighten on his arm in response as he talked. "It turned out Mr. McClintock had everything under control. They're being bathed and deloused this morning after breakfast." He could sense her discomfort but continued. "Not a pleasant task, but a rather necessary one which the storm delayed."

Ronnie pointed to a long rectangular building that was under construction. "What is that going to be?"

"That will be the conservatory for the tea harvest."

People milled around as the rooster crowed again. "He must have a built-in alarm every half hour or so!" Ronnie giggled.

Marshall nodded and chuckled. "I'm thinking he does!" They finished their tour of the edge of the acreage that held the tea plantation. "It will take a few more months before it's completed. Being at the mercy of shipments of lumber and supplies, as well as storms, we often play a waiting game."

"I can imagine that to be the case. Do you suppose it's safe for us to head back down to Ocho Rios yet?"

"I think that can be arranged. However, I hesitate to send you and Mavis back there alone." Marshall was being thoughtful, but also had a hidden motive. He was excited about any chance to spend time with her. "It's difficult to know the toll it has taken on the coast, but we can certainly attempt to go back today, if you like. McClintock has things under control here."

Ronnie liked the sound of "we" in his sentence, hoping it meant he would travel with them and said, "I believe Mavis would like to try as well. Perhaps we should make haste to see what's become of the mercantile." She was also worried about Scottie, but thought she'd keep her obsession with a parrot to herself for now.

"Then I'll travel down with you. It may prove difficult to pass with fallen trees and other debris." They walked back to the slave quarters. "Let's get on Rebel and head back to the house for breakfast." He mounted the horse and grabbed her hand to help her climb up behind him. Willie followed and as they rode, both enjoying the innocent closeness on top of Rebel. *Don't get too close to him. You know what happened last time.*

ROSALIE LOOKED OUT the window of the cabin toward the campfire. Smoke rose from the glowing embers. She could see the outline of a few people talking, gathered in the courtyard of the slave quarters. Normally, she would be among those chatting and talking about the day's events. But she didn't want to talk about today. Then she saw him and her pulse picked up, her breath shallowed. She pulled her shawl tighter around her shoulders and shivered despite the warm night. Her body shook with rage. Now she knew what it felt like to want to kill someone. Now she knew.

—Chapter Twelve—

"Does thou love life? Then do not squander time;
for that's the stuff life is made of." —Benjamin Franklin

1720, London

Adria had crossed the Atlantic from Jamaica to London with her mother in a fog that did not rise from the water. The cloudiness saturating her mind and spirit was sinking into her soul. She found it too painful to be present, so she wasn't, and spent most of the journey in her cabin trying to sleep, wrapping herself in the comforting fog.

"Come on, darling, the plank has been lowered and they're ready to disembark." Adria sat on the edge of the bed. She had managed to dress for the first time in a week and looked up at her mother.

"I am ready." Adria's tone was flat with no emotion. Standing up, she grabbed her purse and parasol. Adria followed Sarah out of their room and up the stairs to the main deck. Looking at the busy port with people rushing in every direction, she wished she could go back to bed. Soon enough. She had no plans other than to cloister herself in her room when they arrived at their row house in the city.

London was as it had always been. It was only Adria that had changed. She'd been just a girl when they had left for Jamaica. She returned a wounded young woman. Losing her baby was not only traumatic, but the guilt that had attached itself to her was like a black cloud that refused to leave. She knew she had brought shame to her parents and caused her mother to return to London prematurely. Because of her mistake, her parents were forced to live apart, leaving her father behind in Jamaica to run Ginger Star. She followed her mother off the ship and over to their awaiting carriage.

"William!" Sarah said and walked briskly toward the carriage. William had worked for the Goddards since they were first married.

"Mrs. Goddard, it is wonderful to see you again," William said as he opened the door to the carriage. He was tall with curly brown hair. Sarah couldn't help but notice how time had passed now that William had just a touch of gray at the temples. "And Miss Adria, you left here a young girl and have returned a lovely young woman!" He bowed in respect. Adria stared right through him.

Sarah tried to play down her daughter's aloofness and stood aside for Adria to enter the carriage first. Grabbing hold of the handle on the door, she lifted her skirts and entered the carriage on her own.

Sarah laughed and said, "She always was an independent one!" Leaning over to William she whispered, "She's not feeling herself. Please forgive her."

"Of course, Madam. Please, allow me," he said offering his hand, which she took and climbed into the carriage to sit across from Adria. William closed the door and leapt up top to grab the reins.

The carriage rolled down the bumpy cobblestone streets of the wharfs of London. Seamen walked carrying their worldly possessions on their back headed home. People shouted greetings to one another as they were reunited as Adria stared listlessly out the window, seeing nothing, her head bobbing up and down with the motion of the carriage.

"My, will you look at that?" Sarah asked, pointing to new additions to the downtown area. "It appears as though they have built a new mercantile near the wharf."

"Mmm, hmm," Adria mumbled, refusing to engage in conversation.

Sarah finally gave up and stared out the window as well. *Will God ever forgive me for bringing such pain to my little girl?*

The coach pulled up in front of their row house inside the city of London. William opened the door and lent his hand to both women as they stepped down onto the pavement. Adria looked up at the three-story gray mansion and sighed. Yes, it was home, but not the one she wanted. She missed Ginger Star with its casual elegance and color as opposed to this imposing grandeur.

The staff greeted them as Adria headed straight up the curved staircase. "I will be having dinner in my room," she said to her mother, and continued climbing the stairs.

Sarah looked after her, sighed, and nodded. She looked at Margaret, their head housekeeper, and said, "I'm so sorry, Margaret. She's not been herself this entire trip." Margaret was a treasured, lifelong servant to the family. For Adria to be so distant to her was a shock to both of them, even though Sarah knew why.

SARAH SPENT MUCH of the next few days answering correspondence. Many invitations to social events as well as requests for visits arrived every day as word got out they were back in

London. Sarah carefully crafted her replies declining the biddings so as not to offend anyone. There was just no way they could host or be entertained until Adria recovered. There would be too many questions and far too few answers to give.

Three days passed and Adria had not left her room. Margaret informed Sarah that she had eaten next to nothing from the trays of food that had been delivered to her. So, Sarah climbed the stairs and knocked lightly on her beloved daughter's door. When she didn't get an answer, she slowly turned the knob and quietly pushed it open. The room was dark with only a curtain moving from a cold breeze. "Oh my, it's cold in here, my dear!" She walked to the window, pulled the frame in, and latched the lock. She purposefully left the drape pulled back to let in some light.

Adria groaned in protest and sat up in the bed, rubbing her eyes. "Please close the curtain!" She pushed her tangled hair from her face.

"My dear, you cannot continue to just lie in bed and wither away. Please come downstairs and eat dinner with me."

"Oh, Mama. I'm so tired. I just want to sleep. Food holds no interest for me."

"I understand, my dear." Sarah sat on the bed next to her daughter and stroked her tousled hair. "But you must keep your strength up and try to find your life again."

Unwelcome tears slipped down Adria's face. "Why do I feel as though I left a part of me in Jamaica?" She laid back down, rolling over and pulling the covers back over her head. "I keep longing to just go back. I just need to say goodbye to him."

Sarah's heart broke at her daughter's words and tears threatened to betray her, knowing the answer but unable share it. *Will this battle ever end? Will my little girl ever recover?* Sarah could not get her to respond again, so she leaned over, kissed her head, and slipped quietly out of the room. Sitting at her desk she pulled out a blank note card to send to Jeffrey, Adria's oldest and best friend here in London. He was her only hope.

"AUNTY SARAH!" JEFFREY said using his pet name for Adria's mother. Their families had grown very close over the years, inviting the familiar term. "It's wonderful to have you back in London.

I've missed you both so much." Jeffrey had turned into a handsome young man with black hair and blue eyes that caught one's attention. Sarah had always wondered if he and Adria would marry one day, but their move to Jamaica had changed things.

"Jeffrey, you have grown into such a handsome young man! We have been gone only a few years, but it appears so much has changed."

"Well, I must say, Jamaica evidently agreed with you, Aunty. You are as beautiful as ever." Sarah smiled and quickly recalled his charm.

"I was concerned to think you might have been married off by now, Jeffrey."

The young man laughed and nodded. "Yes, Mother had all but promised me to Beatrice Smith, but calmer heads pre-vailed — mostly mine," he chuckled, "and I remain unattached." He followed Sarah and they both took a seat in the drawing room. "Perhaps it was all those times of playing wedding day with Adria that kept me from going there."

"You were inseparable, and your mother and I sat through more than one mock wedding with you two. Remember the tablecloth train on her dress?"

Jeffrey laughed and said, "Yes! I thought you were going to fall out of your chair when you saw your grandmother's tablecloth trailing her on the floor!" He reached over and gave her a hug. "I must say, you handled it well."

Sarah smiled and said, "Thank you, Jeffrey. I can't remember the last time I laughed. I think you're just what we need to help pull her out of her fog."

A frown crossed Jeffrey's face as he said, "Fog? What do you mean?"

Sarah walked away to try and gather her thoughts before answering. Turning toward him, she said, "She hasn't been herself for a while now, not getting out of bed, eating poorly. I'm really worried about her." *I can't tell him, not yet.*

"Well, I'm excited to see her and will do my best to make her smile." He thought for a second and continued, "Your note stunned me as I did not know you were back in London. Mother hadn't mentioned it." Jeffrey's mother, Chelsea, was Sarah's childhood friend.

"I asked her to keep it quiet as I knew Adria wasn't ready for the social scene just yet." Sarah went back to the settee and sat down; he followed. She leaned forward and poured them both a cup of tea, handing one to Jeffrey. "Again, I must warn you, Adria is not herself since we returned."

"I recall your note alluding to something being amiss. What's wrong?" He looked over his teacup's edge at her.

Sarah looked away and stared out a window to see yet another gray day. "Many things happened in Jamaica that contributed to her broken spirit. I'm hoping your old friendship will be enough to bring her back to us." Sarah's not-so-hidden agenda intrigued Jeffrey. He still cared for Adria and had been quite surprised at his own reaction when she left for Jamaica. The two had exchanged letters while he attended college. The letters had dwindled between them over the three years she was gone as he pursued his education, but the memory of Adria never did. He sometimes wondered if that was why he could never embrace his mother's idea of a marriage match with Beatrice. He and Adria had grown up as best friends since they were six years old. They were inseparable as youngsters, climbing trees, swimming in the river, and riding horses all over the countryside. Jeffrey's family lived on the outskirts of London at Mansfield, their family estate.

"Understandable." He looked around. "Well, where is she?"

"She has pretty much remained in her room since we got back. Let me go upstairs and see if I can beseech her to see you." Sarah started to head for Adria's room. Turning back toward him she added, "Please don't be offended if she refuses right now." Sarah had mentioned Jeffrey's impending visit to Adria the day before but wasn't certain much of what she had said registered with her daughter.

"Not to worry. Please let her know how much I've missed her." Sarah smiled, turned, and walked up the staircase. Jeffrey walked around the sitting room looking at pictures that took him back to his childhood. He ran his hand over the desk where they had played school as kids. Adria was always the teacher and him, the student. He smiled as he remembered her threatening to paddle him with a ruler. He held a gift for Adria and hoped she would see him. Sarah's voice brought him back to the present as she called his name. He walked to the bottom of the staircase. Sarah and Adria stood at the top. Adria looked much as she did a few years ago, but thinner. He suspected it had to do with her ailment, whatever that was. "Adria! You look lovely. Please come down so I can give you a proper greeting, my lady." He bowed.

Adria took a deep breath. Her mother had warned her that Jeffrey might come that day. She had forced herself out of bed and to her dressing table to pull a comb through the tangles in her hair and was surprised she cared.

JEFFREY CAUGHT HIS breath as Adria walked down the staircase. She was thin but had blossomed into a beauty. He walked over and took her hand. "Adria, you're even more beautiful now than when you left!" He'd forgotten how hypnotizing those gorgeous green eyes could be. He bent down and kissed the back of her hand.

Adria shrank back, but just a little. She felt her heart lift at the sound of his voice. "Thank you, Jeffrey. Just seeing you has reminded me of how much I've missed you."

"I brought you this." He handed her the box wrapped in pink paper with a bow on top.

"Oh, my," she said. She hesitated but decided it would be rude not to accept the gift. She pulled the bow and opened the paper to find a box of her favorite gardenia scented perfume. "Jeffrey! You remembered," she said.

"How could I forget? There were some days you had used so much, I thought you'd bathed in it!" he laughed. She giggled, remembering dousing herself.

"Quite true. I had very little self-control back then." She opened the bottle and dabbed some behind her ears and on her wrists. "Mother, look!" She showed Sarah the bottle.

"Oh, Jeffrey, how thoughtful of you," Sarah said.

"Mother had taken to making gardenia scented oils when we were in Jamaica – " Adria's voice trailed. She didn't like to think about the island she'd left behind. "It was a great imitation, for sure."

Jeffrey reached over and lifting her wrist, he sniffed the gardenia scent. "My, how it transports me!" he said.

Their reunion was swift and joyful. Adria's heart soared when he made her smile again, if only for a brief while. Sarah ducked out of the room once she was sure Adria was comfortable. Jeffrey took Adria's hand and led her to the settee where they sat next to each other. They sat and talked about their childhood, although he couldn't manage to get her to speak of Jamaica very much, sensing that was where her pain remained. The more they talked, the more hopeful he became at bringing the old Adria back.

He turned and looked at her, coming a little closer. "Come to Mansfield and we will ride together again. Remember our days of riding through the fields? Noel and Streak are waiting for us." She immediately remembered riding together at his family's estate. Adria thought for a moment as remembrances of the carefree days of their youth that were filled with laughter and adventure filled her mind.

"We're not the same people we were then," she said. Seeing his shoulders droop in disappointment, she decided to try. "But I think that might be a good idea." Taking a deep breath, the edges of her mouth turned into a grin. "It would certainly be a good diversion and get me out of this awful gray city."

Sarah stood at the doorway and peeked in on the reunion. Her heart sang when she saw the slightest hint of a smile cross Adria's face. Just to see her out of bed, talking and making conversation, made hope a welcome visitor. Sarah had begun to believe she would never get her daughter back. Looking at Margaret who stood in the background and winked at her, she was encouraged. Maybe my plan is working. I pray so. Sarah and Margaret slipped out of the doorway, leaving the two alone.

JEFFREY AND ADRIA rode through the countryside. Pressing her heels on the horse's side urging Noel to run faster, her skirts flew behind her, providing a feeling of flight. The wind hit Adria in the face, cold, but welcome, making her feel alive again. She didn't know where the fog in her head had gone but knew she didn't want it to return. It was as if the wind pushing on her face had blown the cloud away and squeezed the negative memories out of her head. "This makes me feel so free! It's been too long since I've ridden like this," Adria said to Jeffrey after they pulled the horses to a stop.

Holding on to Streak's saddle pummel, Jeffrey leaned toward her and said, "It's wonderful to see you ride like the wind again. You were always a better equestrian than me!"

"Let's go!" she said.

Adria and Noel took off again and Jeffrey followed on Streak. She steered Noel toward the overlook where she and Jeffrey had spent countless hours climbing and pretending during their childhood years. She pulled Noel to a stop and slid off the horse. Jeffrey pulled up beside her, dismounted and said, "Well, you remembered how to get here I see. You're still hard to keep up with!"

"It was like balm to my soul. Thank you so much for suggesting this." She took a deep breath and smiled.

"I'm delighted you're feeling better. It's so good to have you home, Adria."

"For the first time since I left Jamaica, I feel perhaps life still holds something for me," Adria said.

"I think you're talking about hope," Jeffrey said. Just from hearing her words, he now had a little more hope too.

She looked at him as he took her hand and led her to their old spot under the oak tree. Her other hand reached out and traced the letters they had carved there years before. "Look at this, Jeffrey."

He reached up and touched the carved letters, "J + A."

"I'd forgotten about your birthmark." He took her hand in his and kissed the heart-shaped birthmark on the back of her hand.

"You used to tease me and say I'd been kissed by Saint Valentine," she said. Remembering her time with him opened up memories that reluctantly made her smile.

"I must admit, I have missed this," Jeffrey said. "I so rarely ride anymore. It must be because you weren't here to share it with me. I am so grateful you're home, Adria." He looked into her eyes, but she quickly looked away. The dark cloud seemed to cover her again. Yet he refused to let it rain on their time together. "Let's enjoy the picnic your mother and Margaret put together for us." He laid down the blanket from his saddlebag and she grabbed the satchel full of food. They sat down to eat and talked about their mutual friends and the social status of each. Many had married and started families.

"Yes, Harold and Amelia are married and expecting their first child next month." Jeffrey worked to catch her up on everyone, but quickly wished he'd waited. The cloud returned again, but this time it rained tear drops down her face. "What's wrong, my love? Did I say or do something to upset you?"

Adria looked at him. She was so tired of feeling this way, of having the secret drag her back into sadness. Perhaps the only way to rid herself of it was to let it out. So, she did. She knew she ran the risk of alienating herself and her family from London society should the secret ever get out, but at this point, she felt she had nothing left to lose. Jeffrey had always been her confidante and now here he was again. She stared down at her hands and poured out her story about what she thought was "love" in

Jamaica and the son she had lost. When she finished her confession, she warily looked up and into his eyes. The eyes that held no judgment for her messed-up life.

"Adria, we all have things we wish we hadn't done. Things we're not proud of, but from what you have told me, the only thing you are guilty of is love and maybe a little impetuousness." He pulled her close and could smell her gardenia scent. "No one knows you better than I. There is nothing to be ashamed of." She let out a deep breath as if she had been holding it inside for years. Her shoulders slumped in resignation and relief all at once. She knew his words were true and to hear them gave her absolution of sorts. "I am so sorry your baby boy died."

She'd never heard those words spoken, at least not that she could recall. His words broke through the heavy exterior shell she had worked so hard to create. Leaning into him, she cried until her soul was wrung out, but her spirit refreshed.

Finally, she sat up and pushed her hair from her eyes. "Thank you, Jeffrey. I don't know what else to say except for the first time in so long, I feel as if I have a life left to live." Wrapping his arms around her, she pulled back a little, sensing his desire to kiss her. "You have been such a blessing to me, but I'm afraid of another relationship just yet."

He stroked her hair. "I understand, Adria. Just know I'm here for you for whatever you might want or need." He kissed the top of her head. He was willing to wait.

—Chapter Thirteen—

*Sudden power is apt to be insolent, sudden liberty saucy;
that behaves best which has grown gradually." —Benjamin Franklin*

1720, Nanny Town, Jamaica

When Amari first arrived at the Maroon village, he had considered running off on his own, but where would he go? He'd listened to the conversations while he was at Ginger Star and deciphered the plan at hand as best he could. Between hand gestures and words, he understood most of the conversations, and communication was getting easier. He knew enough to know the Maroons were his best alternative. A chance to live a free life; if not the freedom of his homeland, at least he would be no man's slave. He hoped it would be a life that was somewhat like the one he left behind. At least a little. Thoughts of Kwasi kept him praying to Mawu and Lisa for his safety, and thoughts of his family kept him sane.

Saying goodbye to Ronnie had been one of the hardest things he'd ever done. She'd saved not only his life but given him hope in the midst of what could have been a horrendous future. He was amazed at this woman who had given so much of herself when he needed it most, knowing he could give her nothing in return except his undying loyalty. His biggest comfort was that

Elijah was still with him. Somehow, he'd found an unconditional love within his heart for this little boy.

Elijah had become a lifeline for Amari, and he wanted nothing more than to be a father to the boy. The baby had brought him to the Maroon village and while it was not his homeland, there were many here like him; those who had been captured and blessed enough to escape the chains of the white man. Stories of abuse and escape were plentiful and linked to their hopes and dreams for the future. They all agreed they could never let themselves forget the bondage of their past in order to ensure the freedom of their future.

He'd asked the Maroon council to allow him to stay with Elijah and help with his care. He could tell it was an unusual request as most men left the raising of a baby to their wife, but since Elijah had no mother, the council had agreed. He and the baby shared a hut and Amari learned to be a father. A wet nurse took care of the baby's feeding needs during the days and Amari fed him from a bottle in the middle of the night. He became quite adept at changing, feeding, and getting him back to sleep in short order. As Elijah grew, so did Amari's love for him. Weeks turned into months and before he was a year old, Elijah was walking everywhere.

Once Amari's physical abilities and loyalties were confirmed, the Maroon warriors trained him in jungle warfare. Amari had some ideas of his own from his days of hunting with his father and friends in his homeland. The village had some weaponry of the white man — rifles, pistols, some ammunition, and gun powder — but they had to portion that out marginally, so practice with those weapons was kept to a minimum. They used some of the white man's tactics with swords, but they always knew their best defense was a good offense. They worked to stay a step ahead of the British.

During raids and battles, the Maroons covered themselves with leaves and branches so they could lie in wait camouflaged as the British soldiers tried to reach their village. There was only one way in, and the Redcoats were easy to spot and pick off. After a while, it seemed the Brits quit trying to get to their village. Nevertheless, the Maroons were always camouflaged — waiting.

AMARI REACHED OUT and took the broom from his mother's hand. She smiled and spoke to him in his native tongue. "You must do this every morning," she said.

"But what if there is no dirt to sweep away?" he asked.

"The dirt is not what is important. It is the negative spirit we must sweep out of our lives."

He reached over to touch her shoulder, but she faded away as if a vapor.

Amari woke with a start to find his hand reaching out to touch her again. He'd had the same dream many times, trying to bring his mother back to him. Here it was, a year after his capture and beginning his life with Elijah and the Maroons, yet still, he yearned for his homeland and family. He shook his head, knowing the longing would never stop. But he took comfort in these now familiar surroundings. He had found solace in Jamaica with Elijah and was no man's slave, and for that, he was forever grateful. Having someone to love and call his own became his joy. Elijah, now a young boy called him "Papa." Amari knew he was where he belonged.

—Chapter Fourteen—

"There was never a good war, or a bad peace." —Benjamin Franklin

Ocho Rios, Jamaica

The trip back to Ocho Rios was fairly easy and uneventful for Marshall, Mavis, and Ronnie. The storm had turned back out to sea before making much of an impact. There were a few downed trees along the way, but nothing that impeded their travel for long, and flooding along the shore had been kept to a minimum.

Pulling up in front of the mercantile, it appeared only the sign out front had blown down along with a few tree limbs here and there. Scottie flew from branch to branch, flapping his wings and squawking, welcoming them home. Mavis pulled out her key and opened the padlock. Pulling the door open, Shadow cried and wove in and out of their legs as they walked in. Both stood in awe of the miracle before them. Everything was intact.

"Nothing short of a miracle, I would say!" Mavis said feeling as if a huge weight had been lifted from her shoulders.

"I'm thinking that is an accurate assessment, my friend." Ronnie put her arm over Mavis' shoulder and squeezed.

"It looks like all the preparations you both did paid off," Marshall said. "If you give me a hammer, I'll pull the wood off the outside of the windows before I leave."

Reaching into her toolbox under the counter, Mavis pulled out a hammer and handed it to him. "All you had to do was ask!" She laughed with relief.

Ronnie saw a second hammer in the box and pulled it out. "Here's another one. I'll lend you a hand so you can get on the road back to Ramble House," Ronnie said.

"Why thank you. I appreciate the help," Marshall said.

Mavis grinned at the two of them. Their attraction to each other was hard to hide.

"Are you alright in here alone?" Ronnie asked Mavis.

"Why of course. Shadow needs some attention and I'll get the store ready to open." She winked at Ronnie letting her know her ulterior motive didn't go unnoticed. "You can use the store ladder instead of trying to drag the bigger one out of the stable."

RONNIE HELD THE door open while Marshall carried the ladder outside and leaned it up against the building. "I'll climb up and pull the nails out on top and you can do the bottom."

"Sounds like a good plan to me," Ronnie said. They got to work and pulled the wooden shutters off the front of the store first. As they started pulling the last shutter down, Ronnie asked, "So, how often do you come into Ochi?"

"Well, it varies, but typically every ten days or so, sometimes more," Marshall said. He stepped off the ladder as she continued to pull the last nail out of the shutter. He grabbed hold of the wood and lowered it to the ground once it was loose. Carrying it over to the stable, he added it to the pile they had assembled in the corner.

"Is there anything we should add to your list of needed supplies for when the next shipment arrives?" Ronnie asked. Mavis kept a list of specific needs for her regular customers.

"Yes, as a matter of fact, I have a list right here." He reached into his pocket and pulled out a piece of paper. "I'll check in with you when I come back next week." Marshall handed the paper to Ronnie. Since meeting Ronnie, he'd always made it a point to stop at the store. He wondered if it showed.

A MONTH HAD passed since the hurricane and the store was as busy as ever. Ships began arriving a few days after they were back in Ocho Rios. Their shelves were stocked once again. Ronnie checked to make sure they put all of Marshall's needed supplies aside and found herself looking forward to his visits. Ronnie opened the shop quietly in an attempt to allow Mavis to sleep late. She'd had a lingering cough ever since they returned from Ramble House and Ronnie insisted Mavis needed some extra rest. Since Ronnie planned to stay in the storefront for the morning, she took down the bell on the door so there would be less chance of Mavis waking from its tinkling. She put some food in Shadow's bowl as the cat curled around her legs and reached in the salt barrel to grab a fish head to keep her from meowing. "Shh!" she hushed Shadow. Not that it helped any. Only food in the bowl would quiet her.

Try as she might, thoughts of Marshall continued to invade Ronnie's days. She thought of questions she wanted to ask him. She wondered when she might see him again and tried to figure out why she cared.

Ronnie readied the cash box and pulled out the account ledger and ink well. The door opened as she bent down to stock the lower shelves that ran along the side of the store. Ronnie stood and said, "Good morning! How can I help you?" She turned to look at the customer, but his back was facing her as he perused the fruit and vegetables displayed on the counter of the opposite wall. He was dressed in traditional pirate garb. She could spot a member of a pirate ship from her days in Nassau and now the north coast of Jamaica, but it was more than that. There was something familiar about the way this person was dressed.

"Just what I was looking for!" He picked up an orange. His voice was somehow familiar. "Are they any good?" He turned around to face her.

Ronnie felt her face blush and stomach tighten. *Could it be?* She looked at the orange in his hand, only the hand did not look like that of a man's. *Too smooth. And the red hair. I wonder if it could be her. It has to be!*

"Yes, I enjoyed one just this morning for breakfast," Ronnie said. Their eyes met and time took a break. Scottie broke the silence and chimed in. He paced back and forth on the window sill.

"Enjoyed one for breakfast!" They both looked at the bird and then back at each other.

"Anne?"

"Ronnie?" She didn't know whether to be excited or scared. It never occurred to Ronnie that she would run into anyone from Nassau here on the north coast of Jamaica in the sleepy little fishing village of Ocho Rios. Let alone Anne. Ronnie had been confident her past was securely locked away where it belonged, in the past. But here it was staring her in the face in the form of an old friend. The only real friend she'd ever had in Nassau.

Mavis' words popped back into her head. "The only way to get over your past is to face it." *Why did she always have to be right?*

The man who turned out to be a woman walked over and hugged Ronnie. "I wondered what became of you!" Anne said. "I was disappointed when we last returned to Nassau and you weren't there." Anne leaned back and looked at Ronnie holding her by the shoulders. "No one knew what happened to you. Jack was afraid you'd gotten caught up in the war." The British had been determined to reclaim Nassau and New Providence Island from the pirates who had reigned there for years. Pardons were offered to encourage their participation, but instead, many pirates who had fought and competed with each other for years banded together to fight the British government. Anne removed her hat. She shook her head and allowed her red hair to fall to her shoulders.

"Well, that is what prompted me. I knew once the violence broke out, anything could happen."

"You were quite right to leave. Although, Ruby's did manage to make it through relatively unscathed." Just the sound of her former employer's name made Ronnie cringe. That part of her life was an unwelcome memory. Anne could sense Ronnie's disinterest in talking about Nassau. She knew her well. She looked behind Ronnie to make sure there was no one else around.

"We're alone for now," Ronnie said.

"So, how did you get out of Nassau? We heard it was hard to navigate the harbor right before the fighting broke out." Woodes Rogers, the new governor of the Bahamas, and the British Navy, had blocked access to the Nassau Harbor making it difficult for anyone with a ship to escape.

"I was able to take on a disguise much like yours and joined the Neptune as part of the crew, right before they closed the harbor." Slicing an orange into four pieces, she handed Anne one and took a bite out of another. "They were headed to Port Royal, but after getting caught in a storm, we were boarded and taken over by the Vulture." *How much should I tell her*? There was a time when Anne was the only person in the world she would confide in.

"So, how did you end up here in Ocho Rios?" Anne asked and took another bite of the orange.

"As we were navigating the north coast of Jamaica toward Port Royal, the captain realized who I was, or was not, I should say." Ronnie knew Anne could relate. Anne Bonny was the most notorious woman of their era, always dressing in men's clothing and taking part in acts of piracy with Calico Jack Rackham, along with another infamous female pirate, Mary Read. "I knew it was either jump ship or endure the consequences. I chose the former." *I should hold off on Amari's story, at least for now.* "I know my limitations. I'm not the fighter you are, although you taught me well." Ronnie grinned, took a deep breath, and continued. She remembered sparring with Anne using broomsticks for swords. Ronnie never beat her but had managed to glean a few of her moves.

Anne recalled recent rumors. "Are you the woman they talked about that escaped with a slave?" Anne's eyebrows raised in curiosity and her head tilted to one side. "The story was all over Port Royal last we were there."

Ronnie stood still. Her mind reeled and she blinked hard and long, trying to gather her thoughts. *They were telling stories about Amari and me? Why didn't it occur to me that Lewis and his shipmates would talk?*

"They're telling stories of me?"

"Sure appears that way." Anne reached over and slapped Ronnie on the arm. "Who was the slave anyway? Where is he?"

Ronnie hesitated and Anne noticed. "You don't have to tell me."

"Well, it really is a sensitive situation, not that I don't trust you." She peeked behind the curtain that led to the kitchen, wanting to make sure Mavis was still sleeping.

Anne could read her old friend well and knew enough to change the subject. "How long have you been here?" Ronnie handed Anne the rest of the orange. She knew she needed all the fruit she could get to ward off the scurvy that weeks at sea could bring.

"Mavis, the owner of this shop, took me in shortly after I arrived." Ronnie tried to steer the conversation away from Amari. "Enough about me, why are you in Jamaica? And on the north coast, no less." She knew most pirates hung out on the other side of the island, in Port Royal.

Ronnie felt a level of trust with Anne that most did not. She knew Anne could be trusted with secrets, but just the thought of telling anyone, even Anne, about Elijah, was too painful. Just thinking about Elijah and Adria choked her up. To verbalize it was unthinkable. She didn't think she could confess it without breaking down.

"We docked in Dry Harbor and are staying at Queenie's. Jack decided he was in need of a few days off the ship for some restoration and Ocho Rios was a great option. Especially now that I have found you once again!" Anne reached over and pulled Ronnie in for a hearty hug. She leaned back and looked at her old friend. "Would you be able to join Jack and me for a meal while we're here? I know he would love to see you again."

Ronnie looked at Anne. Something was different. Something had changed in her attitude, but also her countenance. Nodding she said, "I think I could work that out."

"Why don't you come to Queenie's tonight around 6 and we can eat right there at her pub?"

"I would love that. I'll be there."

Anne picked up six oranges and also a bottle of Jamaican rum. "Here, let me take this stuff off your hands."

Ronnie counted the fruit and added up the cost. Anne reached in her pocket, pulled out coins, and laid them on the counter.

"It was such a wonderful surprise to find you here, my friend. I'll see you tonight. We're in room ten toward the front on the second floor, right side." Anne tucked her hair back up under her hat. Ronnie wondered why she felt the need for the disguise now but decided not to ask. She was half afraid Mavis would walk in and ask questions she was not ready to answer.

"I will be there, my friend!" Ronnie smiled and hugged Anne good-bye.

Anne picked up the sack and headed out the door.

Ronnie stood and stared after her. *What just happened?* She'd found an old friend, and that part thrilled her. But, with that discovery, her past had come back to life. She'd wanted the past to stay in Nassau, but here it was, breathing the same air. She remembered Mavis' words: "The best way to get beyond the past is to face it." So, she did.

RONNIE WALKED UP the street and around the corner to Queenie's. The building was wooden and painted in brown and yellow tones. No building seemed to hold onto its color for very long given the salt air from the sea and strong sunshine it tried to withstand. The lodge stood in the front with a restaurant on the bottom level. The brothel was toward the back of the building in a useless effort to be discrete.

Ronnie walked up a flight of stairs and down the outdoor walkway to room ten. Ronnie raised her hand to knock on the door when it opened fast. Jack stood there with no clothes on. He was a dashing man with dark hair and blue eyes that flew open wide when he saw her. "Why Ronnie, my love, it's wonderful to see you!" He bent over and crisscrossed his arms in front of himself when it occurred to him he was naked. "Yes, excuse me one minute?" He started to lift his hand indicating his quick return but thought better of it. Ronnie recognized that funny quizzical look that belonged exclusively to Jack. He slammed the door in her face.

Ronnie smiled and shook her head as she remembered Jack Rackham, known as Calico Jack to many. Not much had changed. His charm and quick wit got him out of most uncomfortable situations. A swordsman, not so much, but he had a keen sense of knowing which way to duck. Landing on his feet was his specialty. He'd started his career with the then-king of pirates, the crazy and ruthless Charles Vane. Jack encouraged an insurrection when Vane refused to take on a French man-of-war on its way to Hispaniola. Vane was voted out of his position as captain and was left along with fifteen of his men on a small sloop, adrift in the sea.

Jack quickly moved up the ranks until he was named captain of his own ship, formerly the William, now renamed the Vanity. Jack's famous black flag of a skull and two crossed swords flew on his mast. She stared over the railing at women sitting on men's laps at the tables below. Hands roamed and lips teased until one couple at a time headed up the stairs to privacy. Sounds of pleasure floated from behind the thin walls. She heard the door open behind her and she turned to see Anne. She wore in a green dress, highlighting her red hair. "Well, there you are!" Anne said. She stepped back to allow Ronnie to enter. The room was cluttered with clothes and belongings strewn from one end to the other. The sack with oranges from the mercantile spilled out onto the bureau and the bottle of rum sat next to them, half empty. Ronnie recognized Anne's jewelry box that sat next to the rum. It was black onyx with an inlaid mother of pearl design. "I remember your jewelry box." She nodded toward the dresser.

"I always admired it." Ronnie walked over and ran her finger over the design.

"Yes, it is the only thing I have left of my mother," Anne recalled. Ronnie noticed her eyes took a trip to another time, but only for a second.

Jack sat on the edge of the bed that was tossed about and pulled on his boots. He stood, towering over Ronnie, and pulled her in for a hug. "Well, my lady, Anne tells me you escaped Nassau just in time. It's a bloody mess there now." He leaned back and made an assessment of Anne's old best friend and his confidante. Not that long ago, he would go to Ronnie for advice when he and Anne would battle, which was often. "You're looking great, my dear. Life agrees with you, no matter which island you're on."

Jack grabbed a colorful yellow cotton shirt, put it on, and began to button it up. His wardrobe was very different from most pirates that cruised the seas. Refusing to wear the woolen garb in the Caribbean heat, he donned loose fitting Calcutta cotton shirts. They were dyed bright colors and hence the name "Calico Jack."

"I see you are still wearing your signature wardrobe, Jack," Ronnie said.

"Absolutely! How do you ever think I managed to outlast them and take over the William? The Brits were sweating like the pigs they were. After fifteen minutes with the swords, they were easily slammed to the deck!" Jack's arms flailed through the air as he mimicked his enemy. "Had I been dressed in that awful scratchy winter coat of mine I too would have melted into a puddle."

Realizing that Jack could go on forever, Anne stood and said, "I'm famished. I suggest we take our leave and go down for dinner." Anne grabbed Ronnie's arm and pulled her out of the room. Jack walked behind them down the wooden walkway to the stairs. From the stumble in his walk, it was apparent he'd already gotten into the rum. The sun was making its way down behind the top of the mountain that climbed up behind Ocho Rios. Evenings always came early on the north coast as the sun dipped behind the mountain range. A young boy in Queenie's employ walked around and lit the torches placed throughout the grounds providing light and shadows that danced on the walls.

A woman with bright red lips and a bosomy black dress led them to a table. The sea reflected the moon on its surface, commanding everyone's attention, if only for a second. Jack pulled a chair out for both Anne and Ronnie. They sat and listened as the woman laid a hand-written list of the available meals on the table. "The special for this evening is red snapper." Jack looked up and said to the woman with red lips, "These two beautiful ladies will have a grog with lime juice and I'll take my rum straight up." She nodded and took off toward the bar.

Looking at Ronnie, Jack asked, "What's your plan, Ronnie? Will you stay in Jamaica?"

She felt safe sharing her plans, or lack thereof, with her friends. "I believe I will. There's no place else that calls my name and I've begun to feel at home here." Ronnie picked up her glass. "It certainly is a bewitching place, beautiful views from every turn and so far, good people."

"Give it time!" Jack laughed and tossed back the rest of his drink. "Just stay away from the other side of this island. Port Royal is nothing that would interest you." The waitress returned with their drinks. Port Royal was a slave trading capital in the Caribbean, often called Sodom for good reason.

Jack raised his glass offering a toast, "To Ronnie and her great timing escaping Rogers' tyranny!"

Anne chimed in, "And to finding her here in Jamaica!"

"Here, here!" They all said as they clinked their glasses and took a drink.

Anne put her glass down. She asked the waitress for a glass of water and said, "Jack and I rode from Kingston to Ocho Rios once. You're right, the views are spectacular."

"Yes, they are," Ronnie said.

Jack tossed back the rest of his rum and signaled for the waitress to bring him another. "So, Anne tells me you are the infamous female pirate that jumped ship with an escaped slave!" Ronnie jerked forward as he slapped her on the back.

"Well, I neither confirmed nor denied, but it seems the story has leaked, much to my chagrin." Ronnie looked at Anne. "Yes, that's correct. I suppose I should tell you about Amari." The need to share the truth took over. She always was susceptible to Jack's charm. Ronnie went on to explain how she met Amari and what had become of him. She did not talk about Elijah. That was a secret she would not breach. Not just for confidentiality reasons, but because she knew Anne had left her only child behind in Cuba with Jack's mother to raise for her right before Ronnie left Nassau. She wanted to ask if they had been back to visit him but decided to leave that wound untouched.

"So, this Amari now resides with the Maroons. Have they been giving the Brits any trouble of late?" Jack asked. He finished his drink and raised his hand to signal he was ready for another. He was planning a trip to the interior of Jamaica, but decided to keep that idea to himself, for now. Steering clear of the Maroons would be a good idea. "The last time I was here, they had spon-sored a raid on Seville, but Captain Hemmings thwarted them. Just barely." Hemmings was the owner of Seville, the largest plantation on the island. "But then I heard the entire second floor of the Seville great house was damaged in the hurricane."

Ronnie was relieved the conversation had shifted and said, "Yes that's true. It was a terrible mess for him. He has said he won't rebuild the second floor. Instead he plans to modify the remainder and add on to the first floor." She took another sip of her grog and continued. "With regards to the Maroons, I've not heard of any trouble of late. At least we've not heard any Abengs calling from the mountains." The Maroons were famous for using a cow's horn they called an Abeng (a Ghanian term) as a horn to communicate. The British were unable to decipher their codes and never knew what they were saying. Just the sound was enough to put anyone within earshot on edge. Ronnie took a bite of her red snapper. "I don't know that I will ever see Amari again and for that, I am very sad." She put her fork down, suddenly no longer hungry. "If I could only know if he is alright and at least beginning to create a life for himself."

"Well, you never know what fate might bring. Just look at us." Anne raised her glass in a toast. "We certainly didn't envision having your company to enjoy right here on the shore of Ocho Rios," Anne said. "It is wonderful to be able to talk of our plans with someone. It gives me a sense of peace to be able to articulate what it is we want to do." She went on to elaborate on her and Jack settling down in a life on land instead at sea.

"Do you plan to return to Nassau?" Ronnie asked as she took the last bite of her fish. She swallowed what was left of the grog Jack had reordered for her. The warmth of the liquor slid through her.

"Hell no!" Jack said and tossed back another swig of his rum. "The pardons created a world that none would want to live in. At least not me!"

Anne gave him a look making no secret she wished he'd quit drinking. She'd witnessed Anne dumping his drink into a nearby plant, but it proved to be fruitless. He would just order another.

Jack went on, "Given our current disposition to become retired pirates," he said looking at Anne, "we would like to return to Nassau, but I have been told Woodes Rogers has revoked my pardon and issued a warrant for my arrest instead. And all just because I took over a few small fishing boats!" He shook his head and held his glass up to let the woman know he wanted another refill. "So much for living a righteous life in Nassau," Jack said. "Not that anyone ever will."

"Given its history, I tend to agree," Ronnie exclaimed.

"We're planning to return to Cuba and raise Cunningham together." Ronnie was relieved that Anne had finally mentioned their son. Anne looked from Ronnie to Jack and said, "I'm actually looking forward to my role as a mother and one of these days, that of a wife," Anne said. Winking at Jack, she held her hand out toward Ronnie. A large diamond ring glittered in the lamplight.

"Oh my! How lovely!" Ronnie held Anne's hand and stared at the ring. "You didn't have that on this morning," she looked at Anne, "But I suppose it didn't go very well with your disguise." They smiled at each other. Ronnie knew Anne was still married to James Bonny. Jack had appealed to him with a large cash settlement if he would give Anne a divorce by purchase. Bonny refused and tried to enlist the aid of his supervisor, Woodes Rogers, to punish her on the charge of adultery. Anne and Jack fled Nassau and forfeited Jack's pardon by stealing a sloop. They sailed the Caribbean for a few months, taking over other pirate ships before going to Cuba where Anne gave birth to Cunningham.

"When will you wed?" She looked from Anne to Jack and back again.

"Most say, when pigs fly!" Jack laughed. Anne did not. She stared at the table.

"Well, a divorce would be preferable, I'm sure!" Ronnie looked at Anne wishing she had kept the last comment to herself.

"I think you read my mind," Anne said. "James turned Jack's offer down. Again. If ten thousand pounds wasn't enough to get him to agree, I don't suppose it will happen. At least not legally.

But then again," she said looking over at Jack, "We've never been known for being law-abiding citizens before." Anne shrugged. "Why start now?"

'Here! Here!" Ronnie said as she raised her glass in a toast. Her spirits lifted. The grog was having its way with her mood. The thought of a new beginning for all of them suddenly had a grand appeal.

"I look forward to simply worrying about how the fish are running." Anne said glancing at Jack. He raised his eyebrows and nodded in agreement. Ronnie had always recognized the love that passed between these two and here it was again. "We have already secured a few fishing boats." She referred to their capture of a small fleet earlier that week on the north coast of Jamaica. "We plan to open a fish market when we get back to Cuba. At least that way, we will be at sea part of the time," Anne said.

"Truth is, we commandeered a few fishing boats right before we docked at Dry Harbor, so we are indeed ready for business." Jack added. He shared the common trait among pirates, bragging about a conquest. Anne was always wary once Jack had too much to drink. His lips loosened. It was hard to tell what he might share. "I just have to find a way to keep them under wraps and get back to Cuba before anyone figures it out." He looked from Ronnie to Anne and back again.

"Quality problems, I'm thinking." Ronnie said. "The best kind to have." She raised her almost empty glass and they toasted to their future. For once, she was hopeful she might actually have one.

—Chapter Fifteen—

"Sell not virtue to purchase wealth, nor liberty to purchase power." —Benjamin Franklin

October, 1721, Ocho Rios, Jamaica

Well, if it isn't my old friends, Jack and Anne." The three of them looked up to see Queenie standing before them. "I trust your meal has been good." She had a regal air to her that made it hard to remember she was only five feet tall and sightless. She wore a deep purple turban today, but other than that, looked the same as she had the last time Ronnie had seen her. She wore the same dark glasses as before, but Ronnie noticed she did not use a cane. She knew her way around her place well enough so there was no need.

Jack jumped to his feet, shoving his chair back and hugged Queenie. "I wondered when you would show up! You look wonderful, my love."

"Why thank you, Jack. I would say the same, but we all know I would be less than truthful to remark on your appearance." Queenie smiled. "But it is wonderful to hear your voice once again, my dear." Queenie turned and addressed Anne. "And you, my love. How is life treating you?" She reached over and took Anne's hands in hers. She noticed the engagement ring but didn't mention it. Queenie felt the back of the chair in front of her and pulled it out. Jack pushed the chair under her as she lowered herself and he sat back down.

"Well, it's nice to be here in Jamaica once again. We were in need of a holiday." Anne said looking at Ronnie. "I would like to introduce you to our old friend, Ronnie from Nassau."

"Ronnie?" Queenie turned toward her and extended her hand. Ronnie took it. Queenie's fingers felt her hand finding familiarity in her touch.

"I believe we met not that long ago," Queenie said looking toward Ronnie.

"Indeed we did!" *Uh oh, watch your step, you've been drinking.* Ronnie offered up her explanation to Queenie. "My friend Anne here showed up at the store to purchase some oranges. We were both shocked and thrilled to see one another again."

"Well, it is a wonderful day when we encounter an old friend. Welcome to Queenie's." She turned and faced Jack again. Ronnie was amazed at her intuitiveness and ability to make one forget she was blind. "How long will you stay in Ocho Rios, Jack?"

"I don't have a definitive amount of time in mind, but at least a few more days." He finished another drink. "Why do you ask?"

Queenie raised her hand and got the server's attention for a refill. She leaned in closer so she could lower her voice. "I need to warn you." She looked from Jack to Anne, and back again. "I have heard Governor Lawes has issued a warrant for your arrest and licensed Jonathan Barnet to search for you. I would recommend you make haste to exit the island or at least keep out of sight while you're here." Jack scoffed, but when he saw the resolve on Queenie's face, he backed off. Queenie continued, "It's not wise to take a devil-may-care attitude right now, my dear. And it's not only Barnet that is a threat, but some locals along the north coast are less than enamored with you since you captured several of their fishing boats." Queenie raised her eyebrows at them.

While they knew Rogers was looking for him, he was unaware the Jamaican governor had caught his scent. He was confident the Vanity, the former William and sloop he commanded for now, would not be recognized as being his since he had just recently commandeered it right before landing in Jamaica. He purposely didn't hoist his signature black flag with a skull and swords instead of the typical crossbones to keep pirate hunters at bay, lest they recognize it. "We'll be careful, Queenie. Thank you for the warning. Perhaps we will leave sooner than later after all." He looked at Anne in question.

She nodded. The last thing she wanted was another fight onboard a ship. She doubted she had the energy to withstand it. "Well, darling, it appears our activities are drawing unwanted attention. I think you're right, we need to ship out," Anne said. Cuba was only ninety miles from the north coast of Jamaica.

"Where is Mary?" Queenie asked. She referred to Mary Read, the other infamous female pirate that was known to be a part of Jack's crew.

"She's back on board the sloop keeping the crew in check."

"Well, that's good. It appears as if she needs to keep an eye on you as well!" Queenie said and they all laughed knowing it was true. They shared a few stories of past raucous visits after successful captures.

"Remember the time Hornigold pretended to be me?" Jack asked Queenie.

"He sure did. Thought because I was blind I wouldn't know the difference. Tried to get me to tell him Anne's whereabouts."

Anne tossed back the rest of her grog and said, "Yeah, after that Jack tore down the old flag and put up the one you had made for him. It's remained his signature ever since."

Jack was proud of his new flag for the ship, one he had designed on his own. A skull and two crossed swords as opposed to an entire skeleton. "Well, why would we need a bony body to represent our crew? We let the head represent our wisdom and the swords there to ward off those of our enemies who dare to think of crossing our bow."

"I'm afraid it will take more than a flag to hold them off this time. You had best make a hasty exit." Queenie said.

Jack took hold of Queenie's hand and said, "Let's not allow them to 'cross the bow,' if you will. That can be our code should one of us be in distress. How's that?" He was hoping to make Queenie feel more comfortable with his serious tone and make her smile one more time.

His strategy worked. Queenie's smile flashed once more. "Well, my friends. It has been a delight to be in your company once again." Queenie pushed her chair back and stood. "May God ordain your steps and bring your hopes to fruition." They all stood and exchanged hugs. "Dinner is my gift to you."

"Queenie, it is a true pleasure to see you once again," Jack said and took her hand in his and kissed the top. "Thank you for your hospitality, but a free dinner was not anticipated." He knew better than to argue the acceptance of her gift. Queenie was not one to be denied.

"Many things are not anticipated in this life, my dear. Least of all the surprise of enjoying the company of old friends," she looked Ronnie's way. "And new ones. Enjoy the blessings while you can." Queenie nodded and walked away, navigating her way through the dining room.

The three looked at one another. "Well, I suppose we need to make haste on our exit, my sweet," Jack said to Anne.

"Yes, we must not allow them to 'cross the bow'!" Anne laughed and they toasted once again.

Once the three finished their meal, they sat and reminisced about their lives back in Nassau.

"I must say, I do have a difficult time envisioning the two of you living on land," Ronnie said and looked from Anne to Jack.

"I've come to realize how short our lives here really are," said Jack. "As one grows older, you can see the foolishness of the past and recognize where there is hope in the future." He looked at Anne and covered her hand with his, "The love we have for one another is too precious to risk on the open seas." He looked at Anne with unashamed affection. "It's time to retire from this life of adventure and earn an honest living with no iniquitous trade for once."

Finishing her second grog, Ronnie said, "I've forgotten how much I missed spending time with you two. Memories and laughter are indeed the best medicine." She choked up just a little and continued, "It enables one to come totally out of her own problems for just a little while. Tonic for the soul you might say."

"Well, my dear," he took Ronnie's hand. "Know that both Anne and I love you as a sister. Whatever problems you have belong to us as well."

"Thank you, Jack. I hope you do heed Queenie's advice and don't tarry very long here," Ronnie said and hesitated to ask the question that was on the tip of her tongue. *Go ahead. You'll kick yourself if you don't.* She took the plunge. "Do you know if Rogers is still looking for me?" He had wanted to interrogate Ronnie to see what she knew about a certain pirate's whereabouts.

Anne and Jack exchanged one of their knowing looks with each other. "We wondered about that when we couldn't locate you in Nassau. We didn't want to ask a lot of questions and decided it best to let that sleeping dog lie."

Ronnie sighed from relief and said "Well, at least maybe his interest appears to have waned."

"Agreed. We thought the same," Jack said. "Well, we will stay at Queenie's tonight," he looked at Anne. "and go back to the sloop in Dry Harbor Bay tomorrow to get ready for our voyage in the next day or so."

"Will Mary go with you to Cuba?" Ronnie knew Mary and it was never easy to predict what she would do next.

"She doesn't know what she wants to do as yet," Jack said. "I suspect she will follow suit and retire as well, but we're not sure where she will settle down."

Ronnie smiled. She remembered Mary as a tough and serious woman. She dressed as a man when on the seas and often on land. Mary's love for wearing her disguise as a man was legendary. She'd been practicing it since she was a child. "Please give her my regards," said Ronnie. They all pushed back their chairs and stood. Jack left a few coins on the table for the waitress.

"We will. So, I suppose this will be farewell for a while," Anne said. She put her arm around Ronnie's shoulders as they walked toward the exit of Queenie's. "The next time you see us, we will be teaching Cunningham how to catch and sell fish in Cuba!" Ronnie smiled. She was happy she'd mentioned their son. The thought of Anne and Jack reunited with their little boy made her happy. She knew how it must haunt them both not to know their son. Thinking maybe she overstepped her bounds, she tried to lighten the mood by saying, "Just make sure it's how to catch fish and not how to commandeer a ship!" Laughing, Anne gave Ronnie a little punch in the arm.

Anne and Jack exchanged a glance and Ronnie recognized it as one that shared a thought between the two of them. "I suppose I should take my leave," Ronnie said looking over her shoulder toward home. "Mavis will be wondering why I've been gone for so long." Standing on the walkway next to the restaurant, she said, "I'm finding it difficult to say goodbye. I've not had a chance to talk openly about my life for so long. What a blessing to spend time with you both. I hope we can keep our connection through letters and perhaps a visit one day."

A sense of overwhelming gratitude hit Ronnie. Her eyes welled up as Jack leaned over and kissed her hand goodbye. Her eyes met Anne's and with that, the eyes that held her tears betrayed her will and spilled over. Hugging them both, she turned and hurried away.

RONNIE WALKED ALONG the shoreline toward home. The moon has done away with the need of a candle tonight. It was as bright as she had ever seen. She chuckled to herself at some of the things they talked about during dinner. At the thought of Jack and Anne raising their son together, she smiled and shook her head. They were finally going to live the life they had worked hard to obtain, even if their means to achieve that end had been piracy. It was clear that crazy life was now behind them. She never thought anything, or anyone, could tame Jack Rackham or Anne Bonny, but it appeared that the love they had for one another and their son had done just that. She was relieved they had decided to heed Queenie's advice and leave soon. Ronnie was sorry to see them go but would rather they stay a step ahead of the authorities who sought to punish them. Everyone deserved a second chance. Besides, Cuba was only ninety miles across the sea from Jamaica. She envisioned herself spending time with them there one day.

Ronnie turned and walked away from the shoreline and headed toward home. As she glanced at the mercantile, she could see light inside the windows in the rear. Opening the back door, she stepped inside to find Mavis reading a book in her rocker next to the fireplace. "So, how was your visit, my dear?"

Mavis asked as she closed the book in her lap. "Are your infamous pirate friends doing well?"

Ronnie stared at her. "How did you know?" She had told Mavis she was meeting old friends from Nassau, but that was all. She was stunned that Mavis knew who they were.

"Rumor has it that Calico Jack and his woman pirate lover are in town. I gave it some thought and figured they might be the folks you went to meet." Ronnie walked over and sat in the chair across from Mavis in front of the fireplace. The fire was small but still provided light and a little heat to offset the chill in the night air. "There's a bounty on their heads, you know."

Rumors and stories circulated throughout the Caribbean about Calico Jack Rackham and Anne Bonny. The pirates' torrid love affair lent itself to embellished tales. Ronnie knew much of it to be true, but also knew a side of Jack and Anne that most did not.

Ronnie nodded and said, "The Queenie rumor mill is alive and accurate." Mavis smiled sheepishly when Ronnie figured out who her source was. "Queenie warned us tonight. They're preparing to leave as we speak."

Mavis closed her book on her lap. "Be careful, my dear. You don't want to get caught up in their escapades. Especially now with Jonathan Barnet looking for them." Mavis noticed Ronnie was not surprised about the search. Queenie's information was almost always a step ahead of the rumor mill.

"Everyone knows the Anne Bonny and Calico Jack, the news publications have created in their desire to sell papers, but I know the Anne and Jack that most do not. There is much false rhetoric. Yet, some is true, I must admit." Ronnie sat down across from her. "She has this tough reputation and that is not to say she is not, but she also has a softer side that is very kind — very loving and nurturing." Ronnie went on to tell Mavis how

Anne had nursed her when she was ill but felt it best to leave out the particulars. "I owe her a lot."

"Well, it's good to hear that she has a benevolent side."

Ronnie continued, "She and Jack have decided to retire from the seas and live a quiet life on land."

"Well, I'm glad you were able to reconnect. Good friends are hard to find." Mavis stood, cocked her head, and looked down at Ronnie. "Just be careful." She extended her hand, Ronnie took it and stood, looking into Mavis' eyes. "Word has it Barnet is determined to round them up at any cost." Barnet was a well-known privateer for hire. "He is a formidable opponent, and it is said he needs the payday. You don't want to get caught up in that type of fight, my sweet." Mavis cupped Ronnie's face with her hands. "I've grown accustomed to your company," Mavis said leaning over to kiss Ronnie's forehead. *I'm so thankful for her.* Ronnie looked at Mavis and wept. "My dear! What on earth is wrong?" Mavis asked so afraid she had done something to hurt her. Ronnie sobbed for a few minutes and then gathered herself. Mavis poured her a glass of water. "Here, you'll need to replace all the tears you just cried out, child."

Ronnie raised her head and gazed intently at her, "I'm forever saying thank you to you." Gulping a deep breath to collect herself and keep from breaking down again, she smiled.

"What on earth did I say to bring you to such a state?"

"I'm not sure. I'm overwhelmed with a lot of emotions right now. Thankfulness for you and my past showing up in the form of Anne and Jack. And . . ."

"And what?"

"I think I'm falling in love with Marshall."

"Well, it's about time you realized that!" Mavis smiled.

"That obvious, huh?" Ronnie grinned. "I just don't know if I'm imagining he feels the same or what."

"Oh, my dear. I'm no Queenie, but I can tell he's very smitten with you."

Ronnie's heart leapt at the thought that Mavis could see an attraction, but the reality of her past made her reluctant to be very hopeful. Ronnie said, "That would be wonderful, but it's complicated."

"Well, whatever the 'complications', if it's really love, you two will work it out." Mavis knew there was more to Ronnie's story. However, she felt it best not to pressure her. Ronnie knew Mavis was backing up, again — allowing her some space to pull her muddled thoughts together.

"I can't thank you enough for everything you've done for me. I landed here with nothing and no one. Now here you are caring enough to warn me to be careful as well as encourage me when I need it the most," Ronnie laughed and reached out and hugged Mavis.

"I will be careful, Mavis. Anne and Jack will be gone within the next day or so. The town gossips will be scratching their heads wondering where they went." She didn't want to share their plans of Cuba with anyone. Telling Mavis would only put her in the middle of a situation she didn't need to know about.

Mavis wondered if Ronnie were right about Anne and Jack, but she also knew how relentless Barnet could be. He would often spend a week or two in Ocho Rios celebrating his latest capture. The local businesses were happy to cater to him by keeping him informed of pirate activity and thereby helping to make him a successful bounty hunter. Queenie was definitely going out on a limb to warn the fugitives. Queenie's sources were, more often than not, reliable. She also wondered about Ronnie's life in Nassau. From what she could tell, there was a lot more to it than she had shared so far.

"Barnet is good for the Ocho Rios economy. He spends tremendous amounts of money during his celebratory visits after a capture." Mavis said. The mercantile was one of his favorite places to restock his supplies when in town. Mavis knew him well, even though she didn't trust him. She'd witnessed first-hand his underhanded ways: his willingness to lie, cheat, and steal to get what he wanted. While these were not uncommon characteristics of many people of the sea, she found Barnet to be unashamed of his unscrupulous ways. Despite his occa-sional wealth, good looks, and advances, she had made up her mind long ago to accept his money, but nothing more. "Where is Mary?"

Ronnie wasn't surprised that Mavis knew about Mary Read. Rumors were never in short supply regarding Mary's relationships with members of both sexes. Mary and Anne both continued to be a great source of sensationalism in the papers.

"She stayed aboard to keep an eye on things."

Mavis raised her eyebrows. She knew of Mary Read and how she could take charge when needed. "Well, I cannot think of anyone better to keep a crew in check than Mary, but how do the men respond to her when Jack's not there?"

"From what Jack tells me, there is not a man on board who would dare cross her." Mary's ability to fight an opponent was legendary. Her cunning ways of manipulation were second only to Anne's. Ronnie knew how ruthless Mary could be. She'd witnessed it more than once, as had the crew. "Oh, my thought is if they want their share of the latest plunder, they'll behave."

"Well, I hope they manage to get away. Failure to do so would be tempting fate in a dangerous way."

LIGHT PEEKED THROUGH the cracks in the shutters of the room. Jack slowly pulled the covers back and slid out of the bed where Anne laid sleeping soundly. Being careful not to wake her, he walked over to the desk and quietly pulled out the chair. Sitting down, he wrote her a note. He slipped on his pants and shirt and picked up his boots, leaving his colorful wardrobe in the room. He walked silently to the door. It creaked just a little as he pulled it open causing him to wince. He looked back, but Anne hadn't stirred. Picking up his satchel, he looked over and saw Anne's jewelry box. Thinking it was just the right size for what he had in mind, he tiptoed over to the dresser, emptied it of its contents, and tucked the box into the extra sack. He slipped out without making a sound as he closed the door behind him.

Jack borrowed a horse from Queenie's stable. It was early enough in the morning that no one was around to ask. He left yet another note and a generous amount of coins to make up for any inconvenience. In the note he explained that he would leave the horse in Dry Harbor with the local blacksmith when his task was complete. He knew he wouldn't have time to return the horse and then find a way to Dry Harbor. Barnet would be sniffing around the north coast soon enough, if not already.

Jack rode the brown and white stallion up the road that had turned into little more than a path. He remembered vaguely where the falls were that he and Anne had run across on their trip over the Blue Mountains between Kingston and Ocho Rios. Branches and foliage grew too thick to navigate while riding, so he slipped off the horse's back, held onto the reigns, and walked in front. Pushing the branches aside, he led the horse further up the ravine between the mountains. Remembering the little creek that flowed next to him, he followed it until he could hear the falls.

"Well, I believe we've reached our destination," he said to the horse. "Sorry I didn't have the opportunity to ask your name, old boy," he patted his neck. The falls came from about thirty feet above them and crashed down into a pool surrounded by large boulders and plants sprouting up in between. Tying the reigns around the trunk of a tree, he reached into the saddlebag and pulled out Anne's jewelry box. "She is not going to be happy about this." He shook his head and stared at the box. Now, he wished he had chosen a different container, but there was no changing it now. Pulling out the gold bars, gold chains, and pouch of gold coins he'd taken off the ship, he stacked them carefully inside.

In an effort to protect the box, he grabbed a small blanket from the saddlebag, and wrapped it as tight as possible, and bound it with twine to protect it as best he could. He knew there was going to be hell to pay when Anne discovered it gone. Nevertheless, he knew he had to hide at least some of their cache to keep it out of the hands of Barnet were they to be caught. Jack planned to come back and retrieve the box once he was sure Barnet no longer posed a threat.

Jack wrapped the packaged box with a chain and criss-crossed it on top before linking it together with a padlock. He knew the chain and lock were just a wishful measure and was only enough to keep and honest man honest. Shaking his head, he stuffed the key to the lock deep into his pants pocket. Carrying the heavy box with both hands, he carefully navigated his way around the edge of the pool to the falls. Pushing back large limbs of overgrown plants and flowers, his foot slipped, but he maintained control enough to slow down a bit. The sound of the falls crashing in his ears made it hard to hear his own thoughts. He ducked behind the curtain of water, but not without getting drenched. His blue shirt clung to his frame. He had purposely not put on his pirate gear having left them behind for Anne to collect. He didn't want to be identified should he run into someone, knowing his calico-colored garb could give clues he didn't want to offer.

Jack slipped into the cave behind the falls, but not too far. He had no desire to wake any sleeping bats that might be hanging around. He recalled a ledge he and Anne had used for their lantern and, reaching with his right hand, found it once again. He took the wrapped box and laid it as far back on the ledge as it would go. He could feel the wall of the cave behind it and felt confident it would be safe there — out of the way of a flying bat and the eyesight of a human visitor. Jack made his way back out under the waterfall. Once again, the crashing of the water was deafening. He ducked through the curtain of falling water and grabbed onto a limb as he came out on the other side to gain his balance. Making his way around the pool, he walked back to the horse, unwrapped the reins, and jumped onto his back. He slowly guided the horse out of the forest and back onto the road.

The sound of thunder clapped in the distance. He spurred the horse to move a little faster. Talking to the horse, Jack said, "Typical Ocho Rios weather for November and although I am already wet, I would prefer if we didn't have to fight a storm along the way." The sound of thunder always brought back memories of his childhood. Living on the east side near London's docks, he was often caught in a storm rolling in from the sea. Since he was the oldest of seven, he refused to let his nerves show, but thunder and lightning scared him to his core, not a good attribute for a seaman.

As he rode back down the mountain, he reflected on his early days at sea. Jack joined the crew of a ship at thirteen years old to escape the poverty on land that was his undeniable fate. While he learned not to quiver with fear during a storm at sea, he never did acquire the proficient skill of a swordsman or marksman that most of the crew possessed. However, his ability to think on his feet, motivate his crew, and manipulate the political climate wherever he happened to be proved to be his real strength—and one he knew how to use. "One of the best ways to succeed is to own up to one's weaknesses," he was heard to say more than once—usually after a rum or two. "And surround yourself with those that are strong where you are not." He could charm an entire room with his winning smile and quick wit, and he didn't hesitate to use either one. He wondered if it would be enough to assuage Anne's anger this time. Smiling to himself, he realized that he was probably more worried about Anne's reaction with regards to her jewelry box than running into Barnet.

ANNE SLAMMED HER hand on the desk after she read the note from Jack and shouted, "Who in the hell does he think he is?" She pushed her chair back as she stood toppling it over. "How dare he go without me!"

She picked up a candle stick, intending to throw it against the wall as she normally would, but restrained herself. She took a deep breath and looked around the room. In typical Jack fashion, his belongings were strewn everywhere. It was obvious he expected her to pack his things since he did not. Her first inclination was to leave everything here and take off in a huff. Then, she noticed he had not worn his calico coat or gear he wore on the sloop. She shook her head and muttered to herself. "Why would you leave only half-dressed?" Then it dawned on her. He didn't want to be recognized!

Jack was right in his note; she knew she had to get out of here fast and without fanfare. Barnet was actively looking for them. So, she snatched the satchel and stuffed their belongings inside, including the leftover oranges she had bought from Ronnie. She pulled her hair back and, once again, tucked it away under her hat. She remembered her mother's jewelry box. Turning, she looked on the dresser. The box was gone and it's contents were on the dresser. Kicking over the chair, Annie screamed, "You, dirty rotten . . .!"

Setting the chair back up on its feet, she sat down, and pulled on her boots. She knew Jack had paid for the room, so she wouldn't bother to stop at the desk when she left. After she laid the room key on the bureau, she grabbed the satchel with their belongings, and slipped out the door and down a side path that led down to the sea. She followed the shoreline toward the Vanity, their sloop that was docked in Dry Harbor a few miles down the coast. She kept her head down, oblivious to her surroundings. Anne muttered to herself, irritated that Jack didn't include her, not to mention tell her of his plan. *What was he thinking? He could run into all kinds of trouble and have to fend them off by himself! I fight much better than him and he knows it! Damn men! Why do they think themselves invincible?* She knew Jack was no match in a one-on-one fight. And he knew it too.

THERE WAS NO one on the beach with Ronnie this morning — unless you counted Scottie. She couldn't go far without him trailing close behind. The fishing boats had returned with their hulls full. Which meant that the fishermen were busy negotiating prices for their catches with the merchants in town. Belinda and Arnold were in the midst of setting a price for Charlie's morning catch. There was still plenty of talk about the fishing fleet that was captured by the Vanity, Jack's ship. The locals were plenty steamed that an entire local fleet had been commandeered. Ronnie walked in at the tail end of a conversation about the captured fleet. "Folks are plenty mad about them making off with their livelihood. Should make for an easier round up for Barnet, I'm thinking," Charlie said to Arnold.

Ronnie wasn't interested in the local gossip. She had no desire to hear what the outcome might be. She prayed silently that the Vanity would make it away from Jamaica's north coast and on to Cuba and their safety. It wasn't that far. When she could see there was no quick end to the discussion with Charlie, she motioned to Barb to holler to her when her order of grouper for tonight's dinner and Shadow's fish heads for the week was ready. She took the chance to steal down to the beach and her favorite perch on the almond tree branch.

The morning dawned with the sun peeking through patches of heavy clouds floating her way from the rain forest of Port Antonio. The sun's rays shone down on the sea in between the monstrous clouds making it hard for the eyes to watch for very long. A light breeze provided a cool beginning to what promised to be a steamy day.

The irony of Jack and Anne's plan to live an honest life by stealing the means to achieve it didn't escape her. She knew the lifestyle they led was a tenuous one with terrible consequences were they to be caught. Reflecting on her time with Jack and Anne, she was grateful she had run into her old friends. Seeing them so unexpectedly had given her spirits a boost. Since coming to Jamaica, she had held back from becoming too close with those around her. Hesitating to share who she really was and what her past consisted of kept her guarded. She felt like nobody really knew her. After all, while her past might not be something she was proud of, it did help form who she was today. Why should she be ashamed of that? Mistakes only remain so when we don't learn from them, she remembered Mavis saying.

Ronnie saw someone approaching from a distance down the shoreline. She could hear the person muttering in an angry tone. As the person approached, Ronnie recognized Anne. "You need a new disguise. I'm all too familiar with this one for it to work on me anymore," Ronnie said.

Anne looked up to see who was talking. She spotted Ronnie in the shade, put her hands on her hips, shook her head, and walked up to her and said, "Our paths cross at the most unusual times, my friend."

"It would seem so. I didn't think I would see you again quite so soon. I was hoping you had sailed by now." Ronnie scooted over, making room for Anne to sit. "I heard you fussing. What's Jack done now? Where are you headed?"

"I'm on my way back to Dry Harbor—to the Vanity. 'What has Jack done?' you ask?" She pulled off her hat, let her red hair fall to her shoulders, not caring about her disguise. Sitting next to Ronnie, she sighed heavily. Scottie hopped over to a closer branch. "It's difficult to tell exactly what he's done." Her hands flew in description as she proceeded to fill her in on finding Jack gone when she woke that morning. "He had the audacity to leave me a note saying he had gone into the interior to hide part of our cache. He was afraid of Barnet walking away with a big payoff should we be caught."

"Sounds like Jack."

"Yeah, well, yes it does, but the thing that's most infuriating is that he made off with my mother's jewelry box, I'm assuming to bury it in." Anne picked up an almond from the sand and threw it as far as she could.

"Uh oh! I see why you're upset. Maybe he'll think better of it and transfer the gold into something less valuable before he leaves it behind." That was the best scenario Ronnie could fabricate fast enough to try and assuage Anne's notorious rage. "For now, perhaps you should focus on getting back to the Vanity so you'll be ready when he returns." Ronnie looked at Anne, trying to gauge her level of anger. There were legitimate reasons for the rumors that circulated the Caribbean about Anne's inability to control her wrath. Ronnie had witnessed it in Nassau. "He probably wanted to let you sleep and thought he could get it done quicker by himself." She kept making excuses for Jack. *Why am I so quick to defend him?* She knew the answer to that question. Jack had rescued her on more than one occasion. Once from unwanted advances of the notorious pirate, Charles Vane, and again from a thief that had threatened to rob her.

"We both know Jack doesn't think that way. The path of least resistance is always his first choice. It was there and he took it."

"True enough." Ronnie could remember several instances where Jack's path of least resistance cost him dearly. But like a cat he seemed to have nine lives. He could emerge unscathed from even the biggest blunder, over and over again.

Anne dug the heels of her boots deeper into the sand. "I know you're right. I need to get there soon." She stood up, tucked her hair, put her hat back on, and shook her head. "I'm just not sure I can trust my temper right now. Just because I'm with child, he doesn't want me riding a horse. How stupid is that?" Anne stopped and looked at Ronnie who sat on the limb with her mouth hanging open.

"How stupid is that?" Scottie repeated from a higher branch. "Awwk!" He looked from Anne and back to Ronnie.

Anne looked at him and then back at Ronnie. "Is he yours?"

Ronnie laughed and nodded.

Anne shook her head and said, "Good thing, 'cause I'm in no mood for wise cracks from a bird!"

"Wait a minute. Did you say?" Ronnie started to ask and then thought better of it. Sometimes the less one said, the better. This was one of those times.

Anne took a deep breath, pulled off her hat, and sat back down. "Yes. I'm fairly certain. I'm over a month late. My biggest error was even telling him. He gets quite overprotective when I'm in this condition. We didn't want to tell anyone just yet. We were trying to put our lives back on solid ground when we realized I was expecting.

Taking a deep breath, Ronnie shook her head and said, "That's a lot to deal with." Scottie jumped off the branch and walked back and forth in front of them. "Even so, now that I know you're expecting, I can more readily understand Jack's reasoning. Whether his opinion is well-founded or not, it was his love for you and your child that guided his decision to travel alone. That, plus the risk of being seen between here and there, his theory begins to make sense."

"I should've known I would get no reinforcement from you." Anne smiled and elbowed Ronnie in jest. "My rationale and emotions seem to run amuck when I'm in this condition." Anne placed her hand on her belly.

Ronnie was relieved when Anne smiled. Maybe she was getting through to her in some small way. "Yeah, well, finding reasons to side with Jack against you is a dangerous place to be and not one I relish. I hope I survive my misplaced loyalty!" They both chuckled.

"Yeah, I suppose I need to reevaluate his motives," Anne said.

Ronnie felt the need to warn Anne again. "I can tell you the locals are plenty upset about their captured fishing fleet. It is a good thing you sent them on to Cuba, but I fear the Vanity must do the same very soon. I overheard some gossip this morning in the fish market. Mavis also shared the same warning."

Anne hung her head in resignation, sighed and stood up, ready to leave this time. "It sounds as if our time here has expired. I suppose we get to say goodbye twice this visit. May it not be that long until our paths cross again."

"I hope not, Anne. Please write when you can."

Ronnie stood and looked her friend in the eye. "May your new little one be healthy and your life with Cunningham and Jack in Cuba be all you hope for." They hugged. Walking away, Anne wiped the tears from her eyes with the back of her sleeve in an attempt to pretend they'd never happened.

As she watched her trudge down the shoreline, Anne turned, waved, and continued on. Ronnie couldn't fathom what the future held for her and Jack, but fear threatened to grip her if she thought about the possibilities for too long. She loved Anne and Jack, but knew their destinies were far beyond her control, and even their own to some degree. Between them and Elijah she was learning that other people's choices could hurt as much as her own.

—Chapter Sixteen—

"Three may keep a secret, if two of them are dead." —Benjamin Franklin

October, 1720

*O*nce the mercantile was closed for the day, Ronnie sat in front of the fireplace as it warmed up the chilled night air in the kitchen. Seeing Anne and Jack again had unleashed thoughts she had managed to suppress. Her mind swirled with memories that moved in and refused to leave. The only way she knew how to make the chatter in her head stop was to write. So, she opened her journal to a blank page. "I met back up with Anne and Jack," she began, but stared at the page instead of writing more. Somehow, she found the courage to flip back in the pages of her journal to a time she had tried hard to forget. Reminiscing with Anne and Jack had opened a door she'd worked hard to keep closed since she left Nassau.

The words about her life in Nassau were still there, staring back at her in her own script. It was written over a year earlier in August of 1719. I woke to find Anne looking down at me with concern. Anne told me I had been ill for several days and the child I carried was no more.

Ronnie could see how weak she'd been as she tried to read her own shaky script. She looked up from the page and stared at the dying embers in the fireplace. The memory ignited the raw wound that filled her physically and emotionally. When she lost her parents, first her father and then her mother several years later, she'd felt hopelessly alone. Her pain was inexplicable. Then, here it was again. Although, this pain was far different from the loss of her parents. She'd lost a piece of herself. Looking back down on the page, she continued to read.

"What future have I here other than to make a living at Ruby's? Nassau and New Providence Island is one memory after another of my life that offers nothing but sickness and shame. And with the war certain to start between the government and the pirates, there's no telling what might happen." Reading the words she had written gave her renewed hope. She looked up from her journal. Suddenly, she understood that the pain of losing her baby would never go away. Nevertheless, she also knew there was more life to be lived. She continued to read the words she had written a year ago, while in so much pain.

"There is nothing left to hold me here." She put the journal down, remembering the day her sorrow had transformed to desire. The desire to flee Nassau, the island of pirates and pain.

Turning back to the almost blank page, she began to write. October 15, 1720, I now know I will never forget the pain of losing my baby and its repercussions, but I've encountered hope once again. Hope from old friends and new ones. Hope for a new life. Mum Lettie was right, joy does indeed come in the morning.

She continued to read through her troubled thoughts on the worn pages of her journal. Uninvited tears slid down her cheeks. Her words revealed hurts she'd long denied. Closing her eyes, she allowed herself to remember sitting at her mother's bedside as she floated in and out of consciousness, sometimes recognizing her and other times hallucinating about those who had gone before her. At twelve years old, she prayed her mother wouldn't die, but her prayers went unanswered when her mummy left this world for the next. The words on the pages reflected her imaginary arms flailing at God for taking her mother away. First her mother and then her baby. *Why did I have to survive?* She cried again, her tears landing on the page. Finally, she gave in to the heartache and the many months of denying her emotions and who she really was.

Ronnie felt Mavis' hands on her shoulders as they continued to heave at the will of her sobs. The older woman knelt down in front of her and took her in her arms. Ronnie laid her head on Mavis' shoulder. For the first time since she had left Nassau, she allowed her emotions to meet up with her past. "Let it go, child. Let it go," Mavis whispered in her ear. So, she did. She let go of the pent-up anger, sadness, and sorrow. She cried into the towel Mavis handed to her. Once the tears dried up, she raised her head and looked at her friend.

"I'm so sorry. I'm always laying my problems at your feet."

"My dear, we are here for each other. You have been a sooth-ing balm to me when I reached back into my memories with Jared." Mavis sat on the floor in front of Ronnie. She'd shared many happy and painful memories with Ronnie after supper during their walks on the shoreline or early in the morning as they readied the store for opening. "Confronting your past can be painful, but releasing the hurt is always the healthiest thing one can do."

"You're always helping me pick up the pieces of my life." She looked into Mavis' eyes, ready to let go of her secrets. "My sorrow goes much further back than Elijah and Amari."

"I have always known that to be so, I just didn't know what it was exactly."

Ronnie proceeded to spill out the contents of the journal pages to her friend who felt more like a surrogate mother. "Anne nursed me back to health when I lost my baby." She didn't elaborate as to who the father was, and Mavis didn't ask, thankfully. "My life in Nassau ended horribly. I took the first chance I could to sign onto a ship as a crew member. It turned out a ship called the Eagle was heading to South Carolina, so I figured I would search for what little family I had left there." She took a deep breath and continued. "But the Eagle left without me, saying they didn't need the help, and I had no choice but to beg for a spot on the Neptune and here I am.

"I took a page out of Anne's book and disguised myself as a male. The Neptune was desperate for help since they had a full hull of human cargo, so I made it on board. The rest, you pretty much already know." She knew there was still a part of her story left untold. Like who her baby's father was.

"That must have been quite strange pretending to be a man and learning how to work as a member of the crew," Mavis said. "You must have been frantic when the Vulture overtook the Neptune."

"Yes, it was scary, but looking back, I think it helped me focus on other things instead of my personal losses. Once we were taken over by the Vulture, I had Amari to look after."

She stared into space and took a deep breath as the memory raised its hand again. "The Neptune was initially loaded with human cargo. I panicked at first, but realized I had no options. So, then came the Vulture, my twist of fate, and it turned out, one that I am grateful for."

"Well, I for one am grateful as well. I hope you don't mind, but I've never had a daughter and I suspect the protectiveness I feel toward you is much like that." Mavis watched for a reaction from her.

Ronnie broke into a smile and hugged Mavis tightly. "Mind? Why would I mind?" She leaned back and looked at Mavis. "It's been a long time since I've heard any better words spoken."

Mavis knew there was more to Ronnie's story but decided not to press and ruin the moment. Instead, she offered, "I love having you here with me. Please know you can stay as long as you wish. I for one, hope you never leave."

Suddenly, a loud BOOM rocked the store. It rattled the contents of the shelves. "What in the world?" Ronnie asked and looked at Mavis. She grabbed hold of the ladder Mavis stood on restocking shelves to ensure she didn't fall. She climbed down and they both rushed outside. More loud noises came from the direction of Dry Harbor. "You don't think?" She looked at Mavis. They both feared the Vanity had been intercepted by Jonathan Barnet. They were right.

Each successive blast brought knots to her stomach. Every time the guns fired, the sound reverberated and made her insides shake. She looked at Mavis. "You felt that too?"

Mavis nodded, grabbed her spyglass, and looked toward the bay. "Sounds like they are not giving up easily."

Finally, silence fell. "Did it stop?" Ronnie looked at Mavis, eyebrows raised in hope.

Mavis went to the door and looked through the spyglass again and said, "I believe it has. All I can see is smoke."

Ronnie's first impulse was to jump on Stars and hurry down to the harbor to see for herself, but she resisted. "I suppose we wait." A few minutes later, Barnet's ship, the Tyger, glided by with the bright sunshine giving its two sails an unearthly glow. Ronnie grabbed a spyglass to see if she could spot Jack or Ann. All she could see was Jack's flag, the skull and two swords, flying under Tyger's flag, an indication the deed was done.

DAYS PASSED WITH no news about Anne and Jack, other than Barnet had indeed captured them. Before she knew it, weeks had gone by. Rumors turned into newspaper articles. Jack Rackham and Anne Bonny, along with Mary Read, were taken into custody by Jon Barnet and his crew, but not without a fight.

"I could smell the smoke from my veranda," Queenie said. She sat outside in front of the mercantile on a bench with Mavis, leaning on her cane. Marshall stood on the pathway in front of them holding Rebel's reins and tied him to the hitching post. Ronnie stood in the doorway looking toward the shore, not seeing anything. Today, Queenie wore an orange turban and continued with her report. There was no one in town who knew more rumor and had facts to sprinkle throughout a story than Queenie. "They say the trial will soon come."

Ronnie shook her head. "Just when they were planning a real life together."

"Life is not life without its ironies," Mavis said. Shadow wound in between their feet trying to navigate a lap to jump on. Queenie won as the cat jumped onto her lap. Queenie scratched Shadow behind the ears as she walked in a quick circle and settled down.

"Well, I would fancy a life that did not prefer to laugh at the plans we make," Ronnie said, looking from Mavis to Marshall. He put his arm around her shoulder, turned, and led her down the path toward the shore. He looked over his shoulder at Mavis and Queenie, indicating they would soon return. Mavis turned to Queenie and said, "Perhaps he can calm her down a bit."

"Oh, I'm sure Marshall wants to *calm her down* alright." Queenie smiled as she nodded in their direction. "He'll make up any excuse to wrap his arm around her!"

Mavis laughed. "It appears although you cannot see, you do indeed."

MARSHALL HELD ONTO Ronnie's elbow and said, "So, Queenie tells me you have known the infamous Calico Jack and his partner, Anne Bonny, for some time." They sat on her favorite tree branch. The sea was a dozen shades of blue with the sun casting its spell on the surface and below.

She took a deep breath and replied, "Yes, they've been friends of mine for some time. Anne cared for me when I was ill." Ronnie went on to share her story about Nassau and her childhood in South Carolina as well as losing her baby, although the details about the father — well, she just wasn't willing to go that far. Not yet. Her willingness to suddenly share even this much of her past surprised even her. Every time she shared her story, she felt as if another weight had been lifted from her shoulders. "I am just so worried that their stories may be coming to an untimely end."

Marshall reached down and took her hand in his, covering it with his other one. "Living with the consequences of other people's choices can be difficult." He had often wondered about Ronnie's life before Jamaica. He'd heard the rumors about her and an escaped slave. Asking if she was indeed that woman, he was surprised when she confirmed it. Ronnie shared her story of Amari and his release to the Maroons, thanks to Sam's brother.

"I'm so happy he's living the life of a free man instead of that of a slave, but my heart still aches to know how he is doing. His heart still has to hurt from being ripped from his homeland.

I just can't imagine." She shook her head and stared at the sea. Today, she didn't notice its beauty. She couldn't see it at all. "My heart feels like an anchor that's stuck at the bottom of the sea."

Standing up, she walked to the shoreline and looked west toward Dry Harbor.

Marshall was surprised at himself, instead of backing away from this woman with a troubled past, she intrigued him more every day. Her beauty transcended her troubles and her spirit was kind, yet confused at the same time. He found himself drawn to her in a way that was different than ever before. Trying to keep his feelings in check, he stood and tugged her to her feet. Pulling her to him, he slid his arms around her waist, and held her close. Tilting her head with his finger under her chin, he said, "Living with our own choices can be tough enough. I'm happy you made the brave choice to board the Neptune, to seek your future." He stared into her eyes. "And I am even happier that choice brought you to Jamaica, and to me." He kissed her forehead.

She felt so safe as her heart soared with newfound hope. Marshall offered friendship and she felt a genuine sense of protection when he was around. "I am grateful as well." She leaned her head on his shoulder. She had feared no one would ever hold her this way again and she was grateful she'd been mistaken.

"I'm staying at Queenie's while I wait for my shipment of lumber to arrive." He didn't tell her he hoped it would be late. "I'll be heading up to Claremont, near Ramble House, tomorrow to check on things. Would you like to ride along? I'll be back in the late afternoon." He held his breath waiting for her answer. *When did I ever react like this to a woman? To anyone?*

She didn't have to consider the offer for long. "Yes, just let me check with Mavis to see if she can handle things on her own for the day." As she suspected, Mavis was more than happy to give them the time together.

THE NEXT MORNING while the rooster crowed and the sun began to dawn, they readied Stars and Rebel for the trip. Marshall had saddled Stars for her while she packed a picnic sack with scones, fruit, and jerky to carry with them. She tucked the sack in Stars' saddlebag and Marshall held him still while she mounted. She wore the men's pants she had worn on the Neptune, finding it easier to ride in them than in a long skirt. To make up for the pants, she found herself wearing a blue blouse with ruffles down the front and at the cuffs, thinking at least part of her looked like a woman. At the same time, she was surprised that she cared.

They rode side-by-side until the road up the mountain behind St. Ann's turned into a path. She recognized some of the sights from her earlier trip to Ramble House with Mavis. "I should soon be considered a local as I'm beginning to recognize landmarks on my way to Claremont."

"You will wake up one day and find you are a native Jamaican," Marshall laughed.

"Some days I feel as if I already am," she smiled.

The thought of her staying in Jamaica made him grin, if only to himself. Families were leaving Jamaica. The fear of Maroon raids was taking its toll on the island community. His hope of finding a soulmate had grown dimmer every day. But now, he was convinced that finding Ronnie had turned that dimness into light. It was meant to be. He prayed she felt the same way.

"So, we'll take this fork in the road to the left, instead, as we head toward Golden Grove and the new tea fields," Marshall announced as he pulled Rebel's reins to the left. Ronnie followed on Stars.

They rode in silence for several miles. The tea bushes were coming up nicely. "I'm considering planting coffee. Governor Lawes has just introduced some to his fields up in the mountains. They say it will grow well there. Perhaps it will here as well."

They stopped in front of a stone wall that bordered a field of tea plantings and dismounted. "I need to walk through the fields for a little while and check on some things." He handed her Rebel's reins and walked toward the gate, pulling a key out of his pocket, and opened the padlock that was chained to the post.

"Take your time. I'll walk them over to get a drink from the creek." She took both Rebel and Stars by their reins and led them down to the water's edge. The horses drank and she crouched down, cupped her hands, and took a sip for herself. When she stood again, she followed Marshall with her gaze as he inspected his crops until he walked out of her sight.

When he returned, he pulled a piece of paper out of his saddlebag along with a pencil and proceeded to write. "I need to leave Mr. McClintock a message with some instructions before we go." He took a few minutes, wrote his instructions, and placed the note under a rock that was loose on the wall.

They mounted Stars and Rebel and turned to head down yet another path. The horses took them down a narrow passageway with foliage that grew overhead, diminishing the sunlight until it was cool and shady. "Is this anywhere near Hope Falls?" Ronnie asked, thinking they were close to the place where she and Mavis had been.

"Not too far. Just over the next ridge, I think."

Light filtered its way through in patches slowly until the shining sun could no longer be denied. It broke through with a vengeance causing them to pull the brim of their hats down to avoid its glare. Ronnie followed Marshall to a hilltop overlooking the sea. The view of St. Ann's Bay was spectacular, unlike any she had seen before. The sails of ships shone on the cerulean sea in the distance as they slowly drifted by as if floating on air.

Ronnie slid off Stars and held onto her reins as she walked closer to the edge of the hillside. Rebel snorted and followed. "What's up, Rebel?" She reached over and stroked his black forehead.

"He probably wants some shade and an apple." Marshall dismounted and walked alongside her.

Guiding the horses into the shade, they tethered them to a tree. Stars chuffed as Ronnie reached in the saddlebag, pulled out the bag of food and handed Rebel's apple to Marshall.

"What a magnificent sight," she exclaimed as they walked back over to the top of the hill. He spread out a small blanket on the ground. They sat and Ronnie pulled more apples, mangoes, and jerky from the bag. Marshall pulled a knife from his pocket and began to cut up the fruit.

"It's a hidden gem of a view among a million others here on the island," he informed her while handing her a slice of mango. She put it in her mouth, trying to keep the juice from running down her face. She giggled as she wiped the sweet nectar from her chin with her sleeve. He pulled a handkerchief from his shirt pocket and wiped her chin and handed it to her.

She giggled again. "Seems you are always rescuing me with your handkerchiefs."

"It's a good thing that's all that's required, given my lack of sword and pistol expertise!" They laughed, both knowing it was true. He went on to tell her a few stories of how inept he was with a sword. "My father was insistent that I learn. The only result was a few cuts and eventual humiliation." He continued to take punches at his lack of fighting skills as he stood and demon-s⁺ ated. She laughed even more.

The joy of laughter brought her alive again. She'd had so little of it in the past year and a half. "Laughing feels as if I've opened the door and let the demons out. Thank you, Marshall, for bringing it back to me!" She stared at the sea lying at the bottom of the mountain with the bay curving around it as if a mother was holding her baby in the crook of her arm.

"I delight in the sound of your laughter, my lady." He did a mock bow and sat back down beside her on the blanket. "Laughter is definitely the best medicine for a sorrowful soul and that is how I think of you. One that's been wounded but beginning to heal." He reached over and ran his fingers through her hair. "If I can help you feel better with smiles and laughter, I'll gladly take on that role." He looked at her intently as they sat on the blanket. She felt her face blush as she looked back from the view of the sea to find his eyes digging into her private thoughts again. She'd felt that same feeling when they sat on the beach the day before.

Leaning in, he softly kissed her on the cheek and tilted her head, guiding her mouth to meet his. Their souls embraced for a few seconds.

Pulling back from her, afraid that he had pushed her boundaries too far, he said, "I apologize if I was inappropriate."

"Not at all." She took a deep breath and laid her head on his chest and said, "Not at all." They sat in silence which spoke louder than any words as his arms wrapped around her and they gazed at the sea, each lost in their own thoughts.

CANTERING THROUGH THE countryside on their way back to Ocho Rios, the mountain air brought a cool breeze. Slowing to a walk, Ronnie and Marshall talked at length about their childhoods.

"Growing up in the suburbs of London didn't allow for much learning about the rigors of country living, let alone in a tropical setting," Marshall said. They slowed down to cross a small stream that lay in their path. "The lack of social contact here can be daunting when one lives in these mountains. The possibility of being attacked by Maroons is a reality we live with daily, so we can never let our guard fully down." The genteel of Jamaican society built great houses to support their plantations, crops, and cow pens. These days, it was not uncommon to find an overseer living in the great house instead of its owner. Families were shying away from settling down in the countryside where they stood a chance of being raided.

"But why do the Maroons raid plantations, Marshall?" Ronnie asked. "I mean I understand that they don't want to be enslaved, but why the violence?"

"They need to stay stocked in weapons and ammunition as well as free any slaves that they can in the process. It's all about survival. No matter which side you find yourself on."

Riding into St. Ann's they decided to stop for dinner. Marshall tied the horses up to the post in front of Barley's Tavern. He figured they could drink a pint, eat dinner, and then finish their ride back to Ocho Rios. The pub was filled with boisterous conversation and conjectures flew all around. Rumors of Anne and Jack had intensified.

"He hung and is now hanging for all to see on a gibbet in Port Royal, a warning to others that accept the pardon and go back to their evil ways!" a bearded patron proclaimed. Ronnie sat still as she continued to eavesdrop on the table next to them. She quit breathing for a moment and her face went white.

Watching her reaction, Marshall stood and leaned down to whisper in her ear, "I will go check things out and return soon." He strode purposefully to the bar to get the facts. Turning, he looked at Ronnie knowing she would have no appetite after she heard this news. He walked back to the table and sat down next to her.

Taking her hand in his, he looked into her eyes and said, "I am afraid it's true, my dear. Calico Jack is no more."

"Oh my god! I knew it would happen when Barnet caught them." She stared into space. "I just did not know it would be so swift. What has become of Anne?"

"They say she was tried and found guilty, but given she is with child a delay was granted." Ronnie's lack of surprise at the news told Marshall she already knew about the baby. "Mary Read is with child as well and her execution is also postponed."

Ronnie crossed her arms on the table and plopped her head on top of them. "Poor Anne. She must be beside herself. Even I can hardly bear it." She looked up at Marshall, her eyes red, her blonde hair falling across her face. "What will happen next?"

He gently pushed her loose hair behind her ear. "I don't know. Perhaps her punishment will come after the baby is delivered."

"What will become of her child?" One unanswered question after another spilled out of her.

The proprietor, a rugged looking young man with long black hair pulled behind his neck, approached the table and delivered their drinks. Marshall looked at Ronnie as if to ask if he should order dinner for her and she nodded. They each held onto their mug of grog. The cool liquid felt good on Ronnie's throat and the warmth it provided in her belly was both welcome and numbing. She wanted to feel nothing right now. "I'm so weary of tears. So tired of complaining and worrying."

He reached over and covered her hands with his. He wanted to protect her from the pain, but knew this was the best he could do, for now. He had watched her face her past, dealing with the troubles she'd been dragged into since arriving on the island, and now she had to endure the death of one friend, and possibly another. "You've had so much heartache over the past few years and now this. I'm so sorry, my love." The pet name did not escape her. Somehow, deep within her it brought comfort. They continued to drink their grog as they waited for their meals to arrive.

The proprietor returned to their table and placed their plates before them. "I'm sorry. It appears as though my appetite has left me." Ronnie shook her head and stared at her plate of red snapper and yams. "As hungry as I was earlier, I can't even think about eating now."

"I'll make sure you have it to take home." Marshall watched her stare blindly out the little window of the tavern as he ate his meal in silence.

She'd known they would be found guilty. Yet, in her heart she had still harbored hope for a miracle. *Why does everyone I love have to go away?* "Please forgive me, but I need to visit the outhouse." Marshall stood as she left the table and walked outside. Instead of going to the small wooden building that stood at the foot of the mountain, Ronnie walked around to the rear of the tavern and leaned up against the outside wall. She allowed the sobs to take over and sank to the ground. She mourned the death of Jack and unknown fate of Anne. She cried for the loss of Amari and guilt of her part in Elijah's departure into the mountains, as well as those she had left behind in Nassau and South Carolina. Silent screams came from the bottom of her as she cried out to God. After a few minutes, a calm feeling settled on her and the torrential flood of tears stopped. *Thanks for listening . . .* She lifted her head up knowing her prayers were heard. Still, she sat and stared at the ground a while longer. Pulling herself up to her feet, she looked at her reflection in a window. She saw someone that looked familiar. "Well, I do believe I recognize you." She reached up and touched her hair that was pulled back into a knot, freeing it to lay across her shoulders. Shaking her head in an attempt to clear it, she regained her composure as best she could, threw some water from a wash basin on her face, and returned to the table. She knew it was time. Ronnie looked at him and said, "It is time to get on with my life instead of living with the consequences of other's choices." Ronnie looked at Marshall. "It's time to quit feeling sorry for myself. After all, isn't that what grief really is? The self-pity of being the one left behind?"

Marshall nodded and pushed back his chair. "Well, I believe perhaps you are being a bit hard on yourself, but I understand your logic and intention to move on. Now, let's begin by gathering ourselves and getting you back home."

She shook her head and stayed seated. "Please sit down. There's something I want to tell you." Marshall sat back in his chair and looked at her.

"What on earth is wrong?" he asked.

"Remember when I told you about Amari and taking him to live with the Maroons?" She took a deep breath and briefly wondered why she felt the need to tell him. She was finding that she trusted Marshall more and more.

Marshall nodded and said, "Yes, you and Sam took him there, right?"

"Yes, we did, but Amari was not the only one we handed over to the Maroons that day."

Marshall frowned and asked, "What are you talking about?"

"First of all, I have to know you won't share this with anyone. It could hurt so many people. I'm not proud of what happened." Marshall nodded and she continued to explain about Adria's baby and her parents' plan for the child. She worried as the frown on his face deepened as she told her story.

"I must say, I'm stunned. I had no idea Adria had a child." Marshall said. "John and Sarah must have been totally shocked."

Ronnie nodded and said, "Yes, they were. She almost died during the birth, but Mum Lettie was able to keep her with us. Her parents decided the baby would be better off with the Maroons for many reasons, the main one being he was half negro."

Marshall's eyebrows raised from their frown and he stared at Ronnie for several long seconds trying to process what she'd just said. He blinked and shook his head and looked down. Her heart sank. *I've said too much. Why can't I just keep my mouth shut?*

After a minute of processing what she'd shared, he reached over and covered her hand with his. Marshall looked at Ronnie, tilting her head up to look at him. "I can't imagine the pain you've been through. Coming here and getting caught up in a situation over which you had no control and all the while all you'd been trying to do was help both Amari and Adria."

She was stunned at his nonjudgmental attitude. While she'd had the same thoughts from time to time, it was healing to hear someone else besides the voice in her own head speak the truth. She just hoped she could trust him with the truth.

RONNIE AND MARSHALL courted over the next several months. Rumors were flying around Ocho Rios about its most eligible bachelor being enchanted with its newest resident, Mavis' niece, Ronnie.

"So, when do you think he'll propose?" Mavis asked Ronnie.

Ronnie laughed as she reached down from the ladder for another sack to put on the top shelf of the store. Mavis handed her a bag. "Whatever do you mean?" Ronnie smiled coyly and cocked her head.

"I think you know what I'm talking about, Missy. You two are the talk of the town, you know." Mavis picked up the empty crate and put it under the counter. Ronnie climbed down off the ladder.

"Well, there must be a real scarcity of gossip if we've made the top of the list!" Ronnie laughed. "When he does ask, you'll be the first to know. You can count on that."

"I will!" Mavis said and they both laughed.

Ronnie had thought about the possibility of marriage to Marshall. He certainly seemed like he wanted their relationship to go in that direction with frequent remarks about how their lives might be in the future. She was excited to link her life with his. She knew there was more she needed to tell him about her past and wasn't sure how he'd react to yet another secret. Besides, she knew being the mistress of Ramble House and its slaves would be hard for her to deal with. She wasn't sure how well she could acclimate. She'd always been a poor middle-class person without the worry of owning anyone other than herself. Her lack of social status had always enabled her to not take ownership of the reality of the slavery part of their culture. Marrying Marshall would change all that.

MARSHALL HAD BEEN coming into Ocho Rios most weekends to collect supplies, but truth be known, it was to spend more time with Ronnie. They had made a habit of attending church together and spending most of Sunday together. As they came out of the church one Sunday, Marshall took Ronnie's hand and walked her down the steps to a carriage. A footman opened the door and Marshall helped her inside.

"What on earth is going on?" she asked as she sat on the bench inside the carriage. She pulled her skirt out of his way as he jumped inside and sat next to her.

"I thought I'd surprise you and we'd take a little ride and enjoy a meal next to the river where it's cooler." He pulled a basket out from under the bench.

"Well, I must say, I am surprised and delighted. You know I love being near the water and on a steamy day like today, the river will be a perfect respite."

The carriage traveled outside of town and took the rutted road down to the White River. Soon, they came to a stop and the footman jumped down and helped them out of the carriage. Marshall grabbed the picnic basket and Ronnie's hand. Looking at the footman, he said, "Can you come back around 3 o'clock, Martin?"

"Yessir. I will see you then." Martin boarded the carriage and pulled away.

"Come, follow me." They walked down a pathway to an opening revealing a bluish green pool of water at the bottom of a small tumbling waterfall that cascaded over small and large boulders.

"Oh, Marshall. This place is magical. How in the world did you find it?" She walked over behind a bush, kicked off her shoes and pulled off her stockings. Setting them aside, she walked over to the water's edge and dipped one foot in. "Oh, it's delightful!"

He took her hand and helped her sit on the water's edge where she could submerge her feet. She kicked her feet back and forth in the water, making it spray back over each of them and they laughed. "I love how you make the smallest things joyful, Ronnie."

She smiled at him and said, "I've come to know that laughter is a key to joy. I want to experience it as much as I can, and it's easy when I'm with you."

He started to pull the food out from the basket but stopped. Instead, he reached in his pocket and pulled something out. She looked down at a small box in his hand. *Oh no. It can't be. Not already.*

"Ronnie," he said as he slowly opened the box to reveal a ring with an emerald stone surrounded by diamonds. "I've come to love you intensely these past months. I would be most pleased if you would agree to be my wife."

She took a deep breath, not knowing how to respond. She knew she couldn't give him an answer to his proposal until she revealed her final secret. She reached over and touched the ring. "It's absolutely beautiful, but I can't." She closed the lid on the box, unable to look at the glittering gems any longer. She got to her feet and walked away and stared at the sea.

Marshall jumped to his feet and followed her. "Ronnie, what in the world is wrong?" They had both already professed their love for each other over the past few weeks. He was totally confused.

She turned around to face him. "Are you sure you want a former pirate as mistress of Ramble House?"

"You weren't a pirate!" Marshall said.

"But I was." She reached over and lifted his head to look her in the eye. "I was part of an operation that was less than stellar. No, I never killed anyone, but I was there." She let go of his chin and looked away. "I was involved. Marshall, you have to know what you're getting into." She turned back to look at him and let out a heavy sigh. "There's something I haven't told you."

"What would that be?" He put his arms around her waist, but she stepped back a little.

"I can never have children."

Marshall blinked and took a deep breath, but just for a second. "That's not a reason not to marry you, Ronnie. I'll love you forever with or without children." He stepped toward her, but she backed up again.

"I need to tell you why," she said.

"Why what? What do you mean?"

"Remember I told you I was infatuated with a pirate while in Nassau?" He nodded and she continued. "The pirate I told you that had turned my head was Charles Vane."

Eyebrows raised, he said, "You were involved with Charles Vane?" The pirate's reputation as a brutal cold-blooded killer was legendary.

"Yes, and I'm not proud of it. He was a charming, good-looking man who managed to sweep me off my feet when he wasn't on the seas." Ronnie turned away and stared out the window. It was too hard to look him in the eyes. "I was new to Nassau. Easily persuaded out of desperation, I suppose." She turned back to look at him, "Our relationship was brief, but not without consequence."

"So, what was the consequence?"

She looked away, afraid to tell him, but even more afraid of denying her past. "We had an affair."

"Well, you aren't the first woman to fall prey to the likes of someone like him," Marshall said.

She took a deep breath and said, "I discovered I was expecting his child."

Marshall said nothing, and reached out to touch her, but she turned and moved away again. He wanted to ask about the baby but knew she would get to it. *So, it was Vane's baby she lost!*

"My biggest mistake was allowing him to find out." She stared out at the sea but looked at nothing.

"What on earth do you mean?" He reached out and touched her shoulder. This time, she didn't move away.

Turning, she looked at him. "He picked up my journal and read it, but I didn't know. His reaction wasn't a positive one." She shook her head in disbelief and looked down at her hands. "The man was one of the most crazed and irrational pirates in Nassau and all of the Caribbean for that matter. I thought giving him a child would make a difference."

She laughed with a hint of sarcasm in her voice. "Nothing could have been further from the truth." She looked at him again and continued, "That night, after his tirade, during dinner,

I began feeling woozy and couldn't stand. I must have blacked out. The next thing I remember was waking up with Anne hovering over me. I looked down and saw blood all over the bed and thought I'd miscarried." Ronnie took a deep breath and continued, "I didn't realize until that moment that although having a baby posed all kinds of problems for me, for the first time, I had true hope for some kind of happiness. I fell apart when I realized the baby was no more. Poor Anne didn't know what to do and allowed me to believe I'd miscarried for a few days."

"What do you mean, 'allowed you to believe?'" Marshall asked. Marshall shook his head, not following what she was trying to tell him and asked again, "What do you mean 'allowed you to believe?'"

"A few days later, Anne explained that Vane had arranged for a doctor to abort my baby. He put something in my drink when we were at dinner and I passed out."

"What a wretched thing to do!" Marshall said.

"Yes, it was. Evidently, Anne walked in as the doctor was packing up his bag. She almost killed Vane in a nasty brawl, and he was in need of the doctor's help by the time she pushed him out the door." Involuntary tears slid down her cheek. She was so tired of tears. "Because of my recklessness, a doctor later told me I would never have another child." She looked at Marshall, afraid of what she might find.

Turning to find Marshall's back facing her, she realized it was worse than she'd thought. Feeling the blood drain from her face, she was terrorized and swallowed hard realizing the risk she'd taken. He turned to face her but instead of looking into her eyes he looked down at his hands. Her heart sank as she realized she may have taken the risk and lost.

"If he weren't already dead, I'd hunt that savage down!" He reached down, grabbed a rock, and threw it as far as he could into the sea. He shook his head and turned to look at her. She saw a rage in his eyes she didn't recognize. He took a deep breath in an effort to calm himself. Reaching over, he pulled her to him saying, "I'm sorry he robbed you of so much."

It was then she knew she could trust Marshall with her life. It was then . . .

A FEW MONTHS later, they married on a Thursday evening with only a few guests at Ramble House. Ronnie walked down the cobblestone walkway to the trellis covered with orchids where Marshall waited. He caught his breath when he saw her in Mavis' wedding dress with a veil and bouquet donning lilies from his mother's greenhouse. The scent of the flowers preceded his bride, and the sound of Kimar's drums tickled the air with its joyful tune. Mavis lifted Ronnie's veil over her head, stood back, and beamed as she kissed her on the cheek and said, "My darling, may your life be full of smiles leaving you as radiant always as you are today."

Ronnie hugged her and whispered, "I thank God for you every day, my dear Mavis." Her surrogate mother smiled, and Ronnie turned toward Marshall.

Taking her hand in his, they turned as one to face Reverend Smith. Emotions flooded them both as they looked into each other's eyes.

William Bromley, owner of Bromley Pen, and longtime friend of Marshall's stood next to him acting as the groomsman. The Jamaican sunshine peeked in and out of the clouds, giving the perfect respite from the steamy sunshine.

Rosalie stood on the steps of Ramble House, watching and waiting for the ceremony to end. She and her staff had prepared a special meal for the guests. She smiled at the happiness that seemed to land on everyone but her.

William Bromley had given the newlyweds his cottage at Bromley Pen to use for their honeymoon as a wedding gift.

"I hope you enjoy your stay at Bromley Pen," William said to the couple as they sat down at the dining room table. Bromley was located on a mountaintop overlooking the sea on the edge of a rainforest, and its climate tended to be cooler than most of the island.

"Thank you for allowing us to enjoy your beautiful home, Mr. Bromley," Ronnie said.

"Please, call me William. And you're more than welcome as I will be all over the island checking on things and then sail for London in two weeks. You will have all the privacy you desire. Meredith and Victor, my house slaves, will be there to tend to your needs."

Marshall nodded and said, "Yes, we're so looking forward to a few days of rest." He looked at his bride and grinned.

"Well, I don't know how much 'rest' a honeymoon provides, but I trust you will manage!" William raised his glass laughing and the others joined in. Glasses clinked and the port wine flowed in celebration of the newlyweds.

"Rosie (Ronnie's pet name for Rosalie), you've outdone yourself this time," Ronnie said as Rosalie placed slices of the wedding cake in front of each guest.

"Indeed, she has," said Mavis. "I'm as full as a tick, but I assure you I will work my way through this lovely cake." Her love of sweets was all but legendary.

When dinner was over, the guests retired to the veranda while the couple went to their chamber to change clothes for their trip to Bromley Pen. Rosalie handed out handmade lace handkerchiefs full of rice to each guest. Everyone walked down to the landing where the carriage had pulled up.

"So, I see Scottie has made the transition to Ramble House as well," William said. "Everyone that visits the mercantile will miss him, for sure."

"Yes, Ronnie brought both him and his mate, Bossy, here to Ramble House a few days ago," Mavis said.

Scottie tried to fly down the steps to greet the carriage but stumbled instead. "What's wrong with him?" Mavis asked Rosalie. She looked at an empty glass that was toppled over on the top step.

"Me thinks he had too much rum!" Rosalie laughed and the rest joined in. Scottie had been caught dipping into people's drinks before.

"Well, a drunken parrot won't get too far, that's for sure!" Mavis said as she reached over and pet the parrot. For once, he didn't skitter away. He could hardly sit up straight, let alone skitter. And to think she'd been concerned he might try to follow the couple to Bromley.

"He's going to have some explaining to do when he gets home to Bossy tonight!" Mavis said and everyone laughed.

The newlyweds came out and joined their guests. They walked down the steps as everyone, including Rosalie and the rest of the slaves, showered them with rice. Marshall scooped Ronnie up at the bottom step and carried her to the carriage as Thomas, the stableman, opened the door to let them inside. Everyone cheered, shouting their best wishes. The couple leaned out the window and waved goodbye as Stars and Rebel pulled the carriage down the steep driveway.

ARRIVING AT BROMLEY Pen, Marshall helped Ronnie to climb out of the carriage. Thomas pulled Ronnie's trunk from the back of the carriage and carried it inside. Cattle dotted the hills behind them. Bromley was a large plantation that provided livestock to the island.

The sprawling green and white house had a curved staircase in front leading to a veranda that wrapped around the house. The high ceilings inside along with floor to ceiling windows, allowed for continual air flow. The hexagonal balconies on each of the four corners of the house provided a view of everything from the Caribbean Sea to the rain forest.

"He calls this a 'cottage'?" Ronnie asked. "It's way too grand for that lowly title. What a lovely place!"

Marshall walked up behind her as she stared out the window. Wrapping his arms around her waist, he nuzzled his nose in her hair and whispered, "It is a much lovelier place with you here."

She felt her body respond at his suggestive touch while his hands found their way up to her breasts. She closed her eyes and said a silent prayer that she would be able to make him happy. Turning her around to face him, he kissed her as no one ever had before. She found no need to pray anymore as her body responded to his. Scooping her up again, he nudged the French door open with his foot and walked into the bedroom, laying her gently on the bed. As he undressed himself, she unbuttoned her chemise, their eyes locking. He reached down and helped her undress, kissing her body everywhere he exposed her skin. She writhed with pleasure. As he found what seemed to be the middle of her, she exploded with sensations she had never known existed.

Ronnie laid in his arms in the aftermath of their lovemaking. She rested her legs over his hips, faced him, and curled up in his arms. "I've never been loved that way before," she whispered, trying to catch her breath.

"I've never felt this type of love for anyone before," he said, and kissed her forehead. They remained there until sleep found them both.

The couple enjoyed their days at Bromley. "Waking in your arms is the best wedding present ever, although I do love this cottage as well," Ronnie said as they ate breakfast on the veranda. Egrets took their morning flight down the mountain in search of a herd of cattle to perch on for the day. "Do you think we could just stay here forever?"

Marshall laughed and said, "As much as I would love to, duty calls, my dear. Thomas will have the carriage ready in an hour." While she felt wonderful about their newly found oneness, it was time to return to Ramble House and her duties as its new mistress, a title she wasn't sure how to execute.

RONNIE SAT AT the end of the table of Ramble House staring out the French door window. Normally, it would be wide open, but the breeze felt like a possible storm in the offing, so she and Rosalie had closed them. She wasn't used to being the lady in charge. She wasn't used to so many things since she'd become Marshall's wife just a few months ago.

Her gaze went to the bay window seat, seeing nothing at first, and then there it was, right in front of her and not for the first time. Mr. McClintock, the overseer, yelling at a young cook for burning a chicken on the spit. The boy hung his head, trying to avoid McClintock's wrath, keeping his gaze low and his head lower. There were ways to survive, and this young man she recognized as Lawrence had figured that part out. So had she. And she'd had enough. Standing up fast, her chair scraped the floor and fell on its back behind her. She didn't care. Resolutely, she headed out the door.

"Mr. McClintock!" Ronnie waved her fan to gain the man's attention and held her skirt up as she ran down the steps. His anger showed a bit at the interruption, but he recovered quickly. Or so he thought.

Looking a little embarrassed, McClintock took a deep breath and said, "Yes Ma'am! What can I do for you on this fine day?"

"Fine day?" Ronnie looked from McClintock to ten-year-old Lawrence and back again. "Fine day for whom?"

"The lad was playing around and caused the chicken to burn on the spit!" McClintock hollered and then checked himself.

"Well, shall we punish, 'the lad' for being a youngster and wanting to have a bit of fun in the process of cooking my dinner?" Tilting her head, she shrugged her shoulders and just stared at him. McClintock turned slowly, confused, and unsure of what to say or do.

Ronnie looked at Lawrence who shrank back out of habit whenever he was close to a white person. The young boy's eyes betrayed his fear as he looked at her and then back down at the ground. Ronnie's resolve folded as a tear escaped the side of his right eye. *Tears are way too prevalent on this island.* She took a deep breath, shook her head, and knelt down in front of Lawrence. "It's alright. I realize you didn't mean to burn the chicken. You just need to be more careful." She reached up and touched his tear-stained cheek. Lawrence shrank back just a little. She stood up and faced Mr. McClintock. "I think your tongue lashing is quite sufficient given the crime." She looked back toward the house to see Marshall watching from the veranda. Looking back at Lawrence she said, "Now head on back and finish helping Rosalie with dinner." Nodding, the boy turned and ran back toward the kitchen at the rear of the house his bare feet kicking up dust in his wake.

"Pardon me, Mrs. Fergusson." McClintock held his hat in his hands, looking down not sure what to say. "I don't mean to offend, Ma'am, but I was only doin' my job."

Ronnie looked at him with a boldness she didn't know she had and replied, "Well, Mr. McClintock, I understand that and while you were only doing what you thought was right, things around here have changed." She looked over his shoulder to see Marshall still looking on. "My husband and I have discussed my concerns and he's agreed to allow me to handle the discipline of the house servants. I will be meeting with everyone in the morning."

McClintock took note of her using the term "servants" instead of slaves as was used in the past. He'd heard about new mistresses changing the rules for the overseers. Now it was his turn to swallow the bitter pill and he didn't like it one bit. But he was smart enough not to show it. "I understand," he said as he tipped his hat. He knew he'd best leave before he said something he'd regret.

"Mr. McClintock!" Marshall said as he jogged down the steps and over to meet the two of them. McClintock stopped and turned. Marshall looked at him and said, "I'm sorry I didn't fill you in on the changes here at Ramble House before now, but as you've heard, Mrs. Fergusson is now in charge of the household staff." McClintock all but glared at his boss.

"I understand," McClintock said as he climbed on his horse. "Is there anything else?"

Marshall shook his head and McClintock headed back toward the slave quarters. Marshall turned and looked at Ronnie. "Well, my dear, it appears you have a meeting to prepare for in the morning."

RONNIE SPENT THE evening making notes of what she wanted to say and didn't dare say to the staff. She ran her ideas past Marshall throughout the process. "So, do you think I need to go into daily procedures, or just leave the minor details to Rosalie?" Ronnie glanced up from her vanity which she had turned into a desk and dipped her pen back into the inkwell.

Marshall looked up from his copy of the Jamaica Courant. "Well, my dear, I would think Rosalie can handle details of who needs to do what, but whatever you decide, I'm perfectly confident in your judgement." He stood up and walked over to her. "Have I told you how much I appreciate your willingness to step in and run Ramble House as it hasn't been done since my dear mother was here?" Their eyes locked with each other through the mirror. "She would have embraced you so." He leaned over and kissed her on the nape of her neck.

Ronnie shivered. His touch could be electrifying to her and was hard to refute. Dropping the pen, she turned and lifted her head, welcoming his mouth onto hers. Gratitude, hope, desire, and love for each other overtook them. Thoughts swirled in her head as he explored her body. Within minutes, her thoughts were at bay and only her love and desire for him existed. He found the middle of her once again as his body connected with hers. Her body rose and fell with his as they both were transported into ecstasy. Clinging to him, their words were a passionate exchange bringing a heightened sense of being one.

The next morning, Ronnie opened her eyes. The morning sun reminded her they'd forgotten to close the shutters the night before, neither one wanting to let go of the splendid embrace of their union. She laid there remembering their passion from the night before. She'd known joy before, but this was different. It was emotional, yes, but also physical and somehow spiritual.

"WHO DOES SHE think she is?" McClintock said to Thomas, the slave stable hand. Thomas shook his head in agreement knowing well enough not to agree out loud. From what he'd heard his friends saying in private, Thomas knew they were happy with the recent change — McClintock having less control over them.

McClintock continued his tirade, "They're just a bunch of useless mules. Without someone to show them what to do, they will do nothing. She'll find that true soon enough!" He took another swig of his rum. Stumbling to the slave quarters, he hollered for the woman he normally bedded and she followed him as he went into his quarters and the lights went out.

—Chapter Seventeen—

"Marriage is the most natural state of man, and therefore the state in which one is most likely to find solid happiness." —Benjamin Franklin

1724, London, England

Time passed quickly once Adria regained her old self. Her social calendar filled up for both her and her mother. Jeffrey escorted both of them around London when John was in Jamaica. Adria's father had been back to London once since they'd left Jamaica. After a year of courting, Jeffrey and Adria's relationship had taken a serious turn. Her father had been thrilled when he received the letter from Sarah saying Adria's spell of sadness had forever lifted and she'd fallen in love with Jeffrey. Almost a year later, he received Adria's letter announcing her plans to marry. He wasted no time arranging his trip back to London.

Adria, Jeffrey, and Sarah greeted John at the dock and enjoyed a brief dinner together at home. They sat at the dining room table relaxing with a glass of port.

Picking up his glass, Jeffrey offered a toast, "To the most beautiful woman in the world." He looked at Adria and leaned over to kiss her cheek. "Thank you both for raising such an incredible woman." They all clinked each other's glass and took a sip. "So, John, how are things in Jamaica these days?" Jeffrey asked.

"Ginger Star has been operating profitably for the past year, thank you for asking, Jeffrey." John reached over and grabbed the butter dish. "Sam and Mum Lettie are doing well and continue to be indispensable to me." He looked at Sarah and said, "However, the Maroons have increased their raids of plantations over the past few years." He spread the butter on his roll. "The residents are all on edge these days. The sound of the Abeng is all too frequent." John filled them in on the latest Maroon raid.

"That's frightful," Sarah said. "Makes one wonder if it's safe to live there anymore."

"Well, the good part is that things seem to have calmed down," John said. He had hoped Sarah might decide to come back with him, but it was doubtful.

Adria picked up her knife and started cutting her asparagus. "Mama mentioned that Marshall had married. Who is she?"

John and Sarah's eyes locked. It was a question Sarah had been able to dodge, but John could see no way out. "He married Veronica Shepherd. I believe you will remember her as Ronnie."

Adria's eyes flew open in recognition of the friend she had known for but a brief time. "Really? That's amazing." Adria remembered her short-lived friendship with Ronnie fondly. "I'm so happy to hear they found each other. He's a wonderful man and it will no doubt be a good match."

Sarah diverted the conversation by saying, "So, the plans for Adria's wedding and reception are just about completed, dear." She touched her husband's hand and looked at her daughter. "Adria, why don't you tell your father about the wonderful flowers you've secured at the florist!" Her ploy worked and the rest of the evening was filled with wedding plans and details.

ADRIA RECONNECTED WITH several of her old friends. She and Charlotte, her good friend from school lived near-by and the two spent many an afternoon drinking tea and practicing needlepoint. Charlotte was a tall woman with raven shoulder length hair. Her blue eyes attracted a man's attention from across any room.

"Muriel will have my gown ready to try on this Friday. Would you like to go with me?" Charlotte asked Adria.

"I would love to, but Mother has some last-minute shopping she wants me to do with her. I'm sure it will fit perfectly. You'll look gorgeous in that dark red gown. Your black hair will compliment it well," Adria said.

"Well, I sure hope it fits. I've been turning down scones at tea far too long for it to be too snug!" The two laughed and finished up their needlepoint for the day. Adria was grateful for her friend whom she had yet to confide in about her baby. The fewer people that knew about her shame, the better.

"NO MOTHER WANTS more for her daughter than to see her fall in love," Sarah said to John when they had retired to their room. Laying her head on his shoulder, they both stared at the ceiling. Even though they'd been apart for a long while, they still could anticipate one another's thoughts. "Jeffrey has been such a Godsend."

Pulling Sarah closer, John said, "That certainly appears to be true, and now she seems like a mature version of her old self. Her letters have shown a lot of improvement as well." John kissed her on her forehead. "Now that Jeffrey has graduated, he can step into David's printing business with no problem." Jeffrey's father, David Palmer, had long awaited his son taking over his business. They shared no worries at Jeffrey's ability to provide for their daughter.

John had given a lot of thought about his next statement and worried how to propose it to Sarah. He took a deep breath. "I'm considering hiring a full-time administrator for Ginger Star. That way, I would only have to visit Jamaica once or twice a year."

She popped up on her elbow and looked at him, shaking her head. "But John, you always said being an absentee owner was a poor idea."

"Yes, but I'm tired of being so far away from you. I can make it work. I've been talking to a new overseer from Scotland and Sam is very capable of keeping an eye on everyone. I trust him to keep me apprised."

She'd always secretly hoped he would do this. "Oh, darling, if you're sure it could work, that would be wonderful!" Sarah looked down at him. "I would love to have you home again." Leaning down, she kissed him.

ADRIA PICKED UP the comb and tucked a few strands of stray hair under the braids Margaret, her mother's trusted servant, had curled on top of her head. She stared in the mirror. Living in a fog can be comforting at times, but the clarity that came with embracing life had birthed hope in her again. Coming back to London had been terrifying at first, but Jeffrey's friendship and love had pushed the clouds away. The past four years had been a time of healing for her while falling and rising in love with him. After taking their vows today, they would live together at his parents' estate, Mansfield, not in the main house, but in a beautiful cottage that bordered the forest. He would soon take over Palmer Printing House from his father when he retired.

Marrying Jeffrey was the first thing Adria could remember doing that felt totally right. She found she could move past her mistakes. She knew thoughts of her son would never stop but felt as if the storm had passed and the sun was once again indeed shining.

Her eyes looked at the mirror on her vanity and landed on the veil laying on the bed behind her. She stood up, walked over, and felt the lace between her fingers. The veil had belonged to Grandmother Spencer, her mother's mother. "This will be yours one day," Grandmother's words played over in her head as she held up the veil. "When you find your partner and marry, make sure he's the one that makes your heart stop when he walks into a room and makes you laugh until your side hurts. The two most important ingredients of a good partnership." Grandmother had always had a way of sounding profound and funny at the same time. Adria missed her more than ever since she had come back to London. She'd inherited her quick wit and green eyes. Wearing her veil on her wedding day somehow helped her know she was indeed there. She held it over her head and sat back down at her vanity.

"Well, Grandmother," Adria said as she held the veil up over her head. "Jeffrey makes my heart leap and laugh at the same time, how's that?" She could feel her grandmother's smiling approval.

"So, darling, are you ready to put on the finishing touches?" Adria looked over her shoulder in the mirror to see her mother had walked into the bedroom without her noticing. She wore a royal blue ball gown as the mother of the bride. Her blonde hair was pulled up to a bun at the nape of her neck lending to the aristocratic charm Sarah was noted for.

"Well, Grandmother would be happy with your design, Mummy." She stood and handed Sarah Grandmother's veil.

Sarah had added fresh white gardenias and daisies to the veil's crown and made the bridal bouquet to match. Adria picked up the bouquet, closed her eyes, and inhaled. "This scent reminds me of your garden in Jamaica. Your gardenias thrived at Ginger Star." She was learning to embrace memories of Jamaica's beauty instead of pushing them away. Her mother placed the veil on her daughter's head and smiled.

"This reminds me of my mother's love for you. She so wanted to live to see you marry. I have a feeling she is here."

"Indeed, she truly is, and she's letting us know how to make everything just perfect. She'd keep us straight if she were here, no doubt." Adria laughed.

The sound of her daughter's laughter was balm to her soul. Sarah was still not accustomed to Adria talking about Jamaica and Ginger Star. For so long, they had acted like those two years hadn't happened, but over the past few years, her daughter had found a way to embrace the past, or at least not run from it. Sarah had been so relieved when Adria emerged from her depression, the darkness she thought that would take her away forever. She hated not being honest with her, but finally had found solace in Adria's happiness. It was more important than her own guilt.

Not a day went by that Sarah didn't wonder about her grandson. Where he was, how he was, and what he looked like. Did he have a mother or father? Who was raising him? The only thing that made her heart smile now was watching Adria light up when Jeffrey walked into a room. It was never difficult for a woman to spot true love. She was so grateful Adria had found joy. No one deserved it more.

Sarah adjusted the veil on the bride's head and pulled it down in front of her face. She looked into Adria's eyes. "Even the veil can't hide those green eyes. The eyes that stole my heart the day you were born."

John stood in the doorway watching the two loves of his life. The women turned to look at him. "Never have I seen anything lovelier. The two most beautiful women in London standing here before me." He walked over and kissed them both on the cheek. "Are my ladies ready to take my arms and head to the church?"

THE SANCTUARY WAS filled with family and friends from all over the United Kingdom. Jeffrey stood in the front of the church accompanied by his brother, Gordon. Adria's closest friend in London, Charlotte, was her maid of honor and stood on the opposite side of the altar. Charlotte's raven black hair set off her ivory skin against her dark red satin ball gown, but certainly did nothing to detract from Adria's entrance.

The wedding march echoed through the church and the crowd stood and turned to watch the bride walk down the aisle. Adria held onto her father's arm and carrying the bouquet Sarah had created. She looked up through her grandmother's veil and saw no one but Jeffrey. Her eyes fixed on him, a lone tear of gratefulness slid down her cheek. She and John made their way down the aisle and stopped in front of the minister.

"Who gives this woman in marriage?" the minister asked.

"I do," John said and looked at his daughter, her green eyes alive with happiness. Lifting the veil over her head, John leaned over and gave Adria a kiss on her cheek.

"I love you, Papa," she whispered. Turning, Adria reached over and took Jeffrey's hand. The rest of the ceremony was a blur to the bride and groom, each lost in their own thoughts.

Once their rings were exchanged, the minister declared the two man and wife. Jeffrey turned and took Adria's face in his hands, gently kissing her. The crowd applauded as the couple turned to look at them, their joy contagious. They walked back down the aisle smiling at everyone as they passed. Standing together, they greeted their guests as they left the church.

Waiting at the bottom of the steps in front of the church, was an open white carriage, being pulled by Streak and Noel, both donning crowns of flowers, large bows, and streamers, adding to the festive mood. Jeffrey held onto Adria's arm as they ran amidst the rice the guests cheerfully threw as the couple ran down the steps of the church. The carriage driver opened the door while Charlotte and Jeffrey helped Adria secure her dress and train inside. Leaning out the carriage window, the couple waved goodbye as the horses slowly pulled the carriage across the city to the banquet hall at her father's club.

ADRIA MANAGED TO get through the reintroductions to all her parents' friends. Jeffrey did the same with his family. "How are you making out, my sweet?" Jeffrey asked as he walked up next to her and lightly touched her arm.

She looked up at him from the edge of the dance floor, grateful he was there. "I'm doing pretty well. I find I am a good listener. The more questions I ask about them, the fewer I have to answer about myself!"

"That's a great strategy. Are you ready to dance?" He took her hand without waiting for an answer and pulled her away from the guests to the dance floor. She stepped up to Jeffrey and they glided around the dance floor embracing each other. He caught the scent of her gardenia perfume and smiled to himself.

She stared into his eyes that held not only her gaze, but her heart. "What did I ever do to deserve such happiness?" She loved the feel of his hand holding her waist.

He whispered in her ear, "I can't wait to feel your smooth skin beneath this gown."

"Why, kind sir," Adria leaned back, cocked her head in mockery, and rolled her eyes. "It is a good thing you are now my husband. Otherwise, I'd have to reprimand you!"

His joy was reflected by his smile. "I can only suggest we say our how-do-you-dos to all of our guests and make a hasty exit!" He looked around to make sure no one could hear. "I'll chat with those on that side of the room, you do the other." He nodded in her direction. "We'll meet at the end and say our goodbyes to the crowd."

"Divide and conquer! I like your strategy," she said. They finished their dance to a room full of applause. They'd been lost in each other, not realizing they were again the center of attention. Jeffrey walked her over toward his parents, trying to steal away to the other side of the room to finish greeting their guests, but someone stopped him.

"Well, hello there, Jeffrey!" A young man slapped him on the back. Jeffrey looked over to find his father's intern, Mr. Franklin, standing beside them. Before Adria could leave, she was drawn into the conversation.

"My love, I would like to introduce you to my coworker, Mr. Benjamin Franklin." The young man was a rather short average looking chap, but as Jeffrey had told Adria a few days earlier, he had a presence about him that was undeniable. Franklin was about the same height as Adria, several inches shorter than Jeffrey, but intense gray eyes that could capture anyone's attention in combination with his light brown hair.

Jeffrey looked at Adria and then back at Ben and she said, "Oh yes! I remember. I'm glad you could make it to our celebration, Mr. Franklin. Thank you for coming."

The young man extended his hand and she accepted. Kissing the back of her hand he said, "Please, call me Ben. It's

certainly my pleasure to be allowed to impose myself on such
a memorable event. The ceremony was lovely, and I must say,"
he looked from Adria to Jeffrey, "It is a good thing you married
this woman or I would have definitely pursued her myself." Ben
looked back at Adria with admiration. She could feel herself
blush but refused to turn away. He wasn't particularly good
looking, but his personality, the inflection of his words, and
American accent, attracted her, as well as everyone else within
ear shot. Before long, there was a group of onlookers hanging
onto his every word of such a young man. "You know what I've
always said, Jeffrey?"

Jeffrey took the bait and asked, "What is that, Ben?"

Ben chuckled and said, "Keep your eyes wide open before
marriage, and half-shut afterwards!" The crowd laughed.

Adria smiled and said, "I trust your apprenticeship at
Palmer's is going well, Ben." She extended her hand and
Benjamin shook it. She looked him in the eyes and said, "My
new father-in-law says you've been invaluable to his printing
house. I'm told you're a quick study."

"That's most kind of him to say. I hope he doesn't get too
upset by my not working today in order to attend your wedding!" Franklin raised his glass and in jest, looked over his
shoulder as if afraid Mark Palmer would see him there.

"I have very much enjoyed my time here in London. Mr.
Palmer has taught me much that I plan to implement when
I return home."

Adria's father was listening and asked, "So, Mr. Franklin,
how does living in London compare to Philadelphia?"

Franklin looked his way and grinned, "Well, I must say
the weather and cloudiness can be a bit overwhelming here.
However, I've discovered your inhabitants tend to live much by
candlelight and sleep by sunshine!"

"Whatever do you mean, Ben?" Jeffrey asked.

"Well, the northern sun you have here comes up much earlier in the morning than in the colonies. I've noticed most here sleep long after the sun has risen. Perhaps if everyone opened their businesses earlier, folks would get out of bed and begin their day with the sunshine!"

"Well, that's a theory I've never considered. Makes sense."

"Everyone wants to complain about the tax on candles, yet we burn way more of them than needed. Just get out of bed!" The crowd around him laughed.

Jumping in to change the subject before anyone could offer up a disagreeing opinion, Adria said, "So, Mr. Franklin, Jeffrey enjoys your essays and I should say, I have as well."

"Your flattery is appreciated. I'm afraid I've received much criticism for my opinions as they don't flatter our traditional religious institutions." She laughed and nodded in agreement as he continued. "But then again, my opinions do not tend to lend much in the way of fact, but merely opinion." He looked around the circle of friends and family. "And as we all know, everyone has one of those!" The guests laughed and began to disperse when Franklin took Adria's arm and asked for a dance.

He twirled her around the dance floor and they faced each other as the song began to wind down. "Well, Mrs. Palmer, I must say you are a delightful dance partner."

She curtsied in her wedding gown, hoping to make a quick escape to meet Jeffrey at the back of the room, as promised. "Why thank you, kind sir." She spotted Charlotte and grabbed her arm, almost tripping on her dress, but made a quick recovery. "Allow me to introduce you to my maid of honor, Charlotte. She loves to dance as well." Adria linked arms with Charlotte, tilting her head and added "and is not quite as clumsy as I!" She pulled her friend over toward Ben. "Charlotte, this is Mr. Ben Franklin, an intern from Palmer's Publishing House."

Charlotte's eyebrows raised and she cocked her head in question. Adria winked at her asking for her cooperation. Charlotte understood her friend instantly and didn't let her down. "Why, Mr. Franklin." She coquettishly cocked her head to one side. "Your reputation precedes you. May I be so bold as to ask you for the next dance?"

Franklin's eyes lit up at the sight of this taller, lovely woman. Not intimidated in the slightest by her stature, Ben said, "My lady, I find bold women to be most intriguing." He smiled and offered his hand and Charlotte accepted. "I pray your boldness extends to more than just a dance!" He whisked Charlotte to the dance floor, creating the diversion Adria had hoped for. She couldn't help but laugh at the cavalier attitude of this brash American. She shook her head and took to her side of the room, greeting their guests as she kept an eye on Jeffrey's progress. Their plan worked perfectly and they met at the rear of the reception hall. "Darling, wait here for a moment," he said and walked over, whispering something in the ear of the orchestra conductor. The music stopped leaving guests twirling in silence. Everyone stopped and Jeffrey spoke up, "Ladies and gentlemen, thank you so much for coming to celebrate Adria's and my happiness. We will be leaving you now, but want you to continue the celebration long after our departure!" Applause erupted, Jeffrey signaled for the music to continue, and the dancing resumed. The couple made their escape to their carriage that whisked them away, but not before many of the guests gathered their silk pouches filled with dry rice and tossed it on the couple as they dashed to the carriage. Rice tapped on the roof of the carriage. Jeffrey closed the door and they both leaned out the window waving goodbye to their loved ones and hello to their future together.

—Chapter Eighteen—

"Genius without education is like silver in the mine." —Benjamin Franklin

1725, Claremont, Jamaica

Rosalie walked down the dirt path that wound around the edge of one of the Ramble House sugar cane fields. She carried a basket on her head full of food for the field hands' lunch. She stopped and lowered the basket to the ground as she prepared to ring the cow bell telling them their food was ready. Rosalie could hear two voices approaching. She knew Thomas was close by as his horse was tethered to a tree near the path.

"I no, no what 'tis happening," Rosalie recognized Thomas' voice as he said to his fellow slave, "He call and she have to go. Can't say no, or she get whipped."

A sick feeling hit the pit of her stomach. There was no denying the awful truth which Thomas apparently already knew. When he came to the road where she stood, she looked him in the eyes and no words were necessary. Realizing she had over-heard him, he walked over to her, wrapped her in his arms and she wept.

"HOW LONG WILL you be gone?" Ronnie asked Marshall as they sat on the veranda eating breakfast. Rosalie dropped off a pot of tea and disappeared back down the steps. "Thank you, Rosie!" Ronnie called to her as she went down the steps.

"You welcome, Miss Ronnie," Rosalie said as she continued to descend the steps.

"Only for a night or two," Marshall answered, "There are several ships that are due in with supplies. I've already received word that the Archer has already docked," he said and picked up a piece of bread.

"I'm sure everything will be just fine. I don't think I should leave right now. We have so many preparations to make for the holidays," Ronnie said trying to sound confident. She hadn't spent a night without Marshall since they married the previous year.

The next morning, Ronnie followed Marshall to the driveway where Thomas stood holding onto Rebel who was tethered to the wagon. Marshall threw his satchel up on the seat. Turning to Ronnie he said, "I will be home soon." He leaned over and kissed her on the forehead pulling her close.

"I wish you were going to Ocho Rios instead of Kingston." She leaned back and looked at him. "Then I could go visit Mavis," she said. It had been several months since she'd been able to see her surrogate mother. They had traded letters back and forth and it helped, but was it wasn't the same.

"We will make a trip down to see her soon, I promise," Marshall said and hugged her again.

"Don't think for a moment I'll forget, my dear," she said and smiled.

Her smile always lit up his heart. "I never miss a chance to visit Hope Falls with you." The falls always was their special place and was on their way to the north coast where they would stop to picnic. He jumped up on Rebel and headed down the steep road, turning to wave goodbye.

RONNIE ROLLED OVER to go to sleep and just as she drifted off, she heard, "Aww, please, Massa, I no say notin' again," and the voice drifted away screaming its way into the darkness. She rolled over believing it to be a dream and fell into a deep sleep.

Waking with a start, she sat straight up in bed, rubbing her eyes trying to figure out what was happening. She'd thought it was a dream, but it wasn't. It was the sound of agony.

"I'll just bet you won't!" yelled McClintock as he let the whip crack on the man's back again. He took a swig of rum to ease his own lousy excuse of a conscience. The slap of the whip on the man's back set her in motion. She threw off the covers and jumped out of bed. She grabbed her robe and ran down the outdoor hallway to see Thomas crawling back toward the slave quarters. Running down the steps with careless abandon, she ran straight into McClintock who was headed to the liquor cabinet to help himself.

"So, what brings you to our liquor cabinet this time of the evening, Mr. McClintock?" she asked. She'd seen him sneak in late at night before, but had ignored him, as Marshall didn't seem concerned.

McClintock looked up, shocked to see her up at this hour. Usually, the alcohol supply was fair game by this time of night.

"Why, I thought perhaps a night cap was in order," he said hoping to brush her off. She could smell the whiskey on his breath from several feet away.

"Well, I'm not surprised you need a 'night cap' in order to get to sleep," she answered. He knew from her tone, she was serious.

"Let's just say it helps," he said. "Some days more than others."

"I can only imagine what it's like to whip another person into submission," Ronnie fumed, feeling her pulse grow stronger and faster.

"Madame, Fergusson, if I might be so bold as to suggest, you should consider backing off just a bit," McClintock said.

"'Just a bit?'" She stepped up to him not caring what he smelled like. "How much would that be, Mr. McClintock?" She walked over to the sideboard and poured herself a glass of water, purposely not offering him one and slammed the door to the liquor cabinet shut. "And why would you need a night cap just to sleep? I can only imagine," she said with a smirk.

He now knew his mistake had been not taking Thomas to the slave quarters to beat him. He realized she must have heard too much. "It's what your husband pays me for, Mrs. Fergusson." He walked over, grabbed the bottle of rum and a glass from the sideboard cabinet, and pulled out a chair from the table. Sitting down as if Ramble House were his own, he said, "The rum at the end of the day is my reward for doing both of your dirty work."

She felt as if he'd thrown cold water in her face, and perhaps he had. She took a deep breath and said, "Well, that being the case, why don't you explain to me why you felt the need to whip Thomas tonight?"

The overseer was shocked at her forthcoming nature. He'd never met a woman like her before, except for perhaps the prostitute he tried to underpay the previous week.

"Let's just say he was spreading unnecessary gossip, riling up the slaves," he said and downed another shot of rum. "I had to put a stop to it."

"Well, I don't believe gossip warrants a whipping, Mr. McClintock! I will talk to Mr. Fergusson when he returns, you can rest assured." She turned on her heel and headed back to her bedroom. She would allow Thomas his privacy right now but would check on him in the morning. He knew Rosalie would tend to him tonight.

McClintock stayed downstairs and drank until he could barely stand. His chair toppled over as he stood. Not bothering to pick it up, he headed toward the front door.

Ronnie sat on the veranda and waited for McClintock to leave. She had Marshall's loaded pistol in her lap, just in case he didn't leave the house, but was relieved when he finally staggered down the steps nearly falling down. Gathering what little composure he had, he weaved his way back to his cottage near the slave quarters.

Ronnie went back to her bedroom and stashed the pistol in her nightstand drawer. Laying down she tried to sleep. What little rest she was able to succumb to, was fitful. Every time she woke, she would hear Thomas' screams all over again. The nightmare of plantation life was evident every day but dealing with it and McClintock when Marshall wasn't home was something she didn't want to experience again.

SEVERAL MONTHS HAD passed and the holidays came and went. Ronnie was satisfied that the slaves were being treated better since her run in with McClintock. Marshall had a talk with him when he returned from Kingston the day after Thomas' beating. At least as far as she could tell, things had calmed down. The house was running smoothly, and she'd been able to travel the island with Marshall from time to time. She'd thoroughly enjoyed spending time with Mavis while they stayed at Queenie's

for a night. Marshall had been talking about a trip to London.
Intrigued at the idea, she was not too sure how things would run
in their absence.

Ronnie sat at the dining room table working on the dinner
menus for the week. Looking up when she heard Rosalie sigh as
she straightened up the sideboard after breakfast, Ronnie
noticed her laying her hand on her suddenly big belly, and it
dawned on her. *She's pregnant. Oh my*! Ronnie sighed as she
remembered Rosalie feeling poorly a few mornings in a row a
while back, and the question just popped out of her, "Rosie, are
you expecting?"

Rosalie looked over at Ronnie and then down at her stomach. "Yes, Miss Ronnie. I having pickney." Tears brimmed and
spilled over onto her cheeks as she turned away. Hurrying across
the room, Ronnie pulled her in close for a hug. Leaning back to
look at Rosie, Ronnie said, "Is Thomas happy about the baby?"
Thomas and Rosalie had been close for years and often talked
about marriage.

Rosalie looked at her with a quivering lip and softly said,
"I wish, but it not his chile." Ronnie didn't understand, until
Rosalie said, "Me pickney belong to Mr. McClintock." She
lowered her head in shame.

Ronnie felt a shiver of anger grip her realizing Rosie had
been raped by their overseer. She knew without asking that
Rosie had never sanctioned such a relationship. Wiping her tears
with her kerchief Ronnie said, "What did McClintock have to
say about this?"

Rosalie looked at her and said, "He get real mad when I not
take the guinea from Tilly."

A sick feeling hit the pit of Ronnie's stomach. She knew
people believed the guinea plant would bring on a miscarriage.
"Well, I'm sure that was a hard decision." She put her hand on
Rosalie's shoulder and said, "Please let me know what I can do to

help. Do you know when the child will come?" She tried to look Rosalie in the eyes, but she resisted.

"By September, I tink." Ronnie did the math in her head. That was only six weeks away. "Oh, Miss Ronnie! I feel so bad. Cause of me, he whip Thomas!" Rosalie broked down and cried.

A sick feeling hit Ronnie's stomach as she remembered that awful night. "What do you mean?"

"I hear Thomas talk about what happen." Rosalie stared out the window, seeing nothing. "I tell him he need to stop, that Thomas and others know. I hope he stop, but it jes' make him meaner." She shook her head and her shoulders slumped.

"Well, together we can figure this out." She turned Rosalie around by the shoulders to face her. "You're not alone in this." Just what that meant, neither of them really knew.

Ronnie's first reaction was to seek out Marshall, but he was away in Trelawny on business and wouldn't be home until late that night. She hugged Rosalie, turned, and headed out the door, down to the stable to saddle up Stars.

"MR. MCCLINTOCK!" RONNIE hollered across the field and motioned for him to ride over. The overseer turned his horse to face her. He let out a heavy sigh and walked his horse over to greet her as she sat on Stars and waited for him. He'd managed to avoid the mistress of Ramble House since their last encounter regarding Thomas.

"Congratulations, Mr. McClintock," she said staring at the man that had her stomach turning.

"Why thank you, ma'am, but I'm not sure as to what it is you're talking about."

"Are you not about to become a father?"

The overseer turned pale in the steamy sunshine. Reaching into his pocket, he pulled out a kerchief and wiped his brow trying to collect his thoughts. Deciding it might be a good time for a lie, he answered, "What on earth are you talking about, Mrs. Fergusson?" He threw in as much respect as he could muster.

"You know full well what I am talking about. Rosalie is expecting your child." He gulped and Ronnie continued. "What do you intend to do about that?"

"Well, I tried to get her to take the guinea, but she refused. Stupid slave!" He lowered his eyes.

Ronnie stared at him, not believing he really just said that. She had wondered what his reaction would be to her revelation, but this was beyond her imagination. "Well, Mr. McClintock, it's obvious you have no remorse or feelings for what you've done. I am relieving you of your duties effective immediately." Feeling resolve she didn't know she had as he looked at her with hatred in his eyes, she was surprised at her own ability to maintain her composure.

McClintock gathered his thoughts, laughed, and said, "I doubt Mr. Fergusson will agree with your decision. He can't run this place without me!"

"Overseers are easy to come by, Mr. McClintock. However, positions for former overseers with seedy backgrounds such as yours may not be as easy to find on the island I'm afraid." She rode Stars just a little bit closer and said, "Please collect your belongings and evacuate Ramble House Plantation before the sun sets." Then, she steered Stars away and headed back to Ramble House.

"NOW WHAT AM I to do? Once they realize they're not being supervised, the entire plantation could grow unruly!" Marshall's temper flared as never before when Ronnie explained what happened with McClintock. He picked up a vase, threw it at the wall, leaving a dent in the paneling. Ronnie was stunned. They'd been married over two years and she'd never seen this side of her husband. She surprised herself with her resolve once again and walked toward him, refusing to be intimidated.

"What are you to do? What about Rosie? What about her child?" Ronnie's temper threatened to get out of hand. Throwing something would feel good right about now. Walking away from him to the other side of the room, she willed herself to stay calm. Whirling around to look at him, she continued to rant, "McClintock allowed you to look the other way and not worry about discipline. Forget about your slaves being 'unruly,' he was the definition of the word!" Her words hung in the air between them. Marshall could find no words to defend McClintock or himself. The chasm between the world they lived in and the world he wished it was, seemed to be growing. Shaking his head, he turned and walked out of the room, leaving her alone.

They endured a few hours of an uncomfortable silence throughout dinner and the rest of the evening before retiring to their bedroom. She sat on the edge of the bed and blew out the candle on her bedside table. Laying down, she rolled over with her back toward him.

She felt his hand reach over and touch her shoulder. "I'm sorry. I just didn't know what to do, and in the process, I lashed out toward you."

Turning back over to face him, she said, "I understand, but I know we can indeed figure this out."

"Together we will." He pulled her close and breathed in her lavender scent. They fell asleep, each dreaming of the other's thoughts.

THE NEXT MORNING, Marshall woke to find her gone. Sitting up on his elbow, he saw her leaning on the railing. He got out of bed, and walked to the veranda, turned to look at her and said, "I know this world we live in pushes and pulls us in directions we would never choose to go. It insists we accept things we normally would not. How can Christianity sanction slavery as it does?" He sighed and shook his head. He'd tossed and turned all night struggling with the paradox. "How can any of us sanction this?"

She shook her head and said, "How can our beliefs sanction one person owning another, Marshall? Where do we get off playing God to make our greed equal to our righteousness?"

He pulled her close and said, "I agree, my dear. Together, we will figure it out and if we don't, at least we will have tried."

Looking up at him she said, "Perhaps Mavis is right. She always told me that God's Word is never wrong, but man's interpretation often is."

"Sounds like a very probable theory to me," Marshall said, nodding his head.

"Our society has already sanctioned slavery, leaving us to deal with it in our own way. We don't have to be harsh and unfeeling." She hugged him again and leaned back to say, "Have you ever considered emancipation?"

He knew this question would eventually present itself. "I've talked to Jeffrey," he said as he took her hand and led her to the carved wooden bench on the balcony. "He explained how to go through the legal process. Only Sam and Mum Lettie were emancipated at Ginger Star and neither chose to leave. As a result, the rest of their staff seems content, but one never knows what might happen during or even after the next raid."

"The Maroons do keep us looking over our shoulders every day, it seems."

"That's true, but it does nothing to change the circumstances of the culture we find ourselves in. Turning a profit in sugarcane on this island without slave labor is impossible with all that is required."

"When 'profit' leads to death and the eventual waste of a human life through slavery, how can it be for good?" she asked. He turned his blue eyes away from her brown ones. He had no answer.

In her world, there wasn't much she could do about owning another person except be as shrewd as circumstances would allow. She tried to be as instructive as she could without giving actual reading and writing classes that were all but forbidden for slaves. "Not to teach someone to read is a grave injustice, Marshall. Let me show you what I've been doing of late."

Ronnie pulled out the little cards and pencils she carried in her pocket to use when the opportunity presented itself. "I've done it a few times with Lawrence. He learned to read and write 'chicken' the other day."

"Because he's so good at burning them?" Marshall asked and they laughed remembering McClintock's rant.

Tilly walked onto the veranda with a pot of tea and went into the dining room to put it on the table. "Good morning," Tilly smiled and said looking at them as she walked past. She and Marshall followed her into the dining room and sat down at the table.

"Morning, Tilly. Thanks for the tea. How is Rosalie today?"

"She say she fine, but her ankles still swell." Just yesterday, Ronnie had insisted Rosalie go on light duty and stay off her feet until her baby arrived.

"Well, please try and get her to keep her feet up. I know how stubborn she can sometimes be." Tilly smiled and nodded.

"Here, I'll show you what I mean," Ronnie whispered to Marshall. She stood and walked over next to Tilly at the sideboard in the dining room off the veranda where she worked with her staff to serve their breakfast. Ronnie pulled a pencil and card from her pocket.

Walking over to Tilly at the sideboard, she said, "See these words here?" Tilly glanced at the card and Ronnie worked in a brief reading lesson. "They say, 'tea pot.'" She pointed to the pot on the sideboard. Handing the card to Tilly, she said. "You keep it and practice writing it when you can." She slipped a pencil into Tilly's hand. She knew Tilly would share what she'd learned with others. She'd heard the staff whispering about the cards and saw them teaching each other how to write the words.

"That was quite intuitive, my dear," Marshall said as he looked over his newspaper when Ronnie walked back over and sat down next to him.

"I hope what I'm doing is alright," she said as she put her napkin in her lap and took a sip of her pineapple juice, and peeked over the rim of the glass at him.

"It's a labyrinth for sure, Sweetheart, but one I'm sure you can navigate," Marshall said.

"I know it can be precarious, but we have to be practical too, Marshall. Is it not more advantageous for you to have a servant (she refused to use to word, "slave") who can go to market for you and not get taken advantage of? Is it not easier for all if they are able to read written tasks for the day? Think about it!"

"You make a valid point," Marshall replied. "We just need to be careful."

And careful she was.

"MISSUS FERGUSSON!" GEORGE broke into the library as Ronnie looked up from her desk where she was documenting the week's expenses.

"Yes, George. What's wrong?"

"Miss Rosalie. She having pickney!" His eyes were wide with excitement. Ronnie didn't waste a second. She gathered her skirts around her and hurried toward the slave quarters. Ronnie burst into the cabin to see Rosalie lying still while Tilly tended to the baby.

Tilly looked at Ronnie and said, "She 'ave daughter." Ronnie looked at the small baby and then to her mother.

"Rosie?" Ronnie smiled as she walked over and took the woman's hand. "You have a baby girl!"

Rosalie's eyes opened and closed as she spoke in a weak whisper, "Tell her I love her."

"What?" Ronnie asked and looked over at the baby. "Tilly, what's wrong with Rosie?"

Tilly looked over, put the baby down, and rushed to Rosalie's side. "She lose much blood." Rosalie's skin had turned chalky and she labored to breathe.

"Go find the wormwood!" Ronnie said to Tilly as she scooped up the crying baby. She turned toward Rosalie to find her eyes closed. Forever.

WEEKS PASSED AFTER Rosalie was laid to rest on the hillside not far from the slave quarters, joining several others that had passed before her. Ronnie made sure Rosalie's cross was larger than the rest. Tilly cared for the baby at first, but Ronnie soon took over. She couldn't resist the tiny one that grabbed her finger and smiled whenever she picked her up. She'd fallen in love with the baby girl she'd named Hope.

Marshall entered their bedroom, looked from the bedside to Ronnie and said, "Well, my dear, I see we have a roommate."

Ronnie had moved Hope's cradle in next to her side of the bed. She tucked Mum Lettie's purple quilt around the baby. "Yes, I'm so grateful you agreed, Marshall." She turned and smiled at him. At first, he'd struggled with the thought of raising McClintock's illegitimate baby, but his love for Ronnie and grief for Rosalie trumped any reservation he might have had. Now that McClintock had found employment on the other side of the island, it was somehow easier. Once word got out about his being let go from Ramble House, McClintock found it wiser to seek employment on the docks of Kingston instead of on a plantation where his seedy reputation preceded him. Still, Marshall would have preferred the former overseer had returned to his native Scotland.

Seeing Ronnie grieve Rosalie while falling in love with little Hope made it impossible for Marshall to resist. One little baby had brought so many smiles their way in just a few weeks. He soon found himself unable to tell where his love for his wife started and the feelings for Hope began.

For the first few months, Norma, one of the field hands who was nursing her own child, served as Hope's wet nurse during the daytime hours. For the nighttime hours, Ronnie used a makeshift bottle she'd made similar to the one Elijah had used during their trek to Casa Daley. After a few months, she weaned Hope over to goat's milk, giving Norma a welcome break. Ronnie rewarded Norma's dedication to little Hope by bringing her from the fields into the great house to help Tilly.

Hope grew into a sturdy toddler with bouncing reddish brown curls and soft light brown skin. She played contently by herself as well as with Norma's little boy, Oliver. The two were inseparable as they chased each other through the house and grounds. She dragged Ronnie's purple lap quilt with her everywhere. Ronnie filled her days playing games and chasing chickens with the youngsters while Norma tended to her duties in the house.

Utter joy filled Ronnie in the form of a little girl who now called her 'Mummy'."

—Chapter Nineteen—

"If you are always trying to be normal, you will never know how amazing you can be." —Maya Angelou

1727, Nanny Town, Jamaica

Amari and Elijah acclimated to life in the Maroon village. After a year of learning how to be both a father and a Maroon warrior, he had fallen in love with Gabrielle, the daughter of the council chief. She was tall and regal with a beautiful smile that melted him. He was so grateful when she agreed to jump the broom and marry him.

It had been four years since they married and two years since the birth of Kisi. He was grateful every day for his good fortune. He knew, without the refuge of the Maroons, his life could have been horrific as a slave on some plantation.

Amari and Gabrielle walked down to the river's edge. They had put off washing their garments long enough. The water ran swiftly over the rocks and down the river bed. Several people from the village sat on the edge of the water, bathing themselves and their children, washing their clothing in the water that ran with surging force over the large boulders. Laughter floated above the sound of the rushing water. "No go far, stay close!" Amari hollered to Elijah. A few people swam in the slower water. Mothers bathed their children, soaping them up before they slipped away to play. It was normally a time of fellowship and fun, except for days like today. They had a large basket of clothing that would take a few hours to clean and wouldn't leave much time to play around with Elijah and Kisi.

"I will, Papa!" Seven-year-old Elijah waved at his father and jumped in the river.

"He swims like a fish!" the Basket Lady said to Amari and Gabrielle. He looked up at her to see blue eyes unlike any he had ever seen.

"Yes, he do!" Amari said.

"Sorry, I no know your name," Gabrielle said to her shaking her head.

The Basket Lady hesitated, but only for a second. She extended her right hand and took Gabrielle's in hers. "My name is Clara. It's a pleasure to meet you. Elijah is such a dear boy." She smiled at Gabrielle.

"Tank you. He have good time playing wit your son," Gabrielle replied and smiled in return.

"Ramon, here comes your buddy!" Clara called out. The last few times they'd met at the riverside, the boys had become fast friends. She was hoping Elijah's parents would allow the boys' friendship to continue. There were no other children near their home other than Maroons. Clara schooled him at their kitchen table and tried to entertain him, but she knew there was no substitute for being with someone his own age.

The Basket Lady had done business with the Maroons, trading her goods for theirs and tipped them off more than once to the plans of the Redcoats, but the Council had been reticent about her friendship with any Maroon. Mistrust based on the color of one's skin and was something neither side could deny. Over time, despite the village's concerns about Clara and Ramon not being Maroons, the Council relented. They'd determined her allegiance was credible and was of no threat to them.

Clara's house was small but built from solid masonry. No hurricane would claim it easily. The thatched roof sloped and caught the rainwater in a concrete cistern on the mountainside below. She kept in shape by hauling buckets of water into the house and tending her garden. The windows had sashes she had painted in bright colors.

She knew the village women were wary of her because she had no husband. She was white, so why didn't she own a plantation? Why would she be way up in the mountains alone? She had no answers that would placate them, so she didn't try.

As the years passed, the Maroon villagers grew to accept her. She would occasionally let them know of any British activity in the area and shared her basketmaking skills with the village women along the riverbank. Ramon and Elijah had remained good friends over the years, sharing most of their free time with each other. Clara had come to think of Elijah as the brother Ramon would never have.

Amari was ready. He hugged Gabrielle and gave Kisi a kiss on the head. "Be so careful," Gabrielle said. She always worried when he left on a raid.

"I will," he said and hugged her again. He knew the dangers, but so far, had been very lucky. They had not committed any violent acts other than setting a few fires to divert the plantation owners' attention. Amari turned and walked over to join his fellow warriors gathered in the middle of the village yard. The sun was getting lower, and the daylight dimmed.

This afternoon, the Maroon warriors were preparing to raid a tea plantation, but they would wait until they could do so under the cover of darkness. There were a few enslaved men at the great house ready to help them gain the weapons and ammunition they needed to fortify their cache. Their plantation contacts had tipped them off that the owner would be out of town for a few days and not there to protect his property. They would work to free as many enslaved people as they could once the weapons were secured. There was no intent to harm anyone, but he knew their best plans could be altered in the heat of the battle.

Moving through the thick Jamaican forest, covered with foliage tied on their every limb from head to toe, the Maroons were expert at being stealth. They would leave the foliage on until shortly before they arrived at the plantation. Then, they would strip down to their war paint and pants.

The sun faded behind the mountain as Amari and the others followed the order of Danquah, their leader, and pulled off the limbs, tossing them into the woods. Amari crouched down next to Kofi. They could hear voices in the distance. The main house stood a distance away from the slave quarters. They'd decided this was not necessarily a good thing as getting to the weapons cache would be a distance away from those they sought to release. The mission had been planned in two different ways. Kofi sounded the Abeng with two short notes to indicate readiness to head for the weapon shed. Knowing it would be heavily guarded, and locked, they readied themselves for battle. As the sun set behind the mountain, it gave them the shadows of cover they needed. They crawled on their bellies while dogs barked and goats bleated in the distance. Amari hoped the dogs were barking at the goats and not them.

All hid in the bushes until darkness gave them the disguise they needed. One by one, they bent low and scurried closer to the small wooden building. It appeared to be unguarded, at least for the moment. Kofi had an informant at the plantation who indicated the cache was left alone for a short while every evening. The plan was to break into the weapons cache during that time and unload whatever weapons and ammunition they could.

After this mission was done, they would head to the slaves' quarters to help their brothers and sisters to gain their freedom.

After climbing the hill next to the great house, Amari and Kofi ran crouched over and ducked behind a wagon parked in front of the building that housed the weaponry. They both carried an axe to use to help bring the door down when the time came.

Amari suspected George, their main contact at the plantation, may have had something to do with the wagon's position which aided their efforts. Wrought iron grates covered the windows and were impossible to penetrate in the short amount of time they had. They already knew the door was their best hope. Only having a few minutes, he had to be as quiet as possible. Amari took his axe and worked on the hinges first, keeping his swings to a minimum and making every one count. They had practiced the movement hundreds of times during their training sessions. The Maroons did not leave much to the imagination when it came to their raids. Nanny, their leader and sister of Cudjoe (leader of the Maroons on the other side of Jamaica), had drilled them relentlessly in her guerilla warfare style. They worked hard to see her nod in approval. The door was easier to remove than they thought. Kofi and Amari quietly pulled the door off its hinges and laid it to the side.

He whistled as a signal to the rest who were still hiding in the trees. It was time to retrieve the weapons and ammunition. Crouching over, the warriors ran into the building. After a few minutes, making sure the coast was clear, they exited one by one, carrying rifles and boxes of ammo back into the dark countryside.

Voices could be heard coming from the opposite direction. The sound of drums played in the distance. Kofi whistled to retreat from the weapons shed and they all quickly evacuated. Finding bags of rice and flour stored in the shed, they hauled them away on their backs, carrying the weapons and ammunition in their hands. Covering ground as fast as their feet would go they headed for a wagon waiting on the next mountain ridge about a mile away where they would drop their cache. Then, they would head back to the plantation to help set the captives free. They'd counted on a full moon to allow for more brightness to guide their way, but tonight was cloudy and the intermittent moon slowed them down.

Running as fast as he could, Amari ran down the mountain and up the side of the next one, passing others that had already dropped their loads and were heading back. They would all gather around the perimeter of the slave encampment before moving in for the release. Amari found the wagon, and after leaving his cache turned and ran back toward the plantation. He caught up with Kofi and the others and they followed one another down the path they'd created the week before that led to the slave encampment. Voices floated in the air. Trying to keep activity normal, the drums from the plantation slave quarters played a slow tune and smoke floated into the air from the leftover coals from dinner.

The slaves were strategically sitting and standing around the perimeter of their encampment. The drums continued. George had coached them well. Men, women, and children were clustered in small groups. Danquah had coordinated the effort well. He blew the signal with the Abeng, two short and one long blow, now the time was right to begin the escape. One by one, slaves slipped away and followed a Maroon. Amari's job was to sound the Abeng with four short blasts if the plantation owner or overseer were to show up. He reached his hand to his belt to feel its smooth cool surface, ensuring it was still there. He watched as, one by one, the slaves slipped into the darkness of the forest.

As instructed, Amari posted up next to the main cabin at the encampment. He thought it odd the door was closed in the midst of an attempted escape. A light blinked off and on from the side window, but by the time he realized it was a warning signal, the door to the cabin opened. He stood still and held his breath, hoping it was the friendly face of a brother African. Instead, a white woman wearing a blue dress stepped outside. She turned to look back inside the building. "Let me know if he needs another bandage. I'll be back in the morning to see how he's doing." A chill ran up his spine. Amari recognized the voice. It can't be. It was the voice of the one to whom he owed his freedom and his life.

AMARI ARRIVED BACK at the village late that night. Seven slaves escaped from Ramble House during the raid. Gabrielle and a few other women were there to help them get settled. There were three men, two women, and two little boys, with Will and George among them. All were scared, but grateful to be amongst the Maroons.

As the escapees settled in, the sun was rising. Amari and Gabrielle took the chance to walk down to the river's edge and spend some time alone. "Let's go to waterfall since di children still sleep," Gabrielle said. "I so grateful you safe," Gabrielle said as they walked down the pathway to the waterfall. Amari knew he should be tired, but the adrenaline from the night before still held him.

The falls rushed from the top of the hill down to a pool at the bottom. It was up river from where everyone washed their clothes. "I need to wash and cool off," Amari said. "Want to join me?"

She looked around to make sure they were alone. "Yes!" They jumped in the pool to freshen up. He jumped in and hollered,

"Whoop! It cold, but nice!" She popped up out of the water next to him.

"How are the ones that escaped?" Amari asked as they paddled to keep their heads above water.

"They little scared, but happy," she said with her arms working to keep herself afloat. "Me thinks they be fine. Just need rest."

"Shh!" Amari put his finger in front of his mouth. They tried to listen over the sound of the falls. The sound of horses' hooves and shouts of men could be heard in the distance. "Come!" he motioned for her to follow him and climb out of the pool. He climbed out of the water and extended his arm back for her hand. She grabbed hold of him but was swept away by the current. Without a moment's hesitation, he jumped back in and swam toward her. The water from the falls was creating a vortex that threatened to suck her further away. His hand finally reached hers, and he was able to pull her to the side of the pool. Amari helped her out of the water. They could hear the shouts getting closer. Holding onto her hand, he dragged her with him up the side of the mountain rocks that led behind the veil of the falling water. He slid as far back behind the falling water as he could, holding tight onto Gabrielle's hand.

They stood there trying to hear the voices over the rush of the falling water. The shouts died down, but the sound of horses' hooves let them know they were closer. Amari's first reaction was to hold his breath to prevent them from knowing he was there but quickly realized the sound of the water made it unnecessary. He looked at his wife and asked, "Are you alright?" She nodded wide-eyed, afraid to say anything aloud.

Daylight was shining on the falling water. Amari took her hand again and led her further back into the cave so their silhouettes would not show through the sunlit waterfalls. They stood there while it became obvious from the sound of horses chuffing, the men had stopped to let them drink. They could hear conversation but couldn't decipher the words.

After a few minutes, the conversation slowed and the sound of the horses' hooves began to subside as the riders went further down the mountain path.

Amari let out an audible sigh and looked at his wife. "I think they gone, but not sure yet. We stay a bit longer." She nodded in agreement. His eyes had acclimated to the traveling shadows along the wall of the cave. He looked up to see something shiny on a rock ledge above. "What dat?" He pointed up to the ledge.

"I no see nothing," she answered, but he was much taller and could see something shining from the prism of light that filtered through the falling water. He reached up and touched what felt like a chain. He stood on his tiptoes to take a closer look.

"Be careful!" Gabrielle said. "The rocks slick."

He reached up and pulled the chain. It was wrapped around something with a blanket covering it. Carefully, he pulled the heavy object off the shelf. They both stared at it. "Looks like someone hide it der," Amari said. He sat it down on the landing they stood on. Once they were confident the men and horses were well on their way back down the mountain, Amari decided it was safe to come out. "You stay here. I take dis to the river side and come back." He carefully carried the heavy chained box to the side of the water pool, put it down, and went back for his wife. Taking her hand, he guided her safely back to the edge of the pool.

"What do you tink it is?" Gabrielle asked.

Amari shook his head. "No know. We open when we get home." They both knew it must be something valuable. Something someone would be looking for one day. They had heard stories of pirates hiding their plunder and suspected that might be what it was.

Once they were sure the visitors were gone for good, they sat back down on the edge of the water falling over the rocks. Amari was curious about the heavily chained box, but knew he had to tell Gabrielle what had happened during the raid of Ramble House.

"IT STRANGE T'ING to know I owe mi life to anudder person, but is true for sure," Amari said. He sat down next to Gabrielle and dipped his feet in the cool, flowing stream. The rocks his feet landed on were warm from the sun's reflection, despite the cool water traveling over them. "I could not blow the Abeng when I saw it was her." Amari looked down at his feet under the rushing water.

Gabrielle swallowed her jealousy once more. Amari talked about this Ronnie woman often. She hid her feelings as best she could and wished they would disappear, but they seemed to always find a way to show up again. "What did she say when she saw you?" she asked.

Amari looked at his wife. His heart hurt as he knew it was difficult for her to hear his confession of loyalty to Ronnie over her people. Her father was the Maroon council chief, next in line to Nanny, but Amari was confident of her loyalty to him, her husband.

"She no see me," he said.

"So, you risked everyone by not sounding the Abeng?" Gabrielle glared at him as she never had before. "Amari, why does this woman mean more to you than I?"

"My love for Ronnie is not that of a lover, but more of a sister." Amari looked into her brown eyes. The eyes that stole his heart years ago. "My love for you is far different. It is deeper, and totally, how do you say?" He stared at her with that quizzical look he always got when he could not find the right word. "Committed?"

"I know our love not di same, but you turn your back on Maroon people when you no blow di Abeng, Amari!" She stared at him, climbed to her feet, and shook her head in disbelief at the sound of her own words. "I no want to tink what di Council do if dey knew." She took a deep breath and walked away from him. He jumped to his feet and followed her. She knew the Council's reaction would be swift and severe. "Wi be cut off from di village. Mi fadder would be as if he never 'ave daughter!" She twirled around to look at him again. "You must promise mi, if dis eva 'appen again, you choose your children, your village. Me."

He reached out and touched her arm, but for the first time ever, she pulled away from him. Amari was stunned and said, "Mi promise, Gabrielle. I no realize." He walked in front of her and lifted her chin with his finger bringing her gaze to his. "Please forgive me."

She took a deep breath and leaned onto his chest as he wrapped her in his arms. He leaned over and kissed the top of her head and stroked her hair. "As of today, my debt to Ronnie has been paid."

AMARI AND GABRIELLE walked back to the village and into their hut of a home to find Elijah getting ready for school and Kisi sitting at the table eating the breakfast he had made for her. Amari tucked the box in the corner, to avoid any questions from Elijah he couldn't answer. "Sorry we not here when you wake," Gabrielle said to Elijah.

"It fine. I leave for archery practice now," he said kissing his mother on the cheek. "She hungry dis mornin'." He nodded toward his sister, grabbed his satchel, and headed out the door, waving goodbye to his father.

Gabrielle kissed her daughter on top of her head as she took another bite of mango. Amari picked up the box and worked on unlocking the chain with a saw. After a while of filing back and forth, the chain fell free. He unwrapped the chain and took off the blanket that covered the object.

Gabrielle walked over to see. She ran her hand over its smooth black surface with the white inlaid shells on top. "It beautiful," she said.

Amari nodded, undid the latch, and opened the lid. Inside, the gold coins, chains, and solid bars of gold laid there shining in the patchy sunlight that filtered into the room, as if waiting to be discovered.

Amari shook his head in disbelief. "Gabrielle, dis much money." He reached in and touched the gold bar on top, picking up one of the chains. He thought for a second and turned holding the chain up to his wife's neck displaying its beauty against her dark skin. "It look nice on you." He smiled.

She took a deep breath and said, "Yes, but must give everything to council."

—Chapter Twenty—

The weak can never forgive. Forgiveness is the attribute of the strong." —Mahatma Ghandi

1729, London, England

Adria and Jeffrey settled into married life and quickly discovered they were quite the duo when it came to business. They complimented each other easily, she with her administrative and persuasive skills with both vendors and customers, and Jeffrey with his keen eye for editing and chasing the most noteworthy stories in the interim.

Six years had passed since they married. Adria's father was on his way back to London to celebrate his twenty-fifth wedding anniversary with Sarah. Adria and her mother had spent weeks preparing for their silver wedding anniversary dinner. He was excited to return. Being away from Sarah left him alone with his own thoughts far too often. When his plans to manage Ginger Star from London fell through, he'd frequently found himself helping the evenings pass by drowning his loneliness in a bottle of rum.

Adria walked into the study. "Dinner is just about ready. Are you hungry?" she asked her husband.

"I'm famished," Jeffrey said as he looked up from his desk.

They both looked toward the doorway when they heard loud voices coming from the foyer.

"Miss Adria!" Margaret ran into the study. "Your mother is not well. Please come!" Margaret took Adria's hand and they ran to the dining room with Jeffrey following close behind.

Sarah sat in a chair fanning herself. Several servants stood close to her. "Mama, what happened?" Adria rushed over and crouched down in front of her mother.

Margaret answered for Sarah. "She began to feel poorly and almost fainted. The smelling salts seemed to help, but she should probably go to bed."

Jeffrey looked at the crowd of servants that had gathered. "Lester, please hurry and contact Doctor Baker. Tell him Miss Sarah requires his attention."

"Yessir," the footman said and hurried out of the house.

Sarah took to her bed and between Adria and Margaret, someone was by her side constantly. Soon, Doctor Baker arrived and examined her. "I'm not sure what's going on. Give her a tablespoon of this elixir," he said as he handed a brown bottle to John, "three times a day. If her fever doesn't break in 48 hours, send for me."

The elixir didn't seem to help, and the fever refused to leave, making Sarah delirious. After a few days, she refused to eat and could hardly drink. Doctor Baker suggested Adria send word to her father. She posted a letter to Jamaica even though she knew it would take many weeks to arrive. She also knew he was possibly already on his way as he had planned to return sometime within the next month.

Adria slept on a cot in her mother's room and listened to Sarah's ramblings as she thrashed about, trying to sleep. Sarah's condition worsened over the next few days, her fever raging off and on. She wouldn't eat and barely drank any water, despite their prodding. Doctor Baker had no more suggestions when he visited a second time. "We just have to wait and see," he said grimly as he packed up his medical bag.

"John," Sarah looked around the room. "Is that you?" She looked toward Adria. Jeffrey stood behind her, lending to Sarah's confusion.

"No, Mama, it's us, Adria and Jeffrey." She knelt down next to her bed. Sometimes it helped to tell her who she was, but not today.

"Where's John?" Sarah asked.

"Papa is on his way, Mummy." It was the best answer she had to give, not knowing exactly when he would arrive from Jamaica."

Sarah's cold hand grabbed hold of Adria's. She still thought John was there. "I knew you'd come. These shadows are getting harder to navigate, my love. What should we do?"

"What do you mean?" Adria asked. She knew her mother still thought she was talking to her father.

"I must tell Adria."

"Tell her what?" Adria looked from her mother to Jeffrey and back again. She could feel the dark cloud coming back.

Sarah opened her eyes, not sure who it was at first until the scent of gardenias comforted her. She looked at her daughter. Sarah knew the spirit of Adria's baby boy never left her and remained in the form of heartache that had become a part of who she was. Sarah had struggled for ten years wanting to tell Adria the truth, but knew if she did, she stood to lose her daughter on so many levels. Her soul had wrestled with her conscience daily. Laying in her bed she was able to listen to the spirit within her that turned out to be stronger than her desire to protect herself from Adria's reaction. For the first time, she felt at peace about sharing the reality of her grandson's birth.

Grasping her daughter's hand, Sarah tried hard to focus and said, "Adria, your baby did not die." Sarah searched her daughter's verdant green eyes, knowing it may well be the last time.

"Whatever do you mean, Mummy?" Adria frowned and leaned back in the chair.

"Your son. He lives."

But . . . you and Papa said he died at birth in Jamaica." Adria shook her head and looked at Jeffrey, then back to her mother. She felt his hand on her shoulder.

"We told you that so you wouldn't worry. We had many reasons that made us decide to send him with the escaped slave."

Adria's mind tried to grasp her mother's words. "The escaped slave?" Thoughts swirled in her head as she tried to understand what they meant. *My son is alive? Where is he? Who is he? How did I not know?*

"Mama! You allowed me all these years to believe my son had died? Now you're telling me he lives after what?" She did the math. "Ten years? How could you keep this from me?" she screeched. Getting up off her knees, she took a step backwards with her cheeks flushing red. Questions tumbled out of her. She looked down at her mother. "Does Papa know?"

Sarah took a deep breath and coughed a little. "Yes."

Adria walked to the window beside the bed. Her body flared with anger and adrenaline. She stared outside, not noticing the rain pelting the window. She was dizzy with emotions that pierced her heart like arrows; arrows of happiness, anger, hurt, and hope. She wanted to lash out at her mother. Turning back to look at her to say something that would feel good if only for the moment, she saw how frail Sarah was. Her mummy had been her best friend and confidante, but now was someone she realized she'd not known at all.

"One thing I was evidently right about was that you and father would indeed make me give my baby away!" Adria was filled with fury as she tried to process this new truth. "You and

Papa hid the truth from me that would have set me free from my nightmares and pain." She thought about their trip over the Atlantic, ill from her loss and the embarrassment she had caused her Papa. Anger rose up in that moment and took hold of her. Picking up a vase, she hurled it at the wall, shattering glass all over the floor. She was disappointed the broken vase didn't make her feel any better.

"So, Mummy, you and Papa gave my son away and allowed me to believe he was dead?" she shouted. "And now you tell me from your sickbed, you are sorry?" It briefly occurred to her that her mother's fever may have broken, but she paid it no mind.

"But he was a negro baby, Adria! We had no choice." Sarah looked away and stared at the wall. Her little girl that played with dolls, her little girl that rode her horse and won blue ribbons, her little girl that had, not just a baby, but a negro baby out of wedlock. "Society would never have accepted your transgression, Adria. Our transgression."

"Oh, and we know all too well that we cannot cross 'society's lines, Mummy! That is for certain." Jeffrey pulled her arm, but she shook him off. "Am I right, Mother?" She felt Jeffrey touch her shoulder. She ignored him. "Am I right?" she shouted.

Sarah turned her head and looked at her daughter. "Yes, you are right."

Adria turned to Jeffrey shaking as he pulled her to him. She leaned back, looking at him, intending to ask if he already knew the secret, but she could see in his eyes that he did not. Her mother continued to babble. Adria turned back and looked at her. At that moment it occurred to her that her son might just be a slave on some plantation. A sickening feeling filled her belly and refused to leave.

Sarah looked into Adria's eyes. "I'm so sorry we ever took you to Jamaica. It was too isolated and lonely. I know you were longing for companionship and love." Her hand reached over toward Adria, but Adria shrank back.

"You gave away your grandson?" Adria asked her shaking her head. Their eyes locked until Sarah's closed.

Sarah slid back into a silent sleep. Frustrated, Adria turned toward Jeffrey and said, "I have to get out of here!" She wanted to put as much space between her and her mother as she could. Turning on her heels, she left the room, leaving Jeffrey standing there stunned by the revelation.

Running down the steps and out the back door, she found it was another gray day with a low mist that matched her mood. Going inside the stable to find some privacy, she went into Noel's stall. Noel pawed at the ground in welcome, but Adria didn't respond. *How could she? And Papa knows too? How could they keep this from me?* She allowed herself to cry as loud as she wanted, howling from the pain. The pain of betrayal by those she loved the most, other than her husband. *Where is my boy? What if he's enslaved on some plantation?* The thought made her nauseous.

She slid down the side of the stall to the floor and leaned back into Noel's hay that laid in the corner. "How dare they do this to me!" She screamed and laid down in a fetal position on the bed of straw. Tears flowed and frightful thoughts continued to come at her as if darts were being thrown her way, each bringing a different type of pain. She felt Noel's nose nudge her in the back. Sitting up she hugged the horse's neck, "I love you too, girl." She welcomed the love and warmth her dear Noel offered as the mist permeated them both. Hearing the stable door open, she looked up to see her husband walk inside.

He sat down next to her in the straw and said, "I wanted to ask how you are, but I've a feeling I know. Or at least think I do." He hoped she hadn't fallen back in that well of depression, but the look in her eyes assured him she had not. Gratefully, he could see that steel will, sometimes known as the 'anger of Adria', rise up.

"Part of me wants to lash out and hurt them back, but a bigger part just wants to find my son."

"I understand completely. Your mother is awake again if you want to talk to her some more," Jeffrey said. "She's asking for you."

Standing up, she shook off the straw. "I never want to lay eyes on her again! How can she call herself my mother and put me through such misery?" Jeffrey stood, pulled a few pieces of straw from her disheveled hair, and handed over his handkerchief. She blew her nose and looked at him. "She told me my son was dead! She's lived that lie for ten years. Ten years of nightmares and wells of depression. Ten years while knowing full well, my son could be enduring the life of a slave on a plantation. How do I forgive that?"

"Adria, she's your mother. Everything she did, she did out of love and concern for you. Whether it was right or wrong, it was done out of love."

"Everything she did she did out of fear of her own reputation!" She walked toward Noel and stroked her side.

Jeffrey turned her around by her shoulders. "Listen to me!" He stared into her angry green eyes. "I know you're hurting, but I also know that your mother isn't long for this world. She's getting weaker and could pass at any time." She looked down at the stable floor. He stroked her hair and caught her gardenia scent. "The last thing you want is to regret your inability to forgive."

ADRIA KNELT DOWN next to Sarah's bed, took her hand, and laid her head on the bed next to her mother. She took a handkerchief and wiped Sarah's tears from her cheeks. Knowing her mother wouldn't live to see too many more sunrises, Adria felt as if all the air in her lungs had been sucked out. Her face twisted with hurt, and her soul was being torn between rage and sadness. Rage at being lied to about her baby and sadness at saying goodbye to her mother, her friend.

Adria looked up and said, "Mama, do you think I could ever find him?" She clung to Sarah's hand, searching her mother's eyes. Sarah stared through her.

"I am sure he is there, but I wouldn't know how to begin. He lives with the Maroons."

Adria gasped. "The Maroons? Are you sure?" She knew the escaped slaves and Indians were in a constant state of war with the British, yet were free from enslavement, at least for now. She felt a small tug of hope. "How did that happen?"

Sarah looked away briefly and then turned back to study her daughter's face, but her eyes were growing foggy and their lids heavy. "He went with the slave that was hiding at Ginger Star." She struggled to stay awake. "Your friend, Ronnie, and Sam might know. Please forgive me, my love." Sarah reached out with her cold hand and touched her daughter.

"My friend Ronnie? And Sam?" Adria was perplexed.

Sarah's head shook back and forth. "My darling, can you ever forgive me?" Tears flowed down Sarah's cheeks as she gasped trying to catch her next breath. Adria could sense her mother's time was short. Sarah reached up and touched her daughter's damp cheek. "I'm sorry to put the burden of forgiveness on you, my love. You've barely had time to digest the truth."

"That's true, but Mummy, how could I not forgive you? I disgraced the family. I am certain you did what thought was best for me. That is all you have ever done." Adria knew she had the right to lash out, but she couldn't bring herself to do it. Thanks to Jeffrey, she'd realized the need to reconcile. She would save the harder questions for Papa . . . when the time was right. "I will love you always." She sat just holding her mother's hand. *So, he is with Amari*? She discovered the thought of her son being with the African somehow gave her more hope.

She felt her mother's hand release hers as she slipped into sleep. Each time this happened, Adria wondered if it was the coma the doctor had warned them about. He had explained that Sarah would eventually slip into a deep sleep she would never wake from. The sleep that would claim her and take her away to the other side. And this time, it was.

SARAH WAS BURIED in the family cemetery near the rear of the estate. The community had gathered around them to say good-bye to Sarah and offer condolences.

The next morning, Jeffrey walked up to the doorway of their bedroom. Adria stood staring through the open French door overlooking the pond. Swans floated by in a silent whisper. Her hair was pulled up to a bun at the base of her neck. In that moment, he fell in love with her all over again as that old, familiar, pensive look on her face tugged at his heart. Jeffery knew Adria's heart followed her son. He'd do whatever it took to help find him which he hoped, in turn, would help her to discover the love she sought for herself, and perhaps, for them both.

Her father had returned just a day after her mother passed. For Adria, watching him mourn Sarah was hard enough without adding to his angst with confrontation. She found herself visiting her memories of growing up instead. She shared it all with Jeffrey, a lot of it he already knew, but he listened as if it was all the first time he'd heard it. She talked about her father teaching her how to ride on Noel, shoot a gun so she could accompany him on fox hunts, and her mother making sure she possessed all the social graces required to survive in London society.

She also ruminated about her son, wondering what happened and how his life was now. Along with the speculating came hope and fear. She tried to embrace the hope and ignore the fear, sometimes succeeding and sometimes not.

Adria turned to see Jeffrey staring at her from the doorway. "I need to thank you, my dear, for listening to me relive my childhood and all the conjecturing about my son. It's amazing how just voicing things aloud enables me to process what is and is not true." She knew, with all her heart, that everything her parents had done by giving her son away, although misguided and self-centered on their part, was done with love and concern for her.

A week passed while waiting to address her father about her son hadn't been easy, but she and Jeffrey agreed it would be best to delay the conversation until after the funeral. Now that Sarah was put to rest, it was time.

"There's no need to thank me, but I appreciate it anyway." He walked over to her, kissed her on the cheek, and stared at the floating swans with her. "Your father is in his library. Are you ready?"

She turned to look at him, her husband, friend, and strongest ally. "What would I do without you?" She stood on her tip toes, returning his kiss, and leaned onto his shoulder. He always made her feel so safe. "But this is one conversation I believe I should have on my own." She leaned back, looking up at him to gauge his reaction. "Are you alright with that?"

He was not surprised. "Absolutely." He kissed the top of her head and stroked her neck. He hoped the confrontation with John wouldn't shrink her back into that dreaded well of depression.

Stepping back, she looked at him, took a deep breath, and said, "There will be some difficult questions and I'm assuming, tough answers for Papa." Jeffrey took her hands in his and she continued, "I don't want to put him through any unnecessary sadness. He's had enough of that for now."

He bent over and kissed the top of her hand. "Just know I am here should you need me."

Adria reached up, she touched his cheek, "It's time." Then she turned and walked out the door, down the steps to his study, her heels clicking on the shiny wood floor to the open door. Her father stood up from the chair behind his desk when he saw Adria enter the doorway. He had aged well and was still a handsome man, but since he came back a week ago and found Sarah was gone, she'd seen a noticeable decline in his physical state. It was as if his shoulders bent on the corners where they before had not. The emotions of her heart melted her resolve. She had rehearsed the questions she would ask. The taunting accusations would make her feel better, at least she reckoned so. But gazing at her father, she could see no theatrics would make either of them feel better. Her love for her father overruled her anger.

"Adria," he said as he walked around his desk and walked toward her. He took Adria's hands in his. He looked from her eyes to her hands that were shaking.

"What's wrong, my dear? Why are you shaking?"

"Papa, Mummy told me an astonishing truth right before she died." The look in his eyes told her she needed to explain no more.

He knew why she was shaking. Lowering his head, he asked, "Oh, my dear, I am so sorry. How can you ever forgive me?" Slowly raising his head, he looked into those green eyes. *I've always wondered how she would handle the truth. Today, I will know.*

"Papa, it's not a question as to if I will forgive you. I've already done that." She touched his arm. "Jeffrey has helped me sort through my emotions and the facts. We both know you felt you had no other choice. Our society is a cruel one, judging people for their perceived mistakes. We all fell victim to that I'm afraid."

John plopped down on the settee and she joined him. He went into the explanation of how the idea of giving the baby to the Maroons to raise came about. "Not a day has passed that I haven't regretted, and questioned, that decision." He leaned his forehead onto his hands as his elbows rested on his knees. "I wonder and pray for my grandson constantly. How can you ever forgive me when I can't forgive myself?" John raised his head and looked at her with fear in his eyes.

"Oh, Papa, I've had time to reflect on Mama's confession." All of her rehearsing left her, and the love for her father won out. "While I must admit, I've been through the total gamut of emotions, I have come to know there can be no other conclusion than to know in my heart you both did what you thought was best for me." She looked at her father; her robust, energetic, intelligent father, who she knew would give his life for hers. He wept into his hands.

"I'm so sorry, Adria. I can only imagine how much this lie has hurt you." It made her physically hurt to see her father break down again. This time, for her heartache. He blew his nose into his handkerchief. "How can I ever make it up to you?" He looked into those verdant green eyes. He shared what he knew about the events leading up to the baby taking up residence with the Maroons, including that Sam and Ronnie had taken part in the handoff.

"Sam and Ronnie?" She was amazed at the web of deceit and how wide it had spread all around her.

"Yes, Sam's brother was our only connection to the Maroons. Your friend, Miss Shepherd, went along to help with the baby and the African."

The revelation that Ronnie had a hand in the deceit almost took her breath. *How stupid I was to think she was my friend.*

She paused to try and gather her composure and said, "Well, it appears she has done quite well for herself in Jamaica, marrying an upstanding wealthy plantation owner such as Marshall. She certainly played her cards right, it seems," she said. *As I pine for my son, she lives the life of luxury as well as a lie about his fate.* Jealousy grabbed her. "How can she deserve any kind of happiness after giving my son away?"

"In her defense, she did not have much choice but to help. Remember, she wanted to provide a safe haven for her African friend," John said, wiping his eyes and taking yet another deep breath.

She considered his explanation and said, "I suppose so, but she kept it from me all these years. I'm sorry, Papa, I just feel duped and betrayed." She looked and could see how much her father had suffered these past few days. His shoulders slumped and his hair seemed to turn gray overnight. Both the pain of his wife dying and now the fear of losing his daughter was taking its toll on him.

She thought for a moment and said, "Papa, I need to find my son. Will you help me?"

—Chapter Twenty-One—

"Hate, it has caused a lot of problems in this world, but it has not solved one yet." —Maya Angelou

1730

John immediately posted a letter to Sam and Mum Lettie at Ginger Star letting them know about Sarah's passing and their desire to find his grandson. Adria sent thank you notes to all that attended Sarah's funeral and announced their intention to travel back to Jamaica for an extended period of time. Everyone assumed they were doing so in an attempt to get away from so many memories of their mother and wife, making no further explanation necessary.

Their trip across the Atlantic to the West Indies was uneventful. The weather had cooperated for the most part and they had been able to avoid the storms with the help of a stellar crew. After several weeks on board, they'd passed by Cuba and were now skirting the north coast of Jamaica, leaving London in the midst of winter, only to arrive to the warm winds of the Caribbean.

"My dear, you described the sea as a million shades of blue and green. It was truly unimaginable until now." Jeffrey was in awe of the depth of the Caribbean's beauty. He pulled off his overcoat, draping it over his arm.

Adria pointed at the aqua horseshoe-shaped cove. "That is Dry Harbor where you see the pier." Her bonnet shielded her face from the sun. "It has been said Christopher Columbus was marooned here in Saint Ann's for a year back in 1503." Adria and Jeffrey leaned on the ship's rail as she pointed out familiar landmarks. "That's the Seville Plantation where you see the dock." She pointed toward the shoreline.

John had been watching the couple from a distance. He was relieved now that his daughter finally knew the truth. Even though he'd carried the guilt of the lie that had plagued both him and Sarah, he enjoyed the feeling of relief now that Adria finally knew the truth. Having to live the lie of his grandson's fate had given him perspective, especially now that the secret was uncovered. With Sarah's passing, he realized more than ever how short life could be. He was forever grateful to his wife for her brave confession that had set him free and given him the determination to find his grandson.

John walked up behind the two and said, "The Sevilles are quickly becoming one of the largest sugar barons in the Caribbean. When I left Jamaica last, slave shipments were arriving almost daily."

Adria cringed at the mere mention of slaves. After all, her son could one day be captured and become one. Her stomach hurt every time she thought about the possibility. She found anger grabbed her whenever she thought about Ronnie taking part in the deception, as well as Sam. She excused Sam in her thoughts knowing he really had no choice. But Ronnie?

She'd noticed changes in her father over the past few months before their trip across the Atlantic. He was a softer, more emotional man than ever before.

Mountains reached up behind the shoreline to the blue sky full of blossoming clouds. "I'd forgotten how beautiful it is here," Adria said. She took a deep breath.

"The island of wood and water, Xamayca, was the name given by the Tianos Indians," John shared.

Adria nodded and said to Jeffrey, "The Tianos were the original inhabitants of Jamaica. Now, many are part of the Maroon tribes." She'd been researching the Maroons, as best she could, since she discovered her son was, hopefully, among them.

"Jamaica is just as beautiful as you both have described. I'm thrilled to finally be here." Jeffrey reached around her from behind and hugged her tight.

The ship sailed into the dock and jarred as the crew lowered the plank down to the pier. John stepped back and said, "I'll stay here and ensure all of our trunks are gathered together and delivered to the wagon. You go on ahead." Adria and Jeffrey agreed and gathered their smaller belongings.

She held Jeffrey's arm as they disembarked down the wooden walkway. The warm Jamaican sunshine was a welcome change to the cold dreariness of London, and she quickly pulled a fan from her purse. Villagers milled around. Wagons were lined up as they came to greet the ship and gather their deliveries for stores and plantations. "Hey, look out!" Jeffrey yelled to a passerby carrying a large bag of rice. Adria ducked as the man swung around. She fanned herself as she backed away.

"Oh, my apologies, madam," the offender said. He placed the bag on the ground to wait for another as it was off-loaded. The man looked at Adria and immediately recognized her. "Adria! I'm stunned to see you here," Marshall said.

Her eyes flew open with surprise. "Why, Mr. Fergusson, I'm surprised see you as well. It's nice to see a familiar face, even if you did almost knock me down!" She laughed and extended her hand as he planted a kiss on top. Then she remembered who he had married. Her adrenaline kicked in.

Marshall looked up at her. "Mr. Fergusson was my father. Please call me Marshall." He flashed his smile and worried about where Ronnie was. He looked Jeffrey's way and extended his hand. "It's good to meet you, Mr. Palmer, I assume."

"My pleasure to make your acquaintance." Jeffrey took his hand and nodded in return.

"Oh, where are my manners?" Adria asked. "Marshall, this is my husband, Jeffrey Palmer."

"Well, best wishes to you, my dear, and congratulations to your lucky husband!" Marshall scanned the crowd for Ronnie. "What brings you back to Jamaica?" He looked back at Adria afraid he already knew the answer to his own question.

Adria's attention was drawn to someone walking up behind Marshall. She recognized Ronnie who looked up as their eyes locked. Adria's heart jumped and anger took over. Jeffrey tried to pull her back, but she slipped away from his grip.

Taking a deep breath, she said, "I believe your wife," she pointed at Ronnie and said loudly, "could let us both know who it is I seek and where to find him!"

Heads turned their way to see what the ruckus was all about.

Ronnie's face went white and her stomach tightened. Without thinking, she said, "I do know, and I will."

"I would hope so, since you're the one who gave him away!" Adria took a step closer to Ronnie, but Jeffrey took charge and stepped in between them.

"Well, we certainly didn't anticipate meeting you both here," Jeffrey said looking at Marshall, his eyebrows raised. Both men knew their wives and recognized the need to diffuse the situation quickly. "However, perhaps we should arrange a meeting in a more private setting." He looked at the women who stared at one another. Adria's look was more of a glare and Jeffrey recognized the red flushing of her cheeks which meant she was ready to lose her temper in a rare but serious way. He knew there was limited time to make their exit before she said even more.

Marshall looked at Ronnie who had gone pale in the Jamaican sunshine. He put his arm across her shoulder, pulling her close. The women stared at each other. "Why don't we plan to meet you at Ginger Star in a few days, giving you time to settle in?" Marshall asked.

"'A few days?' I've waited ten years, a few more days is a lifetime!" Adria shouted drawing even more attention.

Jeffrey steered her away from the crowd whispering, "I realize that, but we do need to settle in and see what awaits us at Ginger Star." Looking back over her shoulder at Marshall and Ronnie, Adria could see they looked stunned. She didn't care. *Let them worry.* "I should take them before the magistrate for what she has done to me!" She kept walking, her heels clicking on the dock, toward the string of awaiting wagons and carriages.

Jeffrey took Adria's elbow and steered her toward their carriage. He said, "We need to make a plan and they can help us do that. It looks like your father is waiting for us. Is that Sam?" he asked, pointing toward their carriage.

Adria shook her head in resignation. They walked past several wagons and coaches before she recognized Sam holding Chance's reins. "Sam!" She let go of Jeffrey's arm and ran toward the older black man. Gray peppered itself through his hair, but that was his only sign of aging. Sam hopped down from the coach and hugged her tight. She'd struggled knowing Sam was involved with the handoff of her son to the Maroons, but she also knew he hadn't had much choice in the matter. There was no denying the love he had for her, nor her for him.

Sam kissed the top of her head and leaned back to look at her. "Why Miss Adria, you not change much. Still beautiful!" He took his hat in his hand, looked down and said, "I so sorry 'bout Miss Sarah."

"Thank you, Sam. We all miss her so much, especially Papa," Adria said.

"Yes," Sam said as he looked down again and shook his head. He looked back up to see Jeffrey. "And dis must be Mr. Palmer."

Jeffrey shook Sam's hand. "Please, Sam, call me Jeffrey."

"Yasser. Glad you around to take care of Miss Adria. Where Mr. John?" He looked over their shoulders.

"He's helping to deliver our trunks and should be here soon," Jeffrey replied.

"I go help him," Sam said as he turned and walked toward the ship.

"Mum Lettie!" Adria stood on her tip toes looking over Jeffrey's shoulder. She ran down the dock to greet the older woman. Mum Lettie was as tiny as ever. She had not changed much in ten years. She wore her signature blue kerchief over her head and her brown eyes were wide open at the sight of her surrogate daughter she'd not seen in ten years. Adria could tell Mum Lettie was still able to see right through her. She hugged the older woman, leaned back to look at her and said, "My heavens, you are a sight for sore eyes."

Mum Lettie was relieved. She wasn't certain how Adria would react to seeing her now that she knew about Elijah. Mum Lettie knew Adria would be disappointed that she'd known her son lived and didn't tell her. She knew the conversation was inevitable, but was thankful for the reprieve, even if only for the time being. "You 'ave turned into such a likeness of your mum, my dear. So sorry she gone."

"We all are. It is very strange and difficult for everyone, but mostly Papa." They both looked at John as he helped to finish tying the trunks to the roof of the coach. "I think he's happy to be back in Jamaica though. Seems as if he's more at home here than London."

Jeffrey walked up to where they stood and said, "Adria, are you ready?"

Adria turned toward him. "Yes, we are." She turned to look at him. "Jeffrey, this is our dear Mum Lettie."

"Adria has made it clear to me that you are the most valued of friends, Mum Lettie." He bent to kiss the top of her hand, something Mum Lettie was not accustomed to. She smiled and could feel herself blush, grateful no one could tell.

"Tank you, kind sir." She dipped a small curtsy. "And tank you for lovin' our Miss. Adria." Mum Lettie looked at her almost daughter.

"She makes it very easy to love her. Shall we?" He offered his hand to her and led her to the coach, opening the door. Mum Lettie and Adria climbed in with his help. Looking out the window, he could see John greeting Sam with a handshake and slap on the back as they walked toward the carriage.

"Mum Lettie!" John exclaimed as he reached inside the carriage to greet her with a brief hug. "It's wonderful to see you again."

The older woman nodded and said, "Tis a blessing to have you back, Massa John." She looked toward Adria. "I so sorry you lose Miss Sarah." The older woman's eyes brimmed with tears at the thought of her old friend's passing.

"Thank you, my dear. I miss her every day." He looked at Sam. "Well, I think I'll sit up front with you, Sam." He looked back at Adria, Jeffrey, and Mum Lettie and said, "You folks enjoy the ride."

The trip back to Ginger Star helped Adria forget about the confrontation with Ronnie for a while. She had fun pointing out different landmarks and memories to Jeffrey. The shoreline shimmered with sunshine as Jamaica welcomed her home.

They traveled through Ocho Rios which bustled with wagons and horse traffic as folks headed back with their deliveries from Dry Harbor.

They traveled on past the town and further along the shore-line with glimpses of the sea to their left. Sam guided the coach onto the Ginger Star driveway. "My goodness, look how much the vegetation has grown! Mama would be so pleased, Papa," she hollered leaning out the window of the coach.

"I believe she would be, my dear." John smiled at the bright red heliconia blooming in an archway over the Ginger Star sign.

Arriving at the great house, the men carried the trunks inside. She looked out the window of her old bedroom, over-looking the path leading to the sea. Glancing over her shoulder at Jeffrey, she said, "I never realized how much I missed it until now. I wouldn't allow myself to remember too much as it reminded me so much of what I'd lost here. But now, I feel as if I'm home." He wrapped his arms around her waist and nuzzled his nose into her neck, breathing in her signature lavender scent.

"That makes me very happy," Jeffrey said. She turned around to look at him. "I wasn't sure what your reaction might be. Just to see you smile makes everything right with my world."

"Well, running into Ronnie as we did, I was unnerved. I'm sorry I was so out of control."

"Truly understandable. Given the circumstances, I believe you handled yourself as well as you possibly could."

"Well, I'll try to control my emotions better next time we meet," Adria said as she walked past him, touching and remem-bering each piece of furniture. She pulled open the drawer of her desk and noticed a tangled circle of thread and shells lying there. "Oh, my. I've often wondered what became of this." She picked up the tangled necklace. "I found the shells along the Ginger Star shoreline shortly after we arrived here from London."

She remembered asking Mum Lettie to help her string the shells. "Try dis," the older woman had said, handing her a strong thread. "I use it to tie many tings together." She threaded the string through a large needle and handed it to Adria.

She took the needle and thread, and worked it through each shell, some baby conchs, and some scallops, tying a knot next to each one so they were separated on the string. By the time she was done, the string was a good eighteen inches long. She'd knotted the ends together and wore the necklace constantly until one day the string broke and she put it away in the drawer. She hadn't pulled it back out until now. Carefully, she tucked it away in her skirt pocket.

"The sea is just a short walk to the cliff and down the steps." She grabbed his hand, "Let me show you." They walked down the hallway, through the open-air living room to the grounds, and she marveled at the size of the foliage. "Everything has grown so much. Look at Mama's roses!" She walked over to Sarah's rose garden. Blooms in every color stared back as their fragrance wrapped around them. "These were so small when we left. It appears Mum Lettie has taken wonderful care of them." They continued further down the path toward the sea. Suddenly, Adria stopped and stood still when she caught a glimpse of the thatched roof of the cottage.

"What's wrong?" he asked.

She stared as the memories washed over her. Standing in the spot where Mum Lettie found her in labor, the physical pain was but a faint memory, but the emotional ache came back with a vengeance. "I suppose I should have anticipated . . . " She took a deep breath. He stood back to allow her room to remember.

"What is it?" he asked.

Shaking her head, she said, "Nothing. I won't be a slave to my memories any longer. It is time to make new ones." She grabbed his arm and they continued to walk. She turned and looked back at the door of the cottage, sighed, and spun on her heel. "Down this way to the sea."

RONNIE AND MARSHALL rode their horses down the mountain toward Ocho Rios and Ginger Star. Ronnie hoped she was ready to take the lashing that Adria would surely give her; she deserved it. In a way, she was looking forward to the meeting after ten years of dread being her daily companion. Turning down the lane to Ginger Star, memories tapped her on the shoulder, but she took deep breaths and kept Stars moving forward.

They rode up to the front of the house where Sam stood on the steps. Ronnie had managed not to revisit Ginger Star since she and Mavis had been there all those years ago. The memories were everywhere. "Afternoon!" Sam waved and grabbed the reins of their horses, tying them to the hitching post. They dismounted and Jeffrey reached out and shook Sam's hand. Sam walked up to Ronnie, took her hand in his and shook it. He knew how hard this was going to be for her. "Good to see you both."

"It's nice to see you too, Sam." Marshall slapped him on the back as they walked up the steps and into the house.

"Same to you, Mr. Fergusson." He smiled and said, "Miss Ronnie. It been long time. It look like Ramble House treat you well."

"Yes, it does." She wanted to ask about his brother, Danquah, but thought better of it.

They followed Sam to the drawing room where Adria and Jeffrey sat. As if in unison, they stood and welcomed them. After the pleasantries, Adria asked, "Would you gentlemen excuse us ladies while we take a stroll around Ginger Star?"

Jeffrey was surprised and impressed at Adria's ability to take control of the situation. She was stronger than even he'd realized. "Why, of course, my love. Take all the time you need. It'll give Marshal and me an excuse to light up a cigar." He looked at Marshall who raised his eyebrows in obvious approval. "Fresh from Cuba." Jeffrey opened his desk drawer and the scent of fresh cigars permeated the room.

Ronnie took a deep breath and followed Adria out of the room, glancing over her shoulder as she left. Marshall winked at her and grinned, trying to lend some silent support. He knew she dreaded this meeting, but also knew Ronnie was stronger than she thought.

The women walked in silence down the pathway toward the cottage. Thoughts swirled in Ronnie's head wondering what to say, how to start the conversation when Adria walked up to the cottage door and opened it. "I haven't been in here since I've been back," Adria said as she entered the dark room. Cobwebs hung in corners and light filtered through the slats of the shutters. Adria reached up and opened the shutters on one side while Ronnie opened the others.

Adria looked around the room. There was still a knife and a ball of twine sitting on the table. She picked up both and stared at them in her hands. "I suppose these have been here all this time, used to tie off the umbilical cord of my son who does indeed live. To think I really do have a son." She looked at Ronnie as tears overflowed her eyes. Ronnie was so tired of the tears. She'd learned to carry a handkerchief and pulled it out.

"Yes, you do." Ronnie said. "Please, let me explain."

Adria turned away and picked up the knife. "No need for an explanation. Papa told me what happened and said you really had no choice but to go along with their plan." She put the knife down, not trusting her instinct of wanting to harm Ronnie.

"That's true, but I'm not without fault." Ronnie said. She was sure Adria was going to lash out and her former friend didn't let her down.

Adria whirled around to face her. "Well, if you want to know what I really think, I think you used me to protect yourself and, in the end, gave away my son and covered it up!" Adria walked to the threshold of the door and turned back to face Ronnie. "I kept you from getting caught, both you and your African friend. And you thanked me by giving away my son!"

Ronnie backed up and sank down on the edge of a cot. She looked down at her hands. She couldn't look into those green eyes right now. "Yes, that's true." Knowing she didn't have an excuse that would make either of them happy, she continued, "I've lived it over and over again, trying to figure out how it might have been different. I even thought about taking Elijah away on my own, but," she looked up at Adria who now hovered over her and said, "I had nowhere safe to take him."

"Well, I've lived it every day for ten years. Grieving for my baby who hadn't died." She considered slapping Ronnie across the face, something she'd imagined for weeks now, but knew that while it would feel good for the moment, it would have no lasting advantage. "Logic tells me I should give up hope of ever seeing him, but I refuse."

Adria had been through a full range of emotions when she thought of Ronnie's involvement in the cover up. She'd envisioned slapping, screaming, and pounding on her emotionally and physically. She'd run every possible conversation and scenario through her head and finally realized she'd get nowhere with the animosity that had taken up residence in her heart. A calm stillness fell over her. She looked at Ronnie and recognized the pain she suffered. Had they indeed shared the same grief all these years? Adria realized that forgiving was the only way she could survive this. She'd managed to absolve her parents and now, she knew she had to extend the same to Ronnie. Blame and resentment would slowly kill them all as well as any chance she had of ever finding her son.

Ronnie stood up and faced Adria. "I'm so sorry. I should have never allowed the truth to be hidden all these years." Ronnie looked at the green eyes that could capture anyone in their stare. "But I was paralyzed when it came to doing anything about it." Ronnie knew if she tried to place the blame at the feet of John and Sarah, she would just alienate Adria further. They were her only "excuse," leaving her with none.

Adria took in a deep breath. She knew she needed Ronnie's help to figure out how to find her son.

"Well, I've decided you are an essential piece of the puzzle, and I need your help. Papa tells me his name is Elijah."

"Yes, Sam suggested the name," Ronnie said. "It means 'God is strong.'"

"Well, it's a good name. One I'm sure he'll need to draw on someday." She turned and stared Ronnie in the eyes. "So, tell me where you left him." She sat down on a cot and Ronnie joined her.

Ronnie went on to recall the trek to Casa Daley where they handed both Amari and Elijah over to be sent to the Maroons. "We walked in the dark and I carried Elijah in a sling through the forests, up and down the mountains. When we finally arrived at the great house it was almost dawn."

"You went to Casa Daley? Did you meet Melinda?" Adria asked.

"Yes, she helped Sam to coordinate things with the Maroons," Ronnie said. "Do you know her?"

"We met a few times at social events when I was here in Jamaica, but I didn't know her that well," Adria said. "Somehow it makes me feel a little better. Please go on."

Ronnie took a deep breath, let it out and said, "I've relived pulling Elijah's little hand away from my finger," she looked down and held her right pinky finger with her left hand and continued, "and handing him over to the wet nurse countless times." Ronnie stared into space, seeing nothing but her memory, "I so wanted to take him and run, but where could I go?" She shook her head and said, "When his tiny hand wrapped around the woman's breast, I broke down and had to turn away." Her voice cracked as she looked at Adria. "I found I'd fallen in love with your baby. I knew by letting him go, I was betraying you, the only friend I had in the world. But I could think of no alternative." She hung her head and said, "Saying goodbye to him and Amari all at once was almost more than I could bear." Ronnie looked at Adria to see tears sliding down her face, matching those of her own. "Oh, I'm so sorry, I shouldn't have said so much."

Adria pulled a kerchief from her pocket, wiped her tears away and handed it to Ronnie saying, "No, please continue. I need to know all I can about my son."

Ronnie hesitated, slightly, before continuing. "The one consolation I had was that I knew Amari would look after Elijah in every way he could. Amari and I were both nearly hysterical when Sam and I had to take our leave. By the time we returned to Ginger Star, your father refused to let me see you as you were to depart that day for London." She shifted in her chair and continued, "If it had not been for Sam, and later Marshall, I don't know what I would have done. Or how I would have survived any of this."

The sight of Ronnie falling apart did nothing to make Adria feel better as she had thought it would. It was obvious her pain was as real as her own. Was it really necessary to browbeat her further? She decided not. Adria felt unexpected sympathy for the woman who had aided her parents. She slipped her arm around Ronnie's waist, her one-time friend. She was surprised at her own reaction, but now realized Ronnie had only been a pawn in her parents' grand scheme. Adria had made excuses for Sam and Mum Lettie who had no choice but to obey her parents, and now understood Ronnie had endured the same manipulation.

"Perhaps, but there's no need to continue to berate yourself," Adria said.

It took a few seconds for her remark to sink in. Ronnie was stunned at her kindness and turned to look at Adria. "What can I do to make it better?"

"Help me find my son."

ADRIA PULLED THE cottage door closed behind them and the two walked through the grounds of Ginger Star, heading back toward the great house. For a few minutes, they strolled quietly in the same comfortable silence they'd found with each other ten years earlier. They began to talk in earnest trying to get to know one another again. Talking through the situation they found themselves in had knocked down the wall and allowed them to reconnect. They talked about the past ten years and what had happened in their lives, first with polite pleasantries and then on to major events.

Adria realized her anger had prevented her from remembering just how much she enjoyed Ronnie's company.

"So, when you married Marshall, did you leave Ocho Rios and move into Ramble House?"

"Yes, Mavis continues to run the mercantile on her own. I've missed her so much. I'm afraid I don't get to spend much time with her these days. She's very much a surrogate mother to me."

"Well, let's see if she can join us for dinner tonight. I would love to see her again," Adria said. The two walked up to the front steps of Ginger Star and paused. "Mavis was always one of my favorite people here in Jamaica. I'll send a note over to her now." Together, they walked up the steps and inside to the drawing room. Adria walked over to her desk to jot a quick note to Mavis. The task done, she walked to the foyer and handed it to Solomon, the footman, to deliver. The aroma of cigars lingered as Marshall and Jeffrey sat in the soft leather chairs talking. They stood as the women walked back into the room. Adria smiled and said, "We're ready to work on finding Elijah together."

Ronnie walked over to Marshall for a hug. He could see she'd been crying but knew immediately that they had worked things out between them.

Adria stood next to Jeffrey who kissed her on the cheek. "That's wonderful, darling. Shall I call for Sam and Mum Lettie? They're anticipating a meeting with us."

Adria nodded and said, "It sounds like we have some planning to do."

THE SIX OF them sat at the dining room table, each with a cup of tea and scones on a plate in front of them. While the sight of black and white folks sitting together breaking bread was unusual, no one at the table felt as if it were. They all had a common goal. To reunite Adria and Elijah.

"So, Sam," Adria said, "Do you think you could contact your brother, Danquah, and see if we could arrange a meeting?"

Sam had already talked the idea over with Mum Lettie and said, "Yes, I tink I can reach my bredda, Danquah, an' ask to

meet wid dem," He looked at Adria and Ronnie. "I will head up
der in di mornin."

"Thanks, Sam. Ronnie can go with you, if that's alright,"
Adria said and Sam nodded. "Ronnie, do you think it a good
idea if you meet with them first, before I'm introduced?"
Adria asked.

Ronnie looked briefly at Marshall and back again and said,
"I think that's probably the wise thing to do. It might be good
for me to get a feel for the situation. None of us knows what we
might be facing."

"You're quite right," Adria said and looked at Sam, "So, you'll
both leave in the morning?"

Sam looked at Ronnie and he nodded. "Yessum, we should
leave at first light."

It was decided Sam would travel back to Ramble House with
Ronnie and Marshall that night so the two could get an early
start on their trek to the Maroon Village.

RONNIE PUT HER foot in the stirrup and swung her leg
over Stars, turning her in the direction of the Blue Mountains.
A rooster crowed as sunlight peeked through a cloud into the
valley below, giving them enough light to navigate the trail. They
followed the path up the mountain. Sam had already sent word
to Danquah asking for a meeting with Amari and Elijah. "I not
sure if Danquah or anyone be at Hope Falls, but we gonna see."

The climb up the mountain was steep, but Stars and Chance
navigated the little more than a pathway through the steep
hills as if they'd done it before. As they rounded the first mountaintop, clouds hugged the peaks and a low-lying fog shadowed
the valleys as far as she could see. It never ceased to catch her
gaze, as it did again today. They were able to let the horses run as

fast as they wanted until the next ridge slowed them down. The cool moist air invigorated her and Stars as she allowed the horse to run with abandon. Ronnie found herself praying for a good outcome, whatever that might be, as she clung to Stars' back and they flew through the mist.

Sam slowed Chance and Ronnie pulled Stars to a trot. Looking at Ronnie, he said, "We 'sposed to meet Danquah over der." He pointed to a banyan tree a few hundred yards away. "It called Hope Falls." She could hear the roar of the falling water as they rode alongside one another.

Looking past the tree she said, "Yes, I think I was there before. It's a good meeting place."

Sam looked at her and asked, "How you makin' out wid all tis goin' on?" They had run into each other several times over the past ten years, in town or at a plantation party where Sam would have driven John to the event, but they'd never had the opportunity to talk at any length. Their social status had controlled their lives then and now. Sharing an instant connection every time their paths crossed, they had a mutual respect for each other she knew would always be there, making their friendship an easy and comfortable one. She knew Sam was one of the people she could always depend on.

"I'm doing much better than I thought I would be, Sam. Thanks for asking." They pulled their horses to a stop and he nodded in agreement as she slid off of Stars. She'd always known, but it was now solidified in her mind that Sam was an integral part of her life. This man who'd chosen to stay at Ginger Star instead of linking arms with his brother and the Maroons, now caught in the middle. Again.

Ronnie jerked around when something moved in the corner of her eye. Bushes swished and seemed to walk toward them. The next thing they knew, two dark men stood before them pulling off branches they'd used for camouflage. Ronnie recognized Amari immediately. He smiled. Her heart smiled in response. She'd had no idea seeing him again would bring back so much so fast. "Amari!" She walked toward him as fast as she could, flinging her body into his arms, he embraced her as never before. They both recognized their bond could never be refuted. It just was. She leaned her head on his shoulder and felt him hold her tight.

Amari leaned back and looked at her. "You look like fine lady, Miss Ronnie."

"Why thanks, Amari. Life at Ramble House has been good to me."

Amari's heart skipped a beat as he remembered the raid on Ramble House. He did what he could to hide the memory of Ronnie coming out of the slaves' quarters that night. He decided it best to change the subject quickly before his thoughts and face betrayed him. "Miss Ronnie, Danquah tell me Elijah's mudda is back?"

They walked away from Sam and Danquah to talk. "Yes, she returned from London just a few days ago. She knows about Elijah. Her mother confessed the entire story right before she died." Ronnie looked over at Sam and Danquah. They were talking quietly, catching up as brothers do. Looking back at him, she said, "She wants to meet him, Amari."

He shook his head and walked away from her trying to collect his thoughts. He always feared this would happen. Amari just didn't realize how much it would scare him. Watching his son meet the mother he'd never met would be traumatic for everyone, most of all Gabrielle, who he knew loved Elijah as her own. Both of them did and he was surprised at his own fierce need to protect them. But he also knew he owed Adria for taking him in when he needed it most. Taking a deep breath, he turned back to look at Ronnie, a tear sliding out from the corner of his eye. "When this happen?"

"I'd say that's up to you. Does Elijah know about Adria?"

Wiping off the tear with the back of his hand, he nodded and said, "I tell him truth since he small. Gabrielle, my wife, is his mudda now and he love her."

"I understand. I'm so happy you found someone to love and share your life with." She touched his sleeve. "I heard you had married. Tell me about her."

His face flashed a brief smile. He appreciated her interest as he described his beloved Gabrielle. "She a strong woman. More dan me in many ways." He smiled at her. "We also have daughter, Kisi. Elijah is good brudda to her."

"Oh, Amari, that's wonderful." Ronnie touched his arm. "I'll bet she has your smile."

He grinned. "Yes, and my poor temper, I tink!" They both laughed remembering his, sometimes, impatient ways. At the sound of their laughter Sam and Danquah glanced their way wondering what was so funny.

"Do you know when can you bring Elijah to meet Adria?"

"I talk to Danquah now." He turned and walked over to Danquah. Sam joined Ronnie and they looked at each other, each with hope in their eyes.

Amari and Danquah talked for a minute. The two walked over to Ronnie and Sam and Danquah said, "I talk to Nanny and the council to ask. No can bring Elijah 'less dey approve."

"I understand." Ronnie said, looking at Amari and Danquah. "Thank you, both. I know you took a risk to come here." She took a deep breath and swallowed hard.

Amari nodded and turned away. The knot in his stomach grew larger knowing the trauma that was coming his family's way.

ADRIA COULD SEE Elijah behind the veil of the waterfalls. The sheet of water poured in front of him, allowing her to only see his silhouette. A tall man stood beside him; she assumed it was Amari. She called out a greeting, but they appeared not to hear her. "I'm here!" she waved and jumped up and down, but no response. The sound of the falls deafened them. Before she could call again, they joined hands and jumped through the veil of the falls and into the pool below.

"Don't go!" she shouted, but was too late. Her own voice bounced back at her with no ears to hear but hers. Adrenaline coursed through her body. Without thinking, she ran and jumped into the oblivion of coolness and screamed all the way down into the pool of water. She held her breath and reached for the surface.

"Adria, wake up!" Jeffrey nudged her shoulder. Shaking her head, her arm swung over, smacking him in the eye.

"No, I have to get there!" she shouted as her eyes flew open. After a second, she realized she'd been dreaming. Dropping her arm, she looked at Jeffrey as his hand covered his eye. "Oh, my God, are you alright?" She reached over and touched his head.

"Yes, my dear, but are you?" He removed his hand and looked at her. She stared right through him. She could still see the ghosts of Elijah and Amari jumping, going deeper and deeper. She looked toward the window as the Jamaica moon poured its glow onto the bed. Sitting up, she rubbed her eyes, and remembered the vivid dream. "I jumped after them, Elijah and Amari, as they held hands and jumped through the veil of the waterfall." She turned back to look at him. "It was so real. I couldn't get to them."

He tugged on her arm and she laid back down next to him, resting her head on his chest, her heart still beating as though it would burst. "I am real," he said as he stroked her hair and leaned close to kiss the top of her head. "My love for you is real. Your love for your son is real. How it will be defined, we just don't yet know."

"I only get one opportunity to get this right. I'm so afraid things won't go well."

"I wish I could go with you," he said and kissed the top of her head.

"As do I, but I think Sam is right." She turned to look at him. "The more people that show up to the meeting, the less chance there is it will happen. The Maroons will be watching closely." Sam had explained to them how cunning the Maroons could be. He was certain they would have sentries posted all along their route to ensure only those that were supposed to attend were in the wagon. Any extras, and the entire meeting could be called off.

"Yes, I agree. Be sure to feel my prayers. They'll be continuous until you get back to Ginger Star." He was concerned for her safety. The Maroons had been very aggressive of late with their plantation raids and roadside battles with the British. Sam's presence gave him just enough reassurance to remain behind. As she rested in his arms, he prayed his love would carry her through whatever the dawn would bring.

ADRIA SAT BETWEEN Ronnie and Sam in the wagon. Sam guided Chance up the mountain to the now familiar path off the main road. Adria's heart beat so loud she thought for sure others could hear. What will I say to him? How do I go about introducing myself to my own flesh and blood? My own son . . . my own self? She had lived this moment in the depths of her imagination time and again. Somehow, she knew every rehearsed scenario would flee from her when the time came. They traveled up the mountain, bouncing along with the wagon. She wondered what Elijah looked like. How tall he was, what his voice sounded like.

Adria's thoughts turned to when she was pregnant, feeling his little hands and feet roll around in her belly. She recalled how she would talk to him, share her fears and dreams, but nothing she imagined prepared her for this. Today, she prayed she would know the right words. I only get this one chance to connect with him, Lord, please help me to do it right. She reached in the pocket of her skirt and felt the shell necklace she had found when she first arrived in Jamaica. They turned down the pathway toward their meeting place near Hope Falls and she could see a few people in the distance. Is one of them Elijah?

Danquah walked toward them. He motioned for Elijah and Amari to stay a little behind as he approached Sam, Ronnie, and Adria. "We here wid many sentries watching ova our meetin,'" Danquah said and swept his arm around as if to signal those who guarded them. Several Maroons stepped out of the bushes to reveal their presence, camouflaged with branches and leaves. "The chief insisted we take strong precautions given the unrest throughout the island now."

Adria had heard stories that sent chills up her spine telling of the Maroons' revolutionary warfare. They were indeed surrounded, but none of this mattered to her. She would have run through a wall of arrows just to touch her son and talk to him. Nothing would stand in her way. She had no idea the words she would say to him, but none of that mattered. The immense love of a mother swelled inside her. Never, in no any way would she ever bring him harm. Not just physical, but emotional, and in this moment, she realized that what she said and did in the next few minutes would determine just that.

"Wi understan,'" Sam said. Adria nodded and looked around. Her eyes landed on Amari who was standing with his arm protectively wrapped around Elijah's shoulder.

Adria stared at her son. *What a handsome young man he's become.*

Danquah looked at Adria. Stepping toward him, she nodded and extended her hand and said, "Hello, I'm Adria. Thank you so much for allowing us to come."

"Tis only because of my brudda." Danquah nodded toward Sam, "dat di chief allow di meeting. We must be brief."

"I understand," she said. Danquah stepped aside and Adria walked forward. Adria nodded at Amari and extended her hand and said, "I am thrilled to see you again, my friend."

"I know I owe my freedom to you, Miss Adria." He took her hand and kissed the back of it in British tradition. The gesture took her by surprise. She never thought for a minute that Amari owed her anything. "Thank you, but you owe me nothing, Amari. You have spent all these years taking care of and loving Elijah." She looked at her son and back at Amari. "I am the one indebted to you." Amari nodded, let go of Elijah, and stepped back. The boy looked at his father, unsure of what to do.

"Go, tis a'right," Amari said to his son and nodded in her direction. Elijah looked from him to Adria as his father stepped back.

She stared at Elijah. He was almost as tall as her, had deep tanned skin, dark brown hair, and then there were his eyes, her green eyes. She had assumed they would be dark brown, but his eyes told her he was unmistakably hers. She could hardly catch her breath. She could see the confusion and fear on his face. They shared that much, their fear of the next few moments.

She offered her hand and he took it. His palm was sweaty. She shared his apprehension but pushed the feeling aside. The two turned and walked toward the sound of the falls. At first, she thought perhaps she should avoid the noise so they could talk, but slowly, she realized the soothing sound of the water could quite possibly be what they both needed right now. They walked side-by-side until she came to a fallen tree trunk where they could sit. She let go of his hand and sat down on the tree, patting the empty space next to her. He turned and sat beside his birth mother.

"I am so very pleased to finally meet you, Elijah."

The boy looked at his hands and clasped them together. He took a deep breath and said, "Papa says you my real mudda."

Adria saw a tear forming in the side of his eye. "That may be true biologically," then realizing he would not know the meaning, she continued, "on the day you were born I was your mother, but circumstances took you from me that day." Gabrielle is your real mother." The words stuck in her throat, but she knew they were true. He sat still for a few seconds and turned his head up to look at her. She looked into her own eyes and remembered being a ten-year-old girl in London without a care in the world. Just in this moment, it occurred to her that this child was being told he was half white, half British, and half the enemy.

Taking a deep breath to keep from breaking down, she continued, "I didn't know you were alive until just a few months ago. I traveled here from London to find you. I'm so happy to see you are doing so well and have grown into such a handsome young man." A little twist of a smile started at the corner of his mouth and he looked back at his hands in embarrassment. Adria grinned. She was making progress.

"Papa say you save his life. You hide him at Ginga Star till he can find his way here."

"That's true. I met him and Miss Ronnie when they jumped off their ship to escape an awful fate. They stayed in our cottage." She had recalled those few days recently, telling Jeffrey about her pregnancy and how thrilled she'd been to find Ronnie, someone she could help and could confide in. Being able to talk about her plight with Ronnie and Jeffrey had kept her sane. "God knows what we need, when we need it, but it often takes years to realize just that. I will always be grateful to your papa, first for taking such good care of you, and second, for being such a good friend to me. Your mama as well." She was surprised at her own words, but they felt right. Somehow, she knew she was pouring just a little of herself into her son.

"Elijah," he turned his head to look at her again, their green eyes reflecting each other's. "I do not want to change your life. I am not here to take you away. Only to let you know that I love you and now that I've seen you, I know you were mine once, but now you are Amari and Gabrielle's son. It is as God intended." The look of relief on his face gave her the impetus to continue. She pulled the shell necklace from her pocket. "Here, I brought you this." She held up the strand of string that held baby conchs and scallops. "I made it when I first moved to Jamaica, before I knew anything about you."

Elijah looked at the necklace. "Tank you." He looked at each shell and ran his fingers over each one. He looked hard at her hands resting in her lap. He reached over and touched the back of her left hand. "Same heart." He traced her birthmark.

"Yes, it is a heart." She looked at her hand.

"Yes, same as mine." He held up his arm for her to see her heart on his hand. Adria stared at the second unmistakable sign that Elijah was hers.

She reached over and took his chocolate brown hand in her pale white one. His skin was silky smooth. "My goodness, Elijah. Between this birthmark and your eyes, I am truly overwhelmed." Tracing the heart with her finger, she took a deep breath and said, "Think of me whenever you look at this heart and know how much I love you and always will." She gently touched his chin and turned his face to look at her. "I am here for you, no matter what might happen. Please don't ever forget that."

He looked at her. The tear hiding in the corner of his eye, slid down his cheek as he nodded.

While part of her wanted to sit and ask questions about his favorite food and his sister's name, she sensed his confusion. Somehow, she understood. "You know what?" He looked at her, his eyebrows raised in the middle just like she did when inquiring. Resemblance number three. "I think we should make a pact."

"Pact?" He asked as his eyebrows raised again.

She smiled and said, "It's an agreement. An agreement to say a little prayer for each other when we look at our birthmark."

Elijah understood and nodded. "I will."

"Alright, well then, let's get back to the others so they're not worried." She didn't want to leave, but knew pressing for more, would make him uncomfortable. She didn't want that to be his last memory of her. She knew this quite possibly could be the last conversation they would ever have. Their stations in life would dictate no contact. Her emotions tugged at her, but she pushed them back. She wouldn't allow Elijah to see her break down. There was plenty of time for that later.

"Wait, I have somet'ing for you," he said as he reached into the satchel that was slung over his shoulder. His hand pulled out the small black onyx box. He handed it to her. She stared at the black box and despite her best efforts, tears made their way down her face. My son has given me a gift. Her hands shook just a little as she opened the box to the most fragrant of scents, Jamaican pimento. It was filled to the brim with the little pods filling the air between them with its sweet fragrance. She lifted the box to her nose and took a better sniff. "It's heavenly. Did you grow this?" she asked, suspecting he had.

His chest puffed just a little. He lifted his chin and smiled just a little. "Yes. My mama and me." His voice trailed.

She smiled. "I suspected so. Well, she grows wonderful pimento. Does your papa help?"

"Yes, when he not hunting."

She stretched her arm across his shoulder and pulled him close, just a bit. "Thank you, Elijah. You've grown into such a wonderful young man. Your mama has done an amazing job teaching you what is most important, and that shows how God only multiplies love, 'tis something He will never divide."

"You smell like flowers," he said, looking up at her and she smiled.

They walked slowly back toward the others with her arm lightly touching his shoulder. Adria wanted to drag out their time together as much as she could, but knew it was time to leave. "I hope one day our paths will cross again, Elijah."

He looked at her in awe. How is it he could have two mothers? How could he be half white and half Maroon? He still didn't grasp the enormity of it all. But he knew in his spirit this unusual white woman truly cared about him. The knowledge gave him a strength and hope he didn't know he would one day need.

JEFFREY WOKE TO find Adria gone. At first, he thought it all a dream, but the flashes of their lovemaking were too vivid to be that of a fantasy. He put his feet on the floor and walked across the room to the lanai. He ran his fingers through his hair as he always did when he was worried. Finally, he found her standing in the garden of Ginger Star, and just watching her made him realize again just how much this woman owned his heart. They had laughed and cried together over the past years, sharing their darkest secrets with each other. She stood in the garden wrapped in a sheet. Her large-brimmed, straw hat flopped in the cool sea breeze. Chewing her fingernail as she always did when in deep thought, her hair flowed in the wind. He recognized the stare as if she were in a trance. She often fell into it when the cloud reappeared. The cloud of Elijah. But this time, there was something different on her mind. Somehow he knew.

He walked up behind her, slipping his hands around her waist. She jumped just a little and then settled her head back on his chest as he nuzzled his nose in her neck. He always tried to settle her down and soothe her cares. They did the same for one another, but Jeffrey knew the ghost of Elijah would always be with her. "I missed you, my love."

She turned and sighed, looking into his eyes. The eyes that captured her every time. The sight of him always soothed her, gave her a calm sense of confidence and security

"So sorry, I couldn't sleep, so I slipped out. I tried not to wake you." She took a deep breath.

"The same dream?" She often dreamt of Elijah, seeing him grow into a man. It transported her back to her pain for a bit, but this time it was not the reason for her sleeplessness.

"No, not this time." She turned to look at him. She swallowed hard and continued, "Remember when I felt a little sick a few weeks ago?" He thought for a moment and then nodded.

"I believe I am expecting a baby."

His eyebrows raised in surprise and a smile planted itself on his face. "Adria!" He picked her up and hugged her tight. He lifted her feet off the ground and put her back down. "That's wonderful, my love. Are you alright?" He reached over and lightly touched her stomach. He felt a pang of guilt about last night's lovemaking.

She took his hand and said, "I'm fine, just a little shocked is all. When we didn't conceive all these years, I'd given up on the idea of being a mother again. I'm overwhelmed and oh so grateful."

He stared at her, breathless, as emotion flooded over him. "Oh, Adria, I didn't think it possible to love you more, but it seems I do!" He smiled, picked her up, and twirled her around. They laughed as he sat her back down. She smiled, more radiant than ever. His hand went to her stomach. "I hope that was alright."

"Oh yes. More than alright." They held hands and walked back toward the house. "I was a little nervous as first, but joy has pushed it away." She turned and touched his face. "It seems God has given me another chance to be a mother."

She found happiness that day—or maybe it found her.

ADRIA BUNDLED THE pimento pods from the black box into small sachets and put in each drawer of her dresser so every time she opened one, the scent would hug her. When the scent would catch her attention, she'd slowly blink her eyes, and imagine a hug from Elijah, not permitting herself to cry at the memory of him any longer, but to embrace a grin or smile that helped her greet yet another day. She kept the black box on top of her dressing table and touched it with love and a prayer for him whenever she sat before it.

Jeffrey stood in the doorway looking at his wife. She was so in love with the black onyx box Elijah had given her. He watched her finger trace its lid as she sat at her dressing table. "So, darling, how do you feel this morning?"

"I'm doing fine, now. Seems as if the morning spells have passed, thankfully."

"I'm not sure, but the baby should be here sometime in June, or in London, I should say." She turned and looked out the bedroom window, a little disheartened at the thought of leaving Jamaica. "I'd forgotten the spell Ginger Star could cast. The way she wraps her arms around me." Adria looked back at her best friend, her husband, her lover, and the father of her baby. "I never knew I could find peace again, but I believe I have."

"Agreed. I've noticed," said Jeffrey. "Are you feeling good enough to host the dinner next week?" They had invited many of their fellow plantation owners for a harvest celebration.

"Why, of course! I've ordered all the food, and Mum Lettie is already gathering vases for all the tables. Olivia's been making candles all week so we can don the room in soft light. The blooms in the garden will make it spectacular!" She sat back down and continued brushing her hair. "With all the raids lately, the party will be a welcome diversion. How many overnight guests do you anticipate?" Since it could be a long journey, many would stay overnight at Ginger Star and head home the next day.

Jeffrey looked at his wife. "From what I know so far, it looks like we'll need three guestrooms ready; for the Fergussons, the Bromleys, and Mary Baldwin." He stepped back and looked at her a little closer. "But only if you're up to it."

"Not only am I 'up to it,' but I'm looking forward to it." She smiled at him with a love for life she had never expected to experience again.

THE EVENING OF the dinner party was perfect with a light breeze and full moon and no clouds for it to hide behind. Ginger Star bustled with arriving carriages delivering guests and their belongings. Solomon and Sam handled their portmanteau, taking them to their respective guest rooms. Jeffrey and Adria stood at the top of the steps greeting their guests.

"Adria, this is Mary Baldwin," Jeffrey said turning to his wife.

"Why, Mary, it's indeed a pleasure to finally meet you. The Jamaican Courant is a great asset to Jamaica." Adria extended her hand to the older woman who was dressed in a fine blue brocade gown with a gold chain holding a blue topaz stone that glistened in the candlelight. Her hair was black with a gray streak running down both sides as if intentional. Mary had taken ownership of the newspaper when her husband passed away a few years before.

"Please excuse my tardiness. Duty was calling with all there is going on these days up in the mountains," Mary said. She referred to the Maroon raids and the panic that was starting to set in amongst the island population. Mary pulled off her hat, shook her head and said, "Because of what's been going on, we had to take the long route around the mountains."

"Please, don't give it another thought," Adria said. "I'm just so grateful you made it safely to Ginger Star. It's so exciting to get to know a woman that thrives as you do in the business world." Adria was thrilled to meet Mary. She'd had her admiration for a long time. Mary was the trail blazer of the newspaper business in Jamaica.

"My husband left me with a successful business, Adria. Robert shared his knowledge of journalism and we were a great team. Since his passing eight years ago, Peter and Robert have been a huge asset." Mary smiled and said, "And besides, I enjoy what I do." Mary smiled and turned to shake Jeffrey's hand.

"Well, something tells me you were a big part of its continuing success." Jeffrey said and handed her a glass of port.

"I'm very proud to know such a successful woman in the newspaper business — for that matter, in any business." Adria said and looked around the room as they walked inside. "There are far too few of us at the helm."

"Why, thank you, Adria. I appreciate that as well as your invitation to join everyone here at Ginger Star. I've been hearing you've done marvelous things for the plantation since your return to our island."

"Please excuse me," Jeffrey said as he turned away to greet another guest.

"That's very kind of you to say," Adria said as her father walked up beside them.

Looking at Mary, John said, "It's wonderful to see you again, Mary." Adria sensed a familiarity between the two. "Allow me to show you to the drawing room. We're having a glass of port before dinner." John offered his arm and Mary took it.

As they walked away, Adria smiled at the thought of her father finding happiness here in Jamaica. Time marched on and while they all still missed her mother, her passing made them realize just how short their time was. She was enjoying the sudden spark in her father's countenance. Maybe Mary had been the reason for his rebound, she wasn't sure. They'd all endured such sadness and shame this past decade. It was time to embrace the happy side of life again.

John and Mary walked into the drawing room where Olivia's lit candles coaxed shadows to dance on the walls while the port wine flowed. The owners of the Seville Plantation, Captain Samuel Hemmings and his wife, Sally, along with Mavis and Queenie, as well as other local business owners greeted one another. The conversation flowed as the port was doing its job. The guests offered up laughter as Mum Lettie and her staff silently kept the wine glasses full and carried appetizers on silver trays.

"These past few weeks have been so tense with the frequent raids." Ronnie said to Marshall as she walked up to him after mingling with the crowd. She reached over and took an olive and piece of cheese from Olivia's tray. "Everyone's on edge, it seems."

Marshall nodded, leaning down to whisper in Ronnie's ear, "On a lighter note, it appears as though John is enjoying Mary's company this evening."

Ronnie smiled and said, "It appears life goes on, even in Jamaica."

Mary had been seated next to Adria's father in an effort to even out the guests at the table. Jeffrey noticed the alliance, leaned over, and whispered in Adria's ear, "They make an interesting couple, actually." He nodded in John's direction.

Adria looked at her father. Her eyes widened as her face broke into a smile. "Indeed, they do." She watched them enjoy each other's company throughout the evening. It made her sad her mother wasn't here with her father, but her heart was happy seeing him smile again.

"The lamb is exquisite," Sally Hemmings said to Adria.

"Why thank you, and a huge thanks to William," she looked at William Bromley, the owner of Bromley Pen. "He was kind enough to ensure Sam picked up the best he had to offer."

William smiled and said, "You're most welcome and I'm happy to do so anytime you want to have us over to enjoy it with Mum Lettie's special touch!" He raised his glass in a toast to Mum Lettie's cooking. Everyone clinked their glasses and looked at her. The older woman ducked her head in shyness and scurried out of the room carrying a tray of empty dishes.

Jeffrey looked down the table at the Hemmings couple. "Well, Samuel, I'm so sorry for what you and Sally had to endure as a result of the Maroons' latest raid."

"Thank you, Jeffrey. While it was awful, we realize it could have been much worse." Hemmings said looking at his wife. She was still somewhat shaky when it came to talking about the raid. "We lost a few outbuildings and three slaves escaped. Thankfully, none of us were harmed."

Marshall added, "Ronnie and I certainly understand your angst. It took us a while to regain our bearings after the raid at Ramble House. It also appears as if things have really intensified with Governor Hunter's tenure here on Jamaica. It looks as if he's intent on stirring up the Maroons."

"I know he means well, but it's making life here all but unbearable," Sally added, shaking her head.

Mavis knew Sally wasn't enjoying the conversation and she quickly changed the subject. "So, Sally, I believe the Windward will be arriving within the next few days. I'm expecting the fabric you ordered to be on board."

Sally smiled, appreciating the segue, "That would be a welcome diversion. There's nothing like a few new dresses to change one's outlook on life!" She raised her glass and everyone joined in, clinking and drinking.

When dinner was over, the men retired for cigars in John's study. The women congregated on the veranda for another glass of port.

Sally stood next to Ronnie, Mavis, and Adria staring at the sea shining under the full Jamaican moon. "It's so comforting to see and hear the peacefulness of the sea," Adria said.

Continuing to stare at the water, Sally said, "Quite true. With all that's happened of late, silence can sometimes be most welcome."

Ronnie put her arm around Sally's shoulder. "I'm so sorry for the terror you went through in the raid." Sally had shared details. "I can't imagine the terror. When Ramble House was raided, all they did was take the weapons cache. I don't know how we escaped their plundering, but I am grateful."

Sally leaned into Ronnie's hug and said, "I'm just so grateful we didn't lose more than we did. I'm not sure how much longer I can continue living on edge all the time, wondering when the next attack will come. And on whom." She looked around the room.

A few spattering's of leftover rain from a passing shower fell on the ground. All three women stood in silence, understanding the fear in Sally's statement. All four getting lost in the glow of the moon kissing the sea and its silent whisper of hope for peace on the island.

THE SOUND OF the guests' carriages leaving rumbled in the distance.

"It was a beautiful evening and wonderful breakfast, my dear," Jeffrey said, wrapping his hands around his wife's waist as she brushed her hair in front of the vanity mirror. "I have a feeling everyone will be talking about it for some time to come."

Adria smiled back at him through the reflection. "Thank you, I hope it helped to better connect us to our friends on the north coast. The fear of more raids is real, I'm afraid." She reached over and picked up the gardenia perfume bottle and dabbed some on.

"Yes, it is. We had quite the discussion about it last night," Jeffrey said.

"As did we," Adria sighed.

Jeffrey looked at his wife and said, "Well, on a lighter note, I had quite an interesting conversation with Mary this morning right before she left."

Adria put her brush down on the vanity, stood to face him and said, "Really? Please, do tell. I noticed you were talking in earnest with her in the drawing room last night."

Jeffrey knew better than Adria that were they to go back to live in London, the cloud of depression would find her again if she had to leave her son behind. "How would you feel about my going to work for Mary and the Jamaica Courant as their north coast representative?" He watched her face as she processed the thought. She cocked her head and a smile crossed her face. The same smile that always lit up his heart.

"But what about?" Her thoughts raced. Questions poured from her. "London, your position there, your family? We would remain here in Jamaica?"

"Whoa! Slow down, my sweet. One question at a time." He leaned in and kissed her on the forehead. "Enough with the details for now." He leaned in and reminded her of all the ways he could make her smile. "Yes, we would stay in Jamaica. I've seen how this place has brought you back to life. Your love for it is infectious." He frowned a little and said, "Are you alright with staying here to have the baby?"

Adria threw her arms around his neck. She hugged him as tight as she ever had, leaned back, and looked at him. "Darling, are you serious? We could stay here at Ginger Star? I would love to have Mum Lettie next to me while I deliver. What about Papa? What about our home in London?" She was full of questions, but the plan was already in motion. John was pleased to stay in Jamaica to help run Ginger Star while Jeffrey tended to the Courant's interests on the north coast. "What about Noel and Streak?" Their horses were like family to them.

"Not to worry. I'll make arrangements to ship them here along with whatever else you want sent over." Seeing the cloud was gone and her smile back, made everything right in his world.

JEFFREY WAS IN his realm when he began his new position at the Courant. He loved being the first one in on a story and worked hard to stay on top of current events on the island and abroad. He was grateful for the connections he'd made since they arrived in Jamaica. He was in his element, albeit a smaller one than he had left behind in London, but no matter. He was with Adria, and she was smiling again. That was good enough for him.

—Chapter Twenty-Two—

"My wish for you is that you continue. Continue to be who and how you are, to astonish a mean world with your acts of kindness." —Maya Angelou

1730, Nanny Town, Jamaica

The moon led his way up the path. The stars were still bright, but he knew daylight was not far behind. Ten-year-old Elijah picked up his step so he would be ready when the birds took flight in the dawn. He'd been planning this for weeks, carefully calculating his steps. If he weren't careful, he might walk away empty-handed, so Elijah had taken his time. He carried the bamboo limb his father had helped him trim. It was strapped to his back with a sling for easy transport. When Elijah reached the summit of the mountain, he spotted the tallest tree, a sprawling live oak, he had picked out a few days earlier and headed in its direction. Once there, he laid down the limb and the satchel that held his supplies.

Elijah sat on the ground and emptied the contents of the bag on the ground next to him: twine, a knife, and two starfruits. He cut the starfruit in halves and squeezed its sticky liquid onto one end of the bamboo and set the remainder of the fruit aside to eat later. He wiped the excess goo on his pants, but it didn't help much. His fingers wanted to stick to one another. Reaching down, he dusted his palms with dirt. Once done, he picked up his knife and walked over to a stray banana plant, cutting a long palm from its base. Tucking the palm branch under his arm, he slung the bamboo stick across his back, and carried the satchel over his shoulder.

Looking up from the bottom of the tree, he planned his ascent, and started to climb. Beginning on a low-lying branch, he slowly made his way up to the highest limb that would hold his weight. Once there, he wrapped the large banana leaf around the tallest limb of the tree and held onto each end. Finding leverage with the leaf, he shimmied up the tree until he could see a good place to stop where he could plant his feet on the trunk. Holding on to a branch on the tree with one arm, he pulled the bamboo limb out of the sling. He was careful not to touch the sticky part as he grabbed the limb and hoisted it up the tree until the bamboo and its sticky end stuck up above the highest point. He pulled the twine from his pocket and wrapped it around the trunk of the tree and bamboo limb several times until he was sure it would no longer move in a breeze. Knotting the twine, he tugged on the limb to ensure it was secure.

Satisfied, he shimmied back down to the ground, again using the banana leaf to help him down. Once back on the ground, he looked up at his work. Pleased with himself, he packed up his supplies and headed back to the village. He was counting on capturing a nice parrot to take home as a pet for his little sister, Kisi.

AMARI WOKE TO the sun peeking through the slats of the shutter on the window. He could always tell the weather even before he rose from his bed on the floor. He looked over at Elijah, expecting to find him sleeping in his own bed next to the other window, but he was not there. He pulled the cover off, being careful not to wake his wife, wondering where Elijah had gone so early in the morning.

Amari stood and walked toward the door. He saw a note on the table and picked it up to read.

Papa, I have left early to set the trap for Kisi's parrot. I will return in time to finish my chores, Elijah.

Amari grinned at his son's ambitious love for his sister. Elijah had helped to care for her since she was an infant and now that she was running around, beginning to talk, her big brother had a renewed interest in her and was determined to give her a parrot as a pet for her birthday. He was convinced the parrot and Kisi would learn to talk together.

Amari recalled his own time sitting in the little school learning the language when he first arrived. He was grateful he'd not only learned their language, but that he could read and write many of their words as well. He was told slaves in the plantations were not permitted to learn to read and write. The blessings of living with the Maroons were endless. He would be forever grateful to Ronnie for sending him here.

He couldn't believe his son was soon to be ten years old. It was even more astonishing to him that more than ten years ago, he swam ashore to Jamaica. He'd been a terrified young man with no choice but to trust a white woman named Ronnie. She had not let him down. He owed his life to her, but after the Ramble House raid, he considered his debt repaid.

Elijah had grown into a delightful young man, healthy and strong. His bronze-toned skin and green eyes made for a hand-some young man. Tomorrow would be Elijah's tenth birthday, and just four more years until he could take the test to become a grown Maroon warrior. Amari was certain he would pass with no problem. Elijah hunted with Amari several times a week and was a very good shot with a bow.

"Gud morning, mi love," Gabrielle said to him as she slid her arms around his waist. She laid her head on his back, breathing in his scent. Amari turned and looked Gabrielle in the eyes as she said, "I saw his note. It appears we have a little time alone this morning." She cocked her head. "Kisi still sleeps." He smiled as she took his hand and he followed her across the room and back to their bed.

When archery practice let out, Elijah grabbed the birdcage he'd built and tucked behind the building before archery practice had begun. He hurried down the path toward the parrot trap he'd set earlier that day.

"I saw your parrot stuck on your stick, impatiently awaiting you on top of the hill!" the Basket Lady called. Her hair was a nest of curls pulled up into a hat with a blue and white bow woven around and tied under her chin. A few loose curls escaped down the sides and back of her neck.

"You did?" He walked over and stopped next to her little hut in front of the cottage that served as a store. The shelves were filled with bags of charcoal, spices, fruit, soap, pottery, and baskets she'd woven.

She smiled at him and said, "I sure did. A pretty green and white one. He should be getting mighty hungry by now. Do you need some help getting him down? Ramon and I can help."

He smiled at her offer. "I can get him, but I sure could use help to put him in cage." Elijah raised the birdcage he'd made for his little sister's new pet.

"Well, it just so happens I'm available and at your service, sir." She bowed in his direction, pulled off her apron, and hung it on the back of the door. "Let's get Ramon to help too." She called her son who quickly answered. He came running up the hill, happy to take a break from picking pimento.

She was so grateful for Elijah and Ramon's friendship. Otherwise, her son had little social contact since she schooled him at her kitchen table. Neighbors weren't plentiful this far up into the interior mountains of the island.

"Ramon! Let's go get the parrot," Elijah hollered. "The Basket Lady said he's waiting for us!" He realized he'd called Clara by the Maroon's nickname for her and stopped, embarrassed to look at her.

Clara had overheard the whispers of her Maroon neighbors, so the name was not new to her. She laughed and said, "Don't worry, Elijah, I am the Basket Lady for sure!" She pointed to the countertop filled with palm leaves in the midst of being woven into shape. *I've been called far worse, that's for sure.*

All three of them trudged up the hill to its highest spot and sure enough, there was the parrot squawking. Clara supervised and made sure the cage was ready when the boys were able to pull the stick down from the tree as the irritated bird struggled to get free. Elijah grabbed the bird with both hands, holding it away from his body to avoid getting scratched. The bird gratefully escaped his hands into the cage Ramon held open. Clara reached over with a piece of twine and tied the door shut.

"Kisi is going to have a great birthday!" Clara said as she patted Elijah on the back while they walked back to the cottage. The only one not happy about Kisi's birthday present was the parrot.

RAMON AND ELIJAH were inseparable. The boys played and hunted in the forest, swam in the pool of the waterfall, and helped Clara in the garden when they weren't rounding up the goats that had wandered too far.

Ramon sat at the cottage table working on arithmetic problems his mother had written down for him to solve. He sometimes used his fingers to add numbers. "You need to do it in your head, Ramon. You won't have enough fingers and toes if you're in the market trying to make a purchase!"

"If I run out of fingers and toes, I'll just use yours, Mummy." He grinned and Clara shook her head.

A knock on the door revealed Elijah standing there with a basket of mangoes. Clara waved him in. "What have you there?" she asked.

"We had so many mangoes, Papa was afraid they would spoil. He sent these to you," Elijah said and handed her the basket.

"Well, that was very thoughtful! I'll have to make some mango chutney," Clara said as she placed the mangoes on the table in front of Ramon. "So, Ramon, how many mangoes are on the table?"

Ramon looked from Elijah to the mangoes and counted, "One, two," he continued counting in his head. "There are eight," he said.

"That's right. How many are left if I take two mangoes away?" Clara asked.

Ramon looked and counted to himself pointing at the mangoes one, by one. "There's six left."

"Good job!" Clara said.

"Can I sit down and learn to count too?" Elijah asked.

"Here, sit next to me," Ramon said and pulled out the chair beside him. Elijah sat down.

Ramon taught Elijah to count and write the numbers up to ten that day. From then on, Elijah would join Ramon at their cottage table most days. Clara taught them both to read, write, and do their sums. Both boys were quick to learn and eager to challenge each other. She found that together, she accomplished much more than when she tried to school Ramon on his own.

"Elijah, how do your folks feel about you learning to read and write with Ramon?" Clara asked.

"Oh, I haven't told them yet. Not too many in village can read or write," Elijah said.

Clara sighed and wondered what their reaction would be. She knew there could be consequences with the law were she to be discovered schooling a Maroon. The next time she saw Gabrielle at the falls as she was laundering her clothes as the boys swam, she explained what she had been doing at the cottage table. "Is it alright with you and Amari?"

Gabrielle looked around to be sure no one could hear. "I am sure Amari would approve," she said and nodded, "but we need not tell anyone."

"I understand," Clara said and laid her wet apron on a rock to dry.

After Gabrielle gave her blessing on the lessons, Elijah was at the cottage just about every afternoon. He was a quick study and good at learning to sound out words as he learned to read, write, and do sums. Clara worked in the evenings by candlelight after Ramon was asleep to create lessons for the next day.

SEVERAL MONTHS LATER, Clara crouched in the garden, pulling weeds, trying to finish up before the noon sun stole the coolness from the mountaintop for the day. She heard footsteps rushing through the brush. Walking back briskly to her cottage, she was pretty sure it was Maroons skittering their way through the brush. She knew they were probably in retreat after a raid, but most likely coming back from making a trade for goods, but she could never be sure.

Clara was grateful Ramon had gone to Hope Falls with Elijah. After a little while, she ventured out to investigate what had rushed by. There was nothing other than a few leaves here and there beside the road left over from their disguises. It had happened before, so she was fairly confident there wasn't anything to fret about.

Walking back down to her pimento grove, she began plucking the little green acorns that grew on the bushes. She was amazed at how fast the bushes had grown since she'd planted them almost ten years earlier. Their branches provided shade for the goats on sunny days. She pulled the green peppercorn-type seeds off the bush and added them to the tray she kept at the rear of her cottage to dry in the sun until they turned brown, indicating the pimento (some called it "all spice") was ready. She would then grind it with her mortar and pestle to use for flavor while smoking meat. Later, she would bundle up what she didn't use to be sold. She picked up a few fallen branches from the pimento bushes left over from the last storm and carried them under her arm. She'd use the wood to add flavor to the meat while smoking. Careful not to spill the seeds from her apron, she headed back up the hill toward her cottage when she noticed the brush along the road moved. She looked over and saw Elijah and Ramon come out from behind the tree line.

"Mama!" Ramon waved to her as he crossed the lane indicating she should join him inside the house. She waved back. Cupping her hands around her mouth, she hollered, "What are you doing?" He put his finger to his lips so she would lower her voice and waved her inside the cottage. She walked over dropping the pimento into a bowl she'd left on the porch earlier and opened the door. There stood Ramon and Elijah, with a small stranger between them, a little dark girl, maybe five years old. "Mama, this is Millie." Ramon looked from his mother to the little girl. "We're trying to help her get to Elijah's village." Clara looked from her son to this tiny little girl with terrified brown eyes. The girl wore a gray shift with buttons missing and her skirt was torn. "She was separated from the group during the retreat from the raid on Seville Plantation. We found her in the bushes just up the lane."

Clara looked from the boys to Millie who stood biting her fingernails as she waited to hear Ramon's mother's response. Her big brown eyes stared at the floor. Clara walked over to the youngster, bent over, and put her arm around her shoulder. She could feel her little body shaking with fear. "Not to worry, my sweet. We will keep you safe and get you to where you need to be. I promise," she said, not sure she could keep it.

She tilted Millie's chin up to look at her and pulled her close. The girl broke down sobbing, her little shoulders heaving up and down. Clara took a handkerchief from her pocket, wiped Millie's tears, and handed her the kerchief. "T'ank you," was all the little girl could muster as her sobs poured out.

Ramon brought her a cup of water. Her small hands shook as she grasped the cup and slowly took a drink, letting out an audible sigh. Her hair was plaited with ribbons woven through each braid, tying off each one. Clara took a deep breath as she thought she recognized the ribbon design. Sally Hemmings, mistress of Seville Plantation, was well known for styling her house girls' hair the same way.

Clara sat the youngsters down and dished up the stew she'd been cooking in the fireplace. Ramon and Elijah ate quickly while Millie stared at hers with the spoon in her hand. Clara decided to leave her alone for a bit and sure enough, the little girl slowly began to eat. Before long, she'd finished the bowl.

"Elijah, maybe you should wait until the sun begins to set before you take Millie to the village," Clara said. "Less chance of being seen," she added. Thoughts swirled in her head over what to do next.

She walked to the corner where she kept Ramon's clothes and pulled out a pair of pants and a shirt. Looking at Millie she said, "Why don't you go behind that screen," Clara pointed to the corner of the room, "and change into Ramon's clothes. It's best nobody knows you're a girl for now."

Millie looked at her and nodded. She took the clothing and disappeared behind the screen.

When she looked back at Ramon she asked, "Will your parents be worried or should you go and tell them what's happening first?"

"No, they will think I am having luck hunting. As long as I home before dark, it alright," Elijah said.

Millie walked out from behind the screen. The clothes were larger than she was, but Clara tucked the shirt in and folded up the cuffs on the pants. Taking Millie's shaking hands in hers, she crouched down and looked her in the eyes saying, "Everything is going to be just fine. You'll see." Millie nodded and suddenly wrapped her skinny arms around Clara, clinging to her. Clara scooped her up and sat her on her lap at the table.

"Here, let's take the ribbons out of your hair and comb it out a little." Clara massaged Millie's head while she worked on the braids, trying to calm her down. It seemed to be working. Clara glanced out the window. From the look of the sun's position, she estimated she could send Millie and Elijah on to the Village in about an hour.

Clara said to the children, "Let's sing a song. It always makes us feel better, right, Ramon?"

"Yes, Mummy, it always makes everything good." Ramon started to sing and they all joined in, "Jerusalem on High."

Flipping Clara's soup pot upside down, Elijah used it as a drum. As they sang the last verse.

Ah me! ah me!
that I in Kedar's tent here stay;
No place like that on high;
Lord thither guide my way;
O happy place! When shall I be,
My God, with Thee, to see Thy face?

Clara could feel Millie's muscles relax. They continued singing the song over and over while she worked on Millie's hair, removing the soiled ribbons. The hour passed quickly and soon the sun dipped below the mountain.

"Well, I think it's time for you two to head for the village," Clara said to Elijah and Millie. The little girl reached up and grabbed tight onto Clara's hand as they stood. She gently pulled it away and placed Millie's tiny hand into Elijah's.

Stooping down on the porch, she laid the ribbons down and gave Millie a strong hug. "Everything will be fine, Millie," Clara said kissing the little girl on her forehead. She picked up the bowl of pimento she'd left there earlier. "I think the sun is low enough now. Hurry on, you two!" The youngsters rushed up the lane. Elijah turned to wave and Millie did the same. Elijah grabbed Millie's hand again and they ran into the forest toward the village.

Lying in bed that night, Clara's mind went into overdrive as she tried to think of what to do next. She took a deep breath and tried to reel in her imagination. If they were accused of helping Millie, both she and Ramon would be arrested by the British for aiding an escaped slave. She couldn't let that happen.

THE NEXT DAY, the sound of horses' hooves thundered down her lane. Clara stood up, cradling the last of the pimento corns of the season in her apron. She shielded her eyes from the sun in an effort to see who it was. Redcoats. Two of them. She didn't see them often, but when she did, it was rarely a good thing. The horses drew up and stopped in front of her cottage. She walked over to greet them, stopping to dump the pimento into the bowl on the porch. Dusting off her hands, she walked toward them, her heart pounding in her ears. She hoped it didn't show. *Do they know about Millie?*

She took a deep breath and smiled. "Good day, gentlemen. Is there something I can do for you?" She knew they didn't stop here by accident. They always had a reason. Typically, they were looking for an escaped slave.

"Yes, ma'am." He tipped his hat and wiped the sweat from his brow. She always wondered how they managed to wear those wool coats in the Jamaican heat. "We are looking for several escaped slaves from Seville. Two adults and one child. We suspect they headed through here with the Maroons." He looked past her shoulder for any signs. "Have you seen any activity here of late?"

"No sir," she lied. Her heart skipped a beat. "As a matter of fact, I was just thinking it was unusually quiet here this week. Normally, there are folks up and down the lane all day, but not lately. She glanced at him and turned back to focus on the other Redcoat." The younger soldier dismounted and walked his horse around the perimeter of her cottage. "Are you sure they headed up this way?" She was irritated at their lack of respect for her property, but also knew she had best let it go. He stopped as he rounded the last corner and pulled his horse up closer to her. He held the reins in one hand and bent over to pick up the pile of hair ties she had taken out of Millie's hair. Clara's heart skipped a beat and she hoped her face was not flushing with guilt. He examined the strips of cloth. "What are these?" He asked holding up the strips.

She looked at his hand holding Millie's ribbons. Only Seville had hair ribbons of that design. Did they realize that? She could only hope they did not.

"Oh, I weave those into my baskets sometimes. Adds a little color." She wasn't sure where the lie came from but was grateful for it. He took one of the ribbons, tucked it in his pocket, and dropped the others back onto the porch. She cringed, but didn't object or ask why. He seemed satisfied with her explanation and climbed back up on his horse.

The older redcoat continued talking. "Pretty sure they headed up this way." He seemed satisfied for now. "Please send off a few warning shots if anyone shows up in the near future and we will circle back."

"Absolutely," she answered. Again, she hoped the thumping of her heart inside her chest didn't show. They turned and rode up the lane, slowed down and peeked inside her little store. Satisfied there was no one inside, they looked back at her. She waved them on. The younger Redcoat looked back at her a second time. The rush of blood made it to her throat, and she could feel herself blushing. She saw him pull the ribbon out of his pocket and hand it to the older soldier. She took a deep breath, let it out, and plopped back down on the edge of the porch. Leaning over staring at the ground she could feel the past rearing its ugly head. If they pulled the veil of privacy off the well-known Basket Lady, it would expose who she truly was.

RAMON HAD HIS father's, Jack Rackham, good looks, so disguising him as a girl would not be difficult. Anne, the Basket Lady, sighed as she pulled out a large handful of her auburn hair and sheared it off with her sharpest knife. Reaching around for another chunk, she whacked it off and looked in the mirror

Mavis had given her, noticing she now had crow's feet at the edge of her eyes.

She let out a deep sigh, knowing the truth was her only option. Ramon needed to know his identity and who she really was, the vanished pirate, Anne Bonny. She dreaded telling him that she and his father had been pirates. He knew his father was dead, but she had spared him the truth, letting him believe he died in an accident at sea. Ramon now needed to know Jack had been convicted of piracy and died in the gallows of Port Royal. It was time to tell him the truth about her own life as a pirate and that her real name was Anne Bonny. She knew he had heard the rumors and tales about Jack and her. How would he react to knowing that the infamous Calico Jack and Anne Bonny were his parents? He would realize his mother had killed men in fights and lived to talk about it. Will he still love me? Ghosts had haunted her dreams for years. She'd never felt good about what she'd done, but she told herself it had been essential—kill or be killed. She'd been able to keep the memories at bay during the daytime hours, but still woke up in a cold sweat in the middle of the night dreaming about horrible battles and drowning in a bloody sea. She'd even found herself praying that if anything were to happen to her, God would allow Ramon to make it to Cuba safely, if the need arose. Jack's mother's family lived in Cuba and she knew they would take care of him, but just how would she ever manage to get him there if she were to be captured? Now, she had to find a way out for the both of them, or hang.

She plopped into a chair at the kitchen table, letting the knife fall out of her hand, and allowed herself to remember the day her father brokered her release from the Jamaican prison in St. Andrews. She'd been tried and held in the nasty cell awaiting the birth of her baby before they would take her to the gallows. A few weeks after her trial in Port Royal and Jack's hanging, feeling hopeless and sad, a guard led her to a dank room with a small window, a table, and two chairs. She was shocked to see her father standing there as she entered the room, pregnant and ready to deliver. His gray-hair was shorter than she remembered, having not seen him in almost five years. "Well, my daughter, a fine mess you have managed to get yourself into this time!"

Shaking her head, remembering their aloof relationship, she said, "Well, Father, it's nice to see you too. Why are you here if only to insult me?"

"I am here to get you out of this wretched place." He looked around and cringed at the conditions.

"Well, just how do you propose you do that?"

"I've made arrangements for you to leave with me under the cover of darkness, tonight." Looking over his shoulder to make sure the guards were not within ear shot, he said in a low voice, "At midnight, the red-haired guard will bring you to my carriage outside. It is all arranged."

Anne's eyes lit up with unexpected hope. "Are you sure?" She pulled out a chair and slowly sank into the seat, holding onto the table to keep her balance with her large pregnant belly threatening to tip her over.

"Most definitely. From here, we will head to Port Royal and board my sloop to head back to Charles Towne."

Hope drained from her at the mere mention of returning to South Carolina. She had a feeling this would be his plan. There was no way she was going along with it. "I will never go back there!" Anne knew the culture of South Carolina would suffocate her. "I have always hated the constraints of living the life of a woman, both in Ireland and Charles Towne. I will not go back!"

He plopped down in the chair across from her and slammed his palm on the table and she jumped a little. "You have no room to negotiate, my dear. The noose awaits you!" His hand pointed in the direction of the gallows.

"I would rather be hung quickly than live the slow suffocating death of a woman in the colonies." She leaned back in the chair, grateful to stay off her swollen feet. "How have you arranged this meeting? You have no contacts here in Jamaica any longer, have you?" She knew he had purchased slaves from Port Royal many years earlier but had not heard anything more of him for a long while.

"I received a letter from a friend of yours, Veronica Fergusson." He pulled a wrinkled envelope from his breast pocket. "She gave me the names of people to contact here for your release."

She shook her head. "I should have known Ronnie would be my advocate."

"Who is 'Ronnie'?" he asked.

"Same person, just a nickname."

"She also sent this sealed envelope for me to deliver to you in the event I was able to secure a meeting." He slid the envelope across the table toward Anne.

She picked it up and saw Ronnie's seal on the back, "VB." Breaking the seal, she opened the letter and scanned the words. "It says she knows of a place I can live up in the mountains here in Jamaica. A place where few people go." She looked at her father with hope for the first time in months. "She says it will give me a good place to raise my child and make a living off the land." She handed him the letter.

After he read it, he broke out into a sarcastic laugh making her cringe. It brought back unpleasant memories. "I have not come all this way and spent all this money so you can live on an island mountaintop. What foolishness!" Shaking his head, he tossed the letter back across the table toward her.

Anne grabbed the letter and stuffed it in her bosom. "It is my life and that of your grandchild." She put her hand on her swollen belly. "You can choose to help us; or leave now."

He looked down at his hands. "You were always such a difficult one. Hard for me to understand." He let out a deep sigh and looked into her eyes for the first time since he arrived. "I often wonder how different things would have been if your mother were still here." Anne's mother, Clara Brennan, died when Anne was only twelve years old, shortly after their arrival in South Carolina.

The mention of her mother softened her resolve, but just a little. Her father was the only person in her life that had known her mother. The mere mention of her made Anne tear up and that was not something she wanted to do, especially now. "Mother is gone. She would not want for my child what I had to endure as an illegitimate bastard!" She stood and looked down at him, watching her words sink in. His shoulders slumped and his age was apparent to her once again. She almost felt pity for this man that was her father. While he had tried to shield Anne and her mother from the gossips and judgmental friends, there was always someone that enjoyed reminding them of their less than acceptable status in the community. She had decided years ago she would never go back. Her stubborn Irish ancestry was holding fast.

His head bowed for a few seconds, and he looked up at her with tears brimming. "I loved you and your mother more than anything. That's why we left London and tried to build a life in South Carolina. I'm sorry, so sorry." The tears spilled down his face and for the first time in years, Anne felt love for this man that had given her life and had done his best to make it a good one. The culture where they had found themselves trapped threatened to suck the life out of them both.

"I know, Papa. I know." She stood and walked around the table to hug him from behind. She whispered in his ear, "Let us figure this out together." And they did. The contents of Ronnie's letter gave instructions on how to reach her to put the plan into motion. Her father followed the instructions and sent a messenger ahead to let Ronnie know they were coming. He had brought enough gold with him to pay off the guards for her release. Anne and her father left the prison at midnight that night with the understanding they would board his sloop bound for South Carolina. Instead of heading west, the sloop would head around the eastern tip of Jamaica and drop Anne off in Ocho Rios to meet Ronnie and slip up into the mountains. She had daydreamed about escaping to Cuba to raise her son, Cunningham, along with the baby within her, but thought it best not to let her father know he already had a grandson he would never know.

"Are you certain you want to stay here?" Her father pointed at the island as they rounded the east end to sail to Ocho Rios. "It's pretty desolate up in those mountains."

Anne looked from the mountains to her father and grabbed hold of his arm. "I've never been so sure of anything in my life."

"Then here, take this." He pulled a small purple sack from his pocket. "It should be enough to get you settled. Let me know what this Veronica person needs to complete the real estate transaction and I will make it happen."

Anne looked at the bag in her hand. Her first reaction was to refuse his offer, but she did not have the heart to hurt him again. He was disappointed enough that she wouldn't return home with him. "Thank you, Papa. Once again, you show me more mercy than I deserve." She hugged him tight, kissed him on the cheek, and took hold of the mate's hand to disembark. When she looked up she saw Ronnie's silhouette at the end of the dock. For once, she was grateful to walk toward the land instead of the sea.

JACK'S MOTHER HAD sent numerous letters over the years, trying to talk Anne into coming to Cuba to be with Jack's family and Anne's first son, Cunningham, but Anne was never sure they could make it safely. Her heart hurt that she couldn't see her first born, but she had to remind herself that she and Ramon lived a good life in the mountains of Jamaica. She'd been able to make a living with the baskets, spices, tea, and pottery sales, but now there was no other choice. It was flee to Cuba or be executed for aiding an escaped slave. What would happen to Ramon if they didn't make it out of Jamaica? She couldn't even entertain the possibility. She knew Ronnie would help her but, as the mistress of Ramble House, approaching her would be difficult without being discovered. She thought about Mavis and instantly knew she could rely on her for help. Anne had stolen away to visit her a few times over the years, but the risk was too high to go to Ocho Rios very often.

Rather than go into town and risk being recognized, she met Ronnie or Mavis every few months at their favorite waterfall spot they referred to as Hope Falls. Mavis would deliver supplies and Anne would trade her wares in return which sold very well on the shelves of Mavis' mercantile. The two had become good friends and Anne was able to keep up with local news and was comforted knowing the world thought she was back in South Carolina.

Being Ramon's mother had changed her in ways she never knew could happen. She thought back to her life with Jack. Their lovemaking had been electric and soul exchanging. She knew she would never have that again and accepted that fact thanks to the joy she had found in being Ramon's mother.

The door slammed shut and she knew Ramon was home, jolting her away from her memories and into the present.

"MAMA, WHAT ARE you doing?" Ramon's eyes widened as he looked at her long, wavy auburn hair lying on the floor.

"Well, I think I just cut my hair off." She ran her fingers through her now-short hair and looked at herself with the small hand mirror. She turned and looked at her boy. He'd grown more this year than years past. His build was beginning to reflect Jack's too, although somehow her blue eyes had trumped Jack's brown. His black hair and blue eyes gave him the best attributes of the both of them. She was happy he didn't inherit her pale skin that blistered in the sun. Her loose-fitting clothes protected her and rarely was she ever seen without her big, floppy, straw hat. She changed the ribbon around it to suit her mood. Somedays a floral print, others solid, and once in a while, a stripe or plaid. It was her only indulgence when it came to her wardrobe. But now, with having to go back to a disguise, her hats would stay here in the closet. She would probably never see them again but managed to pack up the ribbons to take with her. She could always find another hat.

"Ramon, please wash up for supper."

He walked to the kitchen basin and grabbed the bar of soap. "Elijah found another flock of parrots. Blue and yellow ones this time." He grabbed a towel and dried his hands as he turned to look at his mother. He stopped when he noticed she was staring at him, not seeming to listen.

She shook her head and let out a heavy sigh and said, "I have something I need to talk to you about." He stared at his mother and knew it had to be serious. They sat across from each other at the table, bowed their heads as always, and after she said grace, Anne looked at him. "Ramon, we have to leave Jamaica."

He looked up from his plate of yams and fish. Frowning, he tilted his head. "What do you mean?"

"You remember the recent incident between the British and the Maroons?" Ramon nodded. "Well, the Brits are suspicious and will not be happy when they uncover my involvement with Millie. I'm convinced they're going to come for me."

Ramon considered her words. "How do you know this?" He put down his fork and it clanged on his plate.

"Two Redcoats came here today. They were very inquisitive about the raid." She took a deep breath. "They found Millie's ribbons on the front porch and took one with them. I'm pretty sure they will match it up with the Seville Plantation where Millie came from."

"Yes, but we know you didn't do anything wrong, Mummy."

"That is true. We had to help Millie, but it won't matter when they figure it out. What worries me more than anything is they will discover who I really am." She looked her son in the eyes. Her eyes. He tilted his head, confused. "You see, I have not told you everything there is to know about your father and me." She took a deep breath and continued. "My real name is Anne Bonny, not Clara. There is a bounty on my head for piracy. I escaped prison with the help of my father who bribed the prison guard to let me go while you were still in my tummy." Ramon stared at her, not moving.

"When I met Jack Rackham, your father, I fell so in love with him that nothing else seemed to matter much. He was such a giving person, fun and gregarious. Very much like you."

"But he was a pirate? A criminal?" He'd heard stories down at the riverside about the antics of the seafaring bandits. Ramon's face held a look of disbelief. She could barely believe it herself, as she spoke these truths out loud. Ramon shook his head but said nothing. She was afraid she had told him too much. Anne had been married once before Jack, but decided in that moment, too much truth was not always a good thing. At least not today.

"The life of a pirate is often dictated by one's circumstances. Your father and I sought it only because there was no other way for us to survive. Most of us were misfits. I myself was resisting the constraints of just being a woman." Anne had married John Bonny in rebellion to the arranged marriage her father had set up for her. She ran off to Providence Island with Bonny. A year later, she met Jack and asked Bonny for a divorce, with Jack offering a substantial sum for her legal freedom, but Bonny refused. So, Jack and Anne took off on his schooner. Anne had already decided these were details Ramon did not need to hear. "I was unable to navigate life on land, so escaping to the sea made perfect sense." She leaned back in her chair and took a deep breath before she continued. "I can be pretty stubborn, you know." She winked at him and a small grin tilted his lips, just a little, lifting her hopes that he wouldn't hate her forever. "Life on the sea is difficult. It's a matter of survival. I'm ashamed of many things I've done and have reconciled with God, but again, I'm not proud." She looked at Ramon and her heart sank at the shock on his face.

"Is that why you have bad dreams so much?" Ramon asked.

"Yes, many things come back to haunt my dreams and deservedly so, I must admit." Anne looked down in shame. She felt Ramon's hand cover hers and she looked back into the eyes of her little boy. It was then she realized his love for her wouldn't wane. She covered his hand with her other and squeezed it. "Giving birth to you changed my life. While I had lost your father and the grief of that was all but unbearable, your life gave me hope and the ability to love again. Something I never knew was possible. Now, I feel I know the true meaning of love, thanks to you." She stood up and walked behind him, leaning down and wrapping her arms around him from behind. Leaning her head on his, Anne planted a kiss on top of his head. She sat back down in the chair next to him, realizing she might have alienated the only person in this world that truly mattered to her. Unwelcome tears of relief, loss, and regret slid down her cheeks.

"But where will we go?"

"I'm not quite sure just yet, but we will figure it out. Maybe Cuba," Anne said looking at Ramon trying to anticipate his questions. "We won't know for sure until we meet up with some friends of mine."

"Who are your friends?" Ramon had never known his mother to have any close friends. The Maroons were friendly enough but they kept the "Basket Lady," as he'd heard them call her, at bay. There were no other neighbors close by.

"You will meet them soon," she said and went on to explain her relationship with Ronnie, Mavis, and Queenie.

"When your father died, I found such unexpected solace in you. While you grew inside me, something changed. The grief of losing him and the sudden realization of a chance for a new life as your mother turned out to be an opportunity at an honest life. One that did not involve the sea." She touched his chin and turned it toward her. "Ronnie, Mavis, and Queenie helped me to find our home and have traded with me to help facilitate our lifestyle here." She could see the thoughts swirling in his head. "We've had such a wonderful ten years here on this mountaintop thanks to them. I'm sorry we have to leave, but I promise, all will be good. We will smile again." She pulled him close, hugged him tight, and hoped it was true.

RAMON CAUGHT UP with Elijah but didn't have much time to spare. His mother had given him strict orders not to be out of her sight for more than thirty minutes at a time. That way, if they had to depart suddenly, they could.

Elijah hurried to meet Ramon. He'd been delayed when his mother asked him to help Millie finish picking the ripened guavas from the tree outside their hut. Millie wasn't very tall and could only reach so far, even with the ladder. She had acclimated well to the Maroon culture. Her father had escaped the same time as she, so her fears had abated. Gabrielle had helped serve the roll of surrogate mother since Millie's mother had died a few years before. She and Elijah had become fast friends, despite their age difference. Elijah was almost out of breath as he ran down the lane to meet Ramon.

"I can't stay long. I want to say goodbye and give you this." Ramon handed Elijah an Abeng he had designed for his friend's birthday, a few weeks from now. "I sanded it down myself and painted it blue, your favorite color."

"Goodbye?" Elijah heard nothing Ramon had said after hearing that word. He was gasping for air from running and this news didn't help.

"My mother and I have to leave. We are moving away." Well, at least that was true. He couldn't reveal their situation lest his mother be prosecuted.

"But why?" Elijah wiped the sweat from his brow with the back of his hand.

"There's no reason that I'm able to share with you now. I want to say I will miss you, Elijah." Ramon extended his hand, but Elijah stepped back shaking his head. When he looked at his friend and realized he was serious, he pulled him into a tight embrace.

Leaning back, Elijah looked Ramon in the eyes and asked, "Is it because of Millie?"

Ramon was not anticipating Elijah's question and gave a quick nod, immediately worried he'd done the wrong thing by being truthful. "Yes, but how did you know?"

"I hear my parents talk about di Brits and di Seville raid. Now it make sense."

"When will you leave?" Elijah asked wiping away his unwelcome tears with his sleeve.

"I don't know yet. It could be soon, but I'm not sure."

"Perhaps we could send letters like you talk about?" Elijah asked. Ramon had explained soon after Elijah began lessons with him that one of the reasons to learn to read and write was to be able to communicate by letter writing.

Ramon considered the idea, and for the first time in two days, a smile crossed his face. "That is a great idea!" Hope raised its head for a few seconds and he didn't want to let it go.

"Now when you write, do not start making up stories to impress me, my friend," Elijah said, trying to make Ramon feel better. He could see the pain in his eyes. "I will know when you're stretching the truth about how many fish you caught or how big they were!" Elijah was always trying to make jokes when things went sour. The boys laughed through their tears remembering the time they told Ramon's mother how big the fish was that got away.

"He was this big!" Elijah imitated Ramon, his green eyes wide with wonder and they both laughed at the memory. They both feared memories were all they would have from now on.

—Chapter Twenty-Three—

"Each time a woman stands up for herself, without knowing it possibly, without claiming it, she stands up for all women." —Maya Angelou

1730, Claremont, Jamaica

Marshall heard the horses' hooves approaching as he tied the wagon up in front of Ramble House. He looked up to see Mavis ride up on Moxie.

"Afternoon, Marshall." She slid off of Moxie, shook his hand and hugged him. "Is Ronnie here?"

"She is." Marshall said.

"It's urgent I see her right away." He could see she was worried.

Marshall turned toward the great house and hollered, "Rosalie!" She turned and looked down from the verandah. "Please ask Mrs. Fergusson to join me in the library."

"Yes, Massa Fergusson." Rosalie turned and walked back into the great house.

Mavis followed Marshall into the library. She laid the envelope from Anne on his desk and sat down. Ronnie walked in and said, "Well, look who's here. I thought I recognized Moxie outside!" She walked toward Mavis and stopped short of giving her a hug when she saw the look on her face. She knew her surrogate mother well.

"Here, my dear. This was delivered this to me this morning." Mavis slid the envelope across the desk.

Ronnie picked it up, looked at the envelope, and turned it over and recognized the broken seal. "It's from Anne!" Ronnie said and locked eyes with Mavis. She pulled the paper out of the envelope, the only thing it said was "Cross the bow" with the initials of AB. Ronnie looked from Mavis to Marshall. Her face paled.

"My dear," Marshall stepped up to her. "Are you alright?" She handed him the paper, but the words made no sense to him.

"Where is she?" Ronnie looked at Mavis and cocked her head. "Do you know?"

"I'm not sure, but I suspect she would be at Hope Falls to meet us where she normally does."

Turning to look at Marshall, Anne said, "I have to go with Mavis. Anne needs help." She had told him the stories about Anne and Jack, how they had been so good to her when she had needed it most.

"But, how do you know?" he asked.

She pointed to the note. "It's a password that shows she's in trouble. Probably something about her true identity." She looked at Mavis for more details.

"I know nothing more than what the password conveys, except that we need to make haste to find her. Are you able to come with me?" Mavis asked.

"Absolutely!" Ronnie said and then remembered to include Marshall in her decision. She looked his way.

"I don't pretend to know what is going on," he said, "but I know the two of you will do what's needed. Would you prefer I come along?"

Ronnie looked from Marshall to Mavis. "It's most likely best we go alone so as not to raise inquiries or scare Anne away," Mavis said.

Marshall nodded and looked back at Ronnie. "Please be careful. Is there anything I can do to help?" He looked at Mavis.

She had given it some thought on the way up the mountain to Ramble House and had her answer ready. "Yes, we'll need an extra horse and supplies for a few days of travel. Maybe some cash? I was not thinking all that clearly when I left Ochi."

Marshall turned and strode over to the railing. He leaned over and called for Thomas to pull the wagon around. "Go to the barn and bring back supplies and a horse for a five-night trip for four people."

"Yessir!" Thomas said. He jumped on the wagon and headed down toward the stables to gather the horse and supplies. Turning, Marshall walked to the picture behind his desk. He pulled it off the wall, put it down, and opened his safe. Reaching in, he pulled out a blue satchel with a drawstring, loosened it and spilled the contents, coins clattered all over his desk. "Take whatever you need," he said to Ronnie.

Looking him in the eyes, she said, "She may never be able to repay you."

"It is not 'you' but us, my love. What is mine is yours. Do as your heart leads you."

She hugged him tight and buried her head in his shoulder just for a second. He squeezed her arms, leaned back, and let her go.

RONNIE CHANGED INTO riding clothes, threw more in a satchel, and rushed down the steps of Ramble House. Thomas had returned with the extra horse and supplies. They all pitched in and filled the saddlebags. Marshall walked over to see them off.

"Are you ready to go?" Mavis asked Ronnie.

"Just as soon as I kiss my husband and daughter good-bye." She loved calling Hope her "daughter." It made her heart smile every time.

"Good and with that, I'll go freshen up." Mavis grinned and headed toward the outhouse.

Marshall looked at his wife and said, "I know better than to beg to come along, but I would sure feel better if I could." He pulled her close and kissed the top of her head. He was above questioning her capabilities — she was as capable as any man he knew. "Please just be careful and stay safe."

She looked up at him, so grateful for this man who knew her past, present, and was invested in her future. While they didn't agree about everything, she knew that with him in her life, she was safe and loved. "I will. I promise. Take good care of Hope."

"You know I will." He grinned and hugged her hard. They walked around the side of the house to find Hope and Oliver sitting on her purple quilt, pretending to have tea. Norma was close by, hanging up laundry on the line. "Here, you have some," Hope said as she pretended to hand Oliver a tea cup.

Ronnie walked over and stooped down. "Hope, Mummy has to go for a short trip. I should be home soon."

The little girl looked up and smiled. "Alright, Mummy. I take care of Papa?"

Ronnie laughed and said, "Yes, please. Take good care of him and look after Oliver and Norma too."

Hope looked at Oliver and said, "So, I am in charge."

Ronnie smiled, stood up and walked over to Marshall and linked arms. They walked back around to the front of the house. "Sounds like Hope has everything under control." Turning toward the sound of an approaching horse, they saw it was Sam riding up on Chance.

"Oh, good. It appears Queenie had my message delivered to Ginger Star," Mavis said as she walked back around the side of the house. "I thought in the event we had to deal with the Maroons, we could use Sam's help."

"Well, that was a good call, Mavis," Marshall said. "I'll feel much better knowing he is with the two of you."

"Sam!" Mavis waved. "Thank you for coming!"

Sam tipped his hat but didn't bother to dismount. He knew time was precious. "Miss Adria send me as soon as she gets your note."

"Well, let's get on our way and see what it is Anne needs," Mavis said.

With that, Ronnie let go of Marshall's hand, mounted Stars, and grabbed his reins. Mavis hugged Marshall goodbye and mounted Moxie. They took off down the road toward the Blue Mountains.

"What do you suppose is going on?" Ronnie asked Mavis as she turned her head to wave goodbye to Marshall. She pulled Stars up alongside Moxie as Sam and Chance led the way.

Mavis shook her head. "I wish I knew. I've imagined just about everything."

"I would think so." She pulled the reins to the side to guide Stars around the ruts in the road. "Do you suppose she needs to leave?"

"I believe that could be the case. I sent the message back to Queenie asking her to have it delivered to Jack's mother in Cuba." She knew Queenie could find someone who was headed that way. Mavis and Ronnie had always agreed Anne would probably head to Cuba should her identity ever come into question.

They navigated the mountains using the map Marshall had given her. He'd marked their path in a blue chalk, but Mavis was sure she knew the way. "We should bed down for the night soon," Ronnie said as the sun began to set behind the mountain ridge.

Sam nodded. "Yes, Miss Ronnie. I know a good spot not far away." He pointed up the road which was little more than a path now. They could hear a waterfall in the distance. Sam and Chance led the way to a small waterfall with a pool at the bottom.

"This is perfect, Sam," Mavis said. "A good place to freshen up too."

They all slid down off their horses. Ronnie and Mavis reached into their saddlebags and pulled out supplies. Sam worked to start a fire while the women prepared their tent and bedding for the night. They took turns bathing in the waterfall pool before darkness descended. By then, Sam had the fire going strong.

Laying in their makeshift bedroom, the candle's shadow danced on the canvas ceiling. They could hear Sam softly snoring as he laid next to the campfire with the embers fading. "Alright, now that we're alone, you have to fill me in. What is happening?"

Mavis rolled over to face Ronnie and said, "I really don't know much more. You know I've met her several times to trade wares to sell, but we both knew it was too risky to do it very often. I purposely didn't share it with you as I felt the fewer people that knew, the safer we all were."

"I suspected that several times. Yet, I understood your reluctance to share." She sighed, "I can't imagine what Anne must be going through."

"I know what you mean. I'm wondering if it had something to do with the Seville raid," Mavis said. "I heard the Maroons freed three of their slaves." They both knew Anne lived close to the Maroon village and often traded with them.

"I know the hair-raising fear that a raid can bring. Ramble House was so very fortunate not to sustain much damage, but we lost seven slaves." Ronnie took a deep breath and continued, "Part of me was sad for us, but a bigger part is happier for them. I often think about George and the others, hoping they're safe and happy." Marshall had been deeply disappointed that George, a valued slave, had chosen to leave. Evidently, he was a big co-conspirator with the Maroons, and was integral in facilitating the raid, managing to get his family off the Ramble House plantation. It had solidified Marshall's position in not emancipating anyone anytime soon, much to Ronnie's chagrin.

"Have you ever wondered if Amari was involved in the raid?"

"Many times. Marshall seems to think he probably was."

"We may never know. I'm just grateful no one was hurt."

"So am I. It makes me shudder when I think of what could have happened." Yawning, Ronnie added, "Well, we're going to need a good night's sleep. I have a feeling tomorrow will be a long day."

"Quite true. Pleasant dreams, my friend." Mavis said as she rolled over on her other side and closed her eyes.

Laying there in comfortable silence, the sound of the waterfall lulled Ronnie into dreams she hoped would not come true.

RONNIE WOKE AT dawn thanks to the aroma of the coffee Sam brewed over the leftover coals. Grateful it was just a dream, she stretched her arms above her head watching the sunshine hide behind the clouds of the rainforest in the distance. Their cool shadow shaded the mountainside and would travel their way soon, providing some relief from the certain to show up, steamy Jamaican sunshine. She crawled out from under her blanket and stretched her arms up to the sky. Yawning, she walked over and sat on a felled tree trunk next to Sam. "Morning."

"Mornin' to you, Miss Ronnie. How you sleep?"

"Not as good as you, I must say." She winked at him.

"Sorry if my snorin' wake you." He winced at the thought.

She smiled and jabbed him with her elbow. "Your snoring told me all was right with the world, Sam. I knew if you were sleeping, then we were all safe." Looking at the ground, he nodded and grinned at the compliment.

Mavis walked out from behind a bush. Ronnie handed her a cup of coffee. "What time do you suppose we will get to Hope Falls, Sam?" she asked.

"Noontime or so," he said.

They drank their coffee and each ate a biscuit to stave off hunger pangs for a few hours. Sam poured water over the camp-fire to extinguish the coals. They packed up their bedding and mounted their horses. Sam led the way back to the road and the women followed on their horses until they came to the road. Ronnie and Stars followed at the rear of the group. They rode single file for about an hour.

"We're making good time," Mavis said, pointing across the mountain ridge. "That's Anne's yellow house on the other side." While they could see the cottage, they would not go there. Mavis and Ronnie agreed Anne would be at Hope Falls, not too far from her home. For them to stay at the cottage could prove too risky if the Brits were looking for her. They could see the jagged mountain behind the cottage where the Maroon village hid.

Riding in silence, each wondered what they would find when they saw Anne again. The horses labored slowly up the side of the mountain. The sound of the waterfall guided them, growing louder and louder. They looked toward the falls to see the silhouettes of two people. One taller than the other.

Anne and Ramon walked toward them as they stopped. Chance snorted in relief. Ronnie hopped down off of Stars while Sam offered his hand to Mavis who took it and slipped off of Moxie. Sam stepped back as Anne embraced both women at once. The strength of their grip on each other drew their circle in close.

"Thank you for coming!" Anne cried, tears of relief streaming down her face. Tears of grateful welcoming to her rescuers. Tears of joy at seeing her old friends. Tears of fear of what the future might hold.

"What happened?" Mavis asked.

"I'm pretty sure the Redcoats suspect that I helped a young female slave escape to the Maroons."

"Was she from Seville?" Ronnie asked and Anne nodded. "There's been a lot of talk about that raid." Ronnie looked at Mavis confirming their suspicions.

"Yes, she was. If they find out who I really am," she looked back at Ramon who, gratefully, was talking to Sam and helping to cool the horses down, "they will hang me."

"Not to worry, my dear. We have a plan." Mavis put her arm around Anne's shoulder and guided her over to a rock by the waterfall pool and they sat. "By the time they realize your identity, you will be halfway to Cuba." Mavis laid out the plan she was sure Queenie and Adria already had in motion.

Anne pulled her hat off. "Oh my, your hair!" Ronnie gasped at the sight of Anne's short haircut; her hand flew up to cover her mouth. The last time they met, Anne's hair had been long and curly.

Anne laughed. "Yes, I am back to my old self. Funny how easily I stepped into my old identity."

Sam came up with Ramon at his side. Ronnie walked back over and reached into Stars' saddlebag. She pulled out a satchel. Handing the bag to Anne, she said, "Assuming Ramon would need a disguise, I brought some girl's clothing that should fit him."

Ramon looked at his mother confused. Anne laughed and took the clothing out of the bag, holding up a blue dress. "We will now call you, 'Ramona'!"

"But, Mama, I am not a girl!" He stomped his foot.

"I know my sweet, but it will only be for a little while."

Anne took Ramon by his hand and went behind a bush to change his clothes. She placed the bonnet on his head as they walked back toward the group. "Mama, please!" and he yanked it off.

"Alright, but keep it handy and put it on when I say." He nodded up and down, sighed and looked away.

"But if we go to Cuba, I will never see Elijah again," Ramon said.

Anne looked at Mavis and sighed. She pulled her son close and kissed the top of his head. It occurred to her that she didn't have to bend over as far as she used to. He was growing tall like his father. " Ramon, I've lived long enough to believe anything can happen. I don't want to leave either, but we must." She stood up and he slowly joined her. They mounted their horses with Ramon jumping up on Chance and holding on to Sam. They started their trip back down toward Ocho Rios. Anne's mind swirled with what she might find, a path to freedom or the gallows; there didn't seem to be much room between the possibilities.

ELIJAH WAS NOT used to this deflated feeling. He supposed it was sadness because Ramon was gone and he would probably never see him again. He'd already started a letter hoping one day he would have an address in Cuba to send it to. Somehow, writing the letter made him feel as if he'd had a conversation with his buddy.

As he walked home from the morning hunt, he broke off from the group to walk past Ramon's now-empty cottage where no one lived. Yesterday, it appeared they had gone, doors closed and windows shut. Today, he sat on their back porch staring at the tea bushes and pimento plants. Their goats bleated and ran up to him, hoping for a snack and followed him around the house until he came to the retaining wall at the side of the cottage. He'd found a note Ramon had left under the same rock they always used to communicate with each other. "Mama wants you to take the goats home with you as well as anything else in the cottage that might be of use to you and your family." Tears betrayed Elijah, sliding down his cheeks, and he sobbed knowing Ramon was really gone. He thought back to the last time he'd seen his friend just a few days earlier.

Elijah had run up to the tree behind the cottage where Ramon waited. His new Abeng Ramon had made hung from his belt. "So, no school for you today?" Elijah asked.

"No, Mummy's been packing up all day," Ramon had said as he drew a star in the dirt with the stick in his hand. "We will leave soon, it seems." He stared at the ground.

"Here," Elijah said as he handed a small brown satchel to Ramon.

"What's this?" Ramon asked.

"Just a few coins to help you in your journey."

Ramon looked at his friend. "We can't take your money, Elijah," he said shaking his head.

"My parents insist. Please accept their gift." Elijah reached in his pocket and pulled out a folded paper. "And here is my first letter. You can read it on your journey. Be safe, my friend."

The two boys looked at each other, each lost in their thoughts. Each unable to imagine a world without the other.

"Don't forget our code," Ramon said, looking at the Abeng hanging on Elijah's belt.

Elijah wiped the tears from his face with the back of his arm and smiled. "Never!"

Pulling the Abeng from his belt, he raised it to his lips and played. They'd used this code as they hunted in order to locate one another and as a way to lose the other kids in the village as they followed each other into the hollows. Somehow, they knew one day, he would need it for a more important reason.

THE SOUND OF horses approaching yanked Elijah back to the present. He ducked into the bushes on the side of the road, knowing how to camouflage himself quickly. He kept his breath shallow, as his father had taught him. Two Redcoats rode up and tied their horses to the hitching post in front of the cottage. The taller Redcoat walked across the porch, boots scuffing on the wooden platform as he swung the door open.

"Hey, Joseph, find anything?" asked the older Redcoat as he pulled a pipe out of his pocket, wishing he had a flint to light it with. He stuck it in his mouth anyway.

Joseph walked out of the cottage. "They're definitely gone. Not much left to pilfer either," Joseph said holding up a satchel he had stuffed a few leftover pottery pieces Anne had made.

Elijah couldn't hear everything but heard enough to know they were looking for Anne and Ramon. The Redcoats mounted their horses taking the satchel with them. As they disappeared over the ridge, Elijah slowly came out of the bushes. He ran as fast as he could. Once at the village, he burst into his home and went straight for it. Grabbing the Abeng, he turned and ran back to the fork in the road that led to Ramon's cottage. He put the Abeng to his lips and played their code. He stopped, took a breath, and blew on the Abeng again.

Just as he finished the second time, a white hand clamped down on his arm. He gasped, turned, and looked into the blue eyes of the Redcoat.

—Chapter Twenty-Four—

"In the flush of love's light, we dare be brave, and suddenly we see, that love costs all we are, and will ever be. Yet it is only love which sets us free," —Maya Angelou poem, "Touched by an Angel"

1730, Ocho Rios, Jamaica

The unlikely caravan slowed down as Sam guided everyone up the hill toward the waterfall where they had stayed the previous night. He stopped, hopped off, and tied his horse to a broken tree stump. Ramon jumped off, holding his skirt. "Please, Mama, can I take this awful dress off?"

"Let's wait until the sun goes down, alright?" Anne reached over and patted him on the shoulder. Ramon shook his head and sighed.

They pulled the overnight gear from the saddlebags and began to set up camp. The sound of the waterfall hovered like a thick blanket. They talked about where to set up the lean-to and who would sleep where. Sam stopped and held his hand up for everyone to quiet down. There it was, the sound of an Abeng. They all knew that could mean trouble between the British and Maroons.

Sam shook his head and said, "Hope no trouble come dis way.

"Shh!" Ramon said and mimicked Sam's "quiet down" hand signals. The young boy's eyes widened. "That code is from Elijah. Our secret code." He looked at his mother. "He is telling us the Redcoats are looking for us. We should not stop." He looked at the others.

Anne looked from Ramon to Sam. "Well, that settles that," Anne said and stood to her feet. "Sam, I think we should continue on to Ochi now. If we're careful, we should make it there by dawn."

"I think we have enough lanterns to light the way," Ronnie said, holding hers up in front of her. Mavis reached in her saddlebag and pulled out hard tack and some of her jerky, handing some out to each person. "Dinner will have to be on the road tonight, folks." Mavis said. They hastily repacked their saddlebags and mounted their horses.

The caravan followed Sam with Ramon sitting in front of him on Chance, holding a lantern in front of them as best he could, shedding light on the path.

Riding for several hours around the mountain ridge, they could now see the lights of Ocho Rios guiding the way. A rooster crowed in the distance. "Di sun ready to wake by di cockerels' crowin'," Sam said as the dawn peeked over the ridge. As the sun rose, beams of light shone down on the sea in spots as if to say, "This way."

Sam pulled Chance to a stop until the others caught up. "I tink maybe wi break up fi a while." He looked at Mavis figuring she would agree, and she did.

"You're right, Sam. If we try to ride into town together, we'll surely draw unwanted attention."

"You ladies take the southeastern trail. Dat will bring you down through the back way."

"Sounds like good strategy." Ronnie said and turned Stars around. "The pass is right up here." She held her lantern up and blew out the flame. Morning was beginning to lend a hand with finding their way through the Jamaican jungle.

"We can meet at the mercantile. Queenie will be waiting there, I'm sure." Mavis said.

Sam and Ramon continued down toward Ocho Rios where the town still slept. A few candles and lanterns dotted windows here and there. The sounds of the docks greeted them with fishermen sailing off for a day's work and a few seamen stumbling back to their boats from the brothels. Sam saw no one he recognized and breathed a sigh of relief as they hitched Chance to the post in the back of the mercantile.

MAVIS WAS RIGHT, Queenie was there and ushered them into the back of the store, pointing at the table for them to sit. "Help yourself to the porridge," she said. Sam scooped them each a hot bowlful.

"It look like you was hungry!" Sam tossed Ramon's hair as he scraped the bowl clean. "Want more?"

"No thank you, sir," he said. Sam grinned. He wasn't used to being called "sir." Ramon looked up to see his mother walk into the room with Mavis and Ronnie following close behind. He stood up and ran over wrapping his arms around her. She buried her nose in his hair.

"I'm so happy you're here safe and sound!" Anne looked at Sam and Queenie and said, "Thank you so much for taking good care of him for me."

Sam nodded and took another bite as Queenie said, "No need to thank me. He was hungry and I assume the rest of you are too." She pointed to the wood burning stove and Mavis dished up three more bowls of porridge.

Queenie cleared her throat, turned toward Anne and Ramon and said, "The schooner that will deliver you two to Cuba will be leaving at dawn." She picked up a satchel with supplies she'd gathered. "There's hard tack and jerky along with some oranges." She grinned and raised her eyebrows. "You can thank Mavis, as I robbed her blind in the mercantile!"

Anne walked over to Queenie and wrapped her in her arms. "It seems as if you have thought of everything, my Queenie." She leaned back and looked at her friend of many years. "Once again, you save the day."

Queenie shook off the compliment and continued barking orders. "Alright, folks. That is enough of dat. Eat up and get some rest." She looked back at Anne and Ramon. "You have a long day in front of you. Make sure you eat all you can."

"So grateful, Queenie." Anne said. She was not used to taking hand outs and knew none of her friends would accept her money. When no one was looking, she slipped a few gold coins under a pot sitting on the counter to cover the cost of the food the mercantile had provided. Ronnie saw her hide the money and was reminded of the satchel she had brought to give her.

Pulling her aside, Ronnie slid the bag of coins into Anne's pocket. "This is from Marshall and me. I hope it helps you to get settled into your new life, my friend."

"But," Anne felt the heavy pouch inside her pocket and knew it was more than enough. "I don't know that I will ever be able to repay you!"

Ronnie took her by the hand and pulled her toward the back of the room for privacy. "Anne, you saved my life more than once. You brought me through the loss of my baby and held me while I cried through my grief. I can never repay you, not even with money."

Grabbing Ronnie, Anne hugged her hard and said, "If it weren't for the letter you sent my father all those years ago,

I would be dead for sure." She looked toward her son and said, "God only knows what would have happened to Ramon."

"Knowing you and Ramon arrive safely in Cuba will be the only thanks I need," Ronnie said.

Returning to the table, they sat and dug into their dinner. Everyone ate in silence, each one thinking about what the next few hours might hold. Ronnie and Anne cleared the table as Mavis pulled a box of draughts out of the cupboard. "So, who wants to play?" She laid the mat down over the table.

"Count me in!" Queenie said as she helped to clear the bowls from the table.

"Watch out for her," Mavis nodded toward Queenie. "She can clean out your pockets!"

"Comes from hanging out with pirates!" Ronnie said and immediately wished she had held her tongue, worried she might upset Ramon.

Anne laughed helping her to feel better. "Well, draughts is one thing this pirate never mastered, so I don't anticipate any success, just so you know!" She looked at Ramon. "Why don't we be partners and I will show you how to play?" She hoped the game would help take the worried look off his face. She'd never seen him as serious as he had been the past few days. All she wanted was a smile from him, but so far, not much luck.

"Well, if you're not going to help me win, Mummy, perhaps I should be Sam's partner instead." Ramon nodded and moved his chair closer to Sam as they all broke out laughing. Sam reached over and tossed Ramon's hair.

They played a few games and sure enough, Sam and Ramon were in the lead. "Stick with me, lil' man, we whoop these ladies yet!" Sam said.

Mavis looked up from the game as they gathered the pieces to put back in the box. "Mummy, I need to go use the outhouse," Ramon said.

"Alright, but put your hat back on first." She knew better than to call it a bonnet. He nodded and tied the hat on before he walked out the door.

"I'll keep an eye on him," Ronnie said. She stood at the door making sure no one was around.

"Anne, I'm just curious, but why are you so adamant about not going back to South Carolina?" Queenie asked.

Anne paused and sighed. "Well, watching my mother's shame at giving birth to me out of wedlock broke my heart. I made up my mind when I was about eight years old, I would fight to my death to avoid the constraints of being a woman there." Anne stood and walked to the back of the room. She held a piece of kindling and snapped it into three pieces. As each piece snapped, she visibly shook with anger. "I watched her travel with my father to the New World and step into a hierarchy in South Carolina I knew I never could survive."

"What made you decide to become a pirate?" Queenie asked, surprised that she didn't already know.

"The dictates of society were more than I could swallow. I fell in love with Jack and turned to piracy in an attempt to not have to conform to the dictates of being a woman." She looked at the rest of them, shocked at what she had said aloud. Just the words being spoken had more validation than ever when she'd heard them in her own head.

"And now, I look around this room and realize each one of you has stepped beyond your boundaries as women. And men," she added when her eyes landed on Sam. "And mostly on my account. Every one of you have all gone way above your approved abilities as our culture would dictate."

Mavis walked over to Anne, put her arm around her shoulder and looked at the rest of the group. "The more I live, the more I know that love does indeed give us the determination to make good things happen. Our society loves to pass judgement and, in my humble opinion, only God has that right."

THE FRONT DOORBELL clanged as someone entered the store. Mavis stood and they all looked after her as she disappeared to the front. Voices murmured for a bit and Mavis pulled the curtain back. She held it open for a tall man with silver hair and a beard. He walked in and just his presence commanded everyone's attention. He pulled his hat off, allowing his long hair to tumble onto his shoulders.

Ronnie's eyes landed on the woman standing behind him. "Adria!" Ronnie rushed to her. "I should have known you would be the one to reach in to save the day." She stopped and looked down at Adria's stomach. "And your little one is getting bigger by the day, I must say!"

Adria laughed and said, "Well, the baby is not the only one growing, I'm afraid, but I believe the stars must be aligned to bring us all together this way and for such a good reason." She looked at the unlikely group. "Folks, this is our captain who is here to whisk Anne and Ramon away to Cuba." Anne looked from Mavis to the man and back again. "Most of you know Adria, but Anne, I do not believe you two have met."

Anne walked over and said, "Adria, I certainly know of you, but have yet to make your acquaintance." Anne extended her hand and Adria shook it.

Adria smiled. "I'm pleased to finally meet you," Adria said as her eyes met Anne's.

Anne turned to look at the captain. "Thank you, sir," she hesitated for a second. There was something familiar about him. "Do I know you?" She looked at Adria and then back at the man.

"Augustin, is that you?" Anne cocked her head and took a step in his direction.

"Well, I think it is," he said, "but was beginning to wonder, Anne-chica." He grinned the lopsided grin that could only be his along with his sweet, Spanish accent. The inflection of his voice brought instant recognition. Her eyes flew open and for the first time in a long while, she felt hopeful. She knew she and Ramon were in good hands.

"In my defense, you never had much of a beard and your hair was not so full of silver!" Anne hugged him tight and thought maybe life was not as dark as she had believed just one minute ago.

He tossed his head back and laughed. "I thought you had forgotten who I was, my dear Anne-chica!" He called her by his pet name for her in his thick Spanish accent. "What took you so long?"

She thought for a split second. "The silver hair. I must say." She took a step toward him and tilted her head for a closer look. "Yes, that's definitely you!" They hugged and his strength felt as if it were contagious. Leaning back to look at him, she added, "And quite distinguished!" Anne turned and looked at her circle of friends who were trying to put the pieces together in their own heads.

She swept her arm in his direction. "This is Augustin Blanco, an old friend." She looked over her shoulder at him. "He saved my life twice and now it appears there will be a third opportunity." Plopping down in a chair, she ran her fingers through her short hair, a quick reminder of all that was happening. She was used to twirling a strand of hair around her finger when she was nervous or trying to think something over.

Ronnie stiffened when she recognized Augustin. He was a pirate she'd known in Nassau. He knew her past which was something she didn't relish reliving here in Jamaica in front of her friends. But her angst was assuaged as she watched Anne relax for the first time since they'd met at Hope Falls. It was as if the realization of being who she really was unleashed happiness and she had let go of her fear. *Maybe you need to take a lesson from Anne.* Ronnie knew with Augustin in control, her old friend was in good hands.

Anne looked at Ramon who stood wide-eyed. "You're a real pirate?" He looked from Augustin to Anne and back again. "You knew my dad?" Ramon hesitated and looked at his mother, afraid he might have hurt her by asking.

Augustin reached over and tossed Ramon's raven hair. "For a brief time, yes, I knew your papa. Quite a chatty fellow with charm like no other." Augustin smiled at the lad. "He loved your mother so." He looked from Ramon to Anne. Trying to recover when he saw the emotion in Anne's eyes, he said, "And a pretty good sailor too. With nothing but the stars to guide him around many a hungry pirate ship, whether it be Blackbeard or Vane, Calico Jack managed to safely steer clear many, many times." The boy looked at the retired pirate in awe.

Augustin's eyes landed on Ronnie. "Ron-chica!" he said, surprised to see her. He walked over and hugged her hard.

"Yes, it's me!" said Ronnie, glad she'd waited her turn. She decided she'd take a page out of Anne's book and not worry about what anyone thought of her past.

Mavis looked around the room. "What is this, a pirate reunion?" They busted into a cleansing laughter.

"Well, it is indeed a sweet surprise," Augustin said, "to not only be able to help our Anne, but to see that my Ron-chica is doing well. I've often wondered." He bowed just a little and smiled. Anne hadn't realized Ronnie and Augustin knew one another all that well.

Ramon's eyes widened again as he looked at Ronnie and said, "You were a pirate too?"

Ronnie hesitated, but just for a second. "Well, kind of, for a little while, but I wasn't very good at it. That's why I stayed here in Jamaica."

Augustin looked at everyone and went on to explain. "I met Ron-chica in Nassau before she set sail with the Neptune. "I have often wondered as I had heard the Neptune was overtaken by the Vulture." He looked at Ronnie and said, "But I did not know you landed here in Jamaica." His Cuban accent clipped the air as he shook his head.

"It's a long story." Ronnie nodded toward Anne. "She can fill you in on your journey to Cuba." Ronnie looked around the room. "Augustin was a good friend of many in Nassau." She winked at Mavis. "Rest assured, our beloved Anne and Ramon are in good hands."

Adria walked over and put her hand on Augustin's shoulder and said, "There is talk that with the bounty on Anne's head, the privateers are looking for a good payday. Leaving at dusk is a better idea than dawn."

"Well then, we had best make haste and set sail before dark," Augustin said. "The weather looks favorable, so we should be able to make it to Cuba by morning."

Anne leaned back and looked back at Augustin. In that instant, she knew she and Ramon would survive. It was the best she could hope for. And that was enough.

ADRIA LOOKED AT Mavis, "Oh, before I forget," as she ducked back behind the curtain into the front of the store and picked up the jewelry box she'd left on the countertop when she arrived. "I need to get some more pimento for my sachets." She sat the black onyx box on the table.

Anne stared at the box and reached across to touch it. She took a deep breath. "Where did you get this?" Anne asked. Her hand traced the inlaid mother of pearl on the top.

Queenie said, "You sound as if you've seen a duppy!" A duppy was Jamaica's version of a ghost.

"I think I have!" Anne said wide-eyed. She picked up the box and stared at Adria not knowing what to say. Realizing she sounded accusatory, she added, "It's just that it looks familiar."

Adria looked at Anne. Feeling as if she was on the defensive for whatever reason, she said, "My son, Elijah, gave it to me."

"Elijah?" Thoughts swirled through Anne's head as she connected them slowly. "The same Elijah that lives with the Maroons?" Anne was confused. Adria's face went white.

Ronnie stepped up to help explain. "Anne, remember years ago when I told you Amari had gone to live with the Maroons?" Anne nodded her head. "Well, what I didn't tell you then was a baby was also taken to them that same night. The baby was Adria's son, now called 'Elijah.'" Things were starting to make sense to Anne, but just a little. Ronnie added, "Adria didn't know where he'd gone for many years."

"Oh my. How awful for you!" Anne said, looking at Adria and then again at the box in her hands. "I must be wrong. It cannot be the same box if he gave it to you," Anne said shaking her head and pushed the box back toward Adria.

Anne and Ronnie looked at each other, both were stunned. They both knew there had been a king's ransom worth in gold inside the box. Ronnie stepped up and said, "No, it's definitely the same box. I doubt there's another quite like it."

"When I caught up with Jack on the Vanity, he admitted to hiding some of the cache in it, behind a waterfall," Anne said looking at Ronnie. "They must have found it somehow." She handed the box back to Adria. "Please keep it. It has more meaning for you than me at this point."

Adria felt as if the air in the room disappeared. She took
a deep breath and cocked her head to one side. The box was
precious to her but finding someone who really knew her son
was so much better. "So, you know Elijah?" Her heart pounded
at the possibility.

"Yes, and I believe I recognize your green eyes in his. They're
hard to forget," Anne said. "He's quite an intelligent, respectful,
and personable young man."

"And he's my best friend!" Ramon added. The adults had
forgotten the boy was even in the room.

"He certainly is," said Anne as she pulled him close to her
side. "The very best friend anyone could have." She kissed him
on his cheek while realizing how much he'd matured just in the
past few days. Real life had a way of doing that to everyone, even
her young son. She looked down at Ramon and asked, "Doesn't
Elijah look like Miss Adria?"

The young boy looked at Adria with renewed interest. "Yes,
she does, but he also looks like his dad," he said referring to
Amari. They all smiled at his misinterpretation of Elijah's parentage. Anne and Ramon went on to share a few stories about their
times parrot hunting, fishing, and playing in the falls.

They all laughed as they recalled the time Elijah tried to ride
one of their goats in the backyard. "He finally jumped off and
ran like a rabbit. I don't think he ever tried to ride one again!"
Ramon laughed.

Adria caught her breath and asked, "But wait, you said there
was gold inside the box? Where did it go?"

Anne responded immediately and said, "It doesn't matter
where it went. I hope it will help Elijah," she looked at Ronnie,
"and Amari to remain free."

THE SOUND OF horses' hooves clomped to a stop in the front of the mercantile. Their laughter stopped and they all went quiet as Mavis disappeared through the curtain once again. The bell on the door clanged. Anne looked around the room. They held their collective breath as the sound of boots scuffed on the floor after the door creaked open.

"Afternoon, ma'am," a Redcoat said as the door slammed behind him.

"Nice to see you, officer," Mavis said hoping to convey who was there to those behind the curtain. "What can I get for you today?" She pretended to wipe the counter as if she cared.

"We are looking for a woman and her ten-year-old son." He looked over Mavis' shoulder trying to sneak a peek through the curtain and continued. "She has long red hair and his is black. Have you seen anyone fitting that description?" He handed Mavis a wanted handbill with sketches that resembled Anne and Ramon, sans their disguises.

Mavis paused and looked at the poster, but just for a second. "Well, I've seen no one looking like this, that is for sure. I'm sorry." She shook her head and was relieved at her own ability to play semantics and stay calm. The drawing was of a long-haired woman and a young boy. "What on earth do you want with a mother and son?" Her boldness surprised even her.

"She's wanted for questioning with regards to aiding an escaped slave," the Redcoat answered and tipped his hat. "Well, Ma'am, if you would put the poster up in your window, it would be most appreciated. The Seville Plantation has also posted a bounty for her capture."

"But of course." Mavis took the poster and looked at a poor sketch of Anne and Ramon.

He turned on his heel, and stepped toward the door before turning to say, "There is a generous bounty on one or both. Just get word to us and we will track them down." Mavis nodded and looked at the paper in her hand. Her stomach tightened. He turned and walked out the door, the bell tinkling in his wake. Her heart skipped a beat and she took a deep breath before turning to head back behind the curtain.

Mavis looked at Augustin and Anne whose arm was around Ramon's shoulder. Augustin said, "Adria is correct. We cannot wait until dawn. As soon as the sun sets, we must go." No one moved, each thinking of the future, hoping Anne and Ramon had one.

RONNIE PULLED ANNE aside as the others stepped out with Augustin and said, "Your largesse is something I can never forget, Anne. Your caring for me as no one else did when I lost my baby is an experience that has never left me and never will."

"I did nothing for you that you wouldn't have done for me, my friend." Anne pulled Ronnie in for a tight hug. The two knew their friendship would always be.

Anne looked over her shoulder and said, "So, my dear, I'm afraid Augustin is going to have my neck if I don't make a hasty exit. The sun has dipped behind the mountain."

Ronnie laughed and said, "Yes, I remember the time I kept him waiting at the pier in Nassau. He made me jump six feet onto the side of the ship to get on!" They both laughed remembering Ronnie's panic. Kissing Ronnie on the cheek, Anne turned and rushed out the door to the rest of her life.

THE LIGHTS OF the Jamaican north coast winked at Anne as she bid its beauty goodbye. The island of her love affair with Jack, Hope Falls where they were first intimate, and the mountaintop where Ramon was born and raised. It was the only home Ramon had ever known. Living in the mountains of Jamaica had taught her to be content on the land instead of the sea. Now, the sea was under her feet, but she felt no draw to it. She only wanted to find a new life for her, Ramon, and Cunningham. She knew in her heart it would be on land and not the sea.

She talked to God that night, thanking Him or Her for giving her a new life. For not making her go back to South Carolina and be squeezed back into a culture that never welcomed her or her mother. And for avoiding the gallows. She wasn't sure what they would find in Cuba, but she was grateful for the chance of a new beginning.

"Mama," he tugged on her shawl. "May I take off this horrible bonnet?" His question pulled her back to the present.

She looked at him and laughed, pulling the bonnet off his head. She tossed it into the dark blue sea, thanking whatever God there was, believing more than ever before that Someone was listening.

—Chapter Twenty-Five—

"A bird doesn't sing because it has an answer. It sings because it has a song." —Maya Angelou

1730, Ocho Rios, Jamaica

Turn this way toward the window," said Jonas, the artist Jeffrey had commissioned to finish painting the portrait her mother had started years before. Jonas took her hand and pulled her around. Adria was getting tired of posing. He looked down to see her heart-shaped birthmark. "What is this?" He touched her hand.

"It's my birthmark. I used to wish it would go away, but no longer." She thought of Elijah's matching heart.

Jonas was almost half finished with the portrait. "The sunlight is better today," he said.

Adria stood as still as she could, staring at the sea, wondering how Anne and Ramon were. They'd left soon after dark the night before. She'd spent a fitful night tossing and turning, wondering how they were doing on their voyage of only ninety miles, yet a lifetime away.

"Miss Adria," Mum Lettie said as she walked in, wiping her hands on her apron. "Der 'tis someone at de door that want talk to you." The older woman's eyes revealed her worry.

"Who is it?" Adria asked as she turned toward Mum Lettie.

"He say he wit da magistrate's office."

Adria nodded at Jonas as he stepped aside for her to walk past and headed down to the foyer. A tall, official looking man in a uniform with a badge stood holding his hat. "Good afternoon, sir. How may I help you?" she asked as she held onto the railing with one hand, while she descended the staircase holding her dress with the other.

"We have arrested a young Maroon for aiding and abetting an escaped slave from Seville Plantation."

A sick feeling hit the pit of her stomach. "Why would you be here to tell me this?" She stared at the man, her stomach churning while she awaited his response.

"He claims to know you, Ma'am." He looked at his hands. "His name is Elijah."

She took a deep breath and knew now what it felt like for chills to run up her spine during a steamy Jamaican afternoon.

"I need to see him now." Adria said. Her green eyes were intense, revealing her determination.

The officer nodded. "I'm sure that can be arranged. You can follow me back to the station, if you like."

"Yes indeed. Let me change my clothes and saddle my horse." She looked at Mum Lettie who was always good at anticipating her needs.

"I fetch hot tea for de officer while he wait an' ask Solomon bring Chance 'round front while you change." Mum Lettie turned and hesitated, but only for a second. She'd wanted to voice her concern about Adria riding a horse while expecting a child but knew better. Adria would not let anything keep her from Elijah and his troubles, that much she knew. She let it go, turned, and walked briskly toward the kitchen where she was sure she'd find Solomon.

Adria rushed to her room, but before she changed, she sat down to write a note to Ronnie. If the government had arrested Elijah, they would want to use him as a pawn to strike a deal with the Maroons. The faster she could set the wheels in motion, the better. She finished the note and changed her clothes. Looking at the clock, she realized Jeffrey wouldn't be home for a while yet. Knowing Mum Lettie would be able to fill him in, she left the bedroom door open and rushed down the stairs. "Sam!" The aging Sam looked up from his whittling as he sat on the front steps. "Please take this to Mrs. Fergusson at Ramble House right away!" She quickly explained Elijah's plight to him, knowing he would make haste.

Sam put down his carving, rose and took the envelope from her. "Yes, Miss Adria." He turned and took off toward the stable.

"Thank you!" she called after him as she grabbed Chance's reins from Solomon and mounted her horse. The officer tipped his hat and took off, leading the way toward town.

They pulled up in front of the building that was little more than a hut. It was masonry with bars on every window. Adria dismounted and followed the officer inside.

"Here is the mistress of Ginger Star," the officer said to the jailor that sat with his feet propped up on his desk while reading a pamphlet. Adria was repulsed by his greasy hair, and from the stench in the room. She pulled her handkerchief from her pocked and covered her nose, trying not to offend. The jailor tossed the pamphlet aside, put his feet back on the floor and stood.

"Well, it's Mrs. Palmer, I believe. Am I correct?" the jailor asked.

"Yes, sir, you are correct," Adria said.

"I am Sergeant Montgomery," he said and extended his hand.

Adria hesitated, but only for a second. You need this man's help. She shook his hand and stepped back just a little.

Montgomery wanted to probe to see what her connection was to his Maroon prisoner, but decided he'd best not interrogate a woman of such stature in the community. He had other ways.

ADRIA LOOKED OVER her shoulder to make sure no one could hear. Looking at him through the bars, she'd imagined many scenarios about their next meeting, but this had never crossed her mind. "Elijah?"

The young man looked up from sitting on the side of the cot in his cell. He was wearing the shell necklace she'd given him. Just one night in this awful place surpassed the worst nightmare he'd ever had, but holding on to the shells on the string, had given him hope. His eyes flashed briefly with excitement as he stood and hurried toward the one that could rescue him. "Miss Adria?"

"Yes, my dear, it's me. What in the world happened?" He explained.

"I only try to help my friend, Ramon, and his mum." He went on to explain that he was accused of aiding and abetting a wanted felon who was his best friend, charges that could land him in prison for many years or maybe even the gallows.

"Please know I'm working on your release, but what on earth happened, Elijah?" She grabbed hold of the bars in an effort to prevent herself from falling. Just the sight of him in this cell made her knees want to buckle.

"I use Abeng Ramon give me to send warning. I know Redcoats on way." His green eyes looked into hers. Her motherly instincts were stronger than she'd thought. Her fierce desire to protect him was surprising, even to her.

She looked over her shoulder to make sure no one could hear and in a low voice said, "Well, while what you did was dangerous, it certainly did help. The story I was told is when they heard your Abeng, they didn't stop, but kept going on to Ocho Rios. Further delay, and they would have been caught."

Elijah grinned, but just a little. "Ramon and his mother have left for Cuba?"

"They should be there by now, thanks to you. Now, all we have to do is figure out a plan to get you released from this awful place." Adria looked around them.

A tear slipped down Elijah's cheek. Adria thought it was because he was scared. She reached her hand through the bars and touched his shoulder. "Please try not to worry. We will get you out of here."

"No, tis not dat. I sad because I never see Ramon again."

Adria sighed. She couldn't argue with his worry but wanted to give him some hope. "Well, my dear, I've lived a little longer than you and can honestly say, there is always a possibility. Life can take away, but it certainly gives blessings back to us when we least expect them." Reaching through the bars, she touched his cheek, wiping away his tear with her hand, the one with their birthmark. "Let's figure out how to get you out of here first." She kissed her hand and touched him on the forehead saying, "And let God handle the rest." And they did.

She smiled at him and turned his chin up to look at her. He took a deep breath, nodded, and grinned. It was the best he could do and that was good enough for her.

RONNIE READ ADRIA'S note that described Elijah's plight. She scribbled something on the bottom of Adria's note and left it for Marshall who was out surveying the fields. She took off on Stars, following Sam on Brownie, heading over the ridges of the Blue

Mountains. She pulled Stars to a stop as they approached the Maroon village.

Pointing toward the smoke and thatched roofs on the next hill, Sam said, "Di village is right der on di next ridge." They had stopped in a clearing with a fork in the path. It was a steep climb up the side of the mountain to the village.

"Perhaps we'd be less threatening on foot," Ronnie said.

Sam nodded as he slid down off Brownie. Ronnie dismounted Stars who snorted and stomped the ground. "What's the matter, girl?" She pulled Stars' head toward her and stroked the star on the palomino's head. Before she could look around, she heard the rustling of leaves. The trees and bushes shook as five Maroons appeared from behind the foliage, their bows and guns pointed at them.

Ronnie gasped as she felt hands grab hers from behind. She turned to look behind her, but before she knew it, someone slipped something over her head and everything went dark.

She could hear Sam plead with them in Patois as he tried to wrestle with his attacker. Struggling to decipher the conversation, she heard a thud and a grunt. Sam fell quiet. Brownie whinnied and took off, the sound of his hooves fading in the distance. All she could imagine was Sam with his face in the dirt and his arms tied behind him.

"Sam!" she shouted. "Are you alright?" The only sound she heard was mumbling from her attackers. "Please let him go! He's here to help you get Elijah back!" One of her captors grabbed her shoulders and shook them, jerking her head. He shouted something in Patois she didn't understand and realizing she had best cooperate, she tried to be still.

Her heart raced, but she willed herself to utter no other sound, taking deep breaths trying to remain calm. Hoping her cooperation would settle her captors down, she prayed she would see Amari soon and this nightmare would end. She could see only darkness poked with holes of light through the sack they had put over her head. Where was Sam? She couldn't hear him anymore. His silence grew louder with every passing minute.

"WAT DIS?" RONNIE couldn't see, but the tone of the man's voice told her someone new was in the room. A voice she recognized. This time, she understood the comment and for the first time, she was hopeful.

"Wi find her coming to village. She look like one Danquah say." Ronnie couldn't discern what they were saying, but what they were saying gave her an inkling. She recognized Danquah's name as she heard someone else come into the room.

"Where my brudda?" She then recognized Danquah's voice.

"He der in da back."

Suddenly, the hood came off and she could see. She squinted at the sunlight coming through the window of the rustic hut. "Miss Ronnie!" She looked up to see Danquah with a look of unbelief on his face. He turned to her captor and shouted something in Patois she couldn't come close to deciphering, but she knew he wasn't pleased to see it was her. The warrior made a hasty exit. Danquah reached down, pulled a knife from his belt, and cut the straps that held her hands behind her.

"I sorry, Miss Ronnie! You alright?"

"Yes, I think so." She rubbed her wrists and squinted, adjusting to the light. Danquah nodded as someone opened the curtain that was used for a door. They looked over to see Amari. She started toward him but stopped short when Gabrielle walked in behind him. Ronnie said with a shaky voice, "I came to see if I can help you get Elijah back." She looked from Amari to Gabrielle, whose eyes were swollen from crying. A Maroon had witnessed Elijah's arrest from a distance and reported it back to the tribe hours earlier.

Ronnie couldn't help but notice the green jade stone that had once belonged to her mother, hanging from a gold chain around Gabrielle's neck. Somehow, it made her feel better. "I'm so sorry for what you're going through," she said to Gabrielle. It was the first time they had ever spoken.

Gabrielle nodded and looked Ronnie in the eye. Ronnie, the woman Amari loved like a sister. This she knew and for once, she wasn't threatened by her husband's feelings for her. She just wanted her son back.

"I think the authorities will want to strike a peace treaty with you," Ronnie said. Amari and Danquah looked at each other. "We no interest in treaty. Maybe trade him for you and Sam?" Danquah said.

Her heart sank knowing this would not be an easy trade. The government had no vested interest in her or Sam, but she hoped Marshall and Adria had connections that might help. Ronnie looked at Sam who was still woozy from the blow to his head. He floated in and out of consciousness. "Is Sam going to be alright?" As soon as she spoke, an older woman walked in and saw the white woman the village spoke about. She looked away from Ronnie and mumbled something to Gabrielle.

Gabrielle looked at Ronnie and nodded toward the older Maroon woman. "This Elet. She a healer an' her will know wat him need." She followed the woman over to Sam. The two talked and Elet reached in her satchel and handed Gabrielle a cloth that held a handful of herbs. "Put dem in pot an' simmer." Gabrielle followed her instructions and the old woman left the hut. When it was ready, they made a poultice containing the herbs and laid it on his forehead. Sam stirred, opening his eyes once again, but quickly closed them again settling into the darkness.

RONNIE LOOKED AT Danquah and said, "My husband, Marshall, may have some influence with the Redcoats, but he doesn't know much of what's happened other than we headed this way and are now missing. How can we get word to him?" Danquah looked at his brother, Sam, still deep asleep in a coma. Ronnie continued, "If we don't get word to them that I am alright, I'm afraid things could spiral out of control." She worried the Redcoats would try to invade the village, but since they'd never had any success before, she doubted that would happen. Knowing that, she knew they would choose to move forward with Elijah's trial and certain conviction in retaliation. "Is there a way to send a note to Ramble House?" she asked.

Danquah sighed and thought for a moment. "I go talk to the elders and see what we do." He motioned for Amari to follow him out the door.

Ronnie pulled her journal from her pocket and tore out a piece of paper. Sitting at the table, she wrote a note to Marshall letting him know what was happening. She was confident he could work things out, given enough time, but knowing how long the Redcoats and the Courant were willing to wait, was something she couldn't predict. Sam began to stir. She put her pen down, walked over, and crouched down next to him.

"Sam, can you hear me?" she asked. The big man nodded slowly and opened his eyes.

"Yes, Miss Ronnie," he whispered.

"Oh, Sam, please don't try to talk. All is going to be fine. Danquah and Amari are here and we're figuring out what to do. Try to get some rest." She picked up his hand and kissed it, the hand of a one-time slave, the hand of a man who would do anything for people he loved and even those he didn't, the man who had saved everyone she knew at one time or another. Now it was her turn to help him. She was determined to find a way.

DANQUAH AND AMARI returned to the hut. Ronnie stood up from the table. "What did you decide?"

Danquah looked at her. "Amari will go to Ramble House to meet with your husband."

"No!" Gabrielle said. "They shoot him!" she cried and ran over, grabbing hold of Amari's arm.

Danquah looked at her and said, "Many warriors go with him. He know our friend, Thomas, there and he help to get him meeting."

Ronnie was stunned when she heard that Thomas was a friend of the Maroons. She walked toward Amari and handed him her note. "You can give Marshall this. If he's not there, Tillie will be able to read it and help." She was never so happy Marshall had permitted her to continue to teach Tillie to read. "Make sure you tell him you are Amari. Put your hands in the air like this." She showed him the sign of surrender. "He will know not to let anyone harm you."

Amari pulled Gabrielle to the far corner of the room and discussed the plan with her. His wife could see the resolve on his face and knew nothing would stop him from trying to get their son back. "Go bring our son home, Amari," she said as she wrapped her arms around him and held on tight. Tears were no longer useful, so she held them back and prayed instead as he ran out the door of the hut with Danquah close behind, leaving her face-to-face with Ronnie.

AMARI RAN AS fast as he could over the mountain ridge toward Ramble House. Danquah and several warriors followed him. Jumping across streams and dodging tree branches as they went up and down the hills and across the ravines, Amari's heart beat wildly, but he didn't notice until he stopped and the warriors caught up with him in the brush. "Time for you to stay," Amari said in a low voice. Danquah looked at him and nodded knowing Amari was their best option when it came to approaching the Brits. He and the remaining warriors would spread out and keep an eye on things to be sure Amari was safe.

Amari turned and ran up the steep Ramble House driveway and stopped at the bottom of the steps. Trying to catch his breath, he looked at Tillie and mustered up the strength to say, "I here to see Massa Fergusson." He stooped over with his hands on his knees breathing hard.

"The massa expect you?" Tillie asked and stepped back, not sure what to do. Maroons didn't normally stop by to just say "hello."

"Tillie, go inside!" Marshall shouted as he stood at the top step, pointing his pistol at Amari. Tillie whirled around and ran back to the kitchen area. Marshall had seen Amari run up the driveway right after he'd read Ronnie and Adria's note saying Elijah had been arrested and she left with Sam to help. He'd instinctively known this was a Maroon if only by the way he was dressed. Marshall couldn't fathom why one would come here in broad daylight, but having just read Ronnie's note, it was beginning to become clear. "McCready! Get over here and fast!" he hollered. Tillie had tipped him off and the new overseer was already on his way, running up from the kitchen area. McCready had his pistol now pointing at Amari and was scanning the edge of the forest for signs of other Maroons.

Amari knew things could easily get out of control. He did as Ronnie instructed, raising his hands he said, "My name Amari."

Marshall blinked hard taking in his words. "What do you want?" He lowered his pistol, but just a little. The contents of Ronnie's note began to make sense.

Amari knew the answer could literally kill him, but he didn't care. "Miss Ronnie, she at Maroon village. Sam too. I have note." He nodded toward his waist where Ronnie's note was tucked.

"Stay where you are," Marshall said, not taking is eyes off Amari's. He walked down the steps, reached over, and grabbed the note, hoping McCready had his back.

GABRIELLE LOOKED AT Ronnie and said, "I no know what to say." She shook her head in despair. Ronnie looked at Gabrielle, not sure of what she'd meant. "I sorry."

"Sorry? What on earth for?" Ronnie asked.

Gabrielle sat on the edge of the bed and said, "For always being scared of you. Amari love for you strong." Gabrielle looked into the eyes she'd always envied and then down at her own hands. She began to realize all of her insecurities had been wrong. Amari loved Ronnie in a way that was deserving and right.

Ronnie sat down next to her and said, "Please don't feel bad. I'm so grateful that you and Amari found each other. It was all I could have hoped for the night I said goodbye to Amari at Casa Daley." Ronnie reached her arm around Gabrielle's shoulder. "And to think Elijah also found a mother," Ronnie said. "And I believe I have found a forever friend." Gabrielle laid her head to rest on the shoulder of the woman she'd thought she hated.

Their bond began that day. Once established, nothing would ever stand in its way. They were from two very different cultures, yet their humanity surpassed any dictates made by others.

ADRIA ARRIVED BACK at the jailhouse for the third day in a row to spend time with Elijah, trying to keep his spirits up. Jeffrey and Marshall had been meeting with every person with any kind of status all over the island to ensure support were there to be a problem with trading prisoners with the Maroons. They posted letters to those they couldn't visit in person. There just wasn't time. Having popular opinion on their side would certainly be needed if things didn't go as planned. Time was of the essence as it was a trial and decision from a judge, they feared the most. A Maroon would not stand a chance in the British court of law, and they all knew it.

She had shared the news about Ronnie and Sam's abduction with Elijah the day before. After she did, she regretted the decision to tell him, knowing that it would make him worry, but she'd assured Elijah that it helped him to have some leverage with the authorities.

"But I do not even know these people. Who they are?" Elijah asked referring to Ronnie and Sam. Adria immediately wished she had said nothing. She realized it would make him worry even more.

"Ronnie and Sam are the people that took you and your father to the Maroons after you were born. You have folks that you don't even know loving you and fighting for your freedom," she said hoping it would make him feel better. He seemed comforted, but she knew when she left, he would have time to reflect on events more that she wanted him to.

Today, she had good news to share with her son. Gabrielle's son. Amari's son. And she was grateful, so grateful. Marshall and Jeffrey had been successful in brokering a deal with the Brits to exchange prisoners if the Maroons would agree to a treaty or ceasefire, at least.

Adria walked into the jailhouse. A bulky man in tattered clothing sat on a chair waiting to see a prisoner, she assumed. His hat was pulled down over his eyes and a light snore ripped through the air. At least I don't have to make small talk. Here she was, grateful again.

Montgomery came back into the office from the jail cell area. "Well, Mrs. Palmer, it's a pleasure to see you again." He looked down and saw the scones and jar of jam she had placed on his desk, courtesy of Mum Lettie. "I thank you for the delicacies. I don't often receive gifts, but I do appreciate them."

"Thank you, Sgt. Montgomery. I appreciate your kindness allowing me to see Elijah as you do. May I see him now?" Adria smiled her best one.

Montgomery looked over at the sleeping man in the chair and sighed. "I have an errand to run, but I will make an exception and allow you to go back while I'm gone." He walked over, grabbing hold of the keys that hung from his belt. He unlocked the door to the cell area and she followed him down the hallway. She noticed another prisoner, she assumed was an escaped slave, and kept walking toward Elijah's cell.

Montgomery pulled the chair over he'd given her to use the day before. "Thank you, Captain," she said with her best smile, grateful for the accommodation.

"Much obliged, Ma'am," he said as he headed back to the front office where the man still slept.

The man woke himself up snoring at the sound of the door closing behind Montgomery. He cleared his throat and asked in a gruff voice, "So, when can I take the African with me back to Kingston?"

"I have to go visit the bank for a minute and will return with the papers for you to sign," said Sgt. Montgomery. "My signature has to be notarized. You can wait here or come back later."

"I guess I don't have much choice but to wait, do I?"

"I suppose not," Montgomery said as he opened the door to the street and slammed it behind him.

The man looked around for a pamphlet to entertain him, but saw none. He decided to walk outside and as he did, lit up what was left in his pipe. He coughed as he discovered it was empty. Leaving the pipe in his mouth to chew on, he walked around the side of the building. Leaning on the wall, he slid down and sat, filled his pipe again, struck his flint, and lit it. He puffed until the cloud of smoke swirled above him as he waited for Montgomery to return.

ADRIA LOOKED AT Elijah. He had pulled his chair over next to hers. She reached through the bars and took his hand. He covered hers with his other hand. She no longer noticed the difference in their skin color as she did before.

"I have good news," she said looking into the eyes that mirrored her own.

"What is it?" Elijah asked, eyebrows raised.

"Well, I don't want to get your hopes up too high, but we may have reached an agreement with your people to make a trade in prisoners. You for Ronnie and Sam."

"When this happen?" Elijah asked. He couldn't get out of this place of doom fast enough.

"I'm not certain, but I pray it will be soon. Maybe the next day or two." She wanted to give him hope, but also didn't want to make any promises she couldn't keep.

"T'ank you so much," he said and hung his head.

"Why do you look so sad?" she asked. "You should be happy!"

"Why you do this for me?" asked Elijah, he looked up at her. "'Cause you my mummy?" He had spent hours upon hours thinking about his parentage. He didn't even know what to call this woman that was his mother.

"Oh, Elijah, I do this because I love you as your birth mother, but your real mother, your mummy, is Gabrielle. Because I am your birth mother, I will always love you as she does. Unconditionally. And always will. Remember, God doesn't divide love, He multiplies it."

Elijah smiled and her heart sang, if only for a moment. It was one smile she'd never forget. She didn't get to witness his countless smiles, so when they happened, she clung to the memory and was grateful.

"But I do not know what to call you," he said.

"You may call me whatever you like, but mummy is Gabrielle's name. How about Adria?"

He nodded and smiled. Again.

ELIJAH TRACED THE heart shaped birthmark on his hand as he stared at it sitting on the cot in his cell. "Think of me whenever you look at this heart and know that I love you and always will," he remembered Adria saying.

He looked up when he heard the same Redcoat who had slid his breakfast of stale bread and hominy under the bars of his cell that morning, walking up to him. The Redcoat said, "Come with me," as he unlocked the padlock. They walked from the dark cell into the light of the jailhouse. Sunbeams streamed through the windows making Elijah blink hard. He'd been there for almost a week and had it not been for Adria's daily visits, he knew he would have lost all hope. Now, today, he was being released to his father and Danquah. A deal had been struck to allow for the trade of Ronnie and Sam for Elijah's freedom to return to the Maroons, along with the promise of no future raids on plantations. At least for now. Both sides knew it was a tenuous agreement at best.

Elijah found himself caught between two worlds. That of his people and the one of his birth mother. He knew had it not been for Adria's love and concern, he may never have been released from this nightmare and may have even been hung in the gallows. He also realized he was truly a Maroon. His love for Amari and Gabrielle was stronger than his gratitude to Adria, but his love for her was undeniable.

The Brits knew they couldn't trust safe access up the mountain to the Maroon Village and Ocho Rios was too much in the public eye, so they were headed to Ramble House to make the trade.

"Get in the wagon, boy," the younger, yet taller Redcoat said. The older officer sat on the wagon, holding the reins, waiting.

"Yes, sir," Ramon replied, remembering how Adria had coached him to answer with respect while in custody. Elijah grabbed the side of the wagon with his cuffed hands. Hoisting himself over the side, he fell into the bed with a thud. He took a deep breath and sat up with his back leaning on the side. Looking up into the blue Jamaica sky, he felt the heat of the steamy afternoon. "T'ank you," he said to whatever God there was. He believed his prayers had been answered. There were days he'd worried he would never feel the sun on his face again. The dank walls of the cell had threatened to squeeze all hope right out of him.

"This should keep us both in the wagon," the Redcoat said. He took the rope that was tied around his waist and connected Elijah to the other end. There was enough in between them for the Redcoat to sit across from Elijah. He pulled out a pouch of jerky and took a bite, offering some to the driver who gratefully took it. Elijah's stomach growled, but he looked the other way. "Here!" the Redcoat said as he tossed the pouch to Elijah who caught it readily.

"T'ank you, sir." He opened the pouch and took a piece. He ate the jerky and thought of the curried goat Gabrielle was sure to cook when he arrived back home. He tossed the pouch back and continued chewing on the beef. The wagon jostled as it climbed the mountain toward Ramble House.

Several hours later, the wagon pulled up the steep driveway of the great house. Horses were tied to the hitching post and there was a crowd gathered out front. Elijah smiled when he saw his father and Danquah standing beside the wagon that held Sam and Ronnie in the back. He tried to wave, but the ropes around his wrists reminded him he was still a captive. Several Redcoats were there standing on the other side of the yard while Adria stood next to Jeffrey and Marshall. A cockerel crowed in the distance as if to announce their arrival. Adria started to walk their way as the wagon stopped, but a Redcoat grabbed her arm and pulled her back. "Not yet, ma'am." She stopped and nodded. Jeffrey put his arm around her shoulder and pulled her close. She instinctively leaned her head on his shoulder.

Danquah walked toward the middle of the yard and the Redcoats escorted Elijah, walking over to meet him. There had been several Maroon sentries posted around the perimeter unseen until now. The warriors stepped out of the trees in the distance and walked closer to make their presence known in typical Maroon fashion. Only this time, there was no attack.

They planned to stand guard over the proceedings and ensure the trade was made as promised.

"What is this?" the older Redcoat bellowed and stopped walking. "We agreed to a certain number of people!"

Danquah stepped over to him. "Dem here to make sure our safe return to village." The Redcoat looked around and realized they were indeed outnumbered.

"I don't care about your man. You can have him back with the promise of no further raids," said the Redcoat. He was sweating in the steamy sunshine.

"Nuh raids won't happen long as there no aggression toward our people," Danquah said and extended his hand.

The Redcoat hesitated, swept his brow with a handkerchief, nodded, and shook Danquah's hand. "Agreed," the Redcoat said. They both knew it was just a matter of time, but at least they had brokered somewhat of a peace treaty, if only for a short while. The frequent plantation raids had the island on edge. Women and children were leaving daily for London as the sometimes deadly raids had them fearing for their lives. Privateers were cashing in by offering frequent trips on their ships back to London.

Amari cut the straps off Ronnie and Sam while leading them to the circle. Sam held Ronnie's elbow as they walked. He could feel her shaking.

The Redcoat cut Elijah's restraints from his hands and nudged him to walk alongside him as they met in the center of the yard. Elijah saw Amari and wanted to dart off to hug his father, but the last few days had made him wiser, so he resisted.

The rest of the crowd gathered in the center of the yard. Once Danquah and one of the Redcoats shook hands, they both nodded and let go of their prisoners. Ronnie ran to Marshall, burying her head in his shoulder. Grabbing hold of her, he stroked her hair. "'Tis fine now, my love. I've got you." He kissed the top of her head.

Elijah embraced Amari as Gabrielle rushed over to share in the reunion. Joyful smiles glowed on all of their faces. "I afraid I never see you again!" Elijah sobbed as they clung to one another.

Adria watched as her son and his family reunited. She knew now was not the time to interrupt, so she went to Sam, wrapping her arms around the man who had looked after her and her family as if it were his own all these years. "Sam, once again, you've saved my son." She leaned back and smiled only to see a touch of sadness evident on the older man's face. She touched the bandage on his head and asked, "Are you alright?"

"Yesumm," he answered and added, "I neva 'av a daughter, Miss Adria, but you one to me." He hugged her tight, never stopping to think it was probably one of the few times he'd ever expressed any emotion toward her. Although he was a free man, the constraints of their culture still held fast.

They looked up as they heard horses running their way, silencing the celebration. Two Redcoats on horseback charged up the hill toward them. They pulled up and stopped, looking into the crowd. "Which one is Sam?"

Sam took an uncertain step in their direction and stopped. "We have a warrant for your arrest," the taller man said as he dismounted and walked toward Sam.

"Wat?" Sam looked from the soldier to Adria.

"What's the meaning of this?" Marshall shouted as he stepped forward, leaving Ronnie to stand behind him.

"He's a slave and aided and abetted the escape of Anne Bonny, a known criminal," the Redcoat said.

Jeffrey stepped up and said, "He is a free man!" He looked at Adria as she stepped toward the officer. He reached over to pull her back, but she was too fast.

"And we've brokered a peace treaty!" Adria said.

"That's nothing to do with this. Free man or not, he's wanted by the magistrate."

"It has everything to do with it!" she shouted as she started to walk closer with Jeffrey following.

Danquah walked briskly toward the officer shouting something in Patois and a shot rang out. Screaming in pain, Danquah jerked and fell face first in the dirt as if in slow motion. Sam ran to him, falling to his knees beside his brother. He rolled Danquah over and locked eyes with him. "Danquah! No!" Sam looked at his hand covered in his brother's blood flowing from his leg. Pulling off his belt, Sam wrapped and tightened it around Danquah's leg.

Shots rang out as the Maroons stepped up and responded, outnumbering the Brits. Jeffrey pulled Adria behind the wagon and nudged her to the ground. He laid his body on top of hers to shield his family from the flying bullets. Everyone scattered as one of the Brits fell to the ground from a Maroon's bullet.

Ronnie grabbed Gabrielle's hand and followed Marshall, crouching behind the stone retaining wall as the bullets pierced the air around them. Amari and Elijah ducked around the corner of the house.

After a few minutes, all went quiet. Another Redcoat had been shot and realizing they were surrounded; the Redcoats stopped shooting and signaled surrender by tossing down their guns and putting their hands in the air.

When Jeffrey stood up, Adria crawled around from the back of the wagon and looked across the yard. Sam laid on the ground next to his brother.

"Sam!" Adria shouted. Jeffrey grabbed for her but missed as she jumped to her feet and ran to the middle of the yard. Danquah was beginning to stir. Sam laid still next to him, face down, shot in the back. Adria rolled him over. "Sam, look at me!"

The graying black man opened his normally soulful eyes, but it was as if he stared right through her. Taking a choppy breath, he said, "Keep," he struggled to talk, "Elijah free." Sam looked at her, trying to focus again and said, "You da daughta I always want."

"No, Sam. Don't go!" She shook her head. "Please Sam, don't. Stay with me!" She could feel his spirit let go of his body as he slumped back. She buried her face in his chest and wept, feeling the blood flow from him in surrender.

Hands touched on her back and she could tell they were not Jeffrey's. She looked up to see Elijah looking down at her. Tears stained his face as she sat up and he knelt to embrace his birth mother. "I so sorry, Mum."

Adria felt such a mix of emotions. Sam was dead, but her son was alive and free; and he loved her. He'd called her, "Mum." She hugged him tight and buried her head on his shoulder, sharing her grief. Leaning back, she looked into her own green eyes and said, "I'm so grateful you're alright!" She held his face in her hands and kissed him on the forehead. "Take good care of yourself and your family."

Standing with courage she didn't know she had, she turned and looked at the Redcoats. "Look what you've done!" She shouted and pointed to Sam. "This man was a hero, not a criminal!"

"It's time to go!" shouted the taller soldier. Two other Redcoats pulled their wounded soldiers up and laid them across their horses. The Brits' weapons remained on the ground as they mounted their horses hastily and left a cloud of dust in their wake.

—Chapter Twenty-Six—

"The good we can do together surpasses what we can do alone." —Benjamin Franklin

1730, Ocho Rios, Jamaica

A week had passed and the mood was somber at Ramble House under the cloud of Sam's death. "Every time I walk out front, I'm reminded of the horrific sight of Sam dying in Adria's arms," Ronnie said to Marshall as she laid in his arms while the dawn broke over the mountains. "It lingers in my mind even when I will it to go away."

"I know what you mean. It's something that will be with us for a long time, I'm afraid." He pulled her closer and kissed the top of her head. "I'm so sorry I can't go to Ginger Star with you for his service and wake." Their new overseer, Mr. Stewart, had been injured when his horse threw him and he broke his leg the day before. "I feel awful not going with you."

"Oh, don't worry about it. I'll be fine. Sam would be the first to say that you should stay behind and tend to your fields. You can pay your respects another day. I will leave soon so I can be home by dark."

"Please stay the night. It's too arduous a trip to make in one day and trying to beat the darkness could prove to be difficult."

"Are you sure?" Ronnie asked. She'd never spent a night away from Hope before.

"Yes, my dear." And as if he could read her mind, he added, "I'll take good care of Hope, don't worry."

She smiled at his intuitiveness and said, "And we both know, she'll take good care of you."

Ronnie sat on the edge of the bed and stretched her arms toward the ceiling. "Hope is excited to spend the day with just her papa and Oliver. I'm afraid I am replaceable!"

Marshall grinned and said, "Don't kid yourself, but I must say, I'm looking forward to riding her around the fields with me for the day." Hope was becoming quite the equestrian. The bigger she got, the more she wanted to ride. Most of her riding time was spent sitting on the horse with either Ronnie or Marshall holding the reins, but lately, they'd been walking alongside her while she rode on Silver, the oldest and calmest of the horses.

"Well, I'm sure she'll be happy to give her opinion on just how things are going," Ronnie said.

"True, our little girl is becoming quite adept at expressing her thoughts," Marshall said and added, "Much like her mother!"

SAM WAS LAID to rest eight days later at the top of the cliff where Ginger Star met the sea. Adria's father built a small memorial, knowing Sam would not want anything elaborate. Reverend Smith officiated as the larger-than-expected crowd gathered around the gravesite. "It's evident by the number of you that have come to show your respect for Sam just how loved he was not only here at Ginger Star, but throughout our community." The diversity of the crowd didn't go unnoticed by anyone. Sam was well respected by people of every color on the island. The reverend led the crowd as they sang the hymn, "Sweet Place."

As she sang the words, "No tears from any eyes drop in that holy choir, but death itself there dies," Adria's heart lifted just a little. The thought that Sam was standing shoulder to shoulder with her mother in that holy choir, gave her comfort. Although Sam had been emancipated, he still in some ways belonged to another person while here on this earth. Now he was truly free.

Reverend Smith then led the crowd through the 23rd Psalm and ended with a brief prayer. "May our Sam now belong to you, dear God, and no one else. In Jesus' name, Amen."

LATER THAT SAME evening, the four women who just a little more than ten years earlier knew nothing of one another, sat around the dining room table of Ginger Star. The soft glow of candlelight danced on the walls as the sun began to set behind the mountains. The open shutters allowed the sound of the Jamaican crickets to add a soft, musical background to the feel of the evening.

The emotional toll of the past few days was evident by the women's silence. Ronnie had mentioned earlier she'd picked up a letter from Anne at the post office on the way to Ginger Star, letting her know she and Ramon had arrived safely in Cuba. Reaching in her pocket, she pulled out another letter addressed to all of them and said, "Here's the letter Anne addressed to all of us. Shall I read it aloud?"

"Please do!" Mavis said, happy that someone finally broke the silence of their shared pain.

Breaking the wax seal, Ronnie pulled out the paper and began to read.

"My dearest friends: Ronnie, Adria, Queenie, and last, but definitely not the least, Mavis.

"How do I begin to say thank you? Words are so difficult to come by as I write this letter. The past ten years, living on my mountain in Jamaica, I was somehow healed of all the hurt I'd ever experienced. The anger was gone and in its place was true gratefulness.

"First, I lost Jack and almost my life. There was a time I truly hoped this life I'd been given would end. Until Ramon."

Ronnie paused and looked around the table. Their collective silence spoke volumes.

She continued, *"Mavis, you loved the very unlovable Anne. The Anne who was angry and hurt. The Anne that had no idea what to do with a baby. Other than the baby saving me from the gallows, I was determined I would not allow myself to love him.*

"Then you helped me birth Ramon. It turned out my son and I were both born that day. He was birthed into a life on a deserted mountaintop, and I was born into motherhood, a profession I didn't want and now realize I never deserved, but am forever grateful. You taught me that all fear can be fine-tuned into faith with prayer."

Ronnie looked up from the letter and chimed in, "Mavis also rescued me when no one else would have or could have." Walking over to her surrogate mother, she put her hand on her shoulder. "There's not a person in this room that doesn't owe you thanks for one type of kindness or another."

Leaning down to hug her from behind, she continued to read, *"Queenie, sometimes it seems as if a lack of sight allows you to perceive that which is otherwise missed by the rest of us. You were the blind baby of a woman and left on the doorstep of*

*a Baptist missionary to raise and of all the ironies, now owns our
local tavern and brothel.*"

Everyone laughed and Queenie said, "Yes, and my adoptive
parents still pray for me every day!" They laughed and giggled
until happy tears showed up.

"Leave it to Anne to bring us laughter when we need it
most!" Mavis said, wiping her eyes from laughing so hard.

Ronnie smiled and continued reading, "*And my dear Ronnie,
a stowaway for lack of a better word. On a ship that tossed
you ashore, only to become the mistress of Ramble House. Proof
enough that God does indeed have a sense of humor.*"

Ronnie stopped reading while they laughed again. She
looked around the room and continued, but only after taking a
deep breath, "*Ronnie, my friend, God is smiling on you. Despite
the loss of your dear Rosalie, Hope has left her namesake inside of
all of us. Without 'hope' in our lives, what is there?*

"*Adria, you were the one who showed all of us how to forgive
and rise above the hurt that life dishes out. Although I'd never
met you until right before we left Jamaica, your love for others has
made a difference in my life for sure. And your son has turned into
a fine young man who should make you very proud. Please know
it gives me great comfort to remember that Mama's jewelry box
now belongs to you with the love of your son tucked inside of it.*"

Ronnie looked up from the letter and said to Adria, "Ha!
All this talk of how sweet you are, and to think I thought you
were going to push me right into the sea when you first saw me
on the Dry Harbor dock that day!" Ronnie laughed and they all
joined in.

"I must admit, the thought did cross my mind," Adria said
and took a bite of another scone. "But the hope that you'd be
willing to help me find Elijah provided me with any grace
I needed and kept you dry!"

She started reading again when the laughter died down. "*I would be remiss if I didn't mention Sam.*" Ronnie's voice choked when she read Sam's name aloud. Taking a deep breath, she continued reading, "*Thank you for deploying him to help get us back to Ocho Rios. There are not too many people I would have trusted to take Ramon to Ochie without me, but that night, he was at the top of my list.*"

Ronnie stopped reading and looked at the shock of hearing Anne mention Sam register on everyone's face. Anne would have had no way of knowing about Sam's death, yet she remembered to acknowledge him.

"To know Sam was to love him," Adria said and sighed.

Ronnie continued reading, "*So, ladies, I thank each one of you for the part you've played in my continued existence. I cannot attest to how things will go here in Cuba, but again there is 'hope' that all will come together. I've not yet met my son, Cunningham, but if I've learned anything, when love is present, just about anything is possible, at the right time. It's waiting for the 'right time' that can be so very difficult. So, once Ramon has acclimated to his new home and Jack's mother feels Cunningham is ready, we will take that leap together.*

"*However, time can slip away from all of us way too soon. Thank you for giving my life more days. My "hope" for all of you is that you are grateful for every day, for we all know that despite how difficult this life can be, joy does indeed, come in the morning.*

"*Thank you from the bottom of my heart.*

"*Forever,*

"*Anne*"

Adria poured everyone another glass of port, declining more for herself, being careful of her pregnancy. She still had not shared it with anyone but Jeffrey and Ronnie. She said, "Were it not for losing Sam, this would certainly be a celebration of Anne's arrival in Cuba."

Mavis raised her glass, tossed back its contents, and said, "I'm so grateful she and Ramon made it there safely. If I know her, she will be exporting her pottery and spices back here before too long."

Ronnie pulled another envelope from her satchel and handed it to Adria. "She also sent a letter from Ramon for Elijah."

Taking the letter from her, Adria hesitated a moment and said, "For a split second, I thought to myself that Sam needed to get this to Elijah." She looked at the letter in her hand as her voice trailed and her fingers traced the seal on the back of the envelope.

Ronnie reached over and patted her on the arm. "Maybe that gives you a reason to go see him for yourself."

Adria grinned at the thought. "Perhaps you're right." Adria looked out the window to see her father still standing there and said, "Sam was such an integral part of our lives, our very existence here at Ginger Star. I certainly took him for granted." She shook her head. "I don't think I'll ever get that awful scene out of my head." She could sometimes still feel the blood flowing out of his body onto hers.

Ronnie nodded, looked around the table and said, "Sam brought us all together in one way or another. To think that not so many years ago, I didn't know any of you. It seems like yesterday, but then again, it feels like a lifetime."

"Well, although I wasn't there when Sam was killed, for once I'm grateful I could not have seen it had I been," Queenie said. She raised her glass and said, "To my sisters who bring me smiles as well as sight." Their glasses clinked again.

Adria grinned as she looked at the unlikely group sitting around Ginger Star's dining room table. Here she was herself, initially an unwed mother, now married to a successful business-man, living in her treasured Jamaica. She pointed toward Sam's memorial where her father still stood. "I'm so worried about Papa. He and Sam were like brothers, so very close." Her father had withdrawn since Sam's death and looked frail to her for the first time ever. "He grieved when Mummy died, but this seems different somehow. Mum Lettie seems lost without him as well."

"And where is Mum Lettie anyway?" Ronnie asked, looking around the room until her eyes landed on her as she walked into the room carrying a soup tureen. "There you are, working as always." She walked over, took the tureen from the older lady's hands, and sat it on the sideboard. "I owe my sanity to this woman. She gave me sage advice and made sure I had a life to live with Mavis." Ronnie hugged Mum Lettie from behind, turned and pulled out a chair. "Here, have a seat at the table, mi lady." Ronnie bowed a little.

Mum Lettie looked at Adria who nodded. She'd sat at this table before, but mostly while polishing Ginger Star silver. As Ronnie slid the chair under her, she sat softly. "It occur to me dat no one ever pull chair out for mi." Mum Lettie's hands traced the embroidered napkin and for once, she was not ironing it as she had so often done. Her fingers traced the cool sides of the flatware.

"Well, it's long overdue, that's for sure," said Adria, grateful for Ronnie's astute intuition to include her. "I also owe her a debt I can never repay," Adria said. "There's no doubt I would have died had Mum Lettie not been there when Elijah was born." Adria grabbed a glass and filled it with port, handing it to Mum Lettie who looked at it in her hand and shyly smiled.

They clinked their glasses and the port flowed as they held them up for a refill and Adria poured, skipping her own glass again. Mum Lettie took a sip, this time from a glass instead of the decanter as she would do when sneaking a drink now and then. "It be betta from di bottle, probably 'cause I's sneakin' sum!" Mum Lettie said, and they all laughed again.

"I always made sure there was some left in the decanter just for you and Sam," Adria said and quickly added, "Sorry, I keep forgetting he's not here." She looked up and noticed her father had sat down on the bench next to Sam's memorial, made by Amari all those years ago.

Mum Lettie looked at her, tears brimming in her eyes. When she blinked they spilled over, but she smiled her semi-toothless grin anyway. "Me hopes you still do dat, jes for me!"

"You can count on it!" Adria said and raised her empty glass and the rest joined in.

"Laughter is balm for the soul, especially on days like this," Mavis said and took another sip. Her cheeks were rosy with a glow from the wine.

Ronnie looked over at Mavis and smiled at her red cheeks, betraying her not being used to drinking spirits. "Here," Ronnie said to Mavis as she handed her a scone in a subversive attempt to add some food to help with the alcohol.

Mavis giggled and looked over at Ronnie. "I would remind you I am watching what I eat and refuse the offer, but we both know that to be untrue." She winked at Ronnie. "First, I don't refuse a chance for some of Mum Lettie's guava jam. And second, my waistline and I have not seen eye-to-eye for quite some time!" She picked up the scone and lathered it with a layer of butter followed by a generous dollop of guava jam.

"Hey, pass that down this way, would you?" Adria's hand reached out and took the breadbasket from her hands. "Nothing like Mum Lettie's scones and jam to fill one up and satisfy a sweet tooth at the same time."

Mum Lettie's head bowed, embarrassed from the flattery.

"Maybe we should all have 'jes a lil bit more!'" Mavis slurred her words just a little, but thanks to the port, it didn't matter. She laughed and filled her glass again, admonishing herself to take it easy.

"Why is it that it takes us women nearly a lifetime to realize the value of bonding together?" Adria asked.

"You're right," Ronnie said, "Seems as if men figured it out long ago."

"I wonder if it's because women have been taught to be seen and not heard?" Mavis queried.

"And then there's always when you're told to be heard and not seen!" Queenie chimed in, laughing at her own joke. Looking around the table as if she could actually see them, Queenie continued talking, staring instinctively at each one, knowing just where they sat at the table, her seventh sense on display. "Ronnie, you've been able to make valuable changes with your staff at Ramble House. Your effectiveness, because of your love for people, is commendable and obvious. And then there's little Hope."

Ronnie nodded and said, "It's true, while Rosie's death was tragic, Hope has brought so many smiles to us at Ramble House. Marshall is as smitten as I. Being Hope's parents has brought us a closeness I didn't know existed."

Adria piped up with her news. "I want to let you all know I'm expecting a baby in December!"

"That's wonderful!" Ronnie exclaimed and jumped from her chair hurrying around the table to hug her.

"Well, there's a good reason to celebrate!" said Queenie as she made her way around the table and the rest followed.

Adria looked toward the doorway as Jeffrey entered the room. "I just shared our news, dear," she said. This time he didn't smile in response to the subject of their baby. "What's wrong?" she asked.

Jeffrey shook his head and said, "There's been another Maroon raid. This time from the Leeward Maroon Village." The Leeward Maroons' village was on the opposite side of the island, led by Cudjoe, Nanny's brother. Rumor had it, they were not happy about the deal that had been struck between the Nanny Maroons and the trade of prisoners.

"Where was the raid?" Mavis asked.

Looking at Ronnie, he said, "Ramble House."

Epilogue

Many ask why I chose to write this book. Well, the idea came to me while lying in a hammock on a resort in Jamaica. I started and stopped work on it several times before sitting down to seriously finish *Ginger Star* in 2020. I had a research trip to Jamaica scheduled for June of 2020 and that trip obviously didn't happen. I knew I had to finish the manuscript without the in-person trip. I was just about finished with the book when George Floyd was murdered in the USA. After that horrific incident, I knew I needed to go back to the drawing board (or writing board, if you will) and not gloss over the issues of the plantations. Characters had to become nefarious, and the culture needed to be exposed for what it was and sometimes, still is.

I first visited Jamaica while doing mission work with my church, Ocean City Worship Center, in 1995. I immediately fell in love with the island and its people. We painted everything that didn't move and did needed repairs and upgrades on an old British great house by the name of Ramble House in Claremont. Hence the focus on Ramble House in the book. You can visit my website to see photos of the great house, then and now.

I've taken liberties with dates and locations throughout *Ginger Star*. Historic information can be minimal and sometimes inaccurate for the 18th Century. For example, Ramble House is believed to have been built sometime around 1748. *Ginger Star* takes place from 1719–1730. They say, "write what you know," so I did and kept my focus on Ramble House.

When I first visited Ramble House, a missionary by the name of Orville Johnston from Michigan, was running a boys' home there with the permission of the Jamaican government and the help of a Jamaican couple, Melvalyn and Donovan Williams.

The boys' home changed many lives, mine included. Orville had found most of the boys wandering the docks and streets of Ocho Rios.

Not being able to visit Jamaica's archives due to COVID, I hope my readers will extend a little grace when it comes to factual dates. Ocho Rios was really not much more than a tiny fishing village before 1950. However, pirates did spend a lot of time hiding out in its coves and tributaries.

Because *Ginger Star* (a fictional plantation and part of my second novel, *My Mother's Apprentice*) is located in Ocho Rios, I had to roll with that. When I wrote *My Mother's Apprentice*, I invented *Ginger Star* and located the plantation near Ocho Rios. I know Ocho Rios and the north coast pretty well. So, that's where *Ginger Star* was born in my sometimes-creative memory, not far from the infamous James Bond Beach. Much of the description comes from that area.

Jamaica will always hold a special place in my heart. Her history is part of her beauty and if I've managed to convey just a small part of that, all the better.

Acknowledgements

WRITING A BOOK definitely "takes a village" and it's only after you're already on that journey, one discovers just how much. I could go on and on, but I'll try to keep this brief.

I want to thank my editor, Bill Cecil, for his encouragement, instruction, mentorship, and friendship throughout the writing (and re-writing) of *Ginger Star*. It seems like every author thanks their editor and I know why.

I owe a debt of gratitude to Ginger Marks of DocUmeant Publishing who remains the one that I lean on over and over again.

Roslyn MacFarland, my cover artist, continues to amaze me with her talents, but mostly because I know I drive her nuts with changes. She still puts up with me.

Robert Jacob, author of *A Pirate's Life*, and his wife, Anne, were my pirate experts and so much help to me when writing about the *Golden Age of Piracy*. They gave me pointers on the factual accuracy and description when writing about the 1720s.

I'd like to thank Brett Ashmeade-Hawkins of the Jamaican Colonial Heritage Society for sharing his knowledge and photos of Ramble House and Jamaica in general. The information he shared made this work so much more realistic and accurate.

Alexandra Edwards was so gracious to have me over for lunch at her lovely home in Sausalito, California. Alex shared amazing details regarding her family's property, Bromley Pen, a lot of which will be great fodder for *Ginger Star's* possible sequel. I'm so excited to visit Bromley Pen in person hopefully in early 2023.

I want to thank several good friends that have helped me get through this process. Cheryl Barnaba has been my marketing guru, drumming up book club invitations among other events. She's even my fashionista (for me, not my characters). Deb Lyman and Linda Goette, have always been my good friends and biggest cheerleaders. Susan Allen, my Jamaican daughter, translated so many phrases into the Jamaican Patois dialect and helped me make the book more "authentic."

The Ginger Star Launch Team consists of twenty people, too numerous to mention here, but you know who you are. Your ideas and energy helped keep me motivated and made the launch of *Ginger Star* what it was.

My children, Adam, Amanda, and Cameron are my anchor and purpose along with my ten grands, two-and-a-half greats, and I can never leave out my former fosters, Juan and Pedro. Too many blessings to count.

I would certainly be remiss if I didn't mention my biggest mentor, Jesus Christ. I can remember wanting to quit my day job all those years ago to write full time. Through prayer, He assured me I'd have time to write to my heart's content in my retirement, and I have. I hope He's okay with what I've written and if the "good Lord's willing, and the creek don't rise," as my grandfather used to say, He approves of what I write in the future.

Patois Glossary

MY JAMAICAN FRIENDS require no explanation for the Patois dialect used in Ginger Star, but everyone else, most definitely will. I hope it helps.

Patois Phrases and Words	English Translation
"Me know the Fante prey pon us,"	I know the Fante prey upon us.
Yuh having di pickney tonite?	Are you having the baby tonight?
How yuh walked. Yuh breast dem get bigga. Yuh sigh when yuh ben' ova an' yuh couldn't even catch yuh breath."	How you walked. Your breasts, they got bigger. You sighed when you bent over and you couldn't even catch your breath.
"Me know seh yuh scared. Yuh wi tell me in yuh own time."	I know you were scared. You would tell me in your own time.
"'Memba to focus and breathe,"	Remember to focus and breathe,
Mum Lettie, yuh here?	Mum Lettie, you here?
Wat in di worl'?"	What in the world?
Mi find har on the pass inna labor and we bring har in here,"	I found her on the path in labor and we brought her here.
A time fi wake di missus and Massa,"	It's time to wake the Missus and Master.
Weh di Massa and di missus deh?"	Where is the Master and the Missus?
"Mi did see di missus inna di dining room."	I did see the Missus in the dining room.
She 'ave pickney dis morning."	She's having a baby this morning.
She hide it from all a wi.	She hid it from all of us.

Patois Phrases and Words	English Translation
Mum Lettie find har on the pass to di cottage in the darkness.	Mum Lettie found her on the path to the cottage in the darkness.
"Dat good, dat good. Now lay back and wen di next pain come, di pickney soon come."	That's good, that's good. Now lay back and when the next pain comes, the baby will soon be here.
Wen di next pain comes, push again an' wi should be finish,"	When the next pain comes, push again and we should be finished.
Yuh 'ave a bwoy.	You have a boy.
Cut it der	Cut it here
Sumtime childbed fever come	Sometimes childbed fever sets in.
"Di pickney need fi eat,"	The baby needs to eat.
She can be di wet nurse 'til Adria wake up."	She can be the wet nurse until Adria wakes up.
It der in a jar on de kitchen shelf. Olivia know which one it tis."	It's there in a jar on the kitchen shelf. Tillie knows which one it is.
Me nuh for certain, but dem things sumtime jus run dem course.	I don't know for certain, but those things sometimes just run their course.
Martha soon come,	Mary will be here soon.
We will be dere in jus' a few miles	We will be there in just a few miles.
Casa Daley jus up roun' di bend."	Casa Daley is just up around the bend.
Keep 'em to di rite	Keep them to the right.
"Here, let's siddung ova there."	Here, let's sit down over there.
Jus up di road	Just up the road.
'Sides, wi only got a little more lef' in dat bottle. We need to get to da wet nurse at Casa Daley."	Besides, we only have a little more left in that bottle. We need to get to the wet nurse. . .
No, a no problem	Not a problem.

Patois Phrases and Words	English Translation
Henry be waitin' for us at the bottom of di drive,"	Henry will be waiting for us at the bottom of the drive,
Me sen' Matthew, the stable bwoy, up here on Chance and him deliver di message before we lef Ginger Star	I sent Matthew, the stable boy, ,up here on Chance and he delivered the message before we left Ginger Star.
They see us. Soon come,"	They see us. Will soon be here.
Soon come (repeated frequently throughout book)	Will be there soon.
The word "da" or "di"	Means "the"
but we're fightin' di dawn,"	But we're fighting the dawn.
The word "har"	Means "her"
Many massas nuh allow slaves to 'av drums,	Many masters don't allow slaves to have drums,
"Wi a go see har tomorrow	We'll go see her tomorrow.
God nuh *let* tings happen. Sumtimes wi mek decisions dat cause these situations. He there to pull us through it an' more often than not, wi learn much."	God doesn't *let* things happen. Sometimes we make decisions that cause these situations. He's there to pull us through it and more often than not, we learn a lot.
The word "wid"	Means "with"
Gud mawning, mi love	Good morning, my love.
The word, "ting"	Means "thing"
The word, "tank"	Means "thank"
I tink I can reach my bredda, Danquah, an' ask to meet wid dem	I think I can reach my brother, Danquah, and ask to meet with them.
We are here wid many sentries to watch ova our meetin',	We are here with many sentries to watch over our meeting.
Wi understan'	We understand
One can neva tell wat might	One can never tell what might

Patois Phrases and Words	English Translation
The sun ready to wake by di cockerels' crowin'	The sun is ready to wake you by the cockerels' (roosters') crowing.
I tink maybe wi break up fi a while.	I think maybe we should break up for a while.
Stick with me, likkle man,	Stick with me, little man,
She a healer an' she wi know wat him need,	She's a healer and she will know what he needs.
no aggression towaad wi people,"	No aggression toward our people
"I neva 'av a daughter, Miss Adria, but you are one to mi."	I mever had a daughter, Miss Adria, but you are one to me.
The word "wat"	Means "what"
The word "'bat"	Means "bath"
The word "pon"	Means "upon
Ewes (pronounced U-Ways)	Amari's tribe in Ghana

CPSIA information can be obtained
at www.ICGtesting.com
Printed in the USA
JSHW042340161122
33325JS00001B/5